Praise for the Rhona MacLeod series

'Forensic scientist Rhona MacLeod has become one of the most satisfying characters in modern crime fiction – honourable, inquisitive and yet plagued by doubts and, sometimes, fears . . . As ever, the landscape is stunningly evoked and MacLeod's decency and humanity shine through on every page' *Daily Mail*

'Lin Anderson is one of Scotland's national treasures . . . her writing is unique, bringing warmth and depth to even the seediest parts of Glasgow. Rhona MacLeod is a complex and compelling heroine who just gets better with every outing' Stuart MacBride

'Vivid and atmospheric . . . enthralling' *The Guardian*

'The bleak landscape is beautifully described, giving this popular series a new lease of life' *The Sunday Times*

'Greenock-born Anderson's work is sharper than a pathologist's scalpel. One of the best Scottish crime series since Rebus' *Daily Record*

'Inventive, compelling, genuinely scary and beautifully written, as always' Denzil Meyrick

'Hugely imaginative and exciting' James Grieve (emeritus professor of forensic pathology)

The Wild Coast

Lin Anderson is a Scottish author and screenwriter known for her bestselling crime series featuring forensic scientist Dr Rhona MacLeod. Four of her novels have been longlisted for the Scottish Crime Book of the Year and she was shortlisted for the Crime Writers Association Dagger in the Library Award in 2022. Lin is the co-founder of the international crime-writing festival Bloody Scotland, which takes place annually in Stirling.

The Rhona MacLeod books in order

Driftnet

Rhona investigates a murder victim who may be the son she gave up for adoption seventeen years ago . . .

Torch

Rhona joins the hunt for a terrifying arsonist on the streets of Edinburgh.

Deadly Code

A horrifying discovery is made off the coast of Scotland's Isle of Skye.

Dark Flight

When a boy goes missing, Rhona is called in to examine a chilling series of clues left behind.

Easy Kill

A sadistic killer is targeting a string of young women in Glasgow.

Final Cut

Rhona is called in when a badly burned body is found wearing a soldier's dog tags.

The Reborn

A pregnant woman is found dead – and the killer is watching and waiting to strike again . . .

Picture Her Dead

A sinister murderer is hiding the bodies of his victims in Glasgow's derelict cinemas.

Paths of the Dead

When a body is found inside a Neolithic stone circle, Rhona is called in to investigate.

The Special Dead

Rhona and DS Michael McNab look into the ancient practice of Wicca following a ritualistic killing.

None but the Dead

Rhona heads to the remote island of Sanday when human remains are discovered beneath an old school.

Follow the Dead

A killer stalks the Cairngorms in the Scottish Highlands after a mysterious plane crashes on a nearby loch.

Sins of the Dead

Rhona is being targeted by a terrifying killer whose methods echo the ancient religious practice of sin-eating.

Time for the Dead

Rhona investigates a series of brutal deaths on Scotland's Isle of Skye.

The Innocent Dead

A decades-old cold case is reopened when a body is discovered in a peat bog south of Glasgow.

The Killing Tide

When three bodies are found on a wrecked ship in the Orkney islands, forensic scientist Rhona MacLeod is brought in to investigate.

The Wild Coast

A killer is preying on campers along Scotland's remote west shoreline.

By Lin Anderson

Driftnet
Torch
Deadly Code
Dark Flight
Easy Kill
Final Cut
The Reborn
Picture Her Dead
Paths of the Dead
The Special Dead
None but the Dead
Follow the Dead
Sins of the Dead
Time for the Dead
The Innocent Dead
The Killing Tide
The Wild Coast

STANDALONE NOVELS

The Party House

NOVELLA

Blood Red Roses

The Wild Coast

A remote shoreline. A lethal killer.

LIN ANDERSON

PAN BOOKS

First published 2023 by Macmillan

This paperback edition published 2024 by Pan Books
an imprint of Pan Macmillan
The Smithson, 6 Briset Street, London EC1M 5NR
EU representative: Macmillan Publishers Ireland Ltd, 1st Floor,
The Liffey Trust Centre, 117–126 Sheriff Street Upper,
Dublin 1, D01 YC43
Associated companies throughout the world
www.panmacmillan.com

ISBN 978-1-5290-8457-3

3 5 7 9 8 6 4 2

A CIP catalogue record for this book is available from the British Library.

Typeset in Meridien by Palimpsest Book Production Ltd, Falkirk, Stirlingshire
Printed and bound by CPI Group (UK) Ltd, Croydon, CR0 4YY

FSC www.fsc.org
MIX
Paper | Supporting responsible forestry
FSC® C116313

The Wild Coast

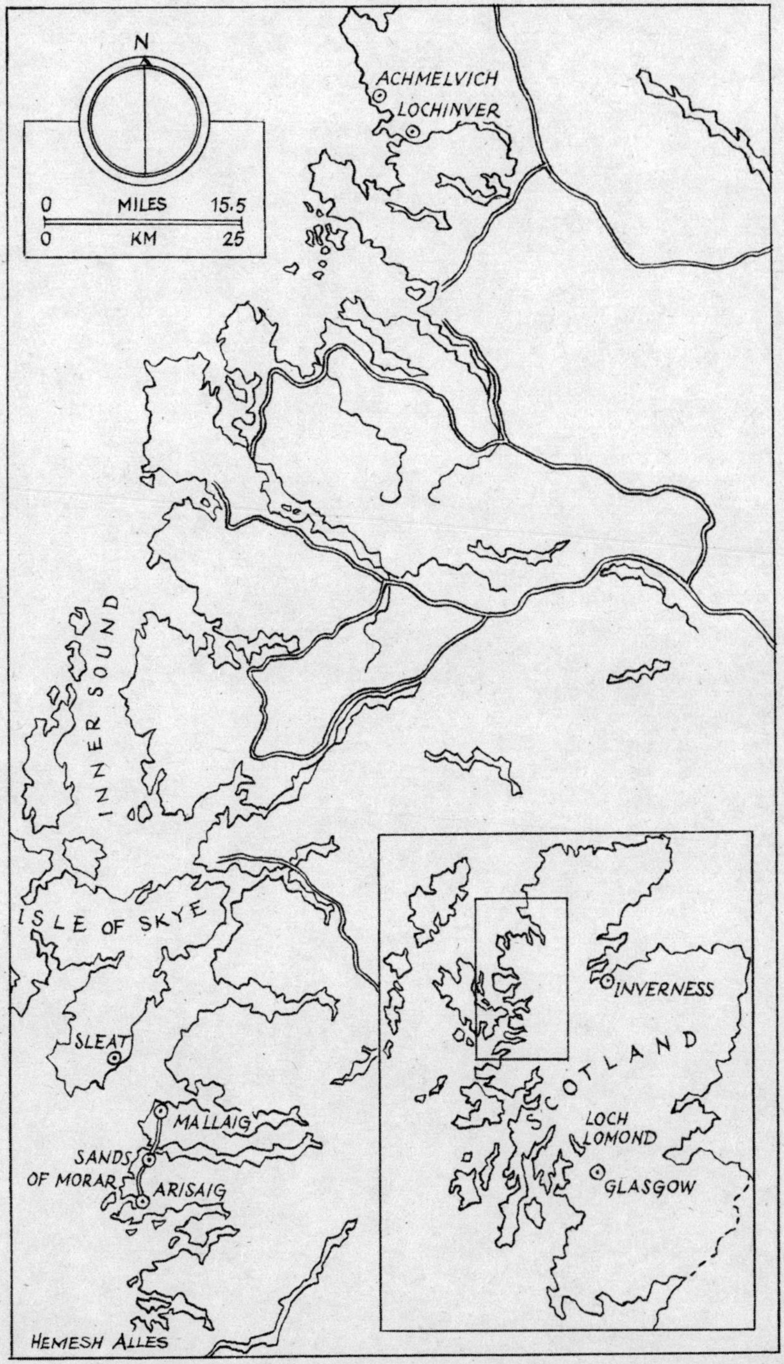
N
0 MILES 15.5
0 KM 25
ACHMELVICH
LOCHINVER
INNER SOUND
ISLE OF SKYE
SLEAT
MALLAIG
SANDS OF MORAR
ARISAIG
INVERNESS
SCOTLAND
LOCH LOMOND
GLASGOW
HEMESH ALLES

1

Arisaig, North-West Highlands of Scotland

Day one

The single-track road wound on, snaking between high flowering hedges. Her fear was that she might miss the turn-off, or worse, meet a car or van, with no way of passing it.

Negotiating the next tight bend, she was relieved to find herself with an open field on her right and a view of the sea beyond.

She slowed, wondering if a distant bungalow might be the croft she was looking for. There was no sign beside the open gate, but there was a campervan making its way past the house and into what she hoped was the campsite she sought.

Deciding to take a chance that it was, she turned in. A few minutes of bumping along the rutted track deposited her next to a tractor parked outside the bungalow. Checking in the rear-view mirror, she noted that the make-up she'd put on earlier to cover the bruise needed refreshing.

Having done that, she pulled her baseball cap down over her eyes before getting out of the van. From where she now stood, she could make out a cluster of vehicles in the field ahead, which bordered a bay fringed by white sand.

She felt her heart lift a little at the sight, and some of the fear at what she'd left behind began to dissipate.

A knock at the blue front door brought a small stocky man in overalls to answer it.

'Can I park up for the night?' she asked tentatively.

'Let me check with the wife,' he told her cheerily. 'I canna read her hieroglyphics in the book for love nor money.'

He disappeared, to be swiftly replaced by a little woman with an equally pleasant smile. She repeated her request.

'I don't have a plug-in spot free, I'm afraid,' she said.

'I don't need electricity.'

'Then you're welcome to the far corner facing the west bay. You know it's cash only?'

She nodded. 'Shall I pay you now?'

The woman waved the offer away. 'No need, we can sort that out in the morning if you decide to stay on.'

And that was that.

The campsite wasn't busy. She'd counted on that, of course. Without much in the way of facilities, and only a few electricity points, it wasn't aimed at the luxury motorhome market, but more the wild camping fraternity, of which she was definitely one.

With no website or email address, you had to phone ahead to make a booking, or else just turn up, as she had.

'Now you can relax,' she told herself as she reverse parked in her allotted spot with her door facing the seaward side.

Her nearest neighbours she registered as a couple with two young children: a little blonde girl who watched her set up camp and take down her kayak from the roof rack, and a boy a bit older who pretended not to be interested, yet undoubtedly was.

Eventually their parents appeared to say hello, and introduced themselves as Francine and Derek Henderson.

'This is Lucy, who looks angelic but isn't.' Francine placed her hand on her daughter's blonde curls. 'And Orlando, who suffers from having a bossy younger sister, but mostly in silence.'

Orlando's solemn expression didn't change at his mother's little joke.

Callie smiled and nodded, but didn't offer up her own name.

'Are you here for long?' the husband asked.

'Depends on the weather and how good the water is,' she said. 'If you'll excuse me, I'm heading out there now.'

The introductions over, she took herself into the van to don her wetsuit. Stripped to her underwear, she tried to ignore the bruises now on view.

Hitting her face had been a mistake. Much better to keep evidence hidden under her clothes. He'd always been careful about doing that, until the last time.

The final time, she told herself.

Emerging from the van, she found Lucy and her brother waiting outside.

'She wants to see you launch your boat,' Orlando explained.

'Well, I'm planning to take off from the beach just across the fence. If you stand there, you can watch me.'

Orlando gave her a little nod.

Locking the van, she slipped the keys into her waterproof bag, then manoeuvred the kayak and her paddle over the fence before setting off towards the only gap, which faced the neighbouring bay.

Passing three medium-sized vans, plugged into the only

electric points, she noted that the rest of the field was empty, bar a couple of small tents, although other campers would no doubt appear before sundown.

A dilapidated static caravan stood in the corner of a neighbouring field near the beach exit with a small fishing boat and a pile of creels on the nearby shore. As she passed it, she thought she caught the twitching of a torn net curtain, but didn't turn her head to check.

Instead, she took three deep breaths and repeated the mantra that she was safe here.

Turning at the corner where her van was parked, she found Orlando standing where she'd left him, behind the wire fence, holding his little sister's hand.

He looked so envious as she lifted her kayak to take it to the water that she found herself saying, 'I'll let you two have a go in it tomorrow if your mum allows.'

The boy's serious look was swiftly replaced by a smile and Lucy gave a little whoop of delight.

'What are you doing?' she muttered to herself as she slipped the kayak into the water. 'You're supposed to be lying low. Not becoming everyone's pal.'

Despite her own entreaty, she found herself turning to wave to the two children, before guiding the kayak across the mirrored water and out of the bay.

2

Day two

Francine carried the two bowls of cereal to the open door of the campervan where she had a clear view of Orlando poking a stick through the fence, but no obvious sign of Lucy's blonde head.

'Where's Lucy?' she called.

Orlando turned and looked at her with a vacant expression.

'I told you to watch your sister while I made breakfast,' she said, perhaps a little too sharply.

His face immediately crumpled under her angry gaze. She tried to calm herself. The field was fenced in apart from the main entrance and the gate to the beach. There was nowhere for Lucy to go.

'Is she hiding from you?' She tried to make her voice light.

They'd played hide and seek before, but with nowhere really to hide in the open field, except inside the campervan, it hadn't gone on for long.

Orlando had picked up on her fear and was standing rigid, his expression blank. It was what he did when worried or disorientated.

Where was Derek? He'd said something about emptying

the chemical toilet, but the disposal unit was only yards away. Perhaps Lucy had followed him?

The field had filled up a little overnight, mostly small vans and tents, and there were a few other children about.

Francine gently took her son's hand and looked into his eyes.

'It's not your fault. I was just surprised that Lucy wasn't here with you. Did she find someone to play with?'

She glanced at the neighbouring blue van. Lucy had been entranced by the kayak yesterday. Maybe she was with the girl, whatever her name was.

'Have you seen the kayak girl this morning?' she asked Orlando, striving to keep her tone unworried.

He shook his head in a 'no'.

'Let's see if she's about,' Francine said. 'Maybe Lucy's in visiting her.'

Taking his hand, she led him round the blue van to the seaward side and knocked on the door.

'Hello? Anyone in there?' she called.

Greeted by silence, she decided to try the door. If it wasn't locked, Lucy may well have gone inside to hide.

As the door slid open she was suddenly engulfed by a sickly smell. Francine found herself gagging and turned away. When she turned back, Orlando was staring in, his small face white with shock.

She pulled him away and told him to go to their van, 'while I check what's wrong'.

She watched to make sure he'd done as ordered before taking a proper look. Someone had vomited, that much was evident by the smell and the puddle just by the door, but there was blood too. Splashes of it across the little table and kitchen surface and more of it on the bedcover and the floor.

Had the girl had an accident? If so, where was she now? She gave a cursory glance at the nearby bay and couldn't see the girl's kayak anywhere on the shore.

Making a decision, she closed the door. Whatever had happened in there hadn't prevented the girl from going out in her kayak. Her job was to find Lucy and she had to do that now.

She began calling Lucy's name, moving out into the field, shouting that her daughter was missing.

3

Day two

The searchers, mostly from their own campsite, had fanned out, walking the machair as directed by the police. The tide had retreated and the rocky promontories that split the fertile sandy shoreline were also being checked.

The tide wouldn't be full in until evening, so that was a blessing, someone had told her.

Francine couldn't remember who had spoken those words, but they'd sounded strange to her terrified ears. How could anything be a blessing in such circumstances?

Her terrified shouts that Lucy was missing had reached the woman from the croft house as she'd driven her car into the field to check who was staying on. Her kind face as she'd listened to Francine's broken words had brought a semblance of brief calm.

'We'll find her,' she'd assured Francine. 'She can't have gone far.'

Producing a megaphone from her car, she'd handed it to Francine. 'Describe your daughter and say you're looking for her.'

Francine did as requested and a few folk came up to speak to her. At that point Derek had reappeared.

'Where the hell were you?' Francine had shouted at him.

'I was emptying the toilet and got talking to someone,' he'd said, looking furious. 'What the hell's happened?'

Knowing she was about to be blamed, Francine had calmed herself before telling him that Lucy had been there one minute and gone the next, and Orlando hadn't seen where she'd disappeared to.

She'd thought Derek would explode there and then, despite the small group of campers that had gathered, eager to help them search, but he'd managed to control himself . . . just.

The field and its current tents and vans had been checked. At least, the ones whose owners were on site and not out on the water somewhere.

Francine didn't want anyone looking inside the blue van, because that might turn the attention away from finding Lucy, so she said she'd checked it and it was empty.

With the main gate shut, and the campsite searched, they'd begun to comb the surrounding beaches. It was then that the police, called by the crofter's wife, had arrived from Mallaig to direct operations.

Francine had been advised to stay behind with Orlando, while Derek went out on the wider search. She'd been left in the care of a female constable, called Anne, who'd quietly reassured her that most children were found swiftly, and that it would be better if she stayed on site in case Lucy turned up again of her own accord.

Orlando had withdrawn into himself, just as he always did when he found life scary or confusing, like when Derek and she had an argument, of which there'd been many of late.

One had been happening when the kayak girl had returned

late last night. Derek, already drunk, had suddenly invited her to join them. She'd briskly refused, saying she was tired after driving here and after her trip out on the water, and was planning some food and an early night.

In the light from the fire pit, Francine had noticed bruising on her face, and had wondered if it had been there when she'd arrived. Thinking back to that now, she wondered if the girl was in some sort of trouble, and that was why she'd come to the remote campsite in the first place.

And then that mess in the van.

Thankfully, Orlando hadn't said anything about it, after she'd made him promise not to.

She'd taken him aside after the search party had set out and explained that they would speak to the police about the blue van once they had Lucy back. The fact that the kayak wasn't there probably meant the girl was fine and already out on the water somewhere.

Orlando had seemed to accept her explanation although, in truth, she'd only half believed it herself.

As the day wore on, she found herself growing more and more agitated. Standing outside, she could see the figures dotted about the various headlands, and up on the single-track road that led to their campsite.

Her mind was plagued by images of Lucy's body lying in a roadside ditch, or floating in the sea, or washed up battered and torn in one of the many coves.

Then a thought occurred. Might there be a chance that Lucy had gone out for a trip in the kayak with the girl, as she'd apparently been promised the previous evening?

Even as she contemplated this, another much worse idea occurred.

What if Lucy had been snatched by someone and removed

from the campsite using the girl's kayak? How easy that would be. She could see it in her mind's eye. Lucy at the fence, being offered a ride in the kayak by some man. She would say yes. Of course she would. Lucy was everyone's friend. And she had been promised a trip today in the kayak.

Shaking almost uncontrollably now, she shouted for the female police officer.

When the young woman came to stand beside her, Francine finally voiced her fear.

'There's something I have to tell you about the blue van.'

4

Sleat, Isle of Skye

Day two

Rhona stood at the open door, mug of coffee in hand, savouring the view.

The water was flat calm, the air crystal clear, giving her a perfect view over the Sound of Sleat to Knoydart on the mainland.

The settled and sunny weather had been ideal for her stay at her family cottage, but the week's holiday was over and it was time to head back to Glasgow. Her plan was to take the ferry from Armadale to Mallaig on the mainland, then drive back to Glasgow via Fort William, making stops on the way to enjoy the sunshine and the west coast scenery.

In truth, she would be sorry to leave, but a week away from work was long enough for her. It was also long enough for her forensic assistant, Chrissy McInsh, who'd made a point of telling her how much she was missed. 'And a ship without its captain . . .' she'd said, in her best serious voice.

Rhona had laughed at that description of herself, well aware that Chrissy was more than capable of being in charge on land or sea.

Walking down to the shore, she settled on a rock to check her mobile messages and found a missed call from Chrissy, which she promptly answered.

'Hey, I'm almost ready to leave,' she promised.

'So you're still on Skye?'

To Rhona's surprise, Chrissy sounded relieved rather than annoyed by that.

'I'm planning on catching the Mallaig ferry back,' Rhona began, before Chrissy cut her off.

'Good, because we've had a call-out to Arisaig.'

Rhona waited while Chrissy explained. 'A police dog located what they believe may be human remains buried on the machair north of the town.'

'Were they searching for someone?' Rhona said, aware that if a police dog had been sent into action . . .

'That's just it,' Chrissy said, her voice breaking a little. 'A wee girl has been reported missing from a nearby campsite.'

'They think it might be the child?' Rhona said, horrified.

'Unconfirmed.' Chrissy, no doubt thinking about wee Michael, her own child, took a moment to regain her composure. 'Once you're on the ferry, you're to give Mallaig station a call and tell them you're on your way. See you soon.' And with that she rang off.

Rhona checked her watch. She'd booked a later ferry, but if she was quick she might just make the earlier one.

As she began to pack her stuff in the car, a familiar jeep appeared on the track leading down to the cottage.

Rhona stopped what she was doing, both pleased and a little perturbed by the arrival of the man who'd been her frequent walking companion on her week's sojourn on Skye. She'd known and liked Jamie McColl since their schooldays together, before her parents had moved the family permanently to Glasgow.

Jamie, despite vowing as a teenager that he would definitely leave the island as soon as he could, had in fact stayed on to take over the family funeral business. He was now as much a permanent resident as the famous Cuillin, and as rock-steady.

'Jamie,' she said as he drew alongside her. 'What are you doing here? I thought we'd said our goodbyes yesterday.' She had no difficulty making her tone one of surprise. Whether she'd managed to disguise her slight concern at his turning up here was another matter.

'I was on my way to discuss funeral arrangements with a family nearby, and thought I'd check in with you before you leave,' he professed with a smile.

It sounded bona fide, but she still found herself a little nonplussed by the surprise visit.

Registering the open boot and her suitcase already inside, he said, 'I thought you were booked on a later ferry?'

'I was, but something's come up at work and I need to try and catch the earlier one.'

'So you're in a hurry?' he said. 'Why don't you get going, then, and I'll lock up for you. Make sure everything's turned off and secure?' he offered.

'Would you?' she said, relieved that this was to be the outcome of their conversation.

'Of course,' he said. 'I'll use the spare key you gave me.'

'Thanks.'

There followed a brief moment of awkwardness on her part before Jamie took the initiative and embraced her. 'You'd better get going, then.'

God, she thought, as she drove away, *Jamie can read me*

like a book. Just as he had back when they were teenagers and more recently as they climbed the hills and walked the remote shorelines of Skye.

Jamie McColl had been and still was a good friend. Or perhaps something more, a small inner voice suggested.

It was a road they hadn't travelled, and yet . . .

Rhona dismissed that thought from her mind, aware that she was toying with it again only as a means to avoid what was truly troubling her at this moment.

That she might be about to exhume a child's body from the sand dunes near Arisaig.

It wouldn't be the first child's remains she'd dug up, the most recent being those of a twelve-year-old girl, discovered in a peat bog south of Glasgow, who'd disappeared fifty years ago.

Regardless of the circumstances, dealing with the murder of a child had to be among the worst experiences for anyone on the front line, herself included.

She found the road through Sleat to Armadale busier than usual, heralding the summer influx of visitors, many of them driving motorhomes. The Sleat Peninsula, being close to the Skye road bridge, was often a choice for day trippers to the second largest Scottish island.

Then again, the motorhomes on the road south might be heading, like her, for Armadale and the ferry back to the mainland. She'd already booked her ticket, but for the later crossing, so there was a strong chance there wouldn't be a place for her on the one leaving shortly.

On finally reaching the harbour, Rhona left the car in the car park and, fingers crossed, went to check if she could change to the ferry currently on approach. The number of vehicles already waiting in the boarding lanes gave her cause for concern, but the fact she only had a car and not a motorhome won the day.

'No bother, Dr MacLeod. We can squeeze your wee car on. Now, if you'd had one of those monstrosities . . .' Eddie, in the ticket office, indicated one such example with raised eyebrows. 'You're in lane one.' He handed Rhona her new ticket. 'And I hope you haven't had reason to shorten your holiday?'

'I haven't,' she assured him. 'I was due back today anyway.'

'Well, we'll see you next time you're home,' he told her with a farewell smile.

It was funny, she thought, crossing back to her vehicle, how folk here referred to Sleat as her home, whereas in Glasgow it was the other way round.

As for herself, she believed she was lucky to call both places home.

Once aboard, she made her way to the upper deck and, choosing a quiet spot, called Mallaig police station.

Identifying herself as forensic scientist Dr Rhona MacLeod, she explained about her assistant's call and that she was on her way to Mallaig on the Skye ferry.

'Dr MacLeod,' the West Highland voice replied, 'I'll just pass you to Detective Sergeant MacDonald. He'll be delighted that you got the message in time.'

The next voice that came on was definitely one Rhona recognized. She'd worked with Lee MacDonald on Skye during an earlier investigation there.

'Lee, have you moved to Mallaig?' she asked in surprise.

'I have,' Lee told her. 'How goes it, Dr MacLeod?'

'Just spent a week on Skye in the sunshine,' she told

him. 'Was about to head back to Glasgow when I got the call.'

She waited as Lee cleared his throat. 'Aye. A bad business, but I'm glad we caught you in time.'

'I understand a police dog located what you believe may be a burial site?' Rhona said.

'Yes, in the machair north of Arisaig. Lucy Henderson, a wee girl of four, had gone missing from a nearby campsite, and we had a search team out looking for her.'

Rhona forced herself to ask the dreaded question. 'You think it could be the child?'

'Thankfully, no. She's safe back at her campervan with Mum and Dad,' he assured her. 'Although we did find her close to the locus – which is an area of disturbed ground, the dimensions of a possible grave. As you're probably aware, machair rarely recovers when dug up.'

Rhona knew exactly what he meant.

'It was the police handler, a local, who alerted us to it.' He paused. 'As for Lucy, how she ended up there, we don't know. And she isn't saying as yet. We have a female PC with the family in the hope that she might have more to tell us.'

The conversation ended at that point and Rhona went out on deck to watch the Isle of Skye retreat, even as the seven peaks of Knoydart approached. Looking out on what was, without doubt, a magical view in both directions, it was difficult to reconcile that fact with what awaited her ashore.

Folk came to the remote bays of the west coast of Scotland both to enjoy the beautiful surroundings and to find the kind of peace and safety not available in the busier UK holiday spots.

She was familiar herself with the area of coastline Lee had referred to. Its sheltered bays and white sands provided a perfect place to swim or to use as a base to explore the coastline in kayaks and small motorboats. In fact, a sea lover's paradise.

But not in this case, it seemed.

The police station was minutes from the ferry terminal, and she found Lee waiting for her in the car park.

'Little point taking you inside for introductions,' he said, 'as most everyone is out at the locus. Chrissy should be there by now. The MIT will set up operations here when they arrive.' He paused. 'Probably better if you leave your car. Chrissy has a forensic van on site.'

Rhona nodded in recognition of all that had been already set in motion. The Highlands had few suspicious deaths happen within its jurisdiction, but, when it did, it was reliably quick off the mark. Whether on Skye to the west or on Sanday – one of Orkney's most remote northern isles – or here on the mainland, it made no odds. She could testify to that.

They had left Mallaig now, which was busy with tourists, and were heading south on the A830, also known as the Road to the Isles.

'Been this way before?' Lee asked.

Rhona indicated she had. 'Sands of Morar are a favourite swim place of mine,' she told him.

'It's an idyllic spot,' he agreed. 'The whole of this coast is, although I won't be taking the coastal route, however beautiful the view. It'll be quicker staying on the main road until we get near to Arisaig.' He pointed to the glove compartment. 'There's an OS map in there. It'll help you get a picture of where we're heading.'

Extracting the map, she unfolded it to feature the coast north of Arisaig.

'We'll take the B road just short of the town,' Lee told her. 'But we're only on it briefly before we meet the single track that leads to the campsite.'

Minutes later, he was doing as promised, turning onto the narrower road but only travelling it for a short distance before another turn brought them onto a decidedly single track, which had, as far as Rhona could see, no obvious passing places.

'Here's where we hope we don't meet anyone coming the other way,' Lee told her. 'Or there'll need to be some reversing. Not by a police car, of course,' he added with a smile.

Eventually the hedges and flowering gardens gave way to an open field on their right, with a view to the sea beyond, shortly after which Lee turned onto a farm track.

'The croft belongs to Donald McIver and his wife, Jean. Jean looks after the bookings. It was Jean who phoned the station when they couldn't find the child. The site has a couple of toilets, fresh water and a place to deposit your chemicals. A few electricity points and not much else, except' – he indicated the beach beyond and the neighbouring blue sea – 'a view of heaven.'

Trundling past the croft house, he didn't stop. 'They know why we're here. Good folks. I hope this won't spoil the season for them.'

Entering by the open gate, Lee pointed to the far left where a blue Transit van sat near a corner fence, the area around it cordoned off, with a white-suited SOCO in view.

'And here's the next part of the puzzle,' Lee said as he drove along the dirt track that crossed the site. 'A young woman arrived yesterday evening. Lucy's family spoke to her, and she apparently promised to take the kids out today in her kayak. When Lucy disappeared, her mother checked the van and found signs of a possible struggle inside. The girl hasn't been located as yet,' he added. 'Although her kayak's not there, so we're hoping she may be out somewhere on the water.'

'You think the grave might be hers?' Rhona said.

'I don't think it's that fresh, but no doubt you'll know.' He tailed off as he drew up outside the crime scene tape that surrounded the blue Transit van. He pointed at the nearest motorhome.

'That's where the wee girl is, with her parents and brother. They're key witnesses, being apparently the only ones who spoke to the young woman, apart from Jean and Donald, on her arrival yesterday evening.'

'And the locus itself?' Rhona asked.

'A short walk west, before the next headland and its campsite. The incident van's in situ, plus Chrissy should be there by now.'

Rhona climbed out of the vehicle. 'I'll get kitted up first, then I'd like a quick word with the SOCO working the blue van.'

5

Arisaig

Day two

From the outside, you might believe it to be an ordinary Transit van.

However, inside it had been lovingly changed into a home from home. Quirky and pretty, with hand-stencilled units, bright sunflower cushions on the bed and an all-round shelf of books above.

Rhona ran her eyes over their spines to find a mix of Booker Prize winners, women's fiction and a selection of crime novels.

All of this air of fun and normality was sadly stripped away, however, when you focused on the blood-splattered surfaces and bedcover. Plus the pool of encrusted vomit on the floor.

She set about taking her own photographs of the scene, before stepping back outside to speak to the SOCO, Isabel, who she'd met professionally before.

'I think there was some sort of altercation in there,' Isabel confirmed. 'A couple of sets of fingerprints. Partial footprints in the blood splattering, one large, one smaller.'

'So possibly a man and a woman?' Rhona said.

Isabel nodded. 'There's blood on the grass at the door side facing the sea. We think the victim may have gone over the fence at that point. The footprints continue on the other side as far as the waterline. The tide was full in around ten last night, so if she was walked along the beach, any indication of that has gone.'

She paused, in case Rhona wanted to ask anything, before continuing. 'We found traces of blood on the bed, and this.' She held up a clear evidence bag. In it was a stick figure, crudely fashioned from twigs.

'It was hanging above the bed, at the pillow end.'

Rhona accepted the bag and took a look through the clear plastic at the face, the open mouth represented by a gouged hole.

'You believe the perpetrator might have left it here?' Rhona said.

'You've seen the way the van has been done up. To my mind, it looks out of place, considering the decor. Creepy, even. Like a talisman.'

'Anything here to provide us with an identity of the owner?'

'Nothing, no wallet, nothing with a name on it. They're checking for the number plate.'

They talked a little further, Isabel confirming that the forensic material they collected would be sent on to the lab, before Rhona returned to the police vehicle, where Lee was on the phone.

'They've found a kayak floating a couple of miles along the coast north of here. It's not been identified as that of the missing girl,' he told her. 'They're going to send a photograph. Maybe the two kids will recognize it, or their parents.'

He checked whether she was ready to go to the locus. 'You can walk from here along the machair. Or I can take the car along to the next campground and head in from there.'

Rhona briefly considered this, before saying, 'I'd like to walk round. I'll meet you there.'

He nodded. 'I thought you would. Just head towards the obvious police presence. No need to climb the fence. There's a path onto the beach halfway along the east bay.'

Rhona waited until he'd driven off, then, accompanied by the haunting cries of seabirds, she headed in the direction Lee had indicated. Mid-afternoon, the tide was out, exposing a long stretch of wet sand with occasional pools, where a couple of children were splashing about with a dog and a ball.

She realized that at low tide it would be perfectly possible to exit here by walking across the sand in either direction, either north or south, and not require a vehicle.

Lee had said they'd interviewed the McIvers and all those who'd been staying at the campsite the previous night, and collected their contact details, after which those who had wanted to go were allowed to leave.

'The site's mostly used for overnight camping,' he'd explained. 'Ideal for folk intent on exploring the west coast. Or maybe heading for the NC500. Small tents predominantly,' he'd added. 'With only three electric points, it doesn't attract the big vans. Although Lucy and her family were planning to spend a week here.'

'Are they staying on?' Rhona had said, wondering how distressing that might be for them, after Lucy's disappearance.

'They've only a couple of days left of their holiday, which gives us a little more time with the girl, just in case she should remember anything useful.'

Some family holiday this had turned out to be, Rhona thought.

Having located the beach entrance, she began her walk back to the corner where the blue van stood. From the beach side of the fence, it looked like an idyllic spot. Parked across the corner, the occupant of the van would have been out of sight of the other campers. Plus, they would have a view of both bays and a perfect place to watch the lovely sunsets of the previous week, which she'd so enjoyed on Skye.

The idyllic nature of the location screamed safety at her. She knew she would have felt safe to camp here, even if she had been alone.

Gathering her thoughts, she set off along the path, turning when she suddenly sensed she was being watched.

The eyes of a little blonde-haired girl and a taller, older, darker-haired boy were studying her intently from the window of the nearest motorhome.

So this was the wee girl who'd wandered off, frightening everyone, and instigating a police search for her. Lucy, Lee had said her name was, and her older brother, Orlando.

Catching her eye, the boy swiftly turned away, but the little girl put her palm flat against the glass as though in greeting. When Rhona held up her own palm in answer, the child responded with a wide smile.

If she had been traumatized by her experience, it wasn't obvious at this moment. Rhona hoped it would remain that way.

The police were always careful about what information they released to the general public, but it would be common knowledge by now, among the search party at least, that the child had been found in the vicinity of a possible burial. And such a story, especially with a photograph of Lucy, would provide a great headline, and a hefty payment for the person who offered it.

As she met and passed a rocky headland, Rhona spotted the locus in the near distance. The low-lying fertile soils in the numerous bays were made up of sand and crushed shells, known as machair. The wild flowers that grew here were specific to their location, the colours changing throughout the season with yellows dominating at first, then fading into reds, whites and blues.

From what Lee had told her, this was the type of soil they would be excavating. The weather was forecast to be dry until the end of the week, and the long hours of daylight would prove beneficial.

Essentially, an excavation should be done in the open and not inside a forensic tent. It was important to photograph the soil layers in daylight as they were carefully removed, with the camera capturing this at each stage.

And every image would tell its own story.

As she walked the path that the victim may have taken, Rhona thought through what she knew about burials in such an environment.

As Lee had indicated, the ground cover often took a long time to recover from being dug up, so the grave outline may well have been obvious to the human eye, as well as to the scenting power of the police dog.

Of course, if it was the young woman missing from the campsite, her body would still be in the early stages of decomposition. If the grave was shallow, the smell of decay alone would have alerted the dog. Although Lee hadn't mentioned any obvious smell.

When, earlier, she'd wondered out loud whether the possible grave might hold a dead dog or sheep, 'Very unlikely' had been his firm answer. He hadn't added that a local simply wouldn't bury their dead animals on the precious machair, which was what he'd meant.

Crossing the final promontory, Rhona caught sight of the locus, tucked in at the head of a small sandy bay, the familiar outline of the incident and forensic vans, with the cordoned-off area and forensic tent indicating she'd arrived at her destination.

6

Day two

A few yards from the tent, Chrissy had already pegged out an area around the suspected grave, the outline of which was obvious to a trained eye.

'So what do you think, boss?'

'It's not new,' Rhona said. 'And certainly not within the last twenty-four hours.'

Chrissy nodded. 'My thoughts too. And look at the cut line. Three sides only. Which suggests the turf was rolled back like a carpet.'

'Making it easy to put back in place,' Rhona added. 'The gravedigger probably hoped that would help retain the grass coverage.'

'Which it didn't,' Chrissy said with a grim smile.

Graves were often spotted because of the difference in the ground cover between them and the surrounding vegetation. That, and sinkage, as the body decomposed below the surface.

In this case, the machair vegetation had died and the ground had slumped a little on the seaward side, probably caused by leaching.

Chrissy had set up the time-lapse camera and laid out a grid across the grave for them to work by. One image would be taken every ten minutes of excavation, then stitched together in an MP4 movie, which could be used in court if required.

'You've photographed it as found?' Rhona asked.

Chrissy nodded. 'We're all set to start taking off the top layer.'

'We'll not try to unroll it,' Rhona said. 'But stick to the grid you laid out.'

Estimating they had around five hours of decent light before they'd have to cover the grave until the following morning, they started the camera.

Like an unsung duet, they set to work, Rhona carefully removing a square of turf at a time, easing it away from the sandy soil beneath, while Chrissy bagged it for transportation to the lab.

Having removed the entire covering of turf, they found the underlying soil to be predominantly dry white shell sand, similar to the nearby upper regions of the beach.

Still sticking to the numbered grid, they continued to dig out the sand a square at a time, numbering and bagging as before.

Eventually Rhona caught a scent she knew only too well. Meeting Chrissy's eyes above the mask, she saw that she too had noted its presence.

It was a smell they'd met many times before. It heralded the moment you knew you were in the presence of death. Immediately recognizable and never to be forgotten, in all its various forms.

It seemed the gravedigger hadn't dug more than two feet down to bury their victim, perhaps through lack of time, or in the belief that what was being buried was unlikely ever to be discovered.

They both remained silent as they painstakingly removed the final layer of sandy soil to completely expose the body.

The victim lay on her back, vacant eye sockets staring up at a summer sky dotted with small white clouds. She couldn't hear the swish of water as it met the shore, nor could she smell the fragrance of the flowering machair, or feel the warmth of the sun on her face.

Although, by what she wore, it was clear that she had likely loved the sheltered bays such as this one that peppered the coastline.

The short, tight, high-necked neoprene wetsuit of black and pink, together with the neoprene boots, appeared unmarked by their time buried beneath the machair. Where encased in neoprene, Rhona knew, the body would be far better preserved than the unwrapped parts.

In fact, the legs, arms, hands and head were already in the third and active decay stage of human decomposition, with evidence of loss of fingernails and teeth, skin slippage, marbling of veins and seepage.

'Well,' Chrissy said, sitting back on her haunches. 'She's not our missing woman from the campsite. That's for certain.'

Rhona agreed.

'So how long has she been here, d'you think?' Chrissy asked.

'Buried in dry sand in warm weather, the exposed parts would suggest maybe a month or so,' Rhona said. 'On the other hand, the body below the neoprene suit could look as though she died yesterday.'

As she said this, something caught Rhona's eye. Bending over the remains of the face framed by curly blonde hair, she saw she was right.

'There's something in her mouth.'

Using her gloved forefinger and thumb, she gently eased the object out.

It was a bundle of twigs fashioned to look like a stick man, the mouth a gouged-out circular hole.

'What the hell is that?' Chrissy said.

'I don't know, but there was one just like it hanging above the bed in the blue campervan. The SOCO bagged it as evidence.'

Chrissy looked at the stick man, then back to Rhona.

'Okay, so that can't be a coincidence, can it?'

Rhona didn't think so, especially since they appeared pretty well identical.

'So, it's not the missing girl's body, but . . .' Chrissy tailed off.

'But it may be the same perpetrator involved,' Rhona finished for her. 'I need to let Lee know what we've found up to now. Wherever the missing girl is, it looks like she may be in danger.'

She found Lee over by the mobile unit, talking to a short man in overalls.

'Dr MacLeod, this is Donald McIver, who runs the wee croft camp.'

'Well, I wouldn't say I run the campsite. That's Jean's business, as I told the lassie in the blue van when she came to the door.' He shook his head. 'Never since we opened the field to campers have we ever had such a thing happen. Jean was beside herself when wee Lucy went missing. Thank God we found her. Then the young woman from the blue van disappears.' He paused to look across at the forensic tent which hid the grave that lay beyond.

Acknowledging his distress, Rhona asked if she might speak to Detective Sergeant MacDonald alone.

'I'll be getting on, then. We're grateful you're here,' he added, before heading back through the field towards the croft house.

'He and the missus are pretty shattered by all of this. As I said, they're good folk.' Lee waited, aware that Rhona had something to say.

'As crime scene manager on this, you should come and see what we've found,' Rhona told him.

'Is it the girl from the van?' Lee asked worriedly.

'No, but it might be connected to her disappearance. You can get suited up in the forensic tent.'

She took note of the remaining light as they walked back together. Approaching midsummer, the sun would set here around ten thirty, although the light needed to work properly by would be gone before that.

An excavation such as this one was a slow and laborious process. They wouldn't reach the point where the body might be removed by the time the good light had gone, so would require to move the tent over the body and secure it until morning.

'So what should I be prepared for?' Lee said as he pulled on his suit.

'It's female. Definitely not the girl in the blue van, though we do think it's a fairly recent burial.' She showed him the bagged stick man. 'This was inserted into her mouth.'

Lee said something in Gaelic under his breath. 'That looks like—'

She finished for him. 'The one found hanging above the bed in the blue van.'

It wasn't the first dead body Lee had seen, although it

might well have been the first excavation he'd dealt with. The smell met them on approach and Lee was doing his best not to comment on it, but the smothered cough and the concentration lines on his forehead signalled how difficult that was proving.

Nevertheless, he knelt beside the shallow grave and took a good and prolonged look at what lay in there.

Eventually rising, he turned away and, facing the serenity of the sea, said, 'How long do you think she's been here?'

Rhona outlined her thoughts on that, and asked, 'Were there any reports of a missing person in the vicinity in the previous couple of months?'

He considered that for a moment, then shook his head. 'Our missing persons around here tend to be elderly and confused folk, or mountain climbers, just as it was on Skye. To my knowledge there's not been a kayaker or a camper reported missing.' He turned back to the body. 'I take it there's nothing buried with her that might give us a clue as to who she is?'

'Nothing so far,' Rhona said. 'But we still have to work the area beneath the body.'

'I'll contact Inverness, get them started on missing persons. Can you draft a broad description of what she may have looked like alive?'

'Of course,' Rhona said.

She walked him back to the tent. 'We'll need to stop work shortly and cover the grave until first thing tomorrow.'

'I thought as much. We've booked you and Chrissy into a hotel in Arisaig.' He smiled. 'Renowned for its food. I remember how much Chrissy likes her grub.'

Chrissy was famous for always being able to eat, despite the forensic circumstances she found herself in.

'She'll be pleased about that,' Rhona said, 'although I understand she already sent one of your constables into Arisaig to fetch her a burger and chips for lunch.'

'Aye, that'll be PC Murray. He's new at the job and keen to please. How long before you're ready to knock off?'

'Another half-hour should see us ready to go.'

Rhona left him then and headed back to the gravesite, where Chrissy had cleared the remaining soil from around the body.

'Anything of interest?' Rhona asked.

'This was tucked in beside her.' Chrissy held up what looked like a small black waterproof pouch.

'Have you checked inside?' Rhona said, hoping it might hold a clue to the victim's identity.

Chrissy handed it over. 'I waited for you.'

7

Day two

'Very nice,' Chrissy declared as she drew up opposite The Old Library. It declared itself to be a 'Restaurant with Rooms', which definitely appealed to someone who'd announced more than once that she was 'ravenous' on the short drive from the locus.

Rhona hadn't admitted the degree of her own hunger as yet, although the further she'd got from the crime scene, the more gnawing it had become.

This was the moment at home in Glasgow, having returned from work, usually late, she would have immediately ordered a takeaway from one of her usual outlets. That was unless she arrived home to find Sean Maguire there to cook for her.

'So no fast food for you tonight, we're dining in style.' Chrissy unfastened her seat belt with a flourish.

'Let's hope the restaurant isn't fully booked,' Rhona said, suddenly realizing how busy the village appeared to be.

'Lee reserved us a table for eight thirty, and we have one of the chalet rooms at the back. Apparently we were lucky to get in anywhere, but someone cancelled. If there had been no room at any inn in Arisaig, we were destined for

Mallaig, hopefully not staying at the police station,' Chrissy finished dramatically.

It wouldn't be the first time she'd had to do that, Rhona thought, especially in the more remote locations she'd found herself in. Still, tonight looked set to be better than a bed in a cell.

'And how do you know all this?' Rhona said, marvelling at Chrissy's ability to learn everything before she'd even thought to ask.

'I was chatting to PC Murray while you were writing up your notes in the tent,' Chrissy told her with a knowing smile. 'Does that earn me first place in the shower?'

'It most certainly does,' Rhona said.

The truth was, she was as keen as Chrissy to be washed clean of death and its associated smells. In fact, on emerging from the tent and seeing how far the tide had come in, she'd even contemplated going for a swim.

She'd envisaged herself walking across the white sand, warmed by the sun, then the cool of the water around her ankles, the snap of cold as it reached her thighs, before she would shallow dive and be swallowed by the fringes of the Atlantic.

Then Chrissy had shouted that they were ready for the off and so she'd reluctantly abandoned her dream, replacing it with the promise of a proper swim once her task here was complete, and the victim's body had been removed to the mortuary.

Now, while Chrissy sang in the shower, Rhona checked out the hotel literature.

Arisaig, she read, *as well as being the name of the village, is also the traditional name for part of the surrounding peninsula south of Loch Morar, extending as far east as Moidart.*

'Arisaig' means 'the safe bay'.

Who, on coming here to stay in the village or its surroundings, would have believed otherwise . . . until now?

They had left the locus under the watchful eye of PC Angus Murray, who would be on guard tonight. Rhona had been introduced to the tall young highlander by Chrissy, who already treated him as a pal, something he appeared quite pleased about.

Rhona smiled as Chrissy's shout announced that she was finished, and that there was only ten minutes until they were due to eat. Rhona suggested she get dressed and head on down, and that she would like a glass of dry white wine. After which she stepped into the shower to wash away the scent of death, until tomorrow at least.

Sean called as she emerged from the shower and, wrapped in a towel, she answered.

'Where are you?' the Irish voice asked.

'Arisaig. Where are you?'

'San Francisco,' he told her. 'So we're both on a west coast, just in different countries and I suspect different planets. Why are you in Arisaig?' he added, puzzled. 'I thought you were on Skye this week.'

'I was, but duty called me to Arisaig,' she told him. 'A body buried in the machair.'

Sean's jokey tone immediately switched to concern. 'You okay?'

'Of course,' she said. 'How about you?'

'I'm good.'

As he fell silent, she caught the sound of music and voices in the background. Thinking of the time difference, she suddenly realized it would be midday where he was.

'You're already at work?' she asked.

'Just about to play my last lunchtime session, then I head for the airport.'

'And I'm just about to go and eat dinner,' she said.

'So I'll see you when I get back?' Sean asked.

'Of course,' she managed.

She rang off then, thinking of all the things they'd left unsaid as she hurriedly dressed, brushed her hair and headed downstairs.

Reading Rhona's expression as she took her seat in the dining room, Chrissy promptly asked if she'd been talking to Sean.

'How—' Rhona began.

'You had that look on your face,' Chrissy said, handing Rhona the menu. 'I'm having the garlic mushroom starter and then fish and chips. Oh, and I ordered a bottle of wine, rather than a glass. We deserve it.'

Rhona was inclined to agree. Glancing at the menu, she chose the mussels followed by the venison.

'So, how is Sean?' Chrissy said.

'Good. It's midday in San Francisco and he was about to play a lunchtime session.'

Chrissy was giving her the eye. 'So all is well between you two?'

Lying to Chrissy had never worked and never would. Rhona shrugged. 'I've been on Skye for the last week. He's been on tour.' She changed the subject. 'So what's been happening in Glasgow while I've been away?'

Chrissy interpreted the question as expected. 'McNab and Ellie are not back together as predicted by you after the dinner party at Janice and Paula's place. The night you and Sean escaped early, using your cat as an excuse to go home for sex.'

God, Rhona thought, *Chrissy even knows about that.*

The dinner party Chrissy was referring to had been the finale to their last case involving a ghost ship gone aground at Yesnaby on Orkney. Three couples: herself and Sean, who was there against his better judgement; DS Michael McNab and on–off girlfriend Ellie, who preferred an open relationship to McNab's closed one; plus DS Janice Clark, McNab's work partner, and her wife, Paula.

They'd managed to avoid discussing work for a while, but just as Sean had predicted, they'd got there eventually. Watching Ellie as they'd inevitably talked shop, Rhona had decided that being the girlfriend of a serving detective wasn't something Ellie relished.

'And,' Chrissy continued, her expression now grave, 'there are rumours of an accusation of sexual assault against a serving officer.'

Now this was worrying news.

'Do we know who?' Rhona said.

Chrissy indicated not. 'No one's talking. It's supposedly linked to the clubbing scene at the top of Sauchiehall Street.'

The stretch of Sauchiehall Street between Charing Cross and Buchanan Street Galleries, once one of Glasgow's main shopping streets, had recently fallen on hard times, especially since the famous Glasgow School of Art had been tragically burnt down twice, endangering a cluster of businesses in the vicinity.

The Charing Cross end was now mainly a night-time area for clubbers. Clubs like the Blue Arrow, Nice N Sleazy and the Priory were the go-to establishments, especially for students. Hence why the area was referred to as the student strip.

Sean had played the jazz club known as the Blue Arrow on occasion, but Rhona had never been inside it, or any of the others. Chrissy, on the other hand, had visited them all.

'Has McNab said anything about this?' Rhona asked.

'Not to me,' Chrissy said. 'But you're the one he usually confides in. Maybe when you get back . . .'

Rhona didn't respond, not wishing her history with Detective Sergeant McNab to be up for further discussion tonight.

Their starters having arrived, they focused primarily on satisfying their hunger. In the interval between the courses, Chrissy topped up their glasses.

'It's a pity that the waterproof pouch only held a ring.'

Rhona agreed, but in truth she hadn't been surprised by that. The pouch had been too light to expect to find a wallet or mobile inside. She also suspected the perpetrator had made a point of emptying the pouch, to ensure there was no means of identifying the victim.

Caught in the seam, the ring, with the inscription *S loves D*, had simply been missed . . . which might be the killer's first mistake.

Rhona's final task, after writing up her notes, had been to draft a description of the victim and email it to Lee as requested. Once the body had undergone a full post-mortem, it would be updated. As it was, she had done her best with what she could determine at this stage.

> Female, possibly mid to late twenties, blonde, with shoulder-length curly hair, height approx. five foot four inches. Wearing a short neoprene wetsuit. Colour black with pink shoulders. Black swim boots, size five. Silver ring found in waterproof pouch. Photo attached.

'Hey.' Chrissy's voice brought her back to the present. 'You haven't told me about Skye. Did you visit ACE Target Sports?'

'We . . . I did,' Rhona said.

Chrissy's eyes lit up. 'We? You mean you and Jamie?'

There was little point in trying to avoid an answer, so Rhona nodded.

'Mmmm.' The shaped eyebrows rose to disappear behind the thick fringe, which was currently blonde in colour.

Rhona waited for what would undoubtedly come next, and was then surprised when she was wrong.

'You saw Blaze, of course . . . and Donald?'

'I did and he asked kindly after you. Donald that is, not the dog,' she added.

'It seems like a lifetime ago we were there,' Chrissy said wistfully. 'I liked Skye a lot. So, what did you and Jamie get up to?' she added, all innocence.

As Rhona rattled off the Gaelic names of the mountains they had climbed together, Chrissy's eyes began to glaze over, which was exactly what Rhona had intended.

'Sounds like fun,' Chrissy said, not meaning a word of it.

Pleased she'd brought an end to her interrogation, Rhona indicated she was heading upstairs to go over her notes from today.

'I said I'd meet Angus in the Arisaig hotel bar,' Chrissy informed her airily.

'Angus?' Rhona repeated. 'You mean PC Murray? I thought he was on duty at the locus tonight?'

Chrissy glanced at her watch. 'Only until ten o'clock. What?' she added, catching Rhona's expression.

'We have to be at the locus first thing tomorrow,' Rhona reminded her.

Chrissy looked unconcerned. 'No problem, boss. And I promise not to wake you when I come up to bed.'

8

Day two

A full moon hung above the waters of the bay, rendering it almost as bright as day.

Francine, unable to sleep, had come out to observe it, and to try to reconcile her feelings for this place and what had happened here.

They were due to head home the day after tomorrow, and Lucy hadn't yet told them why she'd been found next to the grave along the shore. Or if she had seen the kayak girl the morning she'd disappeared.

Lucy, who'd previously been more than willing to chat incessantly, had simply stopped speaking at all. As for Orlando, his usual silence had deepened still further.

Derek, on the other hand, had grown angrier with each passing hour, and now wanted away from here. Regardless of what the police said.

'We leave the day after tomorrow, whether they like it or not,' he'd announced that evening as they'd sat outside, him getting steadily drunker, she withdrawing into her shell, like the molluscs that clung grimly to the nearby rocks, even as the retreating tide tried to drag them with it.

Coming back here was supposed to make things better

between them. It had, in fact, made things worse. And it wasn't only Lucy running off or their neighbour in the blue van disappearing that had caused it.

She'd been watching Derek since they'd arrived, noting his thinly disguised interest in every lone female camper who'd arrived there. His walks about the camp, always in their direction. His chatting to them on the beach.

Derek wasn't going to stop doing what he wanted, regardless of his hollow promises. She'd now accepted this. Knew she must make plans for the future, her future and that of the children. But . . .

She cast a furtive glance in the direction of the blue van, still encased in yellow crime scene tape, as her biggest fear rose to engulf her.

What if Derek had tried it on with the missing girl? What if he'd been in the van with her? Left evidence of that. She shied away from the thought of what that evidence might be.

What if he was in any way responsible for the girl's disappearance?

Then another thought occurred, which tightened her chest still further.

What if Lucy or Orlando knew that, and that was the reason neither of them would speak to the policewoman, or even to her, their mum?

She had become increasingly certain that the children were hiding something from her. Plus they were avoiding Derek. She had thought at first it was because of his constant foul mood. Now she wasn't so sure that was the reason.

Francine turned her gaze in the direction of Arisaig. The forensic woman, a Dr MacLeod, who'd been here checking out the van, was apparently the one in charge of digging up the body. Or so the policewoman had told her.

They hadn't been introduced, but Francine had seen the woman walk past on her way to the grave. Had noted the smile she'd directed at Lucy. Had been surprised when Lucy had smiled back and even more so when they'd exchanged a wave.

She'd been told that Dr MacLeod and her assistant were staying in Arisaig tonight, which meant they hadn't finished with the body yet and would be back tomorrow.

Lucy's reaction to the woman had been surprising. Might Dr MacLeod be able to get Lucy to talk to her about how she'd come to be sitting near the grave?

Would that even be wise, she wondered?

But if it would help Lucy, and Orlando, then surely it would be worth it?

She watched as a red blush in the east heralded the approach of sunrise, and in that moment she made up her mind.

She would speak to the policewoman as soon as she arrived this morning. She would get her on her own and explain that she believed her daughter might be willing to talk to Dr MacLeod.

9

Day three

The hotel had kindly arranged an early breakfast for them, and had also supplied a packed lunch to take to the locus.

Chrissy had looked mildly put out that sandwiches, however delicious, were going to replace her burger and chips of yesterday, but wisely didn't voice her thoughts.

The weather too had remained kind. The sun had returned and was currently burning off the mist that softened the edges of the outer rocks. All being well, Rhona was hoping today would see them complete their examination of the body, although they would still have the material beneath it to excavate.

Reaching the site, they found a smiling PC Murray back in post, having let the night shift go home for a sleep. As he and Chrissy exchanged a few words, Rhona walked on ahead.

Despite the early hour, there were kayaks out on the water, although none venturing into the small bay next to the locus, where crime scene tape had been set up along the line of the beach to discourage visitors.

Walking through the machair brought waves of soft scent to assail her, while the birdsong rang in her ears. She pondered again on the contrast between the idyllic nature of this spot and the horror of what they had unearthed here.

Chrissy appeared beside her. 'Angus wonders if we'll be here another night?' she said, all innocence.

Rhona gave her a look. 'And what did you tell him?'

'Probably?' Chrissy tried.

'Tell him we're booked in for another night,' Rhona said. 'Right, shall we get started?'

Kitted up, they worked in well-rehearsed tandem to remove the coverings that had protected the site overnight.

Now began the critical task of forensically examining the remains in detail, with samples being taken in situ. This scene could never be replicated, so their time here must be spent making sure they had captured every piece of evidence possible, before the body was taken to the mortuary.

It was a task Rhona both loved and hated. Hated that it was required, loved the fact that with this task she might honour the dead, as befit the Gladstone quote she wrote in each of her notebooks.

Show me the manner in which a nation or a community cares for its dead and I will measure exactly the sympathies of its people, their respect for the laws of the land, and their loyalty to high ideals.

In this case there were no obvious signs of how she might have died. No bloodied tears in the neoprene that still encased the trunk. Neither did the exposed flesh of arms and legs show any obvious wounds. There was no sign of blunt trauma to the head either. No evidence of a ligature being used, although the collar of the wetsuit obscured the neck and therefore didn't allow them to check for possible strangulation.

It was Chrissy who spotted what appeared to be an area

of pigmented or tattooed skin on the lower part of the right arm.

Putrefaction had rendered the mark indistinct, but Rhona thought if she removed the loose epidermis, it would be clearer on the underlying dermis. If her hunch was right and it was the remains of a tattoo, it might be another aid in helping to identify the young woman in the grave.

When they stopped for lunch, Chrissy went off to chat to PC Murray, and Rhona decided to walk a little way back towards the croft campsite, planning to eat her lunch on a beach not encased in incident tape.

Here, the world continued as normal. The field held a good number of tents and campervans, including the one housing the Henderson family. From what Lee had said, they were due to leave tomorrow. No doubt with unhappy memories of their stay at Arisaig.

Settled on the grass next to the beach, she ate her sandwiches while watching the comings and goings of those out on the water . . . until she heard someone call her name. Turning, she discovered a young female police officer approaching.

Rhona rose, immediately thinking she might be wanted back at the locus.

'PC Anne Cameron,' the officer introduced herself. 'I work with DS MacDonald at Mallaig.'

'Pleased to meet you,' Rhona said, wondering what was making the young woman feel so awkward.

'I'm sorry to bother you, Dr MacLeod, but Mrs Henderson, Lucy's mum,' she gestured towards the campsite, 'wondered if she might have a word with you.' She halted there for a moment. 'Not regarding what's happening over there.' She cast a glance in the direction of the gravesite. 'It's about Lucy.'

She explained how they were all worried that Lucy hadn't spoken at all since she'd been found, and that Francine, her mother, had noticed her friendly reaction to Rhona yesterday. 'Which surprised and delighted her,' she said. 'Would you have a moment to speak to Lucy?'

When Rhona didn't immediately answer, she added, 'I haven't been able to get a word out of her. No one has.' The note of failure in her voice was reflected in her face.

'I'd be happy to. I take it you've okayed this with DS MacDonald?' Rhona said.

'I have,' she assured Rhona. 'I thought I might send them down here to you. Rather than you come to the van. The husband's a bit angry about it all,' she added.

'Go right ahead,' Rhona said.

The woman and child arrived minutes later. The child's face curious, the mother's worried.

Rhona held up her hand, just as she'd done before. 'Hi, my name's Rhona.'

After a moment's hesitation, the girl repeated the gesture, but didn't offer her name.

'I was planning on a paddle,' Rhona said. 'Want to come with me?'

The child gave a shy smile and nodded.

'Shall we take off our shoes, then, and see how cold the water is?'

Rhona checked with the mother that this was okay. She nodded and took a seat on the grass, while Rhona and Lucy tested the water with their toes and then, with a few oohs and ahhs, walked in.

At first the child was silent, then she began picking up things, seashells and bits of seaweed, and talking to them. Eventually she pointed at a blue kayak being paddled past and said, 'Callie said she would take me and Orly out in her boat.'

'Callie?' Rhona repeated.

'She lived in the blue van, but she's gone.' She looked up at Rhona, the small face puckered as though near to tears. 'Do you know where she is?'

Rhona slowly shook her head.

'Is she buried over there?' Lucy pointed towards the forensic tent in the distance.

'No, she isn't,' Rhona said firmly.

Lucy's face brightened a little and Rhona wondered if worrying about that had rendered the child silent.

'She didn't keep her promise to take us out in her boat, because she's been hurt,' Lucy announced.

'What makes you think that?' Rhona asked quietly.

'Orly saw inside her van. He says there was blood. Was Orly right?' she asked, a tremor in her voice.

Rhona decided she couldn't lie. Not now when the child was confiding in her. 'Yes,' she confirmed.

'It's not nice to hurt somebody.' Lucy shook her head from side to side. 'Mummy says you must always be kind.'

'My mum used to say that too,' Rhona told her.

Lucy nodded, then picked up a pearly seashell and, holding it close to her mouth, she whispered something just loud enough for Rhona to hear.

As Rhona walked Lucy back up the beach, she spotted Orlando watching them from the window of the motorhome. She wondered if he knew what Lucy had been telling her, and thought he probably did.

Lucy's mother came towards them, her face creased by both concern and joy. The joy likely because she'd seen her daughter speaking to Rhona. The concern, Rhona thought, rested on what exactly her daughter had been saying.

Rhona explained. 'Lucy was worried it might be the girl in the blue van that we'd found. I assured her it wasn't.' She looked down at Lucy. 'I'm planning a swim later if the weather stays fine. Would you like to join me?'

Lucy nodded, her eyes lighting up.

'Why don't you and your mum go back to Orlando. I'll let PC Cameron know what we've been talking about.'

PC Cameron, having spotted what was happening, was already on her way back down.

Rhona watched as she and the mother exchanged a brief word, which made the police officer smile.

'You got Lucy to talk,' she said on reaching Rhona.

'Let's walk towards the locus,' Rhona said. 'I'd rather we distance ourselves before I tell you what she said.'

Once out of sight, Rhona described in detail what she'd learnt. She began with the missing girl's name apparently being Callie.

'She must have told the children, but not the parents. Lucy thought she was the one in the grave. That frightened her and was probably why she'd stopped speaking,' Rhona explained.

'Poor wee soul. I knew something was wrong. I just couldn't get her to tell me what it was.'

'She also knew about the blood in the van,' Rhona said. 'Which was why she was so worried about Callie. Apparently Orlando told her he'd seen it.'

'The boy saw the blood? His mother never mentioned that he was with her when she checked out the van.'

'More importantly,' Rhona said, 'Lucy says that Orly thinks he saw someone go into the blue van the night Callie disappeared.'

10

Day three

Francine watched as the two women walked off together in the direction of the crime scene.

What had Lucy said to Dr MacLeod?

She desperately wanted to ask her daughter, but instinctively knew not to. Lucy may have broken her silence, but by the look on her face, things weren't back to normal yet.

Normal, she chastised herself. *What was normal?*

Living with a husband who chased younger women? Worrying about a son whose withdrawal from the world got worse by the day? A daughter so traumatized by what's happened on her holiday that she's stopped speaking altogether?

But she's talking again now, she reminded herself, even if it was to a complete stranger.

'So,' she said as Orlando's worried face appeared at the open door. 'What do you two want to do this afternoon?'

'I'm going swimming with Dr MacLeod when she finishes work,' Lucy informed her. 'D'you want to come with us, Orly?'

Orly's face was inscrutable as he digested those surprising words.

'Can I, Mum?' he asked, anxious, it seemed, that she might say no.

'Of course,' Francine found herself responding, already certain that were Derek back from his fishing trip by then, he would no doubt forbid it.

'Come on,' Lucy told her brother, 'let's check out the rock pools.'

Orlando, looking both surprised and pleased at having his chatty sister back again, immediately agreed.

'Stay where I can see you both,' Francine ordered as they departed, carrying their pails.

She'd kept a tight rein on the two of them since Lucy had disappeared the day before, making them stay in the field and close to the van. In fact, the only one to go wandering since then had been Derek, either saying he was off for a walk or for a swim.

This time he'd taken a fishing rod with him, telling her he'd be back by teatime.

Now should be the moment when she might relax, were her life normal.

As it was, her tortured thoughts would likely occupy her instead.

She made herself a coffee and took it outside, so that she might keep an eye on the children, who were already on the shore, paddling among the rocks, their two heads, one dark, one fair, bent in their search of the numerous pools.

The kids were okay. That was what she had to concentrate on. They would go back to Glasgow tomorrow. They would put what happened here behind them. Derek would be back at work. Things would go on as before.

In her meditation class she'd been encouraged to empty her mind of troublesome thoughts by focusing on one thing and one thing only. Such as the sound of the water lapping the shore. Or birdsong. Or to focus on the rhythm of her own breathing.

She tried that now, and for a short space of time it worked. Her heart slowed and her brain stopped darting about. But it didn't last, not nearly long enough, and when it did go into action again, the unanswered questions had simply grown in number.

Dr MacLeod had said that Lucy had been worried that they'd found the kayak girl's body buried in the machair. That was why she'd stopped talking.

If it wasn't the girl from the blue van buried there, then who was it? And why had Lucy gone there in the first place?

Had her daughter seen something that might put her in danger?

Something to do with the missing girl?

At this point, the recurring image of the blood-splattered van came back with a vengeance.

Had Orlando told his sister about that, despite her ordering him not to? Had that made Lucy think the girl was dead?

But Lucy had disappeared before I checked the van, Francine reminded herself.

Might Lucy have opened the van door herself and, seeing the blood, gone in search of the girl?

God, she mouthed a silent prayer, *please let the kayak girl be alive.*

As her eyes were drawn to the eastern shoreline, where Derek had headed, the final thought arrived, searing her already tortured brain.

What if Derek had anything to do with her disappearance?

11

Day three

The mortuary van had come and gone, leaving them with an empty grave.

'Time for a break,' Rhona announced.

'Good, because the iced doughnuts and coffee should have arrived by now,' Chrissy informed her.

'How . . .' Rhona began, then halted. Chrissy could conjure up provisions at the drop of a hat, wherever they were and whatever they were doing. There was no point in asking her how the current supply had come about.

They pulled the tarp over the open grave and secured it, then Chrissy suggested Rhona find a suitable spot to sit in the sun and she would fetch the goodies.

Their examination and collection of the soil beneath the body would bring an end to their task here, and see their return to Glasgow early tomorrow.

And yet, Rhona thought, there was still the case of the missing girl, Callie, and what appeared, in the form of the stick man, to be a link between her and the body they'd just unearthed.

Would they depart tomorrow, only to be recalled to deal

with her body, either washed up along the coast or discovered in a similar grave?

And what of the child? One thing Lucy hadn't told her, and which Rhona hadn't asked, was why she'd left the campsite and come to the grave.

Had she followed someone there?

'Okay,' Chrissy said as she handed Rhona her coffee and plonked herself alongside her. 'What's going on in that head of yours?'

'The significance of the stick man,' Rhona admitted. 'Plus what more Lucy might know about all of this.'

'Have you heard from Lee yet?' Chrissy asked.

Rhona indicated not. 'I assume PC Cameron will have spoken to him. Told him what I told her.'

'I thought he might arrive with the mortuary van,' Chrissy said. 'Maybe he was following up on what you said at the campsite?'

'The father wasn't there when Lucy came with me. I got the impression that was why we were allowed to meet. PC Cameron said he was very angry about the whole thing.'

'Angry because his wee girl went missing? Or angry that he's still here?'

'I suspect both,' Rhona said, licking icing from her fingers. 'Right, shall we make a start on the undersoil?'

Reverting to their grid pattern once again, they began the rigorous and methodical removal of the soil that had lain beneath the body, which would be sifted and examined in detail back at the lab.

The air had grown clammy and Rhona, encased in the forensic suit, could feel the trickles of perspiration running down her front and her back.

'This is murder,' Chrissy said, her face above the mask a bright and sweaty red.

'It surely is,' Rhona agreed. 'That's why I'll be going for a swim in the cold Atlantic as soon as we finish, and keeping my promise to Lucy.'

She filled what she believed to be the last bag and handed it to Chrissy.

'You might be swimming in the rain,' Chrissy said, indicating a glowering western sky.

'Even better,' Rhona declared, finally standing up with a groan of relief. 'Will you be joining me?' she asked, knowing full well what the answer would be.

The expression told it all, although Chrissy did manage a suitable and much-used Glasgow expletive to emphasize her response.

'Right. So I'll see you back at The Old Library,' Rhona told her. 'You take the van. I'll walk back along the shore path. It's not far.'

'But it'll be pouring by then,' Chrissy said in disbelief.

'A drop of rain never hurt anyone,' Rhona told her.

'Ha ha,' Chrissy said with a dismissive shake of her head. 'And you'd better be back in time for dinner,' she called to Rhona's retreating back.

Rhona changed in the forensic tent. The relief at stepping out of the crime scene suit was palpable, even though she was lightly dressed underneath. Now in her swimsuit, she packed her clothes in a small rucksack and, bidding a still-disbelieving Chrissy farewell, set off across the machair to the croft campsite.

The darkening western sky receded as she walked eastward, although she had no doubt it was already pelting down on the islands of Eigg and Rhum, with a promise to reach Arisaig and herself sometime soon. However, the relief she felt at completing the excavation, plus her desire to keep her promise to Lucy that she would come for a swim after work, exceeded any concern that she might get caught in the downpour.

She just hoped it wouldn't stop Lucy being able to join her.

The scent of the flowering machair had strengthened in the sultry air. Rhona breathed it in deeply, dispelling the lingering smell of the gravesite. Already early evening, the tide was on its way in, the sheltered and shallow bays on this part of the coast offering an ideal place to swim in safety, especially for a child.

On passing the Henderson motorhome she checked for any sign of Lucy, or Orly, but there was no one outside or visible at the window. There was also no sign of PC Cameron's police car, suggesting she was no longer on duty with the family.

Rhona wondered what had happened in the interim between lunchtime and now.

She decided to knock on the door. It might be too late for a swim with Lucy, but she wanted the child to know she hadn't broken her promise.

As she crossed the field, a man emerged to stand outside and observe her approach. From his stance alone, it appeared she would be an unwelcome visitor.

Too bad, Rhona thought, as she continued to walk towards him.

He was tall and wiry, with dark hair and a handsome face, although it wasn't wearing a friendly expression. As she got closer, he appeared to change his mind and almost instantly his appearance changed, and he greeted her with a wide smile. Before she could say anything, he extended his hand.

'Dr MacLeod, I presume?'

'Mr Henderson,' she responded, accepting his firm handshake.

He waited as though expecting her to state her reason for visiting.

'I promised Lucy I would come for a swim with her,' Rhona said.

He gave a little chuckle, then indicated the glowering sky, whose darkness had not yet reached them.

'It's going to chuck it down shortly. Besides, Lucy is already ready for bed. We're heading off early tomorrow,' he added in a determined manner.

As he said this, Rhona caught a whiff of alcohol on his breath.

'If Lucy is still up, may I say goodbye?' she asked.

The pleasant expression was beginning to dissolve, revealing what she thought might be the true nature of the man beneath.

She was immediately reminded of the father of her son, Liam. Edward Stewart, now Sir Edward Stewart, who ticked at least half the boxes that suggested a psychopathic personality, had the most charming of smiles – until, that is, you crossed him.

'No, you may not, Dr MacLeod.' The smile he gave her definitely wasn't reflected in his eyes.

Rhona waited a moment before calling out, 'Lucy, I did come for a swim. Sorry not to see you.' Then turned and walked away.

If looks could in fact kill, I would be dead by now, with arrows sticking out of my back, she acknowledged as she exited the field.

She contemplated swimming in the bay nearest to the

motorhome, in case Lucy wasn't aware she had come, then decided against it. It would certainly annoy Mr Henderson, which might impact on Lucy and her mother. Or it might just make Lucy sad.

Now on the beach, she stood for a moment, registering the dilapidated static caravan abandoned in the neighbouring field. The net curtain at the front window appeared to flutter a little, as though someone might be watching her . . . or the breeze had found its way in, which seemed the more likely explanation, she decided. She assumed Lee had checked it out already, but she would ask him to make sure.

Turning right, Rhona made for the next bay round to have her swim.

12

Day three

When he came back in, his expression was thunderous.

'You should never have let that bitch of a woman near Lucy,' he said in a threatening manner.

'The policewoman suggested it might help Lucy,' Francine lied.

'Bloody police,' he muttered under his breath as he refilled his wine glass.

Lucy was keeking round the door of their bunkroom. Catching her eye, Francine motioned for her daughter to close the door.

'She was the first person Lucy has spoken to since this all happened. That was a good thing, wasn't it?' she tried.

She knew she had crossed a line by the way he drew in a breath before replying. 'But what made-up nonsense did she tell that woman?' he spat at her. 'That's what I'd like to know.'

Francine realized, with horror, what he was about to do next, and tried to get between him and the bedroom door. 'No, Derek, she'll be asleep. You can ask her in the morning, but she already told me they talked about shells and seaweed when they were paddling,' she said, lying again.

Francine hoped she'd spoken loud enough for Lucy to hear. She had no idea what Lucy had told Dr MacLeod, but whatever it was, Dr MacLeod had doubtless repeated it to PC Cameron as they'd walked along the beach together.

When Derek didn't immediately shove her out of way, Francine put a hand tentatively on his arm. 'We're going home tomorrow. We don't need to think about this any more.'

She watched, her heart big in her mouth, as he contemplated this. Then roughly shrugging her off, he returned to the table to open the second bottle of wine.

This is what their life together had become. Bursts of anger amid the sea of distaste that lay between them.

Unsure where to go now, and with no desire to join him at the table, Francine decided to sit outside. He glanced up as she opened the door.

'Where do you think you're going?' he demanded.

'I need some air,' she said. 'It's stuffy in here.' Which was true.

He drank down his wine and refilled the glass. 'If that woman's out there, on no account are you to speak to her.'

He didn't end the command with an 'or else', but she heard it anyway.

Saying nothing in return, she stepped outside. There was no sign of Dr MacLeod on either of the nearby beaches, which meant she must have walked back the way she had come, or gone further round the headland. Francine had no wish to encounter her anyway.

Once on the sand, she sat down to watch as the black clouds moved inexorably towards her. She could smell rain on the wind that felt fresh and cool against her cheek. Eventually she felt the first few raindrops patter her head, then her shoulders.

She could have returned to the campervan before it got any heavier, but chose not to, because she was recalling why they'd come here this summer.

It had been Derek's decision, of course. The reason given was that he'd had a great time here on an earlier jaunt with a couple of his mates from work.

She recalled how pleased he'd been with himself when he'd come home after that long weekend, jabbering on about fishing and campfires on the beach and laughs with the guys.

She'd suspected even back then that he hadn't only spent time with his mates. And watching his performance during the previous week, his attempts at chatting up every lone female camper, had led her to believe something similar had gone on when he was last here.

The pattering was heavier now, spiking the surrounding sand like the pecking of angry birds.

She turned her face up and caught some of the droplets in her mouth, with the desire that the rain might wash her clean inside and out, if she only sat there long enough.

And that was something she craved more than anything. To be free from disgust with herself and fear of him, the man she had once thought she was in love with and now despised.

When she eventually came inside, soaked to the skin, he didn't even look round. She undressed in the bathroom and, putting on her dressing gown, went into the bunkroom and lay alongside Lucy on the bottom bed.

'Home tomorrow,' she said, trying to sound happy about that.

Orly leaned over to look down at her, his eyes big, but said nothing in return.

Lucy reached for her hand.

Francine felt a catch in her throat. 'Okay, my darlings?' she asked, holding Lucy's hand tight.

She waited, but there was no reply.

13

Day three

Rhona had noted the police car outside the hotel as she'd come down the hill into Arisaig, and wondered if that might be Lee come to speak to them. She was right.

She found Chrissy and Lee seated together on the small patio in front of their chalet. Before Chrissy could remonstrate about the time, Rhona assured her she would be changed and ready for dinner in ten minutes.

'You're joining us?' Rhona checked with Lee before heading inside.

'That's the plan,' Lee had told her.

Seated now in the far corner of the dining room, food consumed, plus wine for her and Chrissy at least, Lee ran through what he'd been told by PC Cameron.

'The child said her brother saw blood when his mother opened the door of the blue van. And that he thought he saw someone enter the van the evening before the girl called Callie disappeared?'

When Rhona gave a nod, he considered this for a moment. 'Which confirms, in the first instance, that Mrs Henderson didn't initially give us the full story regarding the van.'

'Have you any idea why?' Chrissy asked.

'She explained to PC Cameron that she delayed telling her about the mess inside because she didn't want folk looking for the missing kayaker when they should be concentrating on finding Lucy,' Lee said.

'Fair enough,' Chrissy acknowledged. 'I may well have done that in the circumstances, if it had been wee Michael that went missing.'

'I don't think that's all Francine Henderson is keeping from you,' Rhona said.

'Such as?' Lee said.

'Lucy told me in a whisper that her father made her mother cry,' Rhona said. 'Having just met the man, I believe her.' She related her encounter with Derek Henderson. 'He definitely didn't want me to speak to Lucy again.'

Lee considered this for a moment.

'He sent PC Cameron away earlier,' he said thoughtfully. 'Said they'd only stayed on to help us, but they'd had enough now. He then accused her of traumatizing his daughter, and informed her that they were going home first thing tomorrow. Plus if we bothered them again he would lodge an official complaint.'

'Bring it on,' Chrissy said with gusto.

'You can't stop them from leaving,' Rhona said. 'But I suspect Derek Henderson has questions to answer.'

'We have the family's address in Glasgow if we need to speak to him further,' Lee said. 'Also, trained professionals to talk to the two kids, but let's just hope Callie turns up alive and well and back in her van in the next couple of days. Kayakers often choose a base then go out on trips, camping wild on the way, before coming back to their vehicles,' he told them.

'What about the blue kayak you found further up the coast?' Rhona said.

Lee shrugged. 'No one's claimed it as yet, although we've circulated an image on social media asking for the owner to come forward. We've also asked anyone who saw Callie to get in touch, using a description of her provided by Jean McIver and of course saying the croft campsite was the last place she was seen.'

'You can't get in touch if you're dead,' Chrissy said bluntly.

'Sadly, accidents and drownings happen all the time in these waters,' Lee said. 'It's the most likely reason for her to disappear.'

'Despite the state of her campervan?' Chrissy didn't look convinced.

'A mess like that could have a simple explanation,' Lee said. 'I remember being called to a house in Portree once where the steps to the back door were splattered with blood and vomit. Turned out the wee boy that lived there had shut his finger in the door and his parents had whisked him off to hospital to have it sewn back on, leaving the house unlocked and looking like a murder scene.'

Rhona knew Lee was playing devil's advocate with his story. She also knew that what he was suggesting could be true.

'What about the missing persons search on the body we just unearthed?' she asked.

'Nothing as yet. Certainly no one local missing that fits the description,' Lee told them. 'Though she was probably a tourist.'

'Since she was wearing a wetsuit, she likely went missing while out on the water. You would think someone would have reported that,' Chrissy added.

'If she was travelling alone like Callie,' Rhona said, 'that might not happen.'

'Well, no female kayaker, swimmer or paddleboarder has been reported missing in these waters over the past year,' Lee said.

'Until now,' Rhona corrected him. 'Plus the female we exhumed had a twig figure inserted into her mouth, almost identical to the one found hanging in the blue van. I don't believe in coincidence in general, and especially not in a case like this.'

As Lee prepared to leave, Rhona remembered that she wanted to ask him about the derelict caravan.

'We checked it, of course,' Lee told her. 'No one has officially lived there for the last year or so, according to Donald McIver. Why?'

'I just had a feeling of someone watching me when I passed it by.'

'Maybe kids from the camp got inside,' Lee suggested. 'I'll ask Donald to keep an eye on it.'

After Lee left, Rhona said she was going back to the room to write up her notes, while Chrissy announced she was meeting Angus in the Arisaig hotel bar.

When Rhona raised a questioning eyebrow, Chrissy gave a shrug. 'I'll be back after I've found out all the stories circulating about this case. Always ask a lowly uniform if you want to know what's really going on. Especially in places like Arisaig.'

Not for the first time did Rhona think Chrissy would make a great undercover cop.

Alone now, she checked her phone to discover a missed call from Sean, followed by a message.

What do you fancy when you get back tomorrow? A meal cooked by me at your place or a table at the Chip? I'm playing later at the jazz club.

Which she translated as: *Sex and food at your place before I head for the jazz club or not?*

She pondered this but only for a moment, because her mind was too preoccupied by the day's proceedings.

Entering the back garden, she discovered the rain had departed, and a flaming sunset now lit up the western sky. It would be just as stunning at the croft campsite, she thought.

Lee had indicated before they'd parted earlier that he intended catching the Henderson family before they left tomorrow. He would express the police's growing concern about the disappearance of their recent neighbour, and establish that they may have to be in touch with the family again in Glasgow.

'Mr Henderson won't like that,' Rhona had told him.

'I think, like you, that Lucy and her brother may well have something more to tell us about all of this,' Lee had said.

Rhona had agreed wholeheartedly with that.

The loud drill of her mobile broke into her thoughts. Glancing at the screen, she was surprised to find McNab's name and hesitated before finally answering.

'Dr MacLeod, I tried your right-hand woman first, but she didn't pick up,' he said, sounding a little disgruntled by that.

'Chrissy's currently talking to PC Angus Murray in the Arisaig hotel bar,' Rhona told him.

'A new love interest?' McNab asked.

'I think it's probably more like an interrogation,' Rhona said, 'regarding local gossip about the body we've just unearthed here. Why did you want to speak to Chrissy?' She didn't say 'at this hour', but that was what she meant.

There was a short silence punctured by background noise

which seemed to indicate that McNab was somewhere outside and wasn't keen to reveal the real reason for his call. Eventually he came back with, 'Just wondered when you two were heading home.'

'Early tomorrow,' Rhona told him.

'Great. I'll see you both after work at the jazz club.' McNab said this as though it had already been agreed.

As he swiftly hung up before she could say yes or no to that, Rhona pondered why McNab had called in the first place. She knew him well enough to judge it hadn't been specifically about their return time. She also found herself doubting whether he'd in fact tried Chrissy first. Something that would be easily checked on Chrissy's return.

She and DS Michael McNab went back a long way, through dark times more often than good. His behaviour had often made her furious, mainly to do with that self-destruct button his finger forever lingered upon. Yet along with the waywardness was his unfailing loyalty to those he worked with.

Ellie, she thought, had been good for him. Made him leave that self-destruct button alone, for a while at least. But Ellie, it seemed, had gone.

14

Glasgow

Day four

McNab groaned and turned over as the alarm music blasted into action. Reaching out, he scrabbled to halt the sound, wondering why on earth he'd chosen that particular song to wake him up of a morning.

A quick glance round told him that he was alone in the bed. Such checking had begun with Ellie's departure and continued since. In this case, after last night, there may well have been a head on the neighbouring pillow. He just couldn't quite recall at the moment.

Throwing back the duvet, he thought he caught a scent of someone more fragrant than himself.

Had he in fact brought someone back with him? Scent was the longest-lasting memory, and Ellie had stayed here a lot. Was it her scent that still lingered in the room, or just the memory of it?

The thought was a stab to his heart and he found himself muttering the same old mantra.

'*You* fucked it up, mate. *You* were the one who fucked up.'

Levering himself out of bed, he walked naked to the kitchen and, going through the well-practised motions, set up the coffee machine before heading for the shower, intent on recalling all that had happened last night, despite the hangover he'd obviously acquired.

His call to Rhona appeared first, and he immediately cursed himself for it. Why had he phoned her when Chrissy didn't answer? She'd sensed he was up to something right away. She must have heard enough background noise to guess he was outside, plus the pelting rain and the laughter of the females in the queue of clubbers in front of him.

The trio had been huddled under a single umbrella. He'd been half listening to their chat, while admiring their fortitude as the rain dripped down their bare backs.

Finally they'd gained entrance, and the brolly was taken down, giving him a clear view of those beneath, while poking him in the ribs in the process.

'Sorry,' the one wielding the brolly had apologized. 'Glasgow rain—' she began.

'You cannae beat it,' he'd finished for her.

Then he was inside and heading for the bar where he'd downed another couple of drinks while sussing out the place and the current clubbers. The males and, of course, the females.

Eventually the brolly owner had come over and introduced herself as Holly. She was slightly built with a head of chestnut hair which she likened to his own auburn, remarking that 'us redheads' should stick together.

It was at that point a guy appeared and asked her to dance, something McNab hadn't managed to do himself, but probably should have. He'd been quietly regretting that when she'd surprised him by turning the guy down, which the bloke hadn't taken well at all.

He'd bridled at the guy's attitude, but she'd just brushed it off, suggesting they take their conversation into the tabled area at the rear. Settling there with a couple more drinks, she'd told him she was a postgrad student at the Glasgow School of Art, whereupon he'd said that meant she was too young for him.

'I'll be the judge of that,' she'd told him, laughing.

That's when she'd asked him what he did. So he'd told her right off that he was a cop.

She'd thought he was joking at first, then realized he was deadly serious.

'Why are you here?' she'd asked, glancing about her as though something was about to go down.

'I like the music and I'm off duty.'

She'd softened at that. 'You like jazz?' She'd sounded unconvinced.

'Now and again,' he'd answered truthfully. 'Some of us hang out at the jazz club in Ashton Lane after work. An Irish mate, Sean Maguire, plays there and here sometimes,' he'd heard himself say, wondering when Sean Maguire had become his mate, when they had often been rivals for Rhona's affections. Or at least he had told himself so.

'So you're not here about . . .' She'd hesitated.

'About what?' he'd urged.

She'd shaken her head then. He recalled the chestnut hair meeting his face with the softness of a cloud.

They hadn't come back here, but had gone to her place, up the hill opposite, passing the sad, burnt wreck of the famous Mackintosh building.

Her flat, which she lived in alone – 'I can't work with others around,' she'd told him – was full of her artwork. Paintings of white beaches and rocky islands with only a single person in the frame, or sometimes two, where one of them looked like a spirit.

'What do you think?' she'd asked.

At that point McNab imagined himself on the edge of a precipice where one false move would send him over the edge. He'd decided to be honest.

'I don't know about art, so whatever I said would be wrong.'

'But what do you feel when you look at it?' she'd urged.

'Lonely,' McNab said. 'Lost in a world I know nothing about.' He remembered he'd given a little laugh then, because that was exactly how he had felt.

She'd nodded thoughtfully at his response, then said, 'Me too.'

She'd brought out wine and they'd sat in the brightly painted kitchen drinking it, after which she'd invited him through to her bedroom. He'd almost accepted, but she hadn't appeared to take offence when he'd indicated that he had to be in court in the morning, so should take his leave.

As she'd let him out, she'd finally brought up the topic she'd avoided before.

'You were at the Blue Arrow because of the sexual assaults that have been happening along the strip?'

'You know something about them?' he'd tried.

'Just rumours,' she'd said, meeting his eye.

'You took a chance inviting me back here,' he'd told her.

'But you're a cop, so you're safe.' She'd given him a half-smile at that. 'Would you like my number, Detective Sergeant McNab?'

He did want her number and had said so.

Dried and dressed now, McNab checked the time. He could

briefly visit the police station and his partner, Janice, before court, or have breakfast out and go straight to court.

Swallowing down the remainder of his extra-strong coffee, he chose the latter.

15

Arisaig

Day four

The detective sergeant arrived early, just as she was giving the kids their breakfast.

Derek was still in bed, comatose. He had sat up well into the night, demolishing the last of the wine they'd brought with them. She'd stayed alongside Lucy in the bunk, determined not to let him come through and start interrogating her.

Seeing the police car draw up, Francine told the kids to stay inside and, trying to disguise her alarm, went out to talk to the male officer.

'Detective Sergeant MacDonald—' he began.

'Everyone's still in bed,' she immediately said. 'It's really early for a visit,' she added, trying not to sound fearful.

'My apologies, Mrs Henderson. I wanted to catch you before you left. The search parties we've had out round the coast haven't manage to locate Callie as yet.'

'Callie?' she said stupidly.

'Lucy told Dr MacLeod that the kayak girl's name was Callie.'

Francine's immediate thought was what else Lucy might have told the police.

'Oh,' she said, 'I didn't know that. The girl didn't tell Derek or me her name.'

'We're growing increasingly concerned for Callie's welfare and we're worried something bad may have happened to her' – he paused briefly – 'considering the blood you and Orlando saw in the van.'

She nodded because she couldn't think of anything else to do.

'Your husband gave me details of how to get in touch with you in Glasgow, which may become necessary, regarding Callie's disappearance and Lucy's presence near the grave.'

'Why has the grave got anything to do with Lucy?' she demanded, her fear growing exponentially.

'We believe Lucy stopped speaking because of us finding that grave. She told Dr MacLeod she was worried it might be Callie that was buried there. Dr MacLeod managed to allay her fears about that, but Lucy never revealed why we found her at that particular place.' He continued, 'We're concerned she perhaps saw some activity there or followed someone to that spot. If it does become necessary to speak to either of your children again in Glasgow, it will of course be done with all the proper safeguards in place, I assure you.' He handed her a card. 'Just in case you need to make contact when you get back to Glasgow.'

She accepted the card, while in her head she was screaming, 'No, you're never going to talk to either of my children again.'

'Thank you again for your patience and cooperation, Mrs Henderson, and have a safe journey home.'

She watched as the car turned and drove off, hoping her

legs might continue to hold her up until it was out of sight. Meanwhile, her brain had gone into overdrive.

Should she tell Derek about the visit? What would she tell Lucy and Orly?

Nothing, she thought. *I'll tell them he was just saying goodbye and thank you, and that we'll never see Detective Sergeant MacDonald again, or PC Cameron for that matter.* That much was true. If they were ever interviewed again, it would be by someone in Glasgow.

As for Derek, if the children mentioned the police visit, she would give him the same story.

She took a series of deep breaths, telling herself that all she had to concentrate on today was not to annoy Derek, and to get the kids home safely to Glasgow.

16

Glasgow

Day four

The jury comprised three women and twelve men. Not a good balance in a domestic assault case, especially since two of the women were young, early twenties McNab guessed, and had appeared intimidated by both the proceedings and the male members of the jury who surrounded them in the box.

Once in the jury room they wouldn't argue with the decision the men would likely take. The third woman was a different kettle of fish. In her fifties perhaps, he'd noted how closely she'd listened to what was being said about the forensic material and crime scene photographs, and had taken note of the injuries inflicted.

The twenty-six bite marks in particular.

Only one man had seemed to reflect her interest throughout the trial. Probably in his sixties, he'd also taken notes and listened carefully. McNab thought he would likely vote guilty too.

Unfortunately, they would be vastly outnumbered.

McNab had identified the jury spokesperson before he'd

been announced, mainly because of the smarmy look on the guy's face. He, no doubt, had taken charge as soon as they'd retired to decide the fate of the accused.

Of the other eleven men, three were in their early twenties; he could see two of them obviously worked out regularly by their body shapes in their fitted shirts. Their facial expressions as McNab had given his evidence as the arresting officer suggested thoughts such as, 'There but for the grace of God go I' and 'Next time it might be my head in that basket', indicating which way they were likely to vote.

After all, if you couldn't give your girlfriend a slap when she needed it . . .

Then there were the other men, who'd exhibited a mix of wishing they weren't there at all alongside 'We'll do anything to get out of here as quickly as possible'.

In a Scottish court, with fifteen on the jury rather than the English twelve, you only needed a majority verdict. Plus you had the possibility of not proven, as well as innocent or guilty, to fall back on.

McNab suspected he knew what they would decide, which would run no doubt against both his evidence and the forensic material which they'd been presented with. Not least the photographs of the woman's injuries, including those bite marks, which the accused suggested she'd acquired from an earlier girly fight with another female and not from him.

He'd noted by the male jurors' expressions at that moment that they believed the defence advocate had just presented them with a way out.

This 'other woman' had not been called as a witness for either the prosecution or defence, because she'd refused to give a statement either way, preferring not to be the next victim herself.

As for the man's injuries, they'd consisted of one possible bite mark on his chest, plus a black eye.

The accused was six feet tall and in good shape. The defendant was five feet tall and as delicate as a bird. She was also Russian, with limited English, something else the men of the jury didn't like about her.

McNab found himself impressed that she'd managed to give the accused a black eye and bite his chest, if only once.

As for the accused, rather than attack her face he had concentrated on biting her body, and pulling out her hair in large bloody clumps, which had been strewn across the kitchen work surfaces. Something he also claimed had happened in the female fight, which undoubtedly, in McNab's opinion at least, had never occurred.

However, the possibility of an earlier cat fight gave the men of the jury a way out. A ploy by the defence, used to cast doubt on the defendant's story. The fact that she was also a pesky Russian had simply been the icing on the cake.

As the jury filed into court, McNab knew by the spokesman's expression that he was right. There would be no guilt found here today. The accused would walk free via a not proven verdict.

It wasn't the first time Charlie Bonar had been up before the court for just such an offence, although the jury weren't aware of that. They also weren't aware of the size of bastard he was. Unless, that is, they'd googled him during the trial, which of course was against the law. Not, McNab suspected, that it would have made any difference. The men of that jury, apart from one, had no intention of locking up one of their own.

As the verdict was announced, Bonar looked towards McNab and smiled his success.

*

'He got off?' Janice said as a glowering McNab strode into the office twenty minutes later.

'How did you guess?'

'The smoke coming out of your ears might have been the giveaway.'

'What a fucking waste of time,' McNab said. 'Twelve men on the jury. Twelve men on a domestic assault case. Half of them looked like they should be in the dock. They didn't listen to my evidence as arresting officer. As for the damning forensics, they went tone deaf at that point.'

'So, no twelve good men and true then?' Janice said sympathetically.

McNab was aware his partner was trying to lighten his load, but it wasn't working.

'Fuck it!' he said as he plonked the coffee he'd brought her on the desk.

'Fuck what exactly?' Janice said.

'The jury system. It should always be fifty-fifty on a jury. Especially in cases of rape and sexual assault.'

'It's fifty-fifty when the hundred potential jurors get contacted,' Janice said.

'But the final fifteen are pulled at random. And look what that meant today.'

'There was a time,' Janice reminded him, 'when it was *only* men on a jury.'

McNab eyed her. 'Are you pissing on me?'

'Easy, soldier,' Janice told him. 'We know you're on our side.'

He caught the smile and nodded. 'Okay, I'll shut up about it now, but he'll do it again. Without a doubt.'

He took a seat and sipped his coffee. 'I'll just have to be patient.'

He swiftly moved aside as the smothered guffaw of

laughter that met this declaration sent a spray of coffee in his direction.

Giving his partner a stern glance, he said calmly, 'So what do we have?'

Janice's expression grew serious. 'There's a possibility that the body Rhona exhumed at Arisaig may be that of Deirdre Reid, the student from Garnethill reported missing two months ago. The broad description fits. Height, hair colour, plus they found a ring in the waterproof pouch buried with the body which could be a match for the one Deirdre's boyfriend Sam said she was wearing when she went missing.'

Now this was something to take his mind off Bonar the biter.

'How the hell did she get to Arisaig from Sauchiehall Street?' McNab said.

Janice appeared as puzzled by that as he was. 'It says here that,' she read from her screen, 'she was wearing a wetsuit and boots, suggesting she'd been involved in water sports of some kind.'

'If she suddenly chose to go sailing up the west coast of Scotland, none of her pals, including her boyfriend, seemed to know anything about it,' McNab said.

The twenty-year-old had been a student at the School of Art when she'd disappeared after a night out with pals on the student strip. Sam Wheeler, her boyfriend, had reported her missing when she didn't come back to their shared flat after twenty-four hours.

'When can we be certain it's her?' McNab asked.

'Apparently, the face isn't in a fit state to be identified, so it'll have to be done by other means via the PM, which is scheduled for this afternoon. The body was brought down late yesterday.' Janice was looking at him with those questioning eyes that said, *You or me at the post-mortem?*

'I'll go,' he offered. 'Anything to make me forget the self-satisfied smile that bastard gave me when the verdict was read out.'

Janice looked pleased and a little relieved by that.

'Check for anything new on the search for Deirdre and I'll see you back here,' McNab suggested.

He briefly considered a stop-off at the canteen for a bacon roll, but swiftly dismissed it. It wasn't wise, for him at least, to eat heartily before attending a post-mortem. Frankly, he couldn't work out how Rhona could stomach being in a tent with human remains for sometimes twelve hours before she even let the body go to the mortuary. Never mind being there when it was cut up on the table.

Still, if it turned out to be Deirdre Reid, then it was his call to be there too.

He and Janice had been on the case from the moment she was reported missing, although they'd fully expected her to turn up at the flat she'd shared with her boyfriend, because folk often went off on a blinder, only to reappear again once the fun and games were over.

When it seemed she wasn't coming back, many – if not all – eyes had alighted on Sam. After all, when women went missing, husbands and partners were often behind their disappearance.

Sam, he remembered, had seemed an okay guy. A wood carver by occupation, he appeared to complement his artistic girlfriend, who specialized in sculpture. Their flat had been filled with her bronze female statues standing atop his finely worked pedestals.

But, as a detective of long standing, McNab was suspicious

of facades, and basically trusted no one on first appearances. The guy's distress had appeared genuine enough. Janice certainly had been inclined to believe in it.

Plus they could find no evidence that Deirdre had ever returned home after she'd gone off on the club trawl with two friends from the Art School. Her DNA was, of course, all over the flat, but there was no evidence of foul play.

According to her mates, Millie and Lisa, they had all been in Nice N Sleazy together. Deirdre had said she was going to the Ladies and had never returned. They'd assumed she was dancing in the crowd, as they were, but when she didn't rejoin them, they'd gone in search of her. An hour later, there was still no sign of Deirdre and their texts and calls to her mobile had gone unanswered.

They'd eventually come to the conclusion she'd gone off with some bloke, or simply gone home. Neither was truly worried, probably because of the drink or drugs they'd no doubt consumed. However, come next day when she didn't appear at the Art School, or answer her mobile, they'd begun to worry and had called the boyfriend, who'd immediately got in touch with the police.

McNab swung into the car park at the Queen Elizabeth University Hospital. On its opening, it had quickly been christened the Death Star by Glaswegians, more because of its *Star Wars* shape than the idea that you were lucky to come back out of it alive.

The mortuary, of course, was something else.

Bracing himself for what was to follow, McNab strode towards the building.

17

Day four

Rhona watched as the wetsuit was carefully cut off. It was a delicate process, one she had chosen not to do in situ, although she would have learnt more at the scene of crime if she had.

As it was, her surmising that the body encased in the neoprene would seem almost untouched by death was true. Karen, Dr Sisson's assistant, gave a little gasp of surprise, suggesting this was something she hadn't seen before.

The assistant forensic pathologist Dr Walker looked entranced by the discovery, as though this might be the first time he too had seen such a contrast between the exposed flesh and the preserved.

As for McNab, he glanced swiftly away, as though the victim's sudden nakedness was an affront to her dignity. Then again, he may have been feeling nauseous. McNab could take being beaten to a pulp himself, but witnessing the dissection of a body on the mortuary slab was something else entirely.

The torso was unmarked by any wounds, although above the left breast was a distinctive tattoo of what looked like a hummingbird.

After Sissons recorded its existence into the overhead mic, McNab caught Rhona's eye, before saying, 'I think this may be the body of Deirdre Reid, who went missing from a club on Sauchiehall Street.'

'You recognize the tattoo?' Rhona said.

He nodded. 'Her boyfriend had a photograph of it. There should be another to match it, though smaller, on the lower part of the inside right forearm.'

Sissons, who had been listening intently, moved to where McNab pointed.

'I photographed a pigmented area there, and removed the epidermis,' Rhona told him. 'It's the same tattoo.'

Sissons looked to McNab. 'Are there any other possible identifying features you might enlighten us on, Detective Sergeant?'

'Your estimated characteristics fit, hair colour, height, weight, etc. A small scar above her left eye but . . .' He tailed off, aware that the face was too far gone to find a scar.

'How long has Deirdre been missing?' Rhona asked.

'Just over two months,' McNab told her.

Rhona looked to Dr Sissons who, reading her expression, said, 'Dr MacLeod is surmising that this body may not have been dead that long. And as she is an expert in buried and hidden bodies . . .'

Ignoring the remark, which may have been either a compliment or an attempt at sarcasm, Rhona said out loud exactly what she'd been thinking.

'The depositional environment has a massive effect on the rate of decomposition. Had you asked me to take a calculated guess when we unearthed her, regarding the stage of decomposition she'd reached, I'd have said she'd been there closer to a month.'

She watched as McNab processed this. 'So she died and was buried around a month ago?' he checked.

Rhona gave a nod. 'The conditions she was buried in suggest that as a probability, yes.'

'Assuming it is Deirdre Reid, this means her captor may have kept her alive for a month or so after she disappeared from Sauchiehall Street?' McNab said.

'That could be the case, yes,' Rhona told him, aware that everyone in that room was thinking the same thing. Where had she been kept and what had been done to her during that time?

Sissons was the first to break the silence. 'I suggest we get back to our job now and try to establish how she was killed.'

At this point, McNab indicated he would contact the station regarding the strong possibility that the body might be that of Deirdre Reid.

Rhona excused herself and followed him into the changing room, where McNab showed her some images of Deirdre that Sam had given him. In one of them, the hummingbird above the breast was clearly visible.

'Janice said there was a waterproof bag with a ring in it?' he said.

Rhona brought up a picture of the ring.

'That looks like the one her partner described,' McNab acknowledged. 'Can you send me that photo and I'll have him take a look at it?"

'The other thing we found was this.' Rhona swiped her screen to display an array of images of the twig figure before and after she'd extracted it from the victim's mouth.

McNab peered at them. 'What the hell is that?' he demanded, grimacing in distaste.

'It's a stick man, fashioned from twigs, with a hole gouged for its mouth,' Rhona told him. 'It was in her mouth, and I'm assuming her killer put it there.'

She watched as McNab digested this. 'A signature, you mean?' he asked.

A signature was the term used for a ritual, something done which was unique to a killer.

'I'm assuming it has some significance to whoever put it there.' She paused. 'And that's not the only place I've seen one of these. A young woman has gone missing from a campsite near the grave we excavated. There were blood splatters inside her campervan, and a stick figure just like this one had been hung above the bed.'

It was obvious McNab didn't like what he was hearing. 'That's way too much of a coincidence,' he said, shaking his head. 'Do we have an ID on this other woman?'

'Inverness has sent out a description of the missing female and the vehicle registration number of her blue converted Transit van,' she told him.

'So we don't have a name? Wasn't she registered at the campsite?'

Rhona explained. 'It's a field on a croft next to the beach. You just turn up. There's no official log-in. It's basically for wild campers.'

'Jeez,' McNab said. 'Folk actually do that?'

Despite the circumstances, Rhona had to smile. McNab's abhorrence of the countryside had obviously not lessened since she'd seen him last.

'All we know is that her first name is Callie, at least according to the two children who were her on-site neighbours.' She explained about the Hendersons. 'Francine, the mother, described Callie as being medium height with blonde hair. Age, early twenties. The family should be back in Glasgow by now and DS MacDonald, from Mallaig police station, will have sent on their details. He and I both think the kids know more than they've been willing to say.' Rhona gave him a quick résumé of her own encounter with both Lucy and her father.

'You think he may have something to do with this Callie's disappearance?'

Rhona shrugged. 'I have no idea, but Orly told his wee sister he saw a man enter the van. Maybe it was his dad he saw.'

'Why would Henderson keep it a secret?' McNab said.

'Exactly . . . unless he made a play for Callie and didn't want his wife to know?' she suggested. 'What I'm more worried about is the significance of the two almost identical stick figures apparently linking the dead woman with the missing one.'

'The one in the mouth of the victim does seem symbolic . . .' McNab halted there. 'Maybe check with your friendly criminal psychologist as to a possible meaning?' he said, his tone dry.

McNab was, of course, referring to Professor Magnus Pirie, who they'd both worked with on a number of occasions, although he hadn't actually said the name. So Rhona did. 'You do mean Magnus?' she said with a smile.

McNab gave an almost imperceptible nod. 'He claims to know about all that sort of stuff.'

It was well known that McNab, like many serving officers, was deeply suspicious of psychology in all its forms, even more so in relation to criminality. He did, however, believe in his own intuition. In fact, the mild-mannered Orcadian professor had once described McNab's intuition as being psychology in action. The compliment, Rhona remembered, hadn't been well received.

'I plan to do that,' Rhona assured him.

'Any ideas on how she may have died?' McNab said.

'Not from my on-site examination. Hopefully now that the wetsuit's off and we're about to open her up . . .'

McNab was already disposing of his own suit.

'Not staying for the finale?' Rhona asked with a teasing smile.

'I'm better used elsewhere. You'll let me know the good doctor's conclusions?'

'Of course.'

'I'll see you later at the club,' McNab called out as the door closed behind him.

Only then did Rhona realize that she hadn't yet asked him what he'd been up to last night.

18

Day four

The dry spell of weather was over, although Glasgow residents were pretending it wasn't, which was par for the course.

The overcast sky was rewarding their disbelief by showering them intermittently. Despite this, there was no evidence of raincoats or brollies. Rather the folk walking through Kelvingrove Park exhibited a certainty that it was only a sun shower, and therefore might be ignored.

The puddles that littered the walkways suggested something different.

Reaching the brow of the hill, Rhona took a last sweet breath of the park air before entering the cool university cloisters, thinking all the time that much as she loved Skye and the west coast, it was good to be back in Glasgow.

By the time she'd left the post-mortem, a conclusion as to how the victim had died had been reached. The hyoid bone fracture, which accounted for only 0.002 per cent of all fractures in humans, was commonly associated with strangulation and rarely occurred in isolation.

The high neck of the neoprene suit had also hidden extensive fingertip bruising to the neck, which Sissons thought reflected more than one choking action prior to strangulation.

There was no water in the victim's lungs or stomach, so despite the wetsuit, although she may have been in the water, she certainly hadn't drowned there.

Their work on the soil and clothing in the lab would hopefully provide them with more information about where she had been prior to her death and burial on the machair.

As for the stick man . . . that might turn out to be the one direct link they had with her killer, she thought, as Chrissy emerged from the lab to greet her.

'Got your text and the coffee's on. Have you eaten at all?' she asked.

Rhona shook her head. 'There wasn't time before the PM,' she admitted.

'Right. I'll warm up a sausage roll in the microwave.'

Minutes later, Rhona had been provided with sustenance, and Chrissy, keen to be told all, was patiently waiting until the last bit of sausage roll had been washed down with coffee.

'Okay,' Chrissy said. 'My guess is she drowned or was strangled.'

'Did you have a spy at the PM?' Rhona demanded.

'Yes, you,' Chrissy grinned, 'although I do know Karen a little, but it's just a guess based on our study of the body in situ. No stab marks in the suit, no obvious injuries. We couldn't see the neck because of the wetsuit—'

Rhona held up her hand to stop the flow of evidence. 'Dr Sissons believes she was strangled. There was extensive bruising to the neck occurring, he believed, over a period of time.'

Both of them were well aware that choking was a form

of domestic abuse that often led to murder. It also played a part in rough sex, sometimes agreed upon, sometimes not.

'Was she ever in the water, or did her killer just dress her like that for some reason?' Chrissy said.

'My thoughts exactly,' Rhona said. 'Once we get the wetsuit, we'll hopefully learn more.'

They had spent some time taping the suit in situ, but a closer examination, particularly of the back, might reveal more clues.

'And is it Deirdre?' Chrissy asked.

'We'll have to rely on DNA to confirm that, but . . .' Rhona explained about the hummingbird tattoo above her breast.

'To match her forearm,' Chrissy nodded.

'Plus the ring,' Rhona said.

They lapsed into silence then, before Rhona mentioned the stick man. 'I spoke to McNab about it. And about the missing Callie. The thing is' – she hesitated – 'I never saw Callie, but Francine Henderson described her to DS MacDonald as medium height, slim, with curly blonde hair, and probably in her early twenties.'

'Which pretty well sums up Deirdre,' Chrissy finished for her. 'And now Callie's missing too, from the place we probably unearthed Deirdre. Weird, eh?' She halted there, her expression darkening. 'God, you don't think the killer might have been on the campsite when the blue van girl arrived?'

It was a question Rhona had been asking herself.

'Lee and his team questioned everyone on the site and took down their details,' Rhona reminded her. 'And no one else works there, other than the McIvers who own the croft.'

'What about that creepy old caravan you told Lee about?'

'The police checked it too and Donald McIver says no

one's stayed there for a long time. Something about it belonging to an old fisherman who's in a home now.'

'Killers have been known to revisit the scene of their crime,' Chrissy said. 'Maybe this one came back by boat or kayak, and poor Callie was just in the wrong place at the wrong time.'

Chrissy was right. Access by water to the site was easier than by foot or vehicle, and escape swifter. Rhona had already played out the image of the live victim being brought to the bay by kayak or small boat from wherever she'd been held, before being strangled and buried where they'd found her.

The likelihood was, she would never have been discovered if little Lucy hadn't gone walkabout and been tracked by the police dog to the graveside.

'Anyway,' Rhona drew her focus back to what she'd discussed earlier with McNab, 'I want to run the stick man aspect past Magnus to see if he has any theories as to its significance in all of this.'

'And McNab encouraged this?' Chrissy's expression said it all.

'He did, in an oblique and slightly disparaging way,' Rhona told her with a smile.

As she brought up the number, she realized she hadn't seen or spoken to Magnus since her last Orkney trip and was unsure if he was back home or still at the university. Although assuming Strathclyde University roughly followed the same dates as Glasgow, formal assessment was usually over by the end of May, and June was marking time.

He answered her call almost immediately.

'Rhona,' he said, the Orcadian lilt in his voice obvious. 'So good to hear from you.'

'Are you here or in Orkney?' she asked.

'Definitely here and up to my neck in grading. I take it you're not elsewhere in Scotland or further afield?'

'Just back from Arisaig,' she told him.

'Holiday?'

'Sadly not. Work.'

A moment followed before he came back in. 'Of course, I should have realized when I saw the news about the body unearthed in the machair that you might be involved.'

Rhona gave him a brief résumé of the stick man aspect of the story. 'McNab suggested I run it past you. It's confidential, of course, so you won't have heard about it on the news.'

'You believe it may be a signature?' Magnus asked.

'I can't think what other reason her killer would have to put it in her mouth.'

'Can you send me an image of this stick person?' he said, his tone serious now.

'Of course. There are two of them.' She explained about Callie's disappearance and the stick man in her van.

'Okay, that is worrying. And there have been no sightings of this Callie?'

'None,' she said.

'Send me what you have and I'll take a look and get back to you,' he promised.

Once Magnus had rung off, Rhona brought up the set of images she'd taken of both stick men and forwarded them as requested.

She'd already googled 'stick men' herself and was aware of their voodoo symbolism. Her search had also pulled up images associated with the 1999 horror movie *The Blair Witch Project*, the film's stick figures looking surprisingly similar to the two in her own photographs. Especially the one from the movie showing the stick figure swinging from a tree, just like the one hanging over the bed in the campervan.

Isabel, the SOCO, had been right. The girl who'd decorated that campervan would not have hung a figure like that above her bed. Which meant someone else had. And that someone, Rhona thought, had likely meant her harm.

19

Day four

Derek had gone out, straight after the kids were in bed.

Francine had breathed a sigh of relief as the door had shut behind him despite the fact that there were still loads of jobs to do. The campervan would need cleaning out, and all the dishes and pots washed and stored on board for the next outing. Then there was the clothes and bedding to wash . . .

She halted there. Who cared about that? She was home. The kids were safe in bed, and Derek, angry or otherwise, was out. And with no likelihood of him coming back until the small hours of the morning when she would be asleep.

She contemplated not bothering with the washing and sitting down instead with a glass of wine, but since she'd already carted all the dirty clothes into the back kitchen, it would be stupid not to load the machine, even if she didn't switch it on until tomorrow.

Pouring a glass of wine, she took it through with her, then set about dividing up the clothes into batches.

With the good weather they'd had, it was mostly lightweight shorts and T-shirts with some added jeans from Derek. Plus all the underwear.

She found the sorting process soothing. It was good to focus on inanimate objects, and not on the worrisome thoughts that had haunted her brain for the latter part of the holiday.

She was aware the time was coming when she would announce her decision, but it wasn't yet, and she need not think about it tonight.

She set up her mobile to play some suitably unfazing music tracks to match her mood, then refilled her glass.

The kids' pile complete, Francine popped those clothes into the machine, then began to sort their own things.

The white T-shirt was a favourite of his. And it had to be white, very white. His orders.

The small marks had been rubbed at to try and erase them. The same way Orly scrubbed at his school sweatshirt when he'd spilt something on it.

For Orly, a stain on an item was like a stain on his life. Something he'd got wrong and needed to fix. Lucy, on the other hand, never noticed anything she spilt. And cared even less.

Francine had halted and was staring at her husband's not-so-white T-shirt.

Were those spots of blood?

Derek hadn't been shaving while on holiday. In fact, he hadn't been close-shaven for years now. Shaving cuts had become a thing of the past since he'd adopted the designer stubble look.

By now she'd spread the offending garment out on the worktop. The marks were like a spray and were only on the front. Where had the blood spray come from?

He'd gone fishing lots of times, she reminded herself. You kill a catch by hitting its head on a rock. Might that cause a fine spray of blood?

Despite all her efforts to the contrary, her brain began to replay the scene in the blue campervan. The splatters of blood, the vomit. She shook her head to dispel the image.

If the T-shirt was evidence of something bad he'd done, Derek would have got rid of it. Not given it up to be washed. She was being ridiculous. Even as she told herself that, she could hear Derek's voice saying the exact same thing.

Francine reached for the stain remover spray, then halted and instead bundled the T-shirt into a pillowcase and put it to one side. For what reason, she had no idea.

His jeans were next. She stared at them. If his T-shirt had blood on it, what about the jeans?

There were dirty smudges and marks, but nothing untoward, until she checked the pockets. The small one at the back did have something in it. She eased the item out, knowing already what it was going to be.

A familiar wash of anger mixed with disgust assailed her at the torn Durex packet, swiftly followed by a 'who the fuck cares?'

She was on the pill and there was no need for precautions with her. So who had the Durex been for? And when exactly?

She did a mental calculation about when the jeans had last been worn, knowing full well that they'd been washed prior to the holiday.

So maybe when he'd been out with his mates the evening before they'd left . . . or else he'd had sex with someone when they were at Arisaig . . . and it definitely hadn't been a fish!

That thought made her laugh as she poured another glass of wine and announced to the world of the back kitchen that he could stick it wherever he liked as long as it wasn't in her.

That small moment of triumph quickly dissipated to be replaced by an image of Derek entering that blue van. Something she hadn't seen, but could imagine well enough.

He wouldn't have brought it so close to home, she told herself. More likely he'd got hold of some girl from the next campsite along. He'd wandered that way often enough.

She found herself methodically checking the other pockets, but there was nothing except a fish hook and some twigs, bound together with fishing line.

Was that some sort of fly to attract a bite? She contemplated binning it, then thought of Derek's angry countenance when he demanded to know what she'd done with his hook and line, and put it, together with the empty Durex packet, in the pillowcase with the T-shirt.

If she could muster enough anger and resentment, she might well present him with the contents of that pillowcase one day soon and ask him to explain.

Otherwise, she would view it periodically herself to help stoke her anger and resolve, in the lead-up to the announcement that she was leaving him.

20

Day four

'Isn't that Sean outside the Chip?' Chrissy said, pointing to a tall male figure standing at the door of the Ubiquitous Chip restaurant, fondly referred to as simply the Chip.

Jolted out of her thoughts, Rhona suddenly realized that it was.

'Shit,' she muttered. 'I didn't get back to him on where we would eat tonight.'

'You had a choice?' Chrissy said.

Rhona shook her head, indicating she didn't want to pursue that question.

'Well, you're about to choose now,' Chrissy informed her as she gave Sean a cheerful wave and continued on her path towards the jazz club.

He was noticeably wet, which suggested he'd been caught in the heavy shower they'd encountered on their way from the university. Rhona found herself experiencing guilt at that before she admonished herself. He could always have stepped inside out of the rain while waiting for her to come along.

Sean's wide smile at her approach served to alter her thoughts. The fact that she hadn't replied to him didn't appear to have either annoyed or upset him, which was, she realized, par for the course. Sean was an easy-going Irishman, which could be both a comfort and an annoyance, depending on the circumstances.

'Hi,' she managed. 'I take it you're waiting for me?'

'I am indeed,' he assured her, drawing her into his arms for a hug. 'You hungry?'

She was starving and the scent of food wafting out the door was only making things worse.

When she nodded, he said, 'Good. Shall we eat?' and held the door open for her.

So that's the way we play it, Rhona thought. *No recriminations. No hurt feelings. No questions.* She smiled. 'Let's go,' she said with enthusiasm.

He looks well, she thought as Sean studied the menu intently. Being a great cook himself, Sean never chose swiftly but gave serious thought to what was on offer.

Once they'd both decided and ordered and the wine was served, he sat back with a smile.

'What?' she said, finding herself bristling a little.

'Nothing.' He shook his head. 'Apart from the fact it's really good to see you.'

'You've only been away . . . what . . . ten days?' She made light of his obvious affectionate declaration.

'Seemed longer,' he stated.

'How was it? The tour, I mean?' she said, swiftly changing the topic.

'Excellent, and I plan to return in a couple of months. A longer stay perhaps next time. Quick trips stateside screw with your head.' He paused. 'How was Skye?'

'Exhilarating,' she told him.

'You climbed mountains?'

'A few. Plus beach walks and swims.'

He openly shuddered at the 'swim' word. 'Where I was, the sea was bath temperature. Not so on Skye, I expect.'

'You learnt to swim in the Irish Sea, or so you told me,' Rhona reminded him.

'That was back when I was trying to impress you.' He gave a grin.

She was waiting for him to mention Jamie as her possible climbing companion. He didn't. She wondered fleetingly whether he had made a friend on his travels, but knew she wouldn't ask, and Sean wouldn't enlighten her even if he had.

Such was their silently agreed arrangement.

'Is there an after-work catch-up planned for the jazz club?' he said.

'McNab seems to think so.'

Sean glanced at his watch. 'I have to be there in an hour anyway.'

It seemed a visit to her flat after this wasn't on his itinerary, so she could stop wondering about that.

The rest of the time was passed in companionable chit-chat, where they each exchanged some amusing tales of their time away from Glasgow. Rhona found it surprisingly soothing after the tangle of thoughts her most recent trip to Arisaig had produced.

Sean never asked about work, knowing she wouldn't discuss it with him, however obliquely.

By the end of the meal, she had to admit to herself that she felt the better for their get-together, and found herself saying, 'Are you heading back to your flat after you play tonight?'

Sean met her eye. 'I can come by yours if you want me to?'

'I may be asleep by then,' she warned.

He smiled. 'There's always the morning.'

And the decision she couldn't make before was now settled.

Sean checked the time. 'Shall we head over before your gang disperses for the evening?'

McNab tried to read the body language as they entered. It was something he often did when he saw Rhona and Sean together. Asking himself why they lasted, despite everything that had happened between them.

Sean looked relaxed, he decided. So his sojourn in San Francisco hadn't done their relationship any harm. And what about Rhona's wee holiday in Skye with, no doubt, the old boyfriend around to entertain her?

Looking up from his musings, he sensed Rhona's eyes on him and felt momentarily exposed. She could do that to him. Too easily, it always seemed.

Back at the PM it had all been business, nothing personal hinted at or otherwise in their exchange. Here was different. Here at the club was where a lot of personal stuff had gone down. Would yet go down.

At this point Chrissy's voice broke into his thoughts.

'Fed and watered, then?' she asked cheekily.

Sean smiled a *yes* and took his leave with a quick word to Rhona before disappearing into the back, where his office was and no doubt his waiting saxophone.

'Anyone for a drink?' McNab offered.

'Yes,' Rhona said.

As McNab ordered up another round, he was aware of Chrissy and Rhona having a short interchange and wondered if it might be about him.

'Sad bastard,' he muttered under his breath. 'You always want it to be about you.'

'So,' he said, handing round the drinks, 'we believe we know who your Callie is.'

Chrissy shot him a surprised look. 'You never told me that,' she said accusingly.

'I was waiting until we were all assembled,' McNab told her, ignoring a look from Chrissy that would have floored a lesser man.

'Who is she?' Rhona immediately asked.

'The keeper of the van is one Caillean Munro. And it's registered at—' He quoted an address off the Great Western Road. 'The property's been visited and there was no one home. A neighbour says Caillean hasn't been seen there for months. Something about moving in with a boyfriend.'

'Who's the boyfriend?' Chrissy said.

'That we don't know, yet. Although if there is one, he hasn't responded to our requests on social media featuring an image of Callie's van. Tech are checking to see if we can locate her online.'

'I take it she's an official missing person now, then?' Rhona said.

'She is. And the coastguard are still searching the area around Arisaig.'

'What about the kayak they found?' Rhona said.

'Still not claimed, so we're assuming for the moment it may be hers. According to DS MacDonald, Francine Henderson said the girl's kayak was blue with enough room for two, which matches the one we found.' McNab looked to Rhona. 'Strategy meeting's set up for tomorrow morning at eleven. DI Wilson has asked the Prof to come along regarding your stick men.'

Rhona's look of gratitude convinced him he'd been right to outline her concerns to his boss despite his own feelings regarding Professor Magnus Pirie.

'Right,' Chrissy said, swallowing the remains of her drink. 'I'm off home to see wee Michael and have my tea. Mum's made stovies for me.' She grinned. 'Not as fancy as what you had,' she told Rhona. 'Plus I won't have a handsome man to share it with.'

'I could come home with you,' McNab said, his smile fading at the looks of disbelief being bestowed upon him by both women. 'Hey, I'm not that bad,' he protested.

Rhona glanced at Chrissy and they both laughed. 'Had you there,' Chrissy announced as she bid her farewells.

'You heading off too?' McNab found himself saying.

'I am,' Rhona said. 'An early night for me.'

His disappointment at her departure was tempered with the thought that Sean, currently about to go on stage, would not be going home with her.

'Am leaving shortly myself,' McNab announced. He wanted Rhona to ask where to. When she didn't, he told her anyway. 'I've a date later at the Blue Arrow,' he lied. 'The jazz place on Sauchiehall Street.'

'I know where the Blue Arrow is.' Rhona gave him a penetrating look. 'Is your visiting Sauchiehall Street anything to do with the rumours Chrissy mentioned?'

'What rumours?' he said cautiously.

'The sexual assault rumours circulating supposedly involving a police officer.'

McNab considered telling another lie, but only briefly. 'Not strictly, no, but the last place Deirdre Reid was seen before she disappeared was on the student strip.'

'That's where you called me from when I was in Arisaig?' Rhona said.

He nodded. No use pretending otherwise.

'Does Bill know you're running your own night-time investigation along the strip?'

Of course the boss didn't know he was hanging about there. He hadn't even told DS Clark about his night-time excursions.

McNab decided to come out fighting. 'If the body you unearthed is confirmed as Deirdre Reid, then there's going to be more than just me down there.'

Rhona gave him one of those looks he believed she kept solely for him, before wishing him goodnight.

'You're a sad bastard, McNab,' he muttered again as he watched her disappear up the stairs. 'And she knows it.'

Swallowing down the rest of his pint, he ordered another, wondering why he'd pretended he had a date for tonight instead of admitting to heading home alone with a fish supper.

What the hell, he thought. He didn't have to go home alone. He could have a date if he wanted one. Someone to eat with at least. He immediately brought up Holly's number and pressed it before he could change his mind.

When she swiftly answered he was momentarily nonplussed, not having decided what to say.

'Detective Sergeant or is it just plain Michael tonight?' she said, a smile in her voice.

'Michael it is. Have you eaten?' he asked cheerily.

A moment's silence, then, 'Not this evening, if that's what you mean,' said with a laugh. 'Why?'

'Do you like curry?'

'Vegan curry, yes.'

'Would you like to come eat some vegan curry with me at Ashoka on Ashton Lane?'

'I would. When?'

'As soon as you can get here,' McNab said, his heart lifting a little.

'I'll head for the underground and text you when I'm at Hillhead. I'm guessing you're at the jazz club you were talking about?' she said.

'You guess right.'

'So, do I get to meet your police pals?' she said with a laugh.

'Just come to Ashoka. I'll be waiting for you there.'

'And after we eat, can we go out clubbing?' she said teasingly.

McNab had greeted her request with a laugh, although he knew that's exactly what they would do. Tonight he didn't feel like turning her down, whatever she might ask.

As he headed for the restaurant, he considered the fact that maybe he wasn't such a sad bastard after all. Not in Holly's eyes at least.

21

Achmelvich

Day four

Faced with a drop on her left and a rock face to her right, plus an incline too steep for her tired legs, Eléa got off her bike.

Now, if she met a vehicle on one of the numerous blind corners on the single-track road, she could step swiftly aside.

The sweat trickling down between her breasts, she promised herself the first thing she would do when she arrived at her destination would be to plunge into the cold waters of the Atlantic.

Swimming in both the dark, peaty Highland lochs and the turquoise waters of the west coast had been a joy. Something her friends at home couldn't understand.

'But the sea off Nice is like a warm bath,' Vivienne had remonstrated with her.

'Exactly,' had been Eléa's response. 'When you've been cycling all day, you don't want a hot bath.'

'It rains a great deal in Scotland,' Vivienne had warned her. 'And they have small biting insects.' She'd made a horrified face.

Eléa had laughed at this point, knowing nothing that Vivienne could say was likely to change her mind.

Her plan to come to Scotland had been hatched over a year ago when she'd first read an article about the North Coast 500 route. Eventually after much online study, she'd settled on flying to Glasgow and picking up a rental bike. She'd located a hire place near Glasgow University which had great reviews.

The guy there, Joe, had got in touch and helped her with her hire and her itinerary. She'd enjoyed a couple of days in Glasgow, sightseeing and checking out the clubbing scene, then headed north via the train to Mallaig.

She'd posted so many images online of that train journey, she'd even made Vivienne, a big *Harry Potter* fan, jealous.

Early evening now, the traffic on the road had lessened, in particular the campervans that had plagued her earlier. No doubt they were already set up in the campsite and enjoying the warm summer evening.

She wondered whether she should have ventured so far in one day. She could have pitched camp earlier. There had been plenty of opportunities along the way, but they hadn't appealed as much as the place she was now headed.

She had, she decided, been right to follow her instincts. Despite the late hour, she would wake up tomorrow exactly where she wanted to be.

Free of the rock face and with a better line of sight, she got back on her bike to enjoy the descent towards the bay, thinking all the time of plunging into the clear blue water that lay ahead.

Fifteen minutes later, she was staring, heavy-hearted, at the FULL sign at the campsite, and the warnings in various languages telling her that she wasn't permitted to camp on the stretch of meadow that led to the dunes.

So where was she going to sleep tonight?

Okay, she told herself, *I may not be allowed to pitch my tent, but there are no rules stopping me from swimming.*

Depositing her bike and gear, she changed into her costume and made her way through the dunes.

Daylight in these northern climes stretched on further than she'd ever experienced. Even now, the sun had not yet set, burning the sky red before dissolving into a creamy pink and blue as it reached the water.

Pleased to find the beach deserted, she set off in a run across the warm sand, anticipating the sharp cold of the water.

Gasping as it met her thighs, she stood for a final moment to watch as the setting sun kissed the horizon, knowing she didn't want to be anywhere else in the world at this moment.

22

Day five

He'd been woken earlier by the rain on the tin roof.

Rising, he'd taken a look out of the window. Through the glass, streaked by rain and the faint beginnings of daylight, he could see that the sea swell had turned the earlier aquamarine waters of the bay to a choppy grey.

Never mind, he'd thought, *at least my tatties are getting a good watering.*

The long hot spell had depleted the stream he used to water the potato patch he'd dug in the grassy cleft that ran from his access road to the small sandy cove below.

Encircled by a high wire fence, the green tops of the plants had avoided the munching of the local sheep, but they did need water. Something the north-west of Scotland wasn't normally short of.

He'd been relieved to see by the rain on the window that things were back to normal.

By the time he'd eaten breakfast and performed his morning chores, the rain had passed, replaced by a Scotch mist that softened all sound, even the excited chittering of the birds as they came to the feeder in the front garden.

Opening the door, he stepped outside and, with a whistle

to his collie, Meg, set off down the path towards the shore. From his vantage point on the hill, he could just make out the distant western headland of Achmelvich with its campsite, the nearby lumpy dunes and the wide curved smile of its golden sands.

The cove he was heading into was mostly bordered by a cliff face, its beach covered at high tide, but, choosing the time wisely, an explorer might locate this path and find themselves with a fine place for a sheltered swim.

It was where he and Meg often came to bathe, but not today, he thought.

Stopping by his potato patch, he noted that the plants looked much the better for their overnight soaking. Happy with that, he whistled for Meg, who was out of sight, then catching sight of her black ears in front of him, he began to wind his way down the steep track towards the shore.

The tide would have turned by now, he knew, leaving at least half the beach exposed. He was intrigued to find out what the rough night might have washed up against the cliffs. The best place for salvage was undoubtedly the most westerly section of the cove with its deep ravine and rough stone steps leading down from the high path that skirted the cliffs round to the main bay.

He'd often gathered driftwood here, plus netting and buoys broken free from fishing boats.

Meg, aware of where he was heading, had gone on in advance. He couldn't see her through the grey mist apart from the bobbing of her white-tipped tail, a feature of collies known as the shepherd's lantern, for good reason. Minutes later, he heard by her insistent bark that she'd found something of interest.

Either that or she'd smelt a rabbit on the grassy but inaccessible headland above.

As he edged round the final rock, he could make out the swishing tail but little else, except it was clear she was agitated about whatever she'd discovered there.

'Come, Meg,' he ordered.

At his command, she came to whine alongside him, giving his hand a concerned lick, staring back at what had obviously disturbed her.

As he continued his approach, he whispered, 'What is it, girl?' as much to himself as to the dog.

Later, he would tell folk that he could pinpoint the exact moment his mind interpreted what he was looking at, although how the jigsaw of blue and yellow plastic netting, small orange floats and the tangle of limbs and hair sorted themselves out in his brain to fire the word *body* at him he didn't know.

He came to an abrupt halt, his boots sinking into the sodden sand, just as his heart sank into the depths of his stomach.

'Jesus, Mary and Joseph,' he whispered to the upturned face of the dog, whose eyes met his own in sympathy. 'It's a lassie, Meg. It's a drowned lassie.'

There was no signal to be had here. He was well aware of that and yet still he stared at his mobile. It was shock, he told himself. Shock that froze him there, his brain unable to function.

Eventually, Meg's eyes still on him, he told her to stay. 'I'll have to go back to the house to phone.'

Meg obligingly did as told, watching him retreat along the beach, half walking, half running, until he turned up into the valley and disappeared. Hurrying past the potato patch, he had to stop briefly to regain his breath before the final steep climb to the house. He had chosen this place to be out of the way of people mainly. And it had worked up to now.

Not any more, he thought, throwing open the door. Not any more. There would be police swarming all over the place. And the coastguard. Was the cove a crime scene now?

He hesitated before lifting the receiver. Did he have to do this? She was obviously dead and perhaps the next high tide would take her away again. The momentary cowardly thought made him feel ashamed.

Was it a 999 call or to the nearest police station? Lochaber or Ullapool?

Eventually he went with 999, and asked to be put through to the coastguard, all the time wishing himself a hundred miles away.

He'd been advised not to touch the body, but to stay on guard nearby until the coastguard arrived.

He had no wish to touch the body, so that was a given, although his eyes were constantly drawn to it as he perched on a nearby rock, a subdued Meg by his side.

The mist had begun to clear, aided by a light onshore breeze, and above him the sun was attempting to escape the clouds.

From where he sat, he could see that the girl wore a short wetsuit of black and pink. Her face was turned from him, the tangled blonde hair shielding most of it. He was relieved about that, having no wish to see what damage the sea and its creatures had already done.

He had heard that a female kayaker had gone missing from a campsite further down the coast near Arisaig. The local radio station had reported it, and the police had been using Twitter to ask folk for information, although they'd only had a first name and a description of the girl they called Callie, plus a photograph of her blue campervan.

The area around Achmelvich was much more exposed than the sheltered bays of Arisaig, so if the girl had ventured this far north, it could be her body that had been washed up here in the bay.

His 999 call had put him through to the coastguard at Lochinver, who'd said they would be with him as soon as possible. He'd mumbled something about the next high tide and how it came all the way up the beach, then felt stupid when they'd assured him that they were aware of that, and just to stay on site.

After what seemed like hours, he eventually heard the thrum of a motorboat and stood up on the rock to watch it make its way into the bay.

'Okay, mate?' a voice shouted as the boat approached the beach and a couple of men jumped out and walked towards him.

'She's there.' He pointed at the tangle of netting and body.

Like him, they took a moment to register what they were looking at, and he could see the reaction on their faces. Unlike him, they didn't swear. He assumed it wasn't the first drowned person they'd encountered.

'The tide will be in here soon,' he repeated. 'Will you take her away?'

The two men were talking together in an undertone. Then they turned to him and one said, 'You can go home now. We have your details if we need to get in touch.'

Despite having wanted to go, he now found himself reluctant to leave. He had sat beside her for so long, he felt bad about deserting her.

'Is it the girl from Arisaig?' he said.

They didn't respond to his question, just repeated their request that he should go and leave them to get on with their job.

Jumping down from the rock, and with a whistle to Meg, he did as ordered.

23

Day five

The dark-blue tent had been pitched on the edge of the dunes, despite the notices forbidding wild camping.

Achmelvich's official campsite occupied a grassy promontory west of its famous beach. At busy times of the year, especially in good weather, the small site filled up very quickly and there was little point in travelling the torturous winding single-track road if you hadn't booked ahead, especially if you came by motorhome.

But if you arrived after dark, on foot or by bike, you might try your luck wild camping among the dunes, and leave before anyone came to remonstrate with you the next morning.

Murdo had spotted the tent on his way to work at the campsite and assumed it would be gone by now. He checked the beach, but there was no one there as yet, not even an early keen wild swimmer.

Deciding the tent's owner had been given enough time to be up and away, he headed across the grass.

A bike lay against the dune directly behind the tent.

So that's how they'd arrived, he thought, probably late last night. With the FULL sign up on the campsite entrance, they'd done what any sensible and tired person would do. Pitched for the night, with a plan to take down the tent early next morning and get out before being confronted.

Approaching the tent, however, he had a strange feeling that something wasn't quite right about it, but wasn't sure why.

'Hey, anyone in there?'

Murdo waited for a minute then called again, a little louder this time. 'Sorry, but you're not allowed to camp here.'

When greeted by a continued silence he tried a couple of other languages, repeating what was already on the signs.

'Camping ist hier verboten,' then, 'Le camping est interdit ici.'

When there was no response to this, he had a sudden thought that if there was anyone inside, they were either choosing to ignore his presence or maybe they were ill.

The campsite had had its fair share of medical emergencies over the years, heart attacks included.

He knelt down and, taking hold of the zip, shouted, 'I'm opening up now.'

He smelt the blood first, the metallic taste of it escaping as he unzipped the entrance. By now, he was convinced that something was wrong. They'd not only had medical emergencies on site, they'd also had attempted and sadly some successful suicides.

Folk escaping to the Highlands to bring an end to their lives. Mostly they took overdoses or walked into the sea. One young lassie had slit her wrists, but they'd luckily got to her in time. She'd returned later to thank them for saving her life.

The dimness of the tent showed him nothing except an

empty sleeping bag, a bundle of cooking utensils and some feminine underwear but no backpack.

The blood smell came from a pool on the groundsheet close to the door.

So the camper was female and she'd been bleeding. If she'd cut herself badly, might she have gone to the nearby toilet block to clean up?

Official campers were given a key to the Gents and Ladies when they arrived, but if you were to hang about the toilet block, it wouldn't be that difficult to have someone let you in. You only had to say you'd forgotten your key. And if you were obviously injured . . .

Murdo decided to check.

The overnight rain had soaked the grass, and the gravel road into the site glistened with puddles. The earlier mist had lifted and he noted that quite a few campers had gone already, no doubt heading further north on the NC500.

On reaching the shower block he found the area around it deserted, as too were the nearby sinks used for dish-washing.

Unlocking the female block, Murdo shouted his presence before entering. A quick check told him there was no one in any of the cubicles or the shower rooms. Neither was there any evidence of someone bleeding in there.

Despite this, the nagging worry that something was wrong refused to go away. His next port of call was the reception and shop.

'What's up?' Esther asked, reading his expression.

'There's somebody camped on the dunes,' he told her.

'Not another one,' she said crossly. 'Can they not read the bloody signs?'

'It's a female cyclist, I think. I shouted the rules about no camping being allowed there, but no one answered.' He hesitated.

'What?' Esther demanded.

'Something made me look inside and there was blood,' he told her

'Blood?' Esther's expression changed. 'You think she's maybe cut herself like that other lassie?'

'I don't know,' Murdo said.

'I think you should call the police,' Esther told him. 'Just in case she's lying hurt somewhere.' She thought for a moment. 'They're still searching for the girl from the Arisaig campsite. I heard they found blood in her campervan.' She halted, alarm on her face as she linked the two incidents together. 'You don't think . . .'

'I'll give Lochinver a ring, just in case,' he told her. 'They'll tell us what to do.'

'You do that, Murdo. You do that right away,' Esther urged him.

Murdo, relieved now to have made a decision, took himself outside to make the call.

24

Day five

The name Achmelvich came from the Gaelic *achadh*, meaning a plain, and *mealbhaich*, the sandy dunes. It was perfectly described, Rhona thought, as the coastguard helicopter settled on the grassy meadow in sight of the said dunes.

She had offered to drive up, but it would have taken five hours or more, and the police wanted her to visit the locus before the next high tide later tonight.

The body hadn't been moved as yet, keen as they were to have her see it in situ first.

The call had come in just as she'd been due to head for the strategy meeting, so Chrissy had been sent in her stead. Since Chrissy had done the excavation alongside her, Rhona had every confidence her forensic assistant could answer any and all queries that might be raised.

Despite that, she was still sorry not to be at the meeting in person.

The helicopter pilot had urged her to take in the view of the coastline en route, kindly pointing out the various islands as they'd made their way north. She'd managed a quick glance as they passed over the Skye road bridge, recalling that it hadn't been long since she'd crossed The Minch via the ferry to Mallaig. A mode of travel she was more comfortable with, if truth be told, although she didn't tell the pilot that, of course.

As the chopper settled onto the grass, and the blades' whirring subsided, she saw the police car parked in the vicinity of a lone tent set up close to the dunes, the area round it marked off with crime scene tape.

'A missing female, who camped here last night,' the pilot explained.

'They think that might be the body found in the cove?' Rhona said, gathering her things together.

'Or maybe the girl from the campsite at Arisaig,' he suggested.

Rhona didn't comment on that possibility, although she'd already considered it. Instead, she thanked him for the lift.

'My pleasure,' he smiled. 'You're not a happy flyer, I could sense that,' he said. 'Hence my running commentary.'

'It's that obvious?' she said apologetically.

'Each to his own. I wouldn't be happy doing your job either. Good luck with that. Maybe see you for the trip back.'

As the chopper took off, a female officer came across the grass towards her.

The young woman offered her hand. 'Dr MacLeod?' she said in a Geordie accent. 'Detective Constable Swanson. Marie.'

'And I go by Rhona.'

She motioned to the nearby one-person tent. 'The pilot said another young woman might be missing?'

'We're assuming it's a female, because of the small size of the hybrid touring bike, plus some clothing items. We think whoever it was arrived last night, saw the campsite was full, and they pitched here . . . against all the rules, of course.

Murdo from the campsite checked the tent this morning and was concerned when he found blood inside. They had a young woman once before who'd attempted suicide by cutting her wrists. Luckily, they got to her in time.'

'Is anyone out searching for her?'

'A few volunteers from the campsite, plus a couple of constables. The coastguard were checking the nearby shoreline until they got the call about the body.'

'Has the tent been processed?' Rhona asked.

'We were hoping you might have time to do that when you're finished with the body . . . just in case it is her.'

'Okay, but I'd like a quick look inside before we head for the locus?'

'Of course,' Marie said, although she looked a little worried by the delay.

Gloves on, Rhona knelt on the grass with her camera and opened the tent flaps. The pool of congealed blood was visible on the groundsheet just inside and some splashes on the walls. There was a rumpled sleeping bag, a few items of clothing and a camping stove with cooking pots.

Conscious of the time, Rhona quickly took some scene shots in and around the tent, including of the bike.

'Do we have any idea as to her identity?'

'Nothing from what's in the tent. No rucksack and the bike panniers are empty, but I took a good look at the bike. Visitors, especially from outwith Scotland, often hire bikes to do the NC500. Hybrid bikes like this one are a common hire. I found what looks like a registration number down near the pedals. I've asked if it can be traced. If we can locate the bike shop it came from . . .'

'Well done, you,' Rhona said appreciatively. 'And for using *outwith*.'

'Can't believe it's not been adopted south of the border,' Marie smiled. 'Although I've introduced my mum and dad to it, so that's a start.'

As they drove the single-track road that climbed the hill east of the main bay, Marie asked if Rhona knew the area.

'I swam off the main beach some years back,' Rhona told her.

'The body was found in a small secondary cove to the east. It's a bit trickier to get to,' Marie said. 'We're on the croft road which gives access to the houses on the nearby hills. One of the occupants, a Trevor Wills and his dog, Meg, discovered the body this morning when he went for a walk on the beach. It was a bit wild here last night, and he was keen to see what the tide had washed up.' She paused. 'According to the coastguard, he was in shock when they got to him.'

'No wonder,' Rhona said. 'Despite the fact that it's my job, I feel much the same every time.'

'How do you deal with all that death?' Marie said, sounding concerned.

'I focus on the victim and try to be their best witness,' Rhona told her.

Marie slowed, then drew into a space beside an old static caravan.

'Mr Wills lives on the hill there. When he first arrived a year ago, he lived in this caravan for a while, then managed to rent an old and slightly dilapidated cottage further up. Not easy to find a full-time rental here these days since Airbnb took over the Highlands.'

They got out and she locked the door. 'Habit,' she explained. 'Can't imagine anyone stealing a police car round here. Now where I used to work, that would have been more likely.' She glanced at Rhona's feet. 'Good to see you're wearing decent footwear. There's a path but it's rough.'

They left the road and took a narrow dirt path downwards, which passed a fenced potato patch, before eventually meeting the beach. As she was led across the wet sand, Rhona spotted the coastguard vessel bobbing nearby in the bay, no doubt on sentry duty.

'When Mr Wills contacted them, two of the crew came ashore and spoke to him, then sent him off. They've been guarding the scene. Now you're here, they'll continue their search and come back when I radio we're finished.'

Rhona nodded. 'The body's lying below the high-water mark, I understand?'

'Partially,' Marie said. 'That's the problem. That and the difficult location, which affects your safety as well as the ability to preserve the scene and recover evidence.'

As they skirted another rock face, Rhona noted a path above. 'There's another way down?' she asked.

'Yes, but it's not for the faint-hearted,' Marie told her. 'A path comes over the clifftop, then along the side of a steep gully with a scramble down the rocks ahead.' She came to a halt. 'We're here,' she said in a hushed tone.

'How long do I have?' Rhona said, looking over at the tangle of body and netting that was now in view.

'The coastguard advises five hours max.'

'Right,' Rhona said, 'if you want to be useful, you should get kitted up too.'

'You want me to help you?' Marie said in a mixture of pleasure and trepidation.

Rhona gave her an encouraging smile. 'I do. Shall we make a start?'

25

Day five

Her face was turned to the east and partially covered by tendrils of blonde hair.

'Rag doll' were the words that immediately sprang to mind as Rhona began to take her photographs. A jumble of limbs, dressed in a short wetsuit, swathed in parts with a network of blue and yellow netting and small round floats.

She lay partially upright against a pile of boulders, which had likely been dislodged from the rock face by the burn that ran down the gully behind. On her right, the stream of water spread out in a fan over the sands before reaching for the sea.

From afar, it had seemed that she was enmeshed in the netting, but on approach that had proved to be wrong.

The net wasn't entangled with her body, but rather laid across it, either by the rough seas of last night or . . .

'The man who found her,' Rhona said. 'What do you know about him?'

Marie shrugged. 'Only that he's a relatively recent incomer with a dog called Meg, and that he was freaked by the find. Really upset, according to the coastguard guys.'

'And the netting on the body?' Rhona asked.

'It's a common enough sight along the coast, why?' Marie said, puzzled.

'Take a closer look,' Rhona told her.

She waited while Marie examined it more keenly now, her brow creased in thought.

'She's not caught in it.' She looked at Rhona in surprise. 'It's been washed over her by the tide, or . . .' She hesitated. 'You don't think Trevor did that? Maybe to cover the horror of looking at her?'

It had been known for a person finding a body to spread something over the victim to stop folk gawking at them, especially if it was a young partially clothed woman. But Rhona didn't think that had happened here.

'If we assume he's not a suspect, for the moment anyway, I rather think a shocked Trevor wouldn't approach her at all,' Rhona said. 'More likely he'd look the other way, towards the sea and hopefully the swift arrival of the coastguard.'

Marie was walking round the body, viewing it from different angles.

'I've seen a couple of bodies washed ashore,' she said. 'They're usually bobbing about at the water's edge or lying face down on the sand.'

'And their injuries normally comprise of superficial parallel abrasions from them rumbling over the seabed or shore?' Rhona said.

'Yes,' Marie nodded.

'So not looking like this one?' Rhona added. 'Which has also not been feasted on by fish.'

'God, you're right,' Marie said, the next thought obviously dawning. 'Her limbs are all crooked. I saw a body like that once on the mountain. The guy had fallen from a great height. He was all broken and twisted.'

'Despite the wetsuit, I suspect this body may not have arrived here with the tide,' Rhona said.

'So where did she come from?' Marie followed Rhona's gaze upwards. 'You think she might have fallen from there?' She pointed up the steep gorge to the path above.

'Or was pushed,' Rhona told her. 'Then arranged to look as though she was brought in by the tide.'

Marie stared wide-eyed at her.

'Once we examine the body in more detail, we may be clearer as to what happened,' Rhona said. 'We'll start with the net. I'd like you to take a series of photographs as we remove it. I'll tell you where and when.'

With the netting removed, it was difficult not to liken the victim to Francine Henderson's description of Callie. Both height and build were similar, and of course the medium-length curly blonde hair. Although the wetsuit colour of black and pink echoed the victim she and Chrissy had exhumed at Arisaig, it was a common enough colour combination for female wetsuits.

They worked on in silence, leaving the wetsuit intact, Rhona aware that the high neckline might well hide a broken hyoid as before.

The body hadn't been long in the water, that much was clear. In the cold water around Scotland, the bacterial action that caused a body to bloat might be slowed enough for it to remain on the seabed for up to a week, the skin absorbing the water and peeling away from the underlying tissues, and of course providing food for the local fish, crabs and sea lice.

None of which had happened here.

If she'd got into trouble while swimming off nearby Achmelvich the previous evening and been washed ashore on the high tide, that might account for her presence here, but it didn't fully explain the injuries they were cataloguing.

A badly broken nose, the nasal fracture to the ridge obvious to the touch and by sight. Other notable fractures, in particular to her left arm and right leg, the ankle twisted round.

Bodies in the sea did sustain injuries, often from passing boats that might even dismember them. A body beaten against a cliff by wave action could result in lacerations, but falling from a cliff would produce more significant injuries. Head, neck, arm and leg breaks such as she was recording here.

Added to that, there were what looked like probable defensive injuries on the victim's lower arms, and Rhona could picture a scenario where the sea had played no part, until after the victim had landed here, on the rocks, and the high tide had washed over her.

Her examination of the body was almost complete when she located the final piece of the puzzle.

The stick man was partially buried just to the left of the victim's head. As Rhona dug it out of the wet sand, she imagined the incoming tide releasing it from the victim's mouth.

The fashioned shape was a replica of the one found in the mouth of the exhumed victim, and the one hanging inside Callie's blue van.

McNab doesn't believe in coincidences and neither do I, Rhona thought, dropping it into an evidence bag.

When she was ready to have both the body and accompanying debris removed, her theory as to how the victim may have died was supported by the two coastguard crew, brothers Jim and Stevie, who'd answered Trevor Wills's 999 call.

'We didn't say anything to the guy who discovered her, but Jim and I knew right away she hadn't been long in the water. As for the buoys and the netting?' Stevie threw Rhona a disbelieving look. 'We didn't buy that one either, but it's good to have it confirmed by an expert.'

'If you're okay to transport the body round to Achmelvich, I'll go with DC Swanson and forensically examine the tent,' Rhona told them.

'You want us to radio the helicopter to come back?' Stevie said.

Rhona nodded. 'Then we'll transport the body, the evidence and me back to Glasgow together.'

The one-person tent looked even more forlorn on their return. Rhona had no direct evidence as yet to link the site to the dead female on the beach, yet the odds against that being the case were low.

If it wasn't the cyclist, then the likelihood of it being Callie grew. Whichever proved to be the case, the stick man linked all three women, that she was sure of.

The idea of a killer travelling the route of the NC500, picking off lone campers, was horrific to contemplate, but it was a valid theory nonetheless.

The signature of the killer was evident in the stick man figure, the modus operandi not so clear. The first victim had been strangled. It had yet to be established at post-mortem how the beach victim had died.

As for Callie, the assumption was that she'd been alive when she'd either left the croft campsite of her own free will or been abducted. Rhona's money was on her abduction, because of the stick man.

But there was a question there too. Why was the stick man left hanging in the campervan when the perpetrator's signature was to place it in the victim's mouth after they died?

Then a sudden thought occurred. Might that mean that Callie wasn't dead . . . yet?

Assuming the buried victim was confirmed as Deirdre Reid, which she thought would happen, then she'd died perhaps a month after she'd gone missing.

If the body on the beach wasn't Callie, did that mean Callie might still be alive somewhere?

That thought brought Rhona a small glimmer of hope.

When she'd first looked in the seemingly abandoned tent, she'd wanted to make sure that nothing in there demanded her immediate collection.

Now, with an hour before her promised ride south, she had time enough to be thorough.

As she worked the tent, the bike and the immediate surroundings, Rhona tried not to dwell on the fact that she would soon be up in a helicopter again.

When she finally did take off, along with the body, bike and all her evidence, she was treated to a spectacular sunset.

'You can't beat seeing that from up here.' The pilot gestured to the layer of blood-lit sky through the glass.

Rhona would have much preferred to have viewed it from Achmelvich beach before heading for a swim but, of course, she didn't tell him that.

26

Glasgow

Day five

'Where have *you* been?' Janice demanded as he sidled up clasping one extra-strong coffee for himself and what he regarded as a lesser brew for her.

'The canteen,' McNab said, motioning to the coffees, one of which he handed over.

Janice looked at her watch. 'Big queues in the canteen?'

McNab tried to look offended. 'I also spent time looking for Ollie in Tech to see if they had anything new on Caillean Munro.'

Janice was regarding him with suspicion, which was always a worry. He soon learnt why.

'You haven't heard, then?' she said.

'Heard what?' McNab tried to look nonchalant.

'Another female's gone missing from a west coast campsite. Rhona headed there by helicopter this morning, when a body turned up in a neighbouring bay.'

'Where was this exactly?'

'A place called Achmelvich,' Janice told him.

'How far from Callie's van?'

'Exact mileage? No idea. But it's a bit further north on the NC500. You can check it out on an online map.'

This definitely wasn't good news. He'd been thinking since the body had been unearthed at Arisaig that a ritualized killing like that wasn't likely to be a one-off.

'So she won't be at the eleven o'clock strategy meeting,' Janice went on. 'Chrissy's coming in her stead.'

McNab nodded without comment, his brain turning over the most recent news about a new body.

'Any idea if the new missing female is from Glasgow?' he asked.

'No idea where she came from, or her identity. No documents left on site, but the bike she was riding may have been hired. We have a number from the chassis we're trying to trace.'

'Folk cycling this NC500 . . . where do they start from?' McNab asked.

'The route is from Inverness heading west, then north along the coast and back down to Inverness,' Janice said. 'Why?'

McNab shrugged. 'Just wondering where she would have hired the bike.'

'A lot of cyclists take the train from Glasgow to Mallaig and go on from there,' Janice said.

'How d'you know that?' McNab said.

'Just because you dislike the great outdoors doesn't mean I have to,' Janice told him.

'Mmmm,' McNab muttered.

'So, are you going to tell me where you were last night that caused you to sleep in this morning?' Janice said.

Suddenly faced with the question he'd been hoping to avoid, McNab attempted an innocent look, which apparently failed.

'Jeez, you do realize how guilty you look?' Janice said with a laugh. 'A female was it?'

'I don't discuss the women in my life, even with you,' he tried. 'Not at this early stage, anyway.' He attempted a laugh in return.

'Where did you meet her?' The enquiry almost sounded innocent.

'Out and about,' he said airily.

'Does she know what you do for a living? Always good to get that out early on,' she suggested.

And at last something he could answer truthfully. 'I told her as soon as we met,' he said.

'And she didn't mind?'

'She seemed quite taken with the idea,' he said, remembering Holly's response when he'd told her.

Now it was Janice's turn to say, 'Mmmm.' Then she added, 'Well, good luck to you, partner.'

He knew she meant that, which made him feel bad, but he couldn't tell her he'd taken up with Holly to try to glean more about what was going on along the student strip. As for last night, he was still trying to work out exactly how he'd got himself into that particular situation and how he was going to extract himself from it.

The callback from Ollie arrived shortly before they were due at the strategy meeting.

'Sorry I missed you earlier,' Ollie said. 'I worked late last night, so had some sleep to catch up on.'

'Tell me about it,' McNab replied, stifling a yawn. 'So what is it you wanted to show me?'

There was the sound of a throat being cleared on the other end of the line. Something that happened when Ollie got nervous. Not a good sign.

'Can I send you an image?' he said.

'Of what?' McNab said.

'I was hoping you could tell me,' Ollie replied.

Ollie was a super recognizer, which meant he could recognize folk in videos and images even if their faces were largely hidden.

McNab realized almost immediately that the likelihood was he'd been spotted somewhere he shouldn't have been. This was Ollie giving him the heads-up in advance of the image going up the line.

'Send it over,' McNab said, trying to sound nonchalant and innocent at the same time.

'Okay to go?' Janice called from the neighbouring desk.

'You go on, I'll follow in a minute,' McNab said.

Once Janice disappeared, heading for the meeting room, McNab clicked on the awaited file.

His first thought was, how could anyone recognize him from such a grainy image, with ninety per cent of his face hidden from view?

Fuck, Ollie definitely was a super recognizer, because it *was* him, and it had been taken last night, at the back exit of the club. He'd checked for a camera before it had all kicked off, but had convinced himself he was out of the picture.

Apparently he'd been wrong. Very wrong.

Christ! If or when the boss saw this . . .

He shut the image and logged off, his mind racing. His first thought was to go see Ollie, but that would look weird. And Janice was already on the lookout for any such behaviour on his part.

Marshalling himself, he rose and headed for the conference room to find that the meeting had already begun. He hung about at the back, not keen to be in the direct eye of the boss. He spotted Chrissy's head near the front, her current hair colour a mix of blonde with red on top. The tall figure of Professor Magnus Pirie stood on her right. No doubt, like Chrissy, waiting for his cue to come forward and say his piece.

DI Wilson was currently confirming that the body found in the grave at Arisaig was that of Deirdre Reid, a twenty-year-old student at the School of Art who went missing two months before from the Nice N Sleazy club on Sauchiehall Street.

No one in the room looked or sounded surprised by that.

'Her immediate family and partner have been informed and I expect the newspapers will be all over it by tomorrow, together no doubt with questions about our investigation into her appearance and why it hadn't advanced in the interim.'

DI Wilson ran his eyes over the assembled audience.

'DS McNab and DS Clark, I'd like a word with you after the meeting.'

McNab had been expecting that to happen, but had hoped he might have gleaned something from his midnight excursions which he could produce at just such a moment. Then again, what if the summons had more to do with the footage from Ollie he'd just viewed?

He tried to focus as DI Wilson continued.

'The young woman who disappeared from the campsite at Arisaig near to the exhumation site has now been identified as Caillean Munro, who has a flat near Kelvinbridge, where she hasn't been seen for some time.

'With the discovery of yet another missing female camper, this time from Achmelvich, further up the west coast, plus the body of a young woman on a beach nearby, this opens up the possibility that we may have a killer targeting lone female campers in the vicinity of the NC500.'

Everyone in the room had been engaged in at least one of the first two investigations. Now it was beginning to appear as though the two may well have become one.

McNab watched as Chrissy was called to the front to give an overview of where their forensic investigation was. He listened as she spoke of the exhumation of Deirdre's body from the machair at Arisaig.

'The victim was wearing a short wetsuit which preserved the parts of the body it covered. From the condition of the subsequent remains and the composition of the soil she was buried in, Dr MacLeod estimated that Deirdre had died and been buried around a month ago. Dr Sissons confirmed this at post-mortem. He also confirmed that she'd been strangled.'

When Janice threw McNab an annoyed look, he shrugged his shoulders, trying to suggest this was news to him, although it wasn't actually, as Chrissy had told him in the club before Rhona had arrived last night.

Various screen images of the exhumation site were on view to Chrissy's right and at this point one of a stick man appeared, to a loud murmur of unease from the assembled team.

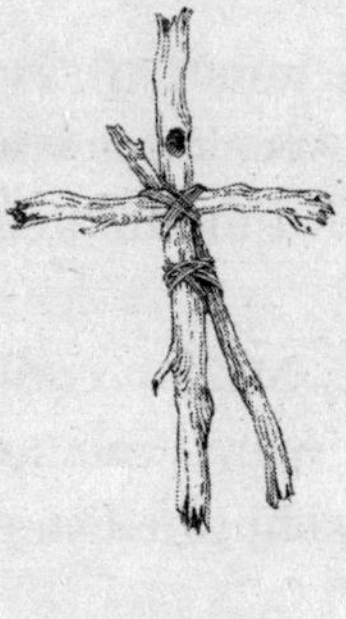

'A stick figure like this one was extracted from the mouth of Deirdre Reid. A similar one was also found hanging in Callie's blue van in the nearby croft campsite,' Chrissy said. 'It was quite out of character with the internal decoration, suggesting it wasn't Callie who hung it there.'

The dismayed murmurs grew even louder, until DI Wilson shushed them enough for Chrissy to finish.

'As to the most recent discovery at Achmelvich, Dr MacLeod is currently on site and working in advance of the arrival of the next high tide. The body and evidence, once retrieved, will come back here to Glasgow sometime later today.'

As Chrissy moved away, DI Wilson thanked her.

'And now if Professor Pirie would like to come up and offer his thoughts on what we may be dealing with here.'

As Magnus weaved his way to the front, the group fell silent again. Many of McNab's colleagues had met the Orcadian professor of criminal psychology during previous investigations. Police officers in general weren't sold on the idea of criminal profiling, himself included, but . . . and there was a but here, McNab thought, because Professor Magnus Pirie had been proved right in more than a few investigations they'd worked on together.

All eyes were now focused on the tall blond figure, waiting for him to begin.

He stood silent for a moment as though mustering his thoughts. When he did speak, his voice was deep and melodious, his Orcadian accent modulated to its west of Scotland counterpart.

Not for the first time, McNab could imagine his students hanging on his every word, the females in particular. It pissed him off as always, but he listened just like the others.

'Most of us have drawn stick figures as children. A circle for a head, lines for body, arms and legs, with or without hands and feet, or a face. It's a universally recognizable symbol, probably one of the best known in the world. It transcends language, location, demographics, and can trace back its roots for almost 30,000 years.' He paused then before continuing.

'This symbol can also be used in other ways, which are not innocent. The one taken from the victim's mouth and the one found in the blue van more closely resemble the Twanas, also referred to as Stick Men or Stick Charms. You might recognize these as a nightmarish theme in *The Blair Witch Project* film franchise, where the wooden stick figures signified black magic rituals and the approaching death of those who met them.

'Both appear to me to denote the signature of Deirdre's killer, and possibly Callie's abductor.'

DI Wilson intervened then to ask, 'You believe the person who killed Deirdre may have also abducted Callie?'

'I believe it to be a distinct possibility,' Magnus said.

McNab saw Janice raise her hand. 'But why would an abductor leave the symbol in the van? Should the signature not be used in the same way as it was with Deirdre? That is, left with the body?'

Magnus acknowledged this, then said, 'It appears from the forensic findings that Deirdre was likely kept for a month before she was killed and buried. I would be interested to learn if she'd encountered or was presented with a similar stick symbol before she disappeared. Also on the basis of our current findings, if Callie's disappearance is linked to Deirdre's it could be that Callie is still alive somewhere.'

Murmurs built up again at that. Abduction always held

the possibility and the hope that they might find the victim alive.

McNab thought back to their search for Deirdre. No matter how thorough the search and for how long, people did disappear and, without any serious lead as to where they went and why, it often resulted in a dead end.

And they had met that dead end in Deirdre's case. Hence his nocturnal visits to the last place she'd been seen in the vague hope that something he heard or someone he observed might provide that elusive clue as to what had happened to her.

His thoughts moved to the boyfriend, Sam. Might he have seen Deirdre with a stick symbol on or before the night she disappeared? Without the police asking such a question, he might have dismissed it as unimportant.

And what about at Nice N Sleazy? Might her pals have seen anything like that? Perhaps the night she disappeared or on a previous visit to the club?

He returned from his thoughts as Janice put a hand on his arm.

'C'mon. Remember the boss has summoned us.'

McNab felt his throat quickly dry up. What if the summons was about what Ollie had just sent him? Had the CCTV recording from the Blue Arrow club already reached the boss?

'You're sure it was for the both of us and not just me?' McNab tried.

Janice shot him a look. 'Why? What have you been up to that I don't know about?'

'Just the usual,' he joked. 'So what does the boss want to see us about?'

'Deirdre Reid, of course,' Janice said. 'Let's go.'

27

Day five

After lunch, she'd encouraged the children to go outside and play in the garden. The sun was shining, so no sitting cooped up in their rooms all day. Right?

They'd both been noncommittal about that, although they had exchanged furtive glances after her announcement.

Now they were back in Orly's room with the door closed. She'd been standing outside for ten minutes, trying to hear what Orly was saying to his wee sister . . . but couldn't.

Eventually she flung open the door, with a breezy, 'What are you two up to? Staying inside on a lovely day like this? Come on, outside, both of you.'

At this Orly had looked anxiously at Lucy who, in her inimitable way, had taken his hand and said, 'Come on, Orly, let's play in the treehouse.'

And that's where they'd gone. So instead of staying out of sight in Orly's room, they were now out of sight in the treehouse. And there was no chance of listening in to what they were no doubt discussing there.

It had been like this since their return from that nightmarish holiday. She'd tried to broach the subject with Orly, but he'd immediately assumed his closed-down look. So she hadn't asked again, just set about watching and listening.

Which hadn't cured her unease one little bit.

Not for the first time she wondered whether she should contact the police on the Glasgow number she'd been given by DS MacDonald, and ask to speak to a family liaison officer. Explain that she felt her two children were still traumatized by what had happened at the campsite at Arisaig.

But did she really want the police to talk to them again? Would that not make Orly retreat into himself even more? At the moment he was talking to Lucy, if not to her, 'And that's a good thing, isn't it?' Francine said out loud.

She made herself a coffee and stood sipping it, her eyes on the treehouse, telling herself that they'd only been back a day. The memory of what had happened at the campsite would fade in time.

But would it, could it, if Callie remained missing? She'd been checking online, not wanting to put the TV news on in case the children heard how worried the police had become for Callie's safety.

Plus the body Dr MacLeod had exhumed on the machair had now been identified as Deirdre Reid, a twenty-year-old Art School student who'd disappeared two months ago from a nightclub on Sauchiehall Street.

How had she got from a Glasgow nightclub to Arisaig?

Francine found herself heading to the wall calendar next to the fridge to flip back two pages. It was as though she couldn't help herself. She stared at the date boxes and the numerous entries swimming before her, the majority of which related to the children and herself. All the time knowing she was really looking to see where Derek had been on the night Deirdre Reid had disappeared.

Had he been out with his mates? Or away somewhere with them?

There was nothing marked on the calendar for Derek during the previous two months, but then there rarely was. He usually just announced on the spot that he was heading out for a pint. If they went out together that had to be marked down, because she needed to get in a babysitter.

She flipped back the pages to find the last time they *had* gone out together, which was over three months before. Then she wished she hadn't, because the memories it invoked sent her to sink down at the table and put her head in her hands.

After that particular evening, she'd vowed never to go out with Derek again. She now wondered in retrospect if he'd behaved so badly that night to make that a certainty. After which he could cheerfully go out alone.

That thought sent her through to the back kitchen cupboard, where she'd stashed the pillowcase containing the blood-spotted T-shirt, the empty condom packet and the roll of fishing line.

She'd pushed it behind the washing powder, but now couldn't see it. Dropping to her knees, she took out the family-size box and knelt to take a better look.

Had she remembered wrongly and put it in another cupboard? No. She was sure it had been in here. So where was it?

Her heart thumping, she checked the neighbouring cupboards. It wasn't in any of them. So who had removed it? It was a stupid question to ask, she thought, because it couldn't have been the children. Could it?

No. They'd been in bed when she'd discovered the stained T-shirt and the other offending objects.

Which only left one possibility.

Derek.

28

Day five

This wasn't the first time he'd been summoned into the boss's office. *And it's unlikely to be the last,* McNab thought. Although the last might be the one that followed that video he'd just watched.

As he listened to what the boss was saying, he found himself replacing the words with some of his own. All the time wondering why he was being told to re-interview Deirdre's partner and not being asked why he'd been caught on camera with an unknown female behind the Blue Arrow the previous night.

When he didn't immediately respond to what was being asked of him, Janice nudged him.

'Yes, sir,' McNab said, hoping that was enough to be going on with.

'And we need to know if Sam Wheeler was aware of Deirdre having received one of these stick figures before she disappeared,' DI Wilson was saying. 'I also want her pals spoken to again on the same topic.'

When McNab didn't respond, Janice came back in with a 'Right, sir.'

'I expect you to retrace the victim's footsteps again that

night, together with what has emerged from the discovery of her body. A body we would likely never have located had the wee girl Lucy Henderson not gone missing from the nearby campsite.' He went on. 'I understand the girl was found next to the grave and that she was afraid the body there might be that of Caillean Munro, who'd apparently befriended her?'

Janice responded again. 'Yes, sir. I believe the family is back now in Glasgow.'

'Right,' DI Wilson said with a decisive nod. 'Make contact with the family and tell them we'd like to interview the girl and her brother in an appropriate setting with the usual safeguards in place.'

After which they were dismissed.

As they headed back to their desks, McNab waited for the inevitable grilling he expected from his partner. It didn't take long before it materialized.

'What's with you this morning?' she demanded seconds later. 'You seemed positively shell-shocked in there.'

'I was expecting to get a bollocking about what we'd not done on the Deirdre Reid case up to now,' he tried.

'Really?' Janice didn't look or sound convinced. 'There's no way we could have known she was taken out of Glasgow, let alone that she ended up buried in a cove near Arisaig with a stick man in her mouth.'

'True,' McNab said, trying a smile. 'I think I'm in need of caffeine. The lack of it has affected my brain.'

Janice appeared to accept that, so he told her he was off to get a double espresso at the machine.

'Fine. I'll contact the Hendersons,' she offered. 'You call Sam Wheeler once the caffeine's hit home.'

'Yes, ma'am.' He went to salute her, then thought that would annoy rather than amuse her, and swiftly dropped his hand.

Jeez, he definitely did crave coffee, McNab thought as he left, although it wasn't the only thing he wanted. He badly needed to speak to Ollie in person about that grainy CCTV image before it went any further.

On a normal visit to Ollie in Tech, he would usually go via the canteen and buy at least one of Ollie's favourites. If Ollie hadn't been put on a diet by his girlfriend, then a sugared doughnut would be the choice. If such things were forbidden and Ollie was sticking to his promise to eat healthily, then a packet of fruit and nuts sufficed.

McNab decided not to take time to purchase either of these, since it would look more like a bribe than the usual reward for help in a case.

As he entered the Tech department, the weight of worry that had landed on his shoulders when he'd first viewed the short video clip now returned heavier than before. Although, he thought, straightening up, Ollie shouldn't be made aware of that.

'Hey, mate,' he said, approaching Ollie's cubicle. 'How's it going?'

The eyes behind the big round spectacles, which usually reminded McNab of a wise old owl, were sending him a different message today.

Without greeting him in return, Ollie gestured to McNab to take a seat next to him. 'Well,' he finally said, his voice kept low. 'Am I right?'

'That is me,' McNab said, 'with my girlfriend, Holly.' He continued, 'Not the most romantic spot, I'll agree, but she chose it, not me.'

'You are aware we've been monitoring the clubs on the student strip because of anonymous accusations of sexual assault by police officers?' Ollie asked.

McNab nodded. 'I was aware of that, yes. But that plainly isn't sexual assault. That's me and my girlfriend doing what couples do. Besides, only *you* could identify *me* from that image,' he added.

McNab watched as Ollie struggled with this for a bit, then said, 'Your girlfriend will confirm this is consensual?'

'Naturally.'

When Ollie looked somewhat appeased by this, McNab found his heart slowing a little in its frantic dance.

'So,' he said. 'I could go directly to the boss with it. Explain the circumstances. That would get you off the hook?'

He watched as relief flooded Ollie's eyes.

'Okay,' Ollie said. 'I'll settle for that. Let me know when it's done.'

'Of course,' McNab promised. 'Right, better get back to work. You'll have heard that the body from Arisaig has been ID'd as our first missing girl, Deirdre Reid?'

Ollie nodded. 'And I know about the stick man. It's all anyone's talking about down here. That and *The Blair Witch Project*.'

'I've never seen it,' McNab admitted.

'Maybe you should,' Ollie said. 'I think her killer probably has.'

McNab forgot about *The Blair Witch Project* as soon as he left Tech, and thought only of what he'd just got Ollie to agree to. He now had a brief window in which to decide what to do about the video.

He'd been honest enough about it being him and Holly, and the fact that she'd taken him outside. However, could he actually ask her to confirm that the sex captured on CCTV was consensual?

Wouldn't she be horrified that they'd been caught on

camera? Or maybe that would excite her? He knew next to nothing about her except for the fact she'd come on to him first in the club and she hadn't minded when he'd told her he was a police officer.

She'd also admitted she knew about the accusations flying around regarding supposed sexual assaults by serving officers. Although he hadn't got her to elaborate on that . . . yet.

He stopped for his double espresso on the return journey. Drinking it down, he carried back the paper cup as evidence.

'Met someone at the machine?' Janice asked pointedly.

'Went to the loo,' McNab told her, throwing his cup in the waste bin. 'Any luck with the Hendersons?'

'I spoke to the mother, Francine. I think she'd been awaiting a call. Said the two children were very subdued still, which worried her. After which she told me she doubted whether her husband would permit an interview. Then she asked if he could refuse. She sounded freaked about that.'

'And?' McNab prompted.

'I told her we could insist, if we believed the children had knowledge that would aid in a murder enquiry.'

'Success, then?'

'Of sorts – she's agreed to come in tomorrow, although she said the father might make it difficult. So what about Deirdre's partner?'

'I was thinking we should maybe just turn up at his door,' McNab said. 'Not give him time to prepare a story.'

'He'll know now that it's Deirdre.'

'Yes, but the report given out to the press doesn't include the stick man,' McNab said, before adding, 'Have you seen this *Blair Witch* film?'

'There's more than one, although the first is the best, in my opinion,' Janice told him.

'I didn't have you down as the horror-film type.' McNab shook his head in wonderment.

'I prefer the fake horror to what we have to face in this job,' Janice said. 'A girl abducted on a night out. Kept somewhere for a month, then forced to don a wetsuit, strangled and buried in sand.'

McNab drew a swift breath. 'You've got a point,' he admitted.

'So when do you want to go see Sam Wheeler?'

'He works from home or the workshop nearby, making *his art*. We could head there now,' McNab suggested.

'What about the clubs along the student strip?' Janice said. 'It's not that far from Sam's place. We could check with them too? See if they've had any sightings of stick men, back when Deirdre disappeared, or even more recently.'

McNab didn't like that idea. Last thing he needed was one of the staff at either Nice N Sleazy or the Blue Arrow to recognize him as a recent regular when he was with Holly.

'I can do Sam and the clubs on my own,' he suggested, 'while you talk to Deirdre's two pals.'

Janice considered this. 'Okay,' she finally said. 'And we meet back here?'

'Agreed,' McNab said, trying not to show his relief.

And there it was. He hadn't actually lied outright to his partner, or to Ollie, but he'd certainly lied by omission.

29

Day five

The cobbled lane behind the flats reminded McNab of Ashton Lane, although instead of eateries and bars and even a small cinema, the old stables here housed a cycle repair shop, an artist's studio, a second-hand book emporium and Sam Wheeler's woodturning workshop.

The previous times they'd met had been at Sam and Deirdre's flat, and Janice had been with him. He remembered thinking back then that Janice had been too soft on the bloke. Most times when a woman went missing or was found dead somewhere, her partner had played a role in it.

Having given evidence in court too often in such cases, just like the other morning, his belief came from experience.

Sam had come over as a nice bloke, but that didn't mean he was one. They would have had to ask Deirdre about that, and sadly that was no longer a possibility.

McNab had no doubt Sam had already been informed that the body dug up at Arisaig was Deirdre. But then again, he may have buried her there himself.

Young woman out with her mates, clubbing. Some blokes

might not like that. Could get jealous. Turn up at the club only to see her messing about with another man and take umbrage. Whisk her away and do the necessary.

But Sam had an alibi for that night. Two mates had come round. They'd watched the footie together, drunk some beer. Mates left and he fell asleep. Didn't miss Deirdre until the morning. But she'd stayed at her pals before, so he wasn't too worried. Or so he'd told them.

McNab wondered how worried he was now.

Eventually Sam, sensing his presence, turned and, seeing McNab standing in the doorway, switched off his lathe and removed his face shield. As silence fell and the two men eyed one another, Sam said, 'They told me as soon as they'd identified Deirdre.' His voice broke a little at that point.

Well it would, wouldn't it, McNab thought. If he's innocent, or if he's guilty. Pretty heart-breaking if you buried your victim somewhere you thought they might never be found. Like a remote beach. Only to have some wee lassie lead the police right to it.

'I'm not here about that,' McNab said.

'Oh.' Sam looked puzzled for a moment. 'Do you have a lead then on who killed her?'

McNab shrugged. 'Maybe.' He made a point of looking around the workshop. There were shavings and offcuts of wood all over the place, but of twigs there were none.

He pulled out his phone and swiped the screen until he located the image of the stick man from the earlier presentation.

'What is it?' Sam said, sounding nervous.

'In the weeks leading up to her disappearance, did Deirdre ever receive something like this?'

He handed the mobile to Sam, who stared at it uncomprehendingly for a while, before saying, 'Isn't that the stick man from *The Blair Witch Project*?'

McNab found himself pissed off by the mention of that bloody film yet again, but managed to reply, 'It resembles it, or so I'm told.'

'Well, the answer's yes, then. There was a special showing of the film a while back, and they were handed out. Deirdre brought one home.'

McNab was sure he heard his own chin hit the floor. 'So everybody got one?'

'Everyone could have one. Not everyone took one, Deirdre said. Some folk thought they were too creepy. Deirdre didn't mind.'

McNab was already imagining Janice's conversation with Deirdre's two pals and likely getting the same story. Fuck it. The lead they'd all bought in to was fast becoming a well-populated dead end.

'Is it important?' Sam was asking.

'It's just a line in our enquiry,' McNab said. Maybe the only one, he thought. 'Did Deirdre keep it?'

'I don't think so. I never saw it after that. It probably ended up in the bin.'

Exactly where this particular lead was heading, McNab thought. Still . . .

'Which cinema was showing the film?' he asked.

Sam looked momentarily nonplussed. 'I'm not sure,' he said.

'So you weren't with her?'

Sam shook his head. 'I'm not into horror films.'

'Who did she go with, then?'

'Deirdre did a class at the Glasgow Film Theatre. Met some folk there who she went to films with.'

'Why didn't you mention this before?' McNab demanded.

'I didn't think it was important.'

'We need to know who these film friends were,' McNab said.

'You'd be better to ask Millie and Lisa.'

'Were they in this film class too?'

'No, but I think Deirdre would have talked to them about it.'

'But not to you?' McNab said, disbelief obvious in his voice.

'I've told you everything I know.' Sam sounded irritated. 'So, if that's all, I have this piece to finish today.' He reached for his face shield in a pointed manner.

McNab nodded as though it was he who'd brought the interchange to an end. 'Thanks for your help, Mr Wheeler. We'll be in touch.'

Outside now, he turned to look back. The lathe was on, but Sam wasn't working it. Instead, he was staring out at McNab, with what he decided was a distinctly angry gaze.

McNab met that look head on. He'd seen such a reaction many times. Sam could be angry at having to face questions again. He could be angry that the police hadn't found Deirdre's killer. He could be angry that Deirdre was dead, having perhaps held out hope that she was alive somewhere. Even if that explanation meant she'd simply walked out on him.

Or he could be angry that they'd found her body and maybe also the stick man.

McNab tried to recall Sam's exact reaction when he'd shown him the image. What had been going on in his brain during those seconds before he'd responded? After which had come the story of the horror film and, conveniently, the mass distribution of stick figures.

Turning their supposed lead into a dead end.

Was what he'd said even true? And why couldn't he remember where Deirdre had watched *The Blair Witch Project*, if it wasn't at the GFT?

They would, of course, check up on the story of when and where the film had been shown. Plus the story of the film club and Deirdre's involvement in it.

Unfortunately, if neither story was true, Sam could easily claim that Deirdre must have been lying to him to cover up where she had been going on her outings and with whom.

Which was as good an explanation as any other.

McNab decided a quick call to his partner was in order. When it went to voicemail, he left a potted version of Sam's story, hoping Janice might get it in time to run it past the two mates.

His next port of call should be the student strip. Without Janice, he was less concerned about being recognized and having to declare his status as a detective. After all, he couldn't imagine for a moment that Holly would have kept that a secret, from her pals at least. And he hadn't asked her to.

Having now learnt that the stick man dolls had been given out en masse prior to Deirdre's disappearance, he had little doubt some of them would have ended up on the student strip. He could check with all the individual clubs or, alternatively, he could ask Holly, and save himself the trip.

She answered immediately. 'Detective Sergeant. What a nice surprise. How's your head?' she said with a laugh.

'Fine. And yours?' he asked.

'Head's fine, but there are other parts reminding me of what we were up to last night,' she said suggestively.

When he didn't immediately respond, she apologized. 'Sorry, mustn't take your mind off your work. Why are you disturbing me when I'm working?'

'A quick question,' McNab said, relieved to get off the subject of sex. 'What do you know about stick men?'

'You mean the band?' Holly asked.

'There's a band called the Stick Men?' McNab said, wondering what fresh horror this was.

'Yeah. They're great. Progressive rock. I'm surprised you haven't heard of them.'

'I said I was too old for you,' he said.

'They're much older than you. In their fifties, I think.'

Mollified, he said, 'What's with the name?'

'Three blokes on various instruments. No vocals. Their outlines are lit up so they look like drawings of stick men. Check them out online. Anyway, if it's not the band . . .' She waited for an explanation.

'The film *The Blair Witch Project* got a special screening a while back where stick dolls were handed out. Did any of them end up in the clubbing scene?'

'Oh, you mean like the creepy twig men that were hanging from the trees?'

'That's them,' McNab confirmed, although he knew nothing about the tree reference.

'I didn't hear about the special screening or I might have gone. Plus I never saw or heard of any stick figures along the strip. Can I ask why?' Holly said tentatively. Then, 'Does it have anything to do with Deirdre Reid?'

'Did you know her?' McNab asked.

'Not personally, no. But I recognized her from the picture you put out as someone I'd seen clubbing.'

'Okay, thanks,' McNab said, thinking it was time to ring off.

'Will I see you tonight?' Holly asked, before he could.

'Working late, sorry,' he managed.

'I'm a late bird myself,' she offered.

'I'll text you when I finish,' McNab told her, aware he would have to reveal that their coupling had been captured on CCTV, probably sooner rather than later.

'Okay.' She sounded placated. 'Now back to work for both of us.'

McNab experienced a mixture of relief and guilt in equal quantities. It was a feeling, he realized, he was familiar with. He would speak to Holly about the CCTV footage, he decided, at the right time. In the right place. Over the phone was neither of those.

He tried to turn his thoughts to what she'd just told him. She hadn't been aware of the circulation of stick man figures. She hadn't known about the special showing of the film. Had it ever really happened?

He found himself intrigued to learn what Janice had discovered, so he headed for the nearest cafe and, ordering up a triple espresso, called her.

This time, she answered. 'Hi, partner, where are you?'

McNab told her.

'Okay. I got your message after I'd spoken to Millie, but before Lisa.'

'And?' he asked.

'Seems Sam was telling the truth. Deirdre liked horror movies. Did join a film group at GFT and did go to a special showing of *Blair Witch* with some of them, where they gave out replicas of the stick men in the movie. Very creepy, Lisa said. Apparently Millie wanted to burn it, but Deirdre wouldn't hear of that. Just laughed.'

When Janice paused there, McNab said, 'Anything else?'

'No, that's it. What about your club trip?' Janice said.

'Same dead end,' McNab told her. 'Although apparently

there's a trio called the Stick Men. Who could have known that?'

'I did,' Janice told him. 'Three musicians. All blokes. Sort of rock. With a light round them . . .'

'Stop,' McNab pleaded. 'You make me feel old.'

'They're older than you,' Janice told him, echoing Holly's earlier words.

'So what now?' McNab needed direction and hopefully from someone who hadn't been lying – or fibbing, as he liked to think of it.

'It's getting late,' Janice said. 'We could meet back at headquarters and prepare a joint report before we finish for the day?'

McNab didn't want to do that. All he could think of now was food and possibly a beer.

'You need to get back to your one true love,' he told her. 'I need to go home and eat. We'll write the report first thing tomorrow.'

'Right. See you in the morning . . . early,' Janice stressed, sounding pleased.

McNab sat, looking into his empty cup. What did he plan for tonight? He thought of Rhona, who should be heading back to Glasgow by now, with the body of possibly the next victim.

He thought of Sean, waiting for her there.

He thought of Ellie, who had so often waited for him, before eventually giving up and departing. He thought of Holly, who for some reason sought his company.

But you haven't been honest with her either, he thought, staring into the empty cup which seemed at this moment to symbolize his empty life.

Lifting his phone, he brought up a picture of Deirdre, alive and smiling for the camera, then thought about her buried on that beach miles from home.

That was what he had to focus on. Rhona, he knew, would be doing exactly that.

30

Day five/six

Now back on solid ground, the body on its way to the mortuary, the evidence en route to the lab, Rhona let herself relax.

She'd found a phone message from Chrissy on landing, telling her briefly how the strategy meeting had gone, including, 'Wait till you hear what Magnus said about the stick man!' and finishing with, 'Am off home now. Come in early so we can talk!'

Rhona was bound for home too, and looking forward to a hot shower and ordering in something to eat.

While waiting for the helicopter to return to Achmelvich, she'd been treated to tea and scones at the campsite's wee cafe. Plus she'd had the opportunity to chat with Murdo MacKenzie, who'd reported the missing cyclist.

He'd seemed aware that she couldn't discuss the body in the cove, nor what evidence, if any, she'd found in the missing girl's tent. So they'd talked of Achmelvich and the shoreline north and south of it.

'The coves around Arisaig are sheltered,' he'd told her. 'Here it's a bit wilder, although just as bonnie. Folk from abroad can't believe they're in Scotland, especially when it's good weather. You should see their faces when they see the white sands and blue water. Mind, if they arrive on a wild day . . .' He'd laughed. 'They don't mind the weather, really. They choose to visit Scotland and sometimes that's what they get.'

Rhona had spoken of her love of swimming along the coast here, and her last visit to Achmelvich.

'Aye,' he'd said. 'It's a wee bit of heaven. Although, after what's happened . . .' His face clouded over.

'Bad things happen everywhere,' Rhona had reminded him.

'But they shouldn't, and definitely not here.' At this point he'd looked directly at her. 'We get a lot of lone campers come to Achmelvich, young women in particular. They feel safe here. Maybe not any more.'

Rhona hadn't responded to this, for what could she say? Except that, according to Lee, Donald and Jean McIver at the croft campsite had voiced the very same concern.

As she was dropped at the flat, she noted the light was on in the sitting room. There were two possible explanations for that: either she'd left it on this morning or Sean had been to the flat – and perhaps was still there.

She checked her watch before slipping the key in the lock. Surely he would be at the club by now? She found herself hoping that was true. All she wanted was to stand under the shower, eat, then write up her notes.

She could manage a few words for Tom, should the cat permit her that privilege, but that was about all.

As it was, she got her wish, with a little extra. The flat was empty apart from Tom, who, perhaps scenting her presence, abandoned his rooftop wanderings to appear at the kitchen window, dropping silently onto the window seat to greet her, briefly but fondly enough to make her feel welcome.

The little extra was a note from Sean to accompany the aroma of marmite de la mer from the slow cooker, with a French stick waiting alongside.

Her plans to order in before the shower no longer required, Rhona headed to the bathroom, emerging fifteen minutes later to ladle herself up a large bowl of fish stew, breaking off half of the French loaf to go with it.

Seated at the table and suddenly joined again by Tom, she noted that it may have been the fish stew that had brought him back from his nocturnal wanderings and not her after all.

Replete now, she poured herself a glass of chilled white wine, ignoring the red already opened by Sean, and took herself through to the sitting room, Tom leading the way.

The setting sun was bathing the room in a dusky glow and from the bay window she could see a reddened cloud hanging between Kelvingrove's twin towers, making them even more magnificent than usual.

She hadn't had the opportunity to write her notes up in situ. No forensic tent, and only five hours to capture the evidence before the incoming tide swept the scene clean, she'd relied on recording her thoughts as she worked, plus the photographs she'd instructed Marie to take.

She studied each captured image, initially without her voiceover, so that she might look at them afresh before listening to her recording.

The smells and sounds that had surrounded them were brought swiftly back to life. The call of the gulls watching them at work, the wash of the sea as it steadily advanced behind them. The veil of salty scent and seaweed masking the smell of decomposition.

And beyond all of this, the face of a young woman who'd undoubtedly been alive not that long before. Her twisted and broken body testament to how she had died.

But who was she? The girl from the tent in the dunes? Or Callie, who'd disappeared from the campsite at Arisaig?

No matter how dispassionately she studied the evidence gathered at the recent locus and wrote her findings down, she knew in her heart and her mind that all three women were linked. The presence of the stick man was testament to that.

Chrissy had stated that the police hadn't as yet revealed the stick man aspect to Deirdre's story, so neither Callie's disappearance nor the body in the cove could be attributed to the work of a copycat perpetrator.

Having finished her notes, she sent a copy to the lab computer and, moving her laptop to the coffee table, slid down to nestle her head against a cushion. Tom, curled by her side, adjusted his position to accommodate her.

She knew it would be better to go to bed, but the thought of rousing herself enough to accomplish that seemed too much of an effort at that moment.

As she dozed off, her brain filled again with the sound of the sea.

When Sean arrived later to scoop her up and carry her through to bed, Rhona thought at first she was merely dreaming. Not until the duvet was pulled over her, and she caught the scent of him, did she realize the truth of it.

'Thank you,' she managed to murmur before she descended into sleep once more, a single image playing out in her head.

The stick man figure, clothed in a strand of slithery seaweed, its end stuffed into the gaping hole of the figure's mouth.

When the early sun woke her, she registered that she was alone in the bed. Had she dreamt Sean's arrival? Rising, she went through to the kitchen, remembering that first night she had brought him home and found him here in the morning, a stark naked man making coffee while whistling an Irish tune.

It made her smile, even now.

She checked the spare room where he would go so as not to disturb her when he arrived late into the night. The mound beneath the duvet, the dark head on the pillow, showed her that her hunch was right.

Stepping out, she quietly closed the door and went for a quick shower. Chrissy had ordered her to come early and she would, of course, obey. Besides, she had no doubt Chrissy would be ready with the coffee and a plentiful supply of well-filled morning rolls.

Earlier than usual, Kelvingrove Park seemed quieter, the walking and cycling contingent she normally met lower in number. The university cloisters were equally empty. Term time was over, as were the exams, and nowadays you didn't have to come read a noticeboard to see if you'd passed.

Rhona enjoyed the bustle of the university campus when the students were around, but there was also pleasure in the empty echo of her footsteps as she walked through the famous cloisters to her lab.

The enticing scent when she entered reassured her that Chrissy had indeed purchased their breakfast rolls and put on the coffee machine, and she found herself grateful once again that Chrissy had abandoned the porridge-for-breakfast phase she'd recently had to endure.

'Black pudding, egg and tattie scone or square sausage, egg and tattie scone?' Chrissy said as she entered.

'Black pudding.' Rhona gave her a wide smile.

Chrissy pushed her choice towards her and went to fetch the coffee.

Ten minutes later, rolls consumed and second coffee poured, they were ready.

'Your story or mine?' Chrissy said.

Rhona could almost taste Chrissy's desire to offload whatever had been said about the stick man, so nodded at her to go ahead.

'Magnus said that the stick figures found in Deirdre's mouth and hanging in Callie's van would be better described as Twanas, which are evil, and are likely to be the killer's signature. Like in the film *The Blair Witch Project*.'

She checked for an indication that Rhona knew which film she was talking about. When Rhona nodded, Chrissy continued. 'Deirdre, as we know, was kept alive for maybe a month before he killed her. Maybe Callie, identified now as Caillean Munro, might be too.'

Chrissy watched her reaction to that for a moment before saying, 'I saw the stick man you found when I logged in the evidence last night. Where was it exactly?'

'Buried a little in the sand close to her head,' Rhona told her.

'So it had been in her mouth?'

'Probably. We can check for her saliva.'

'How did she die?' Chrissy said. 'Was she strangled like Deirdre?'

'Unlikely.' Rhona explained about the broken shape of

the body. 'I transferred my report and the photographs late last night. We can take a look together.'

'Might it be Callie after all?'

'You said she's been identified?' Rhona said.

'They got her name through the vehicle registration. A Caillean Munro owned it . . . owns it,' she said determinedly. 'They checked her address. She hasn't been there for months. A neighbour said she'd moved in with her boyfriend, but didn't know where.'

'And this boyfriend hasn't got in touch?' Rhona asked.

'Not from the van picture the police circulated on social media. Maybe now they have the driving-licence photo of Caillean, he will.'

'So Callie had a boyfriend, who never reported her missing?' Rhona said.

'I wondered about that too. Even if she went off kayaking on her own, surely they would have kept in touch?'

'Can I access the licence photo?' Rhona said.

'Sure thing.' Chrissy brought it up on the computer screen. 'It's not great,' she said.

Chrissy was right, it wasn't a good photo, but could the body on the beach be Callie? Rhona brought up her set of images and, choosing one of the victim's face, sat it alongside for comparison.

'Well,' Chrissy offered eventually, 'it could be, but we can soon find out if this is the Callie from the van, we've got plenty of DNA evidence to compare. What about the missing girl from Achmelvich?'

'No one saw her, but we have various items of clothing and other assorted evidence I retrieved from the tent. The bike, the local police believe, was likely on hire, which is fairly common for folk on the NC500. They have a serial number from the chassis which should hopefully lead to a bike shop.'

Chrissy was viewing the other photographs. 'Same black and pink wetsuit and the stick man . . .' she said angrily. 'This won't end until we get him.'

Rhona nodded. 'So we'd better make a start.'

31

Day six

She hadn't mentioned the missing pillowcase and its contents to Derek, either last night when he finally came home or this morning at breakfast.

In fact, he'd been the one to mention it, just before leaving for work.

'I was looking for my fishing line and eventually found it in the cupboard with the T-shirt I got fish blood on.' He'd looked questioningly at her as he'd said this.

'I was going to steep your T-shirt in bleach to get the stain out. I know it's your favourite,' she'd managed to say.

'Will that work?'

She'd nodded.

'Great. It's in my room on the chair.'

When she'd heard the door close behind him she'd gone up to check and there it was, alongside the pillowcase. There was, however, no sign of the fishing line or the empty Durex sachet.

Derek had moved into the spare room when they'd come back from Arisaig. He hadn't said why and she didn't care. She was more than glad not to have to lie beside him every night. Although every time he went out with his mates, she feared he might crawl back in with her on his return.

If or when that happened, she would go in with Lucy, she decided, just as she'd done at the campsite. The sudden thought of the campsite reminded her of something else she hadn't broached with Derek last night or this morning.

Today's visit to the police station.

If she had, all hell would have broken out. She shuddered at the thought. Of course she could, would have said that the police told her she didn't have any choice, not in a murder enquiry. They needed to talk to the children. Lucy in particular.

She tried to imagine what Derek's expression would have been at that. Guilt? Or just rage?

But if she'd already left him and taken the kids, what could he do about it?

She had a place ready, albeit temporary until she could work something else out. She had a suitcase packed and already in the boot of her car. She planned to tell the kids it was another wee holiday, just with her, because the other one got spoilt.

After the interview, she would head there.

And what about the T-shirt?

She lifted it and, stuffing it back into the pillowcase, decided to take it with her.

When she called the kids for breakfast, she put on her best and most cheerful face.

'Guess what? We're going on another holiday.' She hurried on before they had time to register her words properly. 'A friend of mine doesn't need her holiday cottage for a bit, and she said we could have it.'

She'd expected Orly to look worried by this. In fact, the opposite happened. He adopted what she interpreted as a look of relief.

'Is Dad coming?' Lucy asked.

'Dad has to work, so can't come, but we'll be fine on our own, won't we?' She hurried on, buoyed by the reaction so far. 'I've packed for us and we'll set off in a wee while.'

'Where is the cottage?' Orly said.

'Not far, about an hour away. Beside a big loch, so you can paddle or swim if you like.'

The two children observed each other in that intimate way they had, as though having a silent conversation, before Lucy smiled. 'Okay, Mum.'

So the escape was okay, but . . . what about what they must do before it?

She mustered herself, before continuing, 'On our way out of Glasgow we have to drop in at the police station.'

'Why?' said Orly, with another swift glance at Lucy.

'We promised we would when we left the campsite,' Francine reminded them. 'The police in Glasgow need to have a wee chat to you about—'

She was cut off there by Lucy. 'Will the nice lady be there?' she said. 'The one who wanted to go swimming with me?'

Francine had no idea if Dr MacLeod would be there, but realized she could ask for that to be the case for Lucy's sake.

When she said, 'I'll ask for her to be there,' Lucy looked to Orly with a satisfied smile.

After the children went upstairs to pack their choice of toys, Francine called the number she'd been given by DS Clark. It rang out briefly before she heard the woman's voice from yesterday, giving her name and rank.

Gathering herself, she said, 'It's Francine Henderson here.'

The voice, polite before, now moved to a softer, more welcoming tone. 'Everything all right for this morning, Mrs Henderson?'

'Yes. I've spoken to the children and they seem happy about it. Although there is one request, which seemed important, especially to Lucy . . .' She hesitated there.

'And that is?' DS Clark prompted.

Francine cleared her throat. 'She asked that the forensic lady Dr MacLeod be there. Lucy says she'll speak to her.' She rushed on. 'Lucy stopped speaking after they found the body until she met Dr MacLeod,' she finished.

There was a moment's silence before DS Clark said, 'I'll see if that can be arranged, although Dr MacLeod may already have other commitments this morning.'

Francine thanked her and rang off, aware that that was all she could hope for at such late notice, and, she realized, she could always explain to Lucy that Dr MacLeod was on an important case this morning, and they might have to arrange to see her another day.

Letting out a small sigh of relief, she registered that this was the first time in months she'd had the faintest of feelings that things might work out for her and the kids after all.

32

Day six

McNab listened as Janice explained the reason for Francine Henderson's call.

'So the kid that located the body wants to have Rhona in on the interview? Do we know why?' he said.

'Lucy, that's her name, stopped talking when they found the body. It seemed she was worried it might be the missing girl Callie from the campsite, who she'd taken a shine to. When Rhona explained it wasn't her, she started talking again. She and Rhona became friendly. They were planning a swim together until the father put a stop to that.'

'And what's the dad saying about all of this?' McNab said.

'I'm not certain she's even told him they're coming in today,' Janice said. 'In fact, I'm pretty sure she hasn't. Apparently he was Mr Angry back at the campsite at police involvement with his family. I can't imagine he's changed his mind now he's back in Glasgow.'

'So basically the guy's a prick?' McNab said.

'I suspect so.'

'Or,' McNab thought for a moment, before saying, 'he maybe has something to hide? Did he meet the missing girl?'

'You did read DS MacDonald's report on Callie's disappearance?'

McNab hadn't, but didn't want to admit that his mind had been on other things of late. 'I took a quick look,' he fibbed.

Janice threw him a glance that spoke volumes. 'He apparently gave Rhona a hard time when she came to collect Lucy for the swim. Also he maintains he only saw Callie briefly the night she arrived when he and his wife spoke to her.'

'And we believe him?'

'So far we have no reason not to.'

'Well, if the mother thinks it's a good idea to have Rhona at the interview, we should try and arrange it,' McNab said.

'Do you want to run it past the boss first?' Janice suggested.

McNab knew she was checking how he felt about re-entering the boss's domain after his previous poor performance. Determined to put an end to her silent speculations, he stood up.

'I'll go check with him.'

His bravado, of course, was for show only. In actual fact, he was keen to keep clear of the boss until he'd sorted out the problem of the CCTV footage of him and Holly, especially since last night he'd failed to even broach the subject with her, ending up pursuing more pleasurable pastimes.

Also, first thing this morning he'd received a cryptic message from Ollie which, when deciphered, asked him if he *had* dealt with it.

He could, of course, just use this opportunity to tell the boss about what he now liked to think of as his faux pas. After all, he hadn't exactly broken any laws and he hadn't been seen or recognized, except by a super recognizer.

Be sure your sins will find you out, the voice of his late mother reminded him as his knock was answered and he was commanded to enter.

DI Wilson was seated facing the window, in the old swivel chair they'd tried to replace when his office was refurbished. McNab recognized its legendary squeak as the boss swung round to face him.

'Well, DS McNab. How did your trawl for stick men go?'

'We're just finishing up our report, sir. It'll be with you shortly.'

DI Wilson was eyeing him in that way he had, which made you feel guilty even if you were innocent. Although McNab had rarely been in the non-guilty category.

'So why are you here, Detective Sergeant?' DI Wilson raised a quizzical eyebrow.

McNab attempted to explain about Lucy's request that Rhona be there at today's interview.

When he'd finished, DI Wilson nodded. 'Good idea. Give Dr MacLeod a call, ask if she's willing to oblige. It's scheduled for early afternoon, I understand. In view of the circumstances, I've already made contact with Professor Pirie and he's agreed to be an onlooker, although not in the room.'

The positive nature of this response and the boss's general demeanour caused McNab briefly to reconsider revealing his own sorry tale, before DI Wilson said, 'Get on with it, Detective Sergeant.'

Ordered into action, McNab decided this wasn't the time to bare his soul, so excused himself and exited.

'Well?' Janice demanded on his return.

'I'm to phone Rhona. The Prof's already been recruited as an observer.'

'That's good news,' Janice said, obviously pleased.

'And the boss wants our stick man report as soon as possible,' he added.

'On it now,' she promised.

When he rang Rhona's mobile there was no response, so he tried the lab phone, which rang out a few times before Chrissy eventually answered.

'What's up?' she demanded when he asked to speak to Rhona.

'It's about the two kids from the campsite,' he told her. 'They're being interviewed today.'

'And?'

'The wee girl, Lucy, wants Rhona to be there.'

Silence met his explanation, followed by a clunk as the phone went down, then footsteps accompanied by Chrissy's voice shouting for Rhona.

Chrissy came back on. 'She'll be here in a minute. We were in the lab working through the evidence from Achmelvich.'

He didn't get any more than that before Rhona came on the line. He explained this time in a little more detail, including Janice's thoughts on the angry father.

'I remember Mr Henderson,' Rhona said. 'He deliberately stopped Lucy from speaking to me. What time is this happening?'

'One o'clock,' he told her.

'The PM on the Achmelvich body is scheduled for four. I need to be back for that. Tell Mrs Henderson and Lucy I'll be there.'

'I will, thanks,' McNab said, aware there was quite a lot he'd like to talk through with Rhona himself, should he ever get the chance.

Janice was watching as he rang off. 'All set up?'

'Rhona says to call Mrs Henderson and reassure her she'll be at the interview.'

'Right. Now take a look at your messages. Seems we might have a lead on Caillean Munro's boyfriend. The caller wouldn't give her name. Said she'd seen the licence photo on the news. Also said Callie and she were mates until Callie moved in with a Gus Logan. She gave us an address, although she's not sure if he and Callie are still living there.'

McNab rose. 'Okay, let's go see Mr Logan.'

'I should finish the stick man report first and catch you up. Remember, he might not be there,' Janice added.

'I'm feeling lucky,' McNab declared, although in truth he was only relieved he hadn't blurted out his story to the boss, minutes earlier.

'If he is there, we need to bring him in for questioning,' she told him firmly.

'Understood,' McNab said with a nod.

Exiting the station, McNab found himself more than relieved to be a free agent again. Much as he appreciated having a partner, and one as good as DS Clark, there were times when going it alone was more productive. Just as it had been yesterday morning when he'd talked to Sam Wheeler.

Then he'd felt he'd got a better measure of the man than had been on show when Janice was about.

His partner was inclined to niceness, which could put some suspects at their ease, making them give away more than they intended. He acknowledged that, but as far as McNab was concerned, only men truly knew what their sex was capable of, whatever front they put on.

Janice had read Sam as an okay guy. McNab hadn't been so sure of that back then, and was even less certain now.

The address they'd been given for Gus Logan was in Woodlands, within easy walking distance of the so-called student strip and the School of Art. Could it really be a coincidence that two out of three probable victims lived in the same area? McNab didn't believe in coincidence and definitely not in murder enquiries.

Janice, in her usual efficient way, had also checked for anything they might already have on this Logan guy and apparently he was clean, which didn't mean he was, of course. Plenty of folk succeeded in keeping their heads below the police radar, despite nefarious activities.

McNab had had a quick listen to the recording of the anonymous female caller and there was no doubt regarding the worry in her voice. She didn't like Gus Logan and was fearful for her pal.

Of course, it could all be a hoax. Maybe Gus was an old boyfriend who'd thrown her over, and this was her way of getting back at him. Such things had happened before, but this time, McNab's instinct told him that the pal's concern had been genuine.

Wending his way through the West End, his thoughts moved back to Rhona. What would she say if he asked her advice about the CCTV footage? Even as he posed the question, he already knew her answer. Although, he thought, if he rehearsed his confession with Rhona, she might advise him on how to do it better.

But first you have to tell Holly of the clip's existence.

And that was what he was finding the most difficult. He had told her he was a police officer, right from the start. She hadn't minded that. In fact, she'd seemed excited by it.

Which is probably why she persuaded you outside on that night.

For the briefest of seconds McNab wondered if he'd been

set up. Had she wanted the thrill of perhaps being seen out there? Or even caught on camera?

You were easily persuaded, remember?

And he had been. That first night he'd dropped her home he'd made the right choice, but his willpower hadn't lasted very long. If only Ellie hadn't deserted him, was his next thought, before it was swiftly followed by, *That's right, blame your former girlfriend for something that was all down to you.*

Ellie had been special. He'd forgotten that far too quickly. More fool him.

McNab was glad when he reached his destination, if only to escape his ruminations on his personal life and where it had, and still did, collide with the job.

Focus, he reminded himself as he locked his vehicle. Let's see if Gus Logan was the prick he suspected he might be.

33

Day six

It takes one to know one was the replay in his head as he pushed the appropriate button on the buzzer. The silence following this made him press again, as though that would miraculously result in someone actually being home.

When it didn't, McNab tried one more time, keeping his finger on for considerably longer this time.

A crackle eventually came, swiftly followed by a male voice shouting, 'What the fuck?'

'DS Michael McNab here, wishing to speak with Gus Logan.'

In the silence that followed, McNab could almost hear the brain on the other end trying to decide a response to that. Eventually it did, because the door buzzed open.

The flat was on the second floor of the tenement building, where the right-hand door stood ajar. Just inside was a man of McNab's height, but definitely younger, and possibly fitter. He wore a white T-shirt that did nothing to hide the upper arm muscles or the pecs.

McNab found himself silently promising to hit the gym again as soon as possible.

'Sorry about the language. I was lifting weights in the

back room and couldn't get here fast enough to answer.' The guy smiled and ran his hand over his smoothly shorn head.

At least I have more hair, McNab told himself.

'What can I help you with, Detective Sergeant?'

'May I come in?' McNab said, moving forward as though this was a foregone conclusion.

Logan stepped aside with a wave of his arm. 'Of course.'

Now in a spacious multi-doored hallway, McNab waited to be directed onwards, but wasn't.

Logan closed the front door. 'We can talk here,' he said, as though he should be the one to decide.

'The living room would be better,' McNab suggested.

Logan gave an acquiescent nod. 'Okay.'

He led the way into a large bay-windowed sitting room. A quick glance round told McNab that it in no way resembled his own front room. Much classier and undoubtedly cleaner. Although there was nothing about it that suggested a woman's presence currently or in the immediate past.

Logan gestured to a leather seat and took the one opposite.

'So,' he said. 'How can I help you, Detective Sergeant?'

'Caillean Munro,' McNab said. 'Your girlfriend, I believe?'

Something flickered across Logan's face, but McNab couldn't find the word to describe it. Momentary distaste or maybe rejection?

'Callie?' He now adopted an aura of surprise. 'I haven't seen Callie since we broke up.'

'When was that exactly?' McNab said.

He pulled a face. 'A week ago, I guess. Anyway, that's when she stopped taking my calls from Hong Kong where I was on a work trip. She'd cleared out when I got back, but I have no idea when exactly.' He sounded peeved by that.

'Caillean is reported as officially missing.'

He assumed a look of surprise. 'Who reported her as missing? I know nothing about this,' he said.

'Her photograph's been on the news. Her blue Transit campervan was found at a campsite near Arisaig on the west coast . . .'

Logan interrupted him at that. 'You mean to tell me she went off in that damn campervan again? I assume she had the kayak with her?'

'She did,' McNab confirmed.

'Bloody fool. She went out in all weathers in that thing. It was madness. I told her so.'

Seeing his clenched jaw and tightened fists, McNab wondered if perhaps Logan did more than just tell her so.

'Her disappearance was on the news. You never got in touch with us about it?' McNab said.

'I had no idea about any of this. As you see, I don't have a TV. I don't listen to the news. When I'm working a contract, I don't have the time or the inclination.'

'What about social media? A picture of the van was circulated.'

'Don't do much on social media. As I said, I work a lot. Plus I keep myself fit and I'm often away.'

'What kind of work do you do, Mr Logan?' McNab asked.

'I work in software engineering. I was out in Hong Kong setting up software that I'd designed.' He sounded pleased with himself about that.

'When exactly did you return from Hong Kong?'

'A couple of days ago. Slept on and off since then. Flying long distance does that to me.'

'And Callie wasn't here?'

'I didn't expect her to be, seeing as we'd stopped communicating.' He looked a little pained by that. 'I didn't want to break up with Callie. My work was the problem. Always away on the job. You probably know what it's like, Detective Sergeant, being a police officer?'

McNab did, but he wasn't going to admit it.

'Do you have contacts for any of Callie's friends who we might talk to?' McNab said.

Logan shook his head. 'Callie said she'd left her old world behind when she moved in with me. We just did things together.' He looked crestfallen.

'But not camping or kayaking?' McNab said.

'No,' he replied with obvious distaste. 'Definitely not that.'

'Was Caillean working?'

'She was between jobs when we met. Not long finished her degree in interior design. Textiles were her thing. She was planning on setting up a business. Did a lot of planning, but as far as I know it never got off the ground.' He didn't sound surprised by that.

'May I ask where you met exactly?'

He shrugged. 'In the Blue Arrow on Sauchiehall Street. I like jazz.' He waited in silence for a moment, then said, 'Is that all you need from me, Detective Sergeant?'

'We require you to come down to the station, Mr Logan, to give us a statement regarding your relationship with Caillean Munro.'

Logan didn't like that one little bit. 'But I've told you I wasn't even here when she disappeared. How would I know anything about that?' he demanded.

'You may have been the last person to speak to Ms Munro and presumably knew her well. We need to know whatever you can tell us about her.'

The silent stand-off lasted a little longer, before Logan, his mouth tight with anger, said, 'Very well. Do you want me to come with you now?'

'That would be helpful, yes.' McNab managed an appreciative smile.

As Logan went to get his jacket, McNab moved to wait in the hall. When he'd followed Logan through to the sitting room, he'd made note of the row of coats hanging there, one of which was obviously not Logan's. McNab wondered if it was the only item of Callie's left in the flat.

The apartment would have to be properly searched, of course, and if they held on to Logan for long enough, that could be arranged.

McNab wrote a quick text to Janice as he waited for Logan to reappear, saying simply, Bringing him in.

34

Day six

The family room bore little resemblance to the rest of the police station. Rhona registered the bright colours, the children's toys and books, the warm lighting and comfy chairs, and found her concerns at what was about to happen lessen a little.

'Not bad, eh?' DS Clark said with a smile.

'Makes me feel better,' Rhona told her.

'PC Cope, the family liaison officer, will bring the family in when they arrive. I've watched her in action before and she's very good,' Janice said. 'Professor Pirie will observe by camera next door. DI Wilson wants to chat to you both afterwards. Anything you want to ask?'

'Is the father coming, do you know?'

'I told McNab I thought not. I'm not even sure Mrs Henderson told him of our request to see the children.'

'He's quite intimidating,' Rhona said. 'I think the kids wouldn't talk with him here. Have you run a check on him?'

'Clean as a whistle. Not even a speeding ticket, but hey, as you know, the clever ones often are until we discover what they've been up to.'

'I think Francine is frightened of him, but wants to do the right thing,' Rhona offered.

'My impression too, although I haven't yet met her in person, only chatted to her on the phone.'

The sound of approaching footsteps saw them fall silent. Janice went to open the door, a welcoming smile on her face. Then they were in. Lucy and Orly together, Mrs Henderson following close behind.

Lucy, spotting Rhona, immediately came over, eyes alight. 'Dr MacLeod, you came. I said you would. Didn't I, Orly?'

Orly was studying Rhona closely, as if trying to match her to the woman he'd met back at the campsite. Eventually he gave a little nod, but there was more apprehension in his expression than joy.

'Hello, Lucy and Orly. It's good to see you both again,' Rhona said.

'Did you swim?' Lucy asked, eyes wide.

'I did, but I missed you.'

The eyes clouded over. 'Daddy wouldn't let me come swimming with you.'

'I know,' Rhona said. 'That's why I called in to you, so you knew I came as promised.'

At this, Lucy slipped her hand into Rhona's and, catching Francine's eye, Rhona was rewarded by a grateful smile.

This meeting of herself, Janice and the family liaison officer, with Magnus observing from next door, had been designed to put the children, especially Lucy, at ease. Which seemed to be working, for the moment at least.

Lucy was to be their focus, although Orly's place as his sister's confidant was obvious even now. However, this plan didn't last for long.

Both children listened carefully to PC Hope's explanation as to what was about to happen, then looked to one another in silent communication.

After which Orly said, 'We want to speak to Dr MacLeod on our own.' Despite his anxious look, he sounded determined.

Francine, Rhona suspected, had already been forewarned of this, because she didn't look surprised or even worried by it. In fact, the look she shot Rhona was one of relief.

After a moment's surprised silence, PC Hope responded.

'Okay, we'll leave you to chat to Dr MacLeod on your own for a bit and I'll come and see you later.' She checked with Francine: 'Are you okay with that, Mrs Henderson?'

Francine rose with a nod and an encouraging smile.

The children were silent as they watched the door close behind the adults. Rhona waited, saying nothing, understanding that the children wished to be in charge of this exchange. She wasn't required to ask questions, merely to listen to whatever they were willing to tell her.

After a moment or two, Lucy nodded to her brother to begin.

Fear and worry etched his small face as he began, stumbling over the words at first. 'I saw Daddy go into Callie's van the night she arrived. When Mum and me looked inside the van the next morning there was blood and sick on the floor, so Callie must have been hurt.'

He didn't say he was worried that his father had been the one to hurt Callie, but it seemed from his expression that he might well be.

Rhona felt her heart go out to Orly, realizing he'd been carrying this fear ever since that fateful night.

Lucy took a little longer to begin her own story. Rhona, seeing her distress, squeezed her hand reassuringly.

Eventually, with a little gulp as though she was trying not to cry, she managed to get the words out. 'I . . . I saw Daddy walking along the shore that morning and wanted to go with him. So I shouted but he didn't stop and I couldn't climb over the fence so I had to go round to the opening.

'I tried to catch him up, but he was walking too quickly.' Lucy's face crumpled a little. 'He stopped at . . . that place . . . so I thought he'd heard me calling on him. But then he jumped over the fence and walked back through the fields to the campsite and I sat down.'

So there it was. The reason Lucy had been at the burial ground. But why had her dad gone there? And why did he go into Callie's van?

They were both looking at her, waiting for her response.

'Have you told your mum any of this?' Rhona asked quietly.

They shook their heads in unison. 'No, because it would make her cry,' Orly said.

'And your dad?'

Orly checked with his sister again before answering. 'He doesn't know we saw him.'

The silence that followed was eventually broken by Lucy, who said, 'Mum's taking us on holiday today. We're going to a cottage by a loch.'

Was the child changing the subject because she didn't want any more questions or was this in fact true? Rhona soon found out.

'Dad isn't coming with us. He's got to work,' Orly said in obvious relief.

Did Francine know something or was she just trying to make up for their spoilt holiday? Then again, might she be leaving home altogether? Might that have emerged in her conversation next door with PC Hope?

The two children had dropped into silence. Lucy rose and

said, her voice a little wobbly, 'I want to see my mummy now.'

'Of course,' Rhona said, 'and thank you for chatting to me. You'll be able to swim on this holiday?'

'Mummy says we'll all swim, even if it's cold,' Lucy said in a determined voice.

Lucy gave her a little hug before the door opened and Francine came in.

'Everything okay?' she said to Rhona.

Rhona wasn't sure how to answer that. What both children had revealed to her had thrown an altogether different light on Callie's disappearance and the behaviour of her husband.

'Now they've told me, I think they'll be brave enough to tell you what's been worrying them,' Rhona said. 'Especially since you're going off on holiday together.'

'I'd like that,' Francine said as both children moved to take her hand. 'Will we see you again, Dr MacLeod?'

'I certainly hope so,' Rhona said, before following DS Clark from the room.

Once outside, the door closed behind them, Janice said, 'We watched from next door. Both kids had a startling story to tell.'

'Did Mrs Henderson hear that?' Rhona asked.

Janice indicated not. 'There was always a chance that the kids might have something to say about their mother. Although she was so keen to bring them here, I doubted that. PC Hope chatted to her in another room.'

Rhona nodded. 'Is she really taking them on holiday . . . or is she leaving her husband and just hasn't explained that to them?'

'PC Hope suspects she plans to move out and this is perhaps the first step,' Janice confirmed.

'From what I saw at the holiday camp, she's frightened of him. If he found out she brought the children here . . .' Rhona tailed off.

'She has my number and I've told her to ring me any time she needs to talk, or if she's worried for the children or for herself.' Janice halted there. 'You ready for the boss now? Magnus is with him.'

Rhona acknowledged Magnus's presence on entry, registering his concerned expression, before greeting her long-term friend and mentor, Bill Wilson, who'd been a support ever since she'd entered this job.

'So, Rhona, your thoughts on what the children told you?'

'Up to now Orly only said he'd seen someone enter the van that night. Now he's revealed that he thinks that someone was his father. I think he believes that to be the truth,' she said. 'Plus the relief at being able to say it out loud was obvious.'

'Magnus?' Bill asked.

'I agree, although I think there may be more to come. I believe they'd decided on their lines, and repeated them to you. Sometimes with difficulty because of the upset in saying the words. The boy, Orly, didn't tell you exactly when he saw his father going into Callie's van, or if Callie had willingly let him in. He didn't mention seeing him come out, yet something tells me he would have watched for that. He said he was worried she might have been hurt because of the blood the next day. I think he was worried that his father had hurt her. Why would he think this unless he'd seen his father hurt someone else, his mother for instance?'

Silence followed this before Rhona said what she'd also been thinking.

'Lucy's story about following her father rang true and it

explains why she was found at the burial site, but her father stopping there had really scared her. Why, when she followed him, did she stop there too? Did she realize it was a grave? Or did he do something there that frightened her?'

'Was it recognizable as a gravesite?' DI Wilson asked.

'To Chrissy and myself, yes, and the police dog obviously knew. But to a child like Lucy, I don't think so. The question really is why did Derek Henderson go there in the first place?'

'He could have just been on a walk?' Janice said.

'Or maybe he went to meet someone?' Magnus offered.

'It's time we asked Mr Henderson in for questioning.' DI Wilson looked to Janice. 'I believe we already have Callie's former boyfriend, Mr Logan, on the premises?'

'Yes, sir, DS McNab brought him in,' Janice said.

'Then let's see what both men have to say about all of this.'

'And Mrs Henderson?' Rhona asked. 'Did she tell PC Hope anything more while I was with the children?'

'Only what she'd told us already, although she did explain she hadn't admitted to her husband about coming in today. Or that she was taking the children away to a friend's cottage.'

'We need to know exactly where she's going,' Rhona said. 'I'm not sure it's enough to just know her mobile number. Wherever it is, there may not be a signal. The children mentioned a loch, but not the loch's name or location.'

Magnus nodded, agreeing with her.

'If she is going into hiding from her husband, then she must have a reason for doing that,' Rhona said. 'She's afraid for her children. That much is obvious. I also believe the children share her fear.'

35

Day six

Logan had come quietly enough and was now stewing in the interview room, hopefully worried as hell as to what might happen next.

McNab didn't like the guy and was pretty sure that his story about where he was and when probably wouldn't add up. Instinct suggested he and Callie had had a bust-up and that was why she'd gone off in her van.

On his return to the station he'd chosen not to join the party in with the boss, keen not to face him again until he might sort out the *small* problem of the CCTV footage. Meeting the boss's keen eye when you were either lying or evading the truth was a tortuous business.

With this thought in mind, he decided he couldn't wait any longer to talk to Holly, and took himself outside to make the call before Janice and the others re-emerged.

He stood for a moment, trying to decide how exactly he should frame his story. Play it funny and awkward, appealing to Holly's sense of humour? Or just tell the truth? Which was that he was screwed if she didn't back him up and say the sex was consensual and that she'd been the one to instigate it.

Even as he thought this, he felt embarrassed for himself. Why should he put the blame on Holly, as though he'd been forced rather than led willingly outside to do what he'd done?

As it was, he didn't get to play out either scenario as the call rang out unanswered, before switching to voicemail and Holly's cheery tones asking him to leave a message.

In that split second he decided to tell the machine what he'd planned to tell her. It was much like being in the confessional, where you could reveal all your sins without having to look at the priest as you did so.

Hanging up, he felt a rush of relief because he hadn't had to view Holly's reaction either.

But now you have to wait until she calls you back, he reminded himself, *and what if she doesn't? What then, smart arse?*

As he stood there considering the consequences of his decision, the phone rang, but it wasn't Holly's name on the screen.

'McNab here,' he answered.

'Where's here?' Janice demanded.

'Just popped outside.'

'You're not back smoking, I hope?'

'Don't be daft,' McNab told her. 'I'll be with you in a minute.'

As he walked swiftly back, he chastised himself for stupidly saying he was outside. Why hadn't he said he was at the coffee machine? She would have bought that right away.

Janice, he reminded himself again, was way more astute than he sometimes gave her credit for.

Smiling on entry, he met Janice's quizzical eye.

'So how did it go with the kids' interview?' he immediately

asked, to forestall any more questions regarding his stint outside.

'You can watch the recording, but basically Lucy followed her father to the gravesite, and Orly said he saw his father enter Callie's van the night before she disappeared.'

McNab gave a whistle. 'Jeez, I take it we're bringing Mr Henderson in for questioning?'

'We are. Also, it looks like Mrs Henderson's intent on leaving her husband. She's on her way to a rented cottage at Loch Lomond with the children.'

'The kids told her what they told Rhona?' McNab asked.

'They said they couldn't tell their mother because it would have made her cry.'

McNab expressed his distaste. 'So that wasn't what made her leave?'

'I think she was already scared of him,' Janice said.

'Do we know the address of this cottage?'

'We do. Plus we've alerted the local constabulary to the family's presence.'

He could sense Janice's disquiet about all of this, and now wished he'd gone into the meeting with the boss and heard it for himself. In his attempts to get off the hook, he'd failed in his duty to both the dead and the missing girl.

'What is it?' Janice said, obviously reading his expression.

'Let's go see what Callie's former boyfriend has to say. You take the lead this time,' McNab told her.

'D'you want to let me know what he's told you?'

McNab shook his head. 'This way he has to repeat it all. Let's see if it's the same story.'

By the expression on his face as they entered, Logan was well pissed off at being kept waiting. Taking pleasure from that, McNab formally introduced Janice and apologized for keeping him waiting.

'We were in a strategy meeting regarding your girlfriend's disappearance.'

'Callie's not my girlfriend,' Logan stated stiffly. 'I've already explained that.'

McNab watched as Janice smiled pleasantly and, taking the seat directly opposite Logan, said, 'Nevertheless, Mr Logan, I am sure you want to do everything you can to help us locate Callie, hopefully safe and well.'

Logan's belligerent look faded under Janice's watchful eye.

'Of course I want to help, but I've told Detective Sergeant McNab everything already, back at my flat.' He sounded peeved.

'Then please tell me,' Janice said encouragingly.

McNab relaxed back in his chair, arms folded. His partner had this completely under her control. He only had to watch and listen.

Some forty minutes later, leaving a silent Logan writing up his statement, they headed out.

'Well?' McNab said as they walked back to their desks.

'He's hiding something,' Janice said firmly. 'Possibly a fight before she left. Francine Henderson did say in her statement that Callie's face was bruised when she arrived at the campsite.'

'So he assaulted her and that's why she left?'

'I suspect so.'

'I never told him the exact day she arrived at the campsite,' McNab said. 'He was desperately hoping you would so he could get his dates right.'

Janice gave a little laugh. 'No way was that going to happen. I learnt from the best.'

McNab suddenly realized that the compliment might be directed at him.

Janice, seeing his surprise, quipped, 'You might be an arse at times, but hey, there are things you are good at.'

'Fancy a coffee?' McNab said to cover his embarrassment.

'Please – and maybe a doughnut?' Janice said. 'Keep us going until we knock off.'

Heading for the cafeteria, he relived his shame at the compliment, particularly under the current circumstances. He'd hoodwinked Ollie and now his partner, who should have been the first to know about his shenanigans, even before the boss.

Kidding himself that he'd felt his mobile vibrate, he retrieved it from his pocket and checked. Nothing from Holly. Not a missed call or even a text.

She's not going to answer, he thought. *No way does she want to be involved in my troubles. And I don't blame her. So what now?*

Paying for the coffees and doughnuts, he composed himself. Now would be the time to tell Janice what had happened. Get her on side.

Wait a little longer, an inner voice advised. *You've hardly given Holly time to respond. Text her and ask to meet up tonight. She's never turned down an offer to meet before.*

In fact, she'd seemed keen to see him. Jumped at the chance. But maybe not this time . . .

'What's wrong with your face?' Janice declared as he reappeared. 'Thought you were happy with how the interview went?'

'They didn't have my favourite.' He handed over hers.

'Poor you,' she commiserated, before taking a big bite of the chocolate-topped doughnut.

The moment for revelation having passed, he resolved to do what he'd contemplated earlier. He would find an opportunity to talk to Rhona, maybe later at the club, before he bit the bullet and approached the boss.

36

Day six

As Dr Sissons, the forensic pathologist, recorded characteristics of age, sex and race, hair colour, body length and weight, Rhona found herself comparing them again to the description they had of the missing Callie.

As though reading her thoughts, Sissons said, 'Is this your blue van girl, Dr MacLeod?'

'Facially and physically, it could be,' Rhona told him. 'The wetsuit colour and style match too, although the model is pretty common.'

'So no partner or family member available to confirm this?' Sissons asked in the clipped tone he used when perturbed.

'No family has yet come forward, although the police are interviewing Callie's former partner as we speak,' Rhona told him.

'So, when we tidy up our victim, her partner, be it a he or a she, could come in and identify her?'

'We may know before that, from the DNA samples I took from her campervan,' Rhona said.

He nodded at that. 'Good. So . . .' He paused briefly, as though pondering his choice of words. 'The level of decomposition suggests she hasn't been dead for long, unlike our Arisaig victim. But the similarities between them, the likeness, age and build, do seem to suggest a possible link. However, the visible injuries are wholly different.'

Detailing all the injuries Rhona had already registered in her notes, Sissons eventually said, 'I have viewed your photographs of the scene, Dr MacLeod, and I think you'll agree with me when I say that these injuries did not occur during our victim's time in the sea? Even had she been beaten against the cliff.'

'I believe she was only washed over by the incoming tide,' Rhona confirmed.

'So, she either fell from the cliff or was pushed or thrown from there? Then possibly arranged to look as though she'd come from the sea?'

'She wasn't entangled in the netting,' Rhona confirmed. 'It appeared to have been placed over her.'

Sissons gave an appreciative nod, as though this fitted with his own thoughts. 'The Arisaig victim had been choked over a period of time, then eventually strangled, which was established once the wetsuit was removed. I assume you're keen to know if the modus operandi was the same in this case, since I understand you found a stick man at the scene?'

'I did, in the sand near her head,' Rhona confirmed.

'Then let's see if that is the case.'

Rhona watched as the wetsuit was carefully cut from the body. On the previous occasion the area beneath had been well preserved and bore no resemblance to the exposed and decomposing parts of the body.

Just as before, the torso, protected by the wetsuit, remained intact and unmarked, except for the slim neck, with its telltale circle of dark fingerprint bruising, which stood out against the lightly tanned skin.

There was a moment's silence as this was recorded, before Sissons said, 'I think you may have your repeat offender, Dr MacLeod, which will, I believe, be confirmed on our internal examination of the hyoid bone.'

When she eventually emerged from the mortuary, Rhona gave Chrissy a quick call.

'What's the verdict, then?' Chrissy immediately asked.

'Sissons believes she was recently strangled, then thrown off the cliff,' Rhona told her.

'Any sign of repeated choking?' Chrissy asked.

'There was fingerprint bruising but not as extensive as with the previous victim.'

There was a short silence as Chrissy absorbed what this might or might not mean. Was it Callie they'd found or the girl missing from Achmelvich campsite? Or someone else entirely?

'Are you coming back to the lab or shall we just meet at the club?' Chrissy asked.

Rhona glanced at her watch. 'I'll shower here and see you at the jazz club. We can catch up properly then.'

Discarding her suit, she undressed and stepped under a hot shower. Raising her face to the spray, she rinsed the metallic taste of the mortuary from her mouth.

Under the beat of the water, her thoughts moved to Lucy and what had happened between them. She recalled the child's smile as she'd mirrored Rhona's hand signal from the beach at the campsite. Then again today, when Lucy had entered the family room and immediately run to her.

Why had the child chosen her as her confidante back in Arisaig? And again today at the police station? Was it because

Lucy knew that she'd been the one excavating the body and the little girl had been truly worried that it might be Callie buried on the machair?

Whatever the initial reason, it was clear that Lucy now trusted her enough to reveal why she had been found at the deposition site.

The image of Lucy following her father along the shoreline, calling out to him, was a troublesome one. Had he not heard her? Or had he simply chosen to ignore the calls of his youngest child?

Either explanation worried her. Plus it was clear Lucy had been really upset by it. She pondered what type of relationship Derek had with his children. They were obviously closer to their mother, and Francine, she now believed, had every intention of leaving her husband.

Had that been brewing for a while? Or had what had happened at the campsite been the trigger?

Rhona recalled her own conversation with Derek Henderson. His swift switching of mood from smilingly co-operative to openly antagonistic, even threatening. Mr Henderson, she thought, had something to hide, and Orly's revelation that the figure he'd seen entering Callie's van had been his father might be at the heart of it.

Dressed now, she called for a taxi to take her to Ashton Lane, the police car that had dropped her at the mortuary long since gone out on another job.

The sky had grown dark and heavy, and as they drove up Byres Road the rain came on in earnest.

'I'll have to drop you at the entrance to the lane, I'm afraid,' the driver apologized in advance.

'No worries,' Rhona assured him. 'I'll make a run for it.'

Once out of the cab, Rhona sprinted for the jazz club,

reaching the stairs just as the heavy shower became a downpour. Shaking her head free of raindrops, she went inside.

The gang was standing at the bar. She spotted Magnus's tall blond figure first, then the diminutive Chrissy intently looking up at her favourite Viking. Janice was there, but not her partner, Paula. She found herself checking for McNab's auburn head, but he was nowhere to be seen.

As though sensing her scrutiny, Chrissy waved her over, before ordering a large white wine for her from the hovering barman.

'No McNab?' Rhona asked Janice.

'Gone to the bike shop on Gibson Street. Turns out the bicycle at Achmelvich was hired from there.'

'Will it still be open?' Rhona said, glancing at her watch.

'He called them after we got word and they agreed to stay open to talk to him.'

'Any idea who hired it?'

'Not yet, but I expect McNab will appear here soon to tell us.' Janice paused there, before adding, 'Have you any idea what's going on with McNab, other than this case?'

'I was hoping you could tell me,' Rhona said.

'So, it's not just me thinking something's off with him?' Janice said. 'Maybe to do with the new girlfriend?'

Rhona thought back to McNab's somewhat desperate efforts a couple of nights ago to let her know he was heading out on a date at the Blue Arrow, which had had her quizzing him on what the hell he was doing, hanging around the student strip.

'Have you any idea who she is?' Rhona said.

'None,' Janice assured her. 'I also have no idea where he met her.' Janice studied Rhona's reaction to that before saying, 'But I'm guessing from your expression that you have?'

Rhona decided to come clean. 'The Blue Arrow – or at least that was where he was meeting her the last time we were here.'

'He's hanging about the student strip?' By Janice's expression she wasn't too happy about that. 'God, no wonder he didn't say. You'll have heard about the rumours?'

'I have from Chrissy, which is why I tried to dissuade him from going there.'

'The stupid bastard.' Janice shook her head. 'How long has this been going on for?'

'I think maybe from when Deirdre Reid disappeared.'

'No wonder he said he would be the one to check out the clubs for possible stick men,' Janice said. 'He obviously didn't want staff to recognize him with me about.'

'I should have told you,' Rhona apologized. 'But he said he would do that himself.'

'So that's what all the weirdness has been about. When he arrives, I'll insist he go in to the boss first thing tomorrow and set things straight about his visits to the student strip.'

37

Day six

The rain was drumming the metal roof, the sound filling the room. In truth, she was glad of the rain. The prolonged sunshine had been turning the shed into an oven, and her into a roasting carcass.

She thought how wonderful it would be to be outside, her mouth turned up to the rain. To feel it on her shoulders. To feel it everywhere.

It would be like stepping into the sea again, without the salt taste on her tongue.

The sun had risen and set . . . how many times since she'd come to in here? Maybe four or had it been longer . . . six?

There had been nothing to mark a tally on the concrete floor, even if her hands had been free. The only thing she could count was the number of times he'd appeared. To make her sip water. To spoon food into her mouth. Liquid food. Soup or sometimes porridge. At first she'd gagged at it, until she grew so hungry she ate it greedily.

Then the other thing he came for . . .

She stopped there, desperate not to relive the pressure of his hand around her throat, grinding her head against the metal wall, while he groaned and moaned his excitement.

One time he'd pressed so hard that she must have passed out, because he slapped her face to bring her back to life.

And always his voice, whispering through the mask. 'You want this, don't you? Don't you?' he would demand, even as he choked her attempt to shout 'No'.

But I'm still alive, she reminded herself. *He doesn't want me dead. Not yet anyway.*

'And they must be looking for me. Surely the police are looking for me?'

Even as she spoke the words out loud, she knew they would be searching the coastline, waiting for her drowned body to wash ashore, assuming the worst.

She might still be breathing, but to everyone in the outside world, she was already dead.

38

Glasgow

Day six

McNab made a mad dash for Gear Bikes as the clap of thunder signalled the start of the downpour. Not fast enough – he was already soaked by the time he got there.

Realizing the shop door was standing open and therefore those inside could hear his string of expletives, he set about composing himself before he had to walk in and declare himself to be a police officer.

At that point a voice shouted above the din of the rain, ordering him to come in and 'shut the bloody F-ing door', which he did with alacrity, thinking the owner and himself on an equal footing in the cursing stakes.

Weaving his way through both the standing and hanging bikes, he emerged in front of a long wooden counter behind which a middle-aged guy and what he took to be a more youthful assistant were working on two upturned cycles with the aid of a bright ceiling spotlight.

'Joe?' McNab tried.

'That's me,' the older man said. 'I take it you're Detective Sergeant Michael McNab?'

'You guess right,' McNab said, extending a hand.

'Didn't know Glasgow's finest sported such a colourful vocabulary,' Joe said with a wry smile.

'We have to keep up with those we're arresting,' McNab offered in return.

'Young Jerry here had to cover his ears.' Joe laughed at the lad's open-mouthed expression. 'I'm lying, of course. He's got a few of his own that are new to me, especially when he gets his fingers caught in a bike chain.'

Frivolities over, Joe said, 'I take it you've come about our missing bike?'

'I have,' McNab confirmed.

Joe's expression grew grim as he waved McNab over to a large black notebook attached to the desk by a cord. It was already open, and he pointed at one of the entries.

'This the number you were asking about?'

McNab brought out his own much smaller notebook and checked his number against the entry Joe was pointing to.

'It is,' he said.

Joe nodded. 'Thought as much. A French lassie hired it, name was Eléa Martin. See, here she is in the book with the date she picked it up. I even have a photo of her on my phone taken outside the shop. She was so excited to be here in Scotland. What's happened to the lassie?'

'She was reported missing from a campsite up north,' McNab told him.

'She was planning on doing part of the NC500. That's what she told me.' Joe's expression darkened. 'Is this connected to that other lassie near Arisaig?'

McNab wasn't about to ask which lassie he meant, the buried one or the missing kayaker, so he didn't respond.

Joe nodded, as though he understood what could and could not be said. 'D'you want to see the photo?'

When McNab gave a quick nod, Joe brought it up on the screen.

Eléa was standing next to Joe outside the shop in the sunshine, a wide smile on her face. She came up to his shoulder, slim with blonde hair, and at first glance could have been the missing Callie, or even the dead Deirdre.

Reading McNab's expression, Joe gave a groan of despair. 'Jesus. Who is the bastard going after these young lassies?'

'Can you send me that photograph?' McNab said, avoiding the question.

'Sure thing, son. And I hope you find her alive.'

McNab headed out. Having got rid of its load, the rain had settled down to a steady drizzle, although the gutters were still swiftly flowing burns feeding the waterfalls that tipped into the drains.

He had a fleeting notion that Glasgow was crying for 'these young lassies', as Joe had so eloquently put it.

His next job, having discovered the identity of the camper from Achmelvich, would be to inform Eléa's next of kin, assuming the address she'd given Joe on hiring the bike would lead them to someone who knew her.

Three missing girls, two bodies, and only one – Deirdre – had as yet been formally identified. At least Sam knew Deirdre was dead, and wasn't tortured by thoughts of where she was.

They knew what had happened to her. She'd been kept alive for around a month, during which she'd been constantly throttled. Then she'd been strangled and buried in a sandy field near Arisaig.

How much did Sam know about that? How much did he want to know? How much was the media intent on telling him? If they weren't told the facts, the press just speculated on what might have happened. And since it sold newspapers, they made that speculation as horrific as possible.

Although the stories they spun could never be as terrible as the real truth.

Dispelling such thoughts, McNab now considered his next move. He could make for the jazz club and a welcome pint, or head for Holly's place and see if he might catch her at home, since she hadn't responded to his voicemail.

His mind was made up by the approach of a taxi. He flagged it down and, dashing through the downpour, jumped in and told the driver where he was headed.

39

Day six

They all turned as Janice shouted McNab's name.

He looks pleased, Rhona thought, *as though he's a birthday boy being welcomed into his own party.*

'Where the hell have you been?' Janice demanded.

The smile slid from his face, replaced by puzzlement. 'I told you I was going to the bike shop.' He gazed round at the assembled company and their expressions, from fury to horror and back again.

For a moment it seemed he was playing with the thought that they were all having him on, then reality seemed to sweep in.

'What's happened?' he demanded.

Rhona handed him her mobile. 'Listen to this.'

McNab, still bemused, held the mobile to his ear. It didn't take long before anything resembling normality slid from his face.

'How the fuck?'

'That is you?' Rhona demanded.

'It was a private phone call to Holly,' he said.

'Not so private now,' Janice said. 'Did you talk to Holly about Rhona?'

'I mentioned her in the passing as one of the gang that came to the jazz club . . .'

'She must have had access to your mobile,' Janice said accusingly. 'And seen Rhona's name.'

It was obvious from McNab's expression that he'd already worked that one out, maybe even how and when it might have happened.

'You have to call the boss right now and tell him about this,' Janice said. 'There's no knowing what other numbers she had access to.'

McNab was already turning on his heel and heading for the door, his own mobile in hand.

Rhona had the sudden and terrible thought that he wasn't about to do what his partner had demanded, but something else entirely. Janice, catching her eye, obviously thought the same.

'You call DI Wilson,' Rhona told her. 'I'll go after McNab.'

She left before Janice responded, aware that if she wasn't quick enough she might lose him altogether. Chrissy's voice followed her, but all she made out was the worried tone of whatever it was Chrissy was saying.

Reaching the top of the stairs, she was met with pelting rain, as heavy as when she'd entered the jazz club earlier. Her hope was that McNab might have gone to the pub across the street to make his call, out of earshot of his accusers.

Nipping across the cobbles, now running with water again, she searched among the crowd but could see no sign of him. Re-emerging, she spotted Magnus further along the lane where it turned towards the main road.

Catching up with him, she read his expression and knew what he was about to say.

'He's gone, hasn't he?' she said, defeated.

'Caught a taxi. Maybe he's going to see DI Wilson?' he said hopefully.

'More likely to the girlfriend's place,' Rhona said. 'To find out if she was the one to pass on his voice message.' She turned, conscious now of how wet she was. 'Let's go back inside.'

'No luck?' Chrissy said on their return.

'He jumped in a taxi,' Rhona told her. 'What about Bill?' she checked with Janice.

'He's left the station. They're trying to contact him. I did my best to imply it was something to do with the stick man case. Hopefully, no one else got the recording except you.' Janice didn't sound too confident about that.

In their time outside, Sean had arrived to do his evening stint. Seeing how drowned Rhona looked, he reminded her she had some clothes in the back room, if she wanted to get dried and changed.

Rhona followed him through.

'What the hell's going on?' he said through the bathroom door.

'Suffice to say, McNab's fucked up.' She didn't add 'again', although she briefly thought it.

'Seriously?' Sean sounded truly concerned. McNab and he had had their differences in the past, but they'd also teamed up when necessary for her sake.

'He's been hanging about the student strip. Met a girl there. Let's say she's made life difficult for him.' Rhona wondered if that were in fact true. Hadn't she just heard McNab ask this girl to say the sex in some CCTV video they'd been caught in had been consensual?

Then it came to her. The camera had to be somewhere on the student strip. He'd been caught having sex with a female inside or outside one of the clubs, where rumours were apparently abounding about a serving officer sexually assaulting young women.

'There's no way McNab would do that,' she muttered under her breath. 'No way,' she said more strongly now.

'No way what?' Sean echoed from the other side of the door.

'No way McNab would sexually assault a woman,' she told him as she emerged.

The shock her words produced on Sean's face swiftly dissipated. 'I agree,' he said firmly. 'So how will this play out?'

Rhona had already considered the scenario. Even if the girl he implied he was with in the footage came forward to say the sex was consensual, McNab would likely be suspended, pending further enquiries. The more she considered it, the more she began to think McNab had been set up. Either by the female he was with or someone else.

So where was this footage, and how had McNab viewed it? Her thoughts immediately went to his confidant, Ollie in the Tech department. Had he been given the job of monitoring the clubs, because of the rumours of sexual harassment by officers, and he'd spotted McNab and the girlfriend?

With this thought, bits of the jigsaw began to slip into place.

Suppose McNab had spotted something while hanging about the student strip. Something relating to Deirdre's disappearance? If so, he hadn't mentioned it to her or, it appeared, to Janice. Perhaps he hadn't yet realized how significant it was, but now that McNab's name was blackened, anything he said now was unlikely to be believed.

She paused there in her thoughts, realizing that Sean was still awaiting an answer.

'He'll be suspended until the video, if it exists, is investigated.'

'You think there might not be one?' Sean said, puzzled.

'McNab may have been told it exists, and reacted to that.' She stopped there, aware that her thoughts around Ollie shouldn't be repeated. 'Right,' she said, 'I need to speak to Janice before I head home.'

Sean looked a little put out by that. 'I thought you might stay on for a while and we could grab something to eat after my spot.'

'I have notes to write up,' Rhona said. 'I'll pick up a pizza on the way home.'

She could feel his disappointment, even though he strove not to show it. 'I'll call you tomorrow,' she added as a sweetener.

'Okay.' He gave her a lopsided smile. 'Good luck with everything.'

Janice's shake of the head as she got back to the bar indicated there was nothing new from McNab or the boss. 'Although if the voicemail was distributed to more than just you, I would have heard about it by now,' she added, trying to sound hopeful.

Rhona was inclined to agree. Bad news spread like wildfire among the forces of law, especially regarding one of their own.

'Maybe it was just the girlfriend rattling McNab's cage,' Chrissy suggested.

'Let's hope so,' Rhona said. 'And let's hope he gets in touch with one of us before the night's over.'

'What if the boss does first?' Janice said. 'Should I tell him the whole story, at least as we know it?'

It was a question Rhona had been asking herself. They

had limited knowledge of what had been going on, and hadn't got the opportunity to question McNab about it. They could make things worse for him with what they said.

'Maybe say there's been a development, and you and McNab need to speak to him first thing in the morning,' Rhona suggested. 'That way you get to hear McNab's side of the story first.'

Even as she said this, Rhona silently prayed that McNab wouldn't do anything stupid in the interim.

40

Day six

He'd been set up. From the moment Holly had walked over to join him that night in the Blue Arrow.

He began to replay their scenes together in all their vivid intensity, anger and disgust mounting with every word and image.

And he'd thought he'd been the one leading the dance. Using Holly as his way into the world of the student strip. Congratulating himself on not having had sex with her when he'd first walked her home.

He took a deep breath and forced his hands to release the fists they'd made.

If Holly was there, he would reason with her quietly. Explain that he'd been wrong not to speak to her face to face. Apologize for leaving a message instead.

And all the time the detective in him knew he was wasting his time playing nice. Holly had set him up from the beginning. Why, he didn't know. Or who else might have been involved. He had just made it ultra-easy for her with that voicemail.

The question was, why had he been targeted? For a personal reason on Holly's part? Or was someone else behind the plan for his downfall and she was merely a pawn in the game?

He'd amassed plenty of enemies over the years on the job. Some incarcerated, some still wandering free. Maybe a con had been recently released and fancied screwing with the officer who'd put him away.

Then again, maybe Holly had something against him personally, and it had been all her own work.

The taxi having arrived outside her building, McNab paid up and stepped out into the rain. Glancing upwards, he noted there was a light on, so chances were she was at home.

Pressing the buzzer, he expected an answer, but got none. Looking up again, he wondered if he'd been spotted from the window and Holly had decided not to let him in.

When he buzzed the neighbouring flat, it was answered right away.

'Sorry, mate,' McNab said. 'Forgot my key. Can you let me in?'

Whoever it was didn't reply, but sprang the door anyway. As he climbed the stairs, McNab decided he would gain entry to Holly's, whether she was at home or not.

As it was, he didn't need to use his skill on her lock. The door was off the latch and a small push saw it swing open. His senses immediately on high alert, he called her name, announcing his presence.

McNab stood in the hallway, trying to read what the hell might be going on here.

'Holly?' he tried again. 'It's me, Michael.'

The kitchen and bedroom were empty. She wasn't here, despite the door being left unlocked.

Might she have gone to a neighbour's?

He tried to recall in her often incessant chatter a mention of a friendly neighbour and couldn't.

Using his mobile to call her, he listened as it rang out unanswered. So wherever she'd gone, she'd taken her mobile with her. He checked each of the rooms, looking for anything which might suggest where she'd gone and why the door had been left unlocked.

He eventually found it, a note tucked just under the pillow on the side of the bed she'd insisted laughingly that he use.

It held one word only, and that was *Sorry*.

Picking it up, he stared at it. Had this been left there for him?

Holly would have known he'd come looking for her after his voicemail had reached Rhona. Was that why the flat had been left unlocked so he might enter and find it?

Might Holly have been forced into all of this? Forced to set him up by someone against her will? That might explain the apology.

Then again, sorry could be said in many different ways. It didn't always mean a real apology. Maybe she was simply mocking him for being so gullible.

Then another thought struck. Had she left the flat for good? He realized that it felt wrong. It had always been untidy before. Clothes lying about. Dishes. Much like his own place, though it had always smelt nice, like Holly.

The scent of her had definitely gone and, opening the wardrobe, he found a row of empty hangers, a set of drawers also empty.

It seemed Holly had made herself scarce, so no matter what he told the boss about the CCTV footage, he had no one to back him up that the sex was consensual. Not to mention a recording of him pleading with Holly to say it was, which had been sent out to who knew how many folk besides Rhona.

He checked his mobile, noting a text from Rhona asking where the hell he was. Janice no doubt would have contacted the boss by now.

He recalled Rhona's expression as she'd thrust her phone into his hands. What had he seen there? Anger, disappointment, disgust?

Surely none of the three women would believe he had pressured someone into having sex with him? Never Chrissy, his staunchest ally. Then he thought about the other two, both of whom he'd pestered in the past, Rhona the most. No force had been involved, although persistence had, resulting in strong words to him from the boss.

He felt a little sick at the memory.

He should call his partner, explain his actions. But could he defend them? He brought up Janice's number and wrote a text telling her that he would explain all in the morning, before going in to talk to the boss. He added a sorry, before pressing send.

As for Chrissy, he sent a simple sorry.

Rhona he found the most difficult, which was why he left it to last. Rhona, an inner voice told him, should be spoken to face to face. After all, she'd already warned him about hanging around the student strip. Questioned his stupidity at doing that. Told him to confide in Janice. Urged him to come clean to the boss about his actions and intentions.

As he stood considering what answer he should send to Rhona's text, he suddenly realized what was really wrong with the flat.

How the fuck had he, a supposed detective, not spotted it right away?

Holly's clothes might have gone, her scent too, but no way would she have left her paintings. Not willingly. Paintings of white beaches, and rocky islands with only a single person in the frame or sometimes two, where one of them looked like a spirit.

'What do you feel, when you look at them?' she'd urged.

And he'd been honest, telling her he felt lonely and lost in a world he knew nothing about.

He realized he was in that world now, with Holly as his ghostly companion.

41

Day six

McNab had finally answered her angry text with, Am outside. Can I come up?

She'd considered this for a full five minutes before responding. Not really wanting to see him, nor have him here in the flat.

McNab had always brought trouble with him, ever since they'd met. She chastised herself even as she thought that, reminding herself of all the times he'd stood by her. Saved her even.

At that point she released the main door.

He looks terrible, she thought when she saw him. The green eyes weary, the face shadowed with worry.

Saying nothing, she waved him into the kitchen and closed the door, slipping on the chain, already thinking she would tell him to sleep in the spare room tonight, to make sure he would be at the station first thing.

Before joining him, she texted Janice with, He's here. That at least would allow his partner some sleep.

He'd already brought down the whisky bottle from its known spot in the cupboard, together with two glasses.

Rhona considered this for a moment before accepting that he also pour one for her.

She added water from the tap. He kept his neat.

Taking a seat across from him at the table, she waited. She had nothing to say that she hadn't already said. He was the one with the story here.

Eventually he began. He told her that Holly had gone from her flat, together with her clothes.

'It looked as though she'd just made off so as not to have to face me. But . . .' He hesitated there while Rhona waited in silence.

'The door wasn't locked and this was tucked in under the pillow on my side.' He pushed a scrap of paper across the table to her.

The word *Sorry* was a scrawl, done in a hurry. Was it a real apology for what she'd done or a joke? McNab had never talked about this Holly. Rhona had no idea what she was like. Why she had been with McNab, however fleetingly. Rhona looked up from the note, aware there was more to be said.

'She's an artist. I was in her flat and saw her paintings. We talked about them.' He swallowed the whisky down in a gulp. When he didn't continue, Rhona eventually urged him on.

'She would never have left those paintings behind.' He muttered this almost to himself.

Rhona tried to process this, before saying, 'You think she was made to leave?'

He studied the space in front of him as if it held the answer. 'On the way to her place, I became more and more convinced she'd set me up.' He shrugged. 'But at the time I thought she just liked me. We met in the queue for the Blue Arrow.

She was with two mates. It was pouring. They were huddled under a brolly, all three of them. Drips running down their bare backs.' A ghost of a smile at the memory. 'Once inside, she came over and we got chatting. She was funny.' He took a deep breath in. 'I needed funny. I told her outright I was a police officer. She seemed unfazed by that.'

'So *she* chose you?' Rhona checked.

'Seemed like that. I took it as a compliment.' He halted for a bit before describing how he'd walked her home. 'We had a glass of wine. I left after that. No sex was involved.'

She could tell from the way he'd outlined it that Holly had offered herself but been turned down.

'So when did the sex happen?' Rhona said.

'That night we spoke at the jazz club. You went home. I invited her for a curry. We went on to the Blue Arrow afterwards. It happened out back.' He ground to a halt, his expression a mix of distaste and regret. Eventually he met her eye. 'It was her idea. Not mine.'

Rhona bit her tongue before she said how pathetic that made him sound, before she reminded him that the clubs along the student strip were being watched, because by his expression he knew all of this.

'Ollie saw the CCTV footage,' he said. 'Being a super recognizer he realized it was me, despite the poor image and my face barely visible.'

'And he gave you the heads-up?' Rhona asked.

'So that I could explain it to the boss,' he finished for her.

'Which you failed to do?'

'I had to speak to Holly first, but . . . I didn't get the chance.'

'You mean you chickened out and left her a voice message.' Rhona heard the anger and disappointment in her words.

He swore under his breath and poured another measure of whisky, which he stared at as though he might see an answer to his dilemma in its golden depths.

'What if she says it was a sexual assault?'

His words hung in the air between them.

'Does it look like an assault?' Rhona demanded.

'Sex against a wall in an alley in the dark.' He shook his head as though to dispel the image. 'It doesn't look pretty.'

'You need to go to Bill first thing. Show him and tell all.'

'What about Holly? What if she's not okay? What if it was a set-up?'

'When did she have access to your mobile?'

He shook his head. 'Probably when I was asleep.'

'You went back to her place that night?'

He nodded. 'Slept in. Was late getting to work. As to your number, it was on the recently called list.'

'And no password entry on your mobile?'

'Thumbprint. As you know, I'm a sound sleeper . . .'

She halted him there with another question. 'Why would she send your voicemail to me and not everyone on your list?'

He shrugged. 'She only had time to take note of your number? She knew who you were, because I mentioned you as one of the gang who went to the jazz club.' He halted there, a thought forming. 'She wanted to meet you all, but I turned her down.' His tone had moved through many emotions and was now at seriously pissed off.

Rhona suggested he go to bed. 'Sean's room is free for tonight.'

He threw her a look that spoke of the past between them.

'Thanks but no, Dr MacLeod. I only came here to set the record straight.' He swallowed down the remains of his whisky before rising. 'Can you forward the voicemail to me, please. Then I'll leave you in peace.'

She did as asked, hearing the buzz as it arrived.

A deep silence, full of unsaid things, formed between them, before he gave her a nod and left her there.

Rhona heard the chain being pulled back. The door was opened, then closed, his footsteps rapidly taking the stairs.

She moved to the bay window in the sitting room and watched him stride away from her and into the night.

But where was he going exactly? That was a question she couldn't answer.

42

Day seven

Ollie was a night owl. McNab had counted on this when he'd turned up at Ollie's flat in the early hours of the morning and rung his bell.

Thankfully, Ollie answered.

'Can I come up or are you busy with the girlfriend?' McNab said in what he hoped was a jocular fashion.

Ollie didn't respond, but the door did click open.

As he climbed the stairs, McNab worried that he'd maybe said the wrong thing. Was the girlfriend no longer the girlfriend? He felt guilty that part of him wished that was true, because then Ollie would likely better understand his own state of mind.

The door stood open and waiting. McNab shut it behind him, then, composing himself, followed the beam of light that led to Ollie's equivalent of the *Starship Enterprise*, or perhaps under the current circumstances, like the Queen Elizabeth Hospital, the *Death Star*.

Ollie stopped typing and turned to look at McNab through the round spectacles which made him look like an owl. McNab interpreted that look as a mix of crossness and disappointment.

'I have an appointment first thing in the morning with the boss,' he said, hoping to dispel that image.

The cross look softened a little, or was that only in his imagination?

He rushed on. 'Trouble is, Holly's gone, so she can't back me up.'

'Gone?' Ollie repeated. 'Gone where?' He sounded immediately suspicious. 'Do you actually know the female in that video recording?'

McNab ignored the underlying accusation and brought Ollie up to date on the whole sorry tale. He then let him listen to the voicemail and finished with his concerns regarding Holly's whereabouts and welfare.

Ollie listened to all of this in studied silence.

Finally, McNab concluded with a request to locate the whereabouts of Holly's mobile. 'If she's in trouble, I need to know. If she's decided to screw me over, I need to know why,' he finished firmly.

The starkness of his statement seemed to have hit home.

'You believe you were set up, either by this Holly you're talking about, or someone she's working for or is beholden to in some way?'

'That pretty well sums it up,' McNab agreed.

Ollie eyed him. 'The alternative interpretation might be that you sexually assaulted a young woman at the back of the Blue Arrow nightclub and got caught on camera doing it.'

The simple truth of how others, including the boss, might see both the CCTV footage and the voicemail hit McNab with full force.

'Okay. Send the recording to the boss. Right now. Tell him what's passed between us. I'll explain why I asked you for a delay. This isn't your problem and I don't want you to pay for it in any way, shape or form,' he finished.

Ollie thought about that for a moment.

'Give me the girl Holly's mobile number, full name and address. Let's see what we can find out about her. I take it you didn't check her out before you got into the relationship?'

McNab indicated not. He hadn't intended on a relationship when they'd first met, but perhaps using Holly to glean gossip surrounding Deirdre Reid's visits to the clubbing scene and maybe the rumours of the sexual assaults. Even to his ears that sounded poor, so he didn't say it out loud.

'I'll start with social media. Everyone is on there somewhere. It might take a while,' Ollie told him. 'If you're hungry, check out the fridge. There's pizza . . . cold, but beggars can't be choosers. And bring me a Coke.'

McNab took up his offer of the cold pizza and, after supplying Ollie with a can of Coke, made himself some strong coffee and settled down to eat.

Eventually, as his eyes began to droop, Ollie called him over and pointed at one of the many screens.

'Is this the female we're talking about?'

McNab stared at the photograph. If it was her, she looked very different. Her hair was short and dark in the image. Lots of make-up round the eyes.

'The shape of the face is similar, the smile maybe, but . . .' He stood mesmerized. Was that really Holly?

'What did she look like to you?' Ollie said, seeing his puzzlement. 'Describe her when you first met.'

McNab did as asked and watched as Ollie, going through subsequent images, eventually produced a replacement Holly. One that he knew, with long chestnut hair and green eyes. Hair that had brushed his face in a soft cloud. Looking at the image, he could almost smell her perfume again and hear her laugh.

'That's what she looked like when I met her,' he confirmed. 'So when was the other picture taken?'

Ollie shrugged. 'A couple of years ago, I think. You said she was doing a postgrad at the School of Art?' he asked.

When McNab nodded, Ollie said, 'She's not on their current records.'

McNab's heart, having lifted a little at the recognizable image, plunged again at the possibility that Holly had been lying about that.

'Maybe I got it wrong. Maybe she'd finished it by now. The flat is full of her paintings. She's definitely an artist.' Even as he said this, he knew it might well not be true.

'The flat where you say she lived is currently owned by a Mr Mulligan. We can check with him if she's the occupant. If she left, maybe she gave a forwarding address.' Ollie didn't look hopeful.

'You think she was pretending to stay there?' McNab said, thinking back to the time he'd spent there with her.

Ollie shrugged again. 'I don't think anything. We need facts about this girl if we're going to locate her. Do you know of any reason why she might want to cause problems for you?'

'I'm not short on enemies. Maybe she's involved with one of them,' McNab offered.

Ollie considered this for a moment. 'The only thing she's done wrong so far, that we know of, is to send your voicemail to a colleague.'

McNab knew that to be true. He briefly considered what he, as an investigating officer, might think if faced with both the video and the voicemail, and knew exactly what that would be.

'Are there any other photos of what might be my Holly?' he said.

Ollie busied himself for a bit, then a small collage appeared.

Pulling his chair in closer, McNab ran his eyes over them. 'That one there,' he said, pointing. 'Can you enlarge it?'

It looked like the inside of Nice N Sleazy and it was Holly, despite the dark hair. In this image she was standing next to a guy who had his arm about her shoulders.

'I've seen him before. He's a security guard at Nice N Sleazy.' McNab was about to sit back when a figure behind the pair caught his eye.

'That bloke behind and to the right. Looks like a shadow because of the light. Can you make him easier to see?'

Ollie tried, but it was still like one of the ghost figures in Holly's paintings.

'Can I get a copy of that image to my mobile?'

'Sure thing,' Ollie said. 'What are you thinking?'

McNab shook his head, not sure himself, but something about the ghostly guy's face was ringing a bell.

'This business with the suspected sexual assaults,' Ollie interrupted his line of thought. 'Until now they've just been rumours. Nothing substantiated.'

'But the belief is that police officers may be involved?' McNab said.

'If they are, we need to identify them,' Ollie said. 'And you might be the first.'

McNab understood what Ollie was implying. 'If I was, that takes the heat off the real culprit or culprits?'

'Exactly. It's always good to have a fall guy.'

'And I may be that guy?' McNab asked.

Ollie didn't reply. He didn't have to.

A peep from one of the screens caused them both to turn. A red dot was flashing.

'That's her mobile,' Ollie said. 'She's currently somewhere on the student strip.'

43

Loch Lomond

Day seven

It was still raining. She'd heard the continuous beat of it on the cottage roof during the long hours of the night as she'd lain, wide-eyed, staring at the ceiling.

Unlike her, the kids had slept soundly. She'd risen at least three times to check on them. As she gazed down on their tousled heads and heard the easy breath of their untroubled sleep, she knew she'd done the right thing in bringing them here.

It wasn't getting away from the city that had done it, but leaving Derek behind – or, if she was honest, going into hiding from him – that had relieved their anxiety. That, plus their conversation with Dr MacLeod. Whatever they'd told her seemed to have unburdened them.

The watchful looks they'd observed her with back in Glasgow had dissipated. They were children again. Lying laughing in bed last night, as though not even torrential rain could spoil their holiday. Or their freedom from their father.

She, of course, had not been set free by the journey here.

The calls from Derek remained unanswered. The stream of texts that followed too.

She had told herself not to listen to the voicemails he left, or read the texts. Although she had found herself unable to follow her own advice.

The first voicemail had sounded genuinely worried and puzzled. After which they became, like Derek often was, strident and demanding. The final voicemail blamed her for him having to report to the police station first thing tomorrow morning . . . this morning, in fact.

'You bitch. What lies did you tell them about me?'

She thought of the T-shirt with blood on it. Fish blood, he'd told her with a smile. She hadn't believed him. Nor did she now.

So why didn't you hand it in to the police? she asked herself again. If it was a match for the blood in Callie's van, then he would have to explain himself to them.

Then a thought occurred. If he wouldn't leave her alone, could she use the T-shirt as collateral?

She imagined his reaction to her possible blackmail and it frightened her even more. No. The last thing she wanted was to antagonize him any further.

She reminded herself she no longer cared what happened to him, because she no longer lived with him. She was here now and the school holidays had only just begun. Since she worked as a classroom assistant during term time, she too was free for as long as the children were.

She allowed herself a moment's pleasure at that thought before the nagging doubt returned. And after that, what?

Derek was unlikely to give up easily. Plus he had friends who would support him. The men he now went fishing with. The boys, he called them, like they were twelve and not grown men.

She'd never met them in person. Hadn't been permitted to. They definitely weren't the pals he'd had when he'd first met her. The ones who'd been at their wedding, including Josh, his best man, who seemed to have been discarded.

She'd liked Josh, but Derek said he'd gone to London, after which Derek had taken a job with a security firm and made new friends, who took him fishing.

Had things between them started to change around then?

She couldn't be sure, because she'd blamed his behaviour on losing his job in sales and it taking a while to find something else. She'd openly got on his nerves around then, as had the children.

They were, according to Derek, all holding him back.

She shook her head to dispel the memory of his cutting words, his declaration that she wasn't sexy any more and needed to spice up her act.

The truth was he had no thoughts for anyone apart from himself during their sporadic coupling. If she was undesirable it was because he made her so.

It was around then she'd discovered he was having sex elsewhere. He'd brought the smell home with him as he slipped into bed beside her. At first she'd lain there angry, then became sad and defeated. Eventually, though, the feeling had become one of relief that it meant he left her alone.

'This time for good,' she said to herself as she set to preparing breakfast.

Looking out of the window, she saw that the clouds were rolling past, exposing glimpses of blue sky, which brought a smile to her face. Out on the waters of the loch a small boat came into view, chugging its way past the cottage before it stopped to drop anchor.

Someone come to fish, she thought, pouring out the children's cereal into two bowls.

The image brought the realization that she had never seen Derek actually fishing. She'd seen him load up his gear when he headed out on his trips with his mates. Seen him walk off with the rod when they'd been at the campsite. But she had never actually seen him fish.

As she pondered this, a figure stood up on the little red boat and cast a line. It was a man, she could make that out, but not his face. At first she was only intrigued by the view, then a gnawing thought crept in.

Why had he stopped just there, offshore from the cottage?

She shook her head, trying to dispel such a thought. The man could have been coming to this spot forever and she wouldn't have known about it.

She'd turned to the fridge to fetch the milk, ready for the arrival of the children who she could hear bouncing about above her, when the memory of the twigs and the fishing line suddenly returned and with it the terrible thought that she would never be free of Derek.

Never truly free, no matter what she did and where she was.

At that moment her mobile pinged, indicating that a text message had arrived.

Her first thought was to ignore it, but she found herself unable to do this. When she saw it was from Marion, who'd lent her the cottage, she opened and read it.

> Hope you're settling in well. Let me know if there's anything you need. Enjoy the peace and quiet. Marion x

The message eased her worried thoughts. Marion knew where she was, as did the police. Everything would work out okay. Derek was the one in trouble this morning. He was the one being interviewed by the police.

44

Glasgow

Day seven

Rhona glanced at the clock. She'd arrived at work early, and from when she'd let herself into the lab till now, the intervening time had dragged by.

She'd attempted to work and there was plenty of it to do, but yet she could not shake the last sight she'd had of McNab as he'd disappeared into the darkness.

Where the hell had he gone after leaving her? To search for Holly? But where? She could only hope he hadn't headed back to the student strip. If he was seen there after the shit hit the fan . . . And it would hit the fan. She had no doubt about that.

Better that he should have come clean right away about this CCTV recording and face the consequences.

She chastised herself then because, as far as she knew, he might well be up and showered and on his way into the station right now. Even as she tried to picture that, she saw an alternative image of a worried Janice at the police station alone.

At this point she heard the door open and met the surprised face of Chrissy.

'You're here before me,' Chrissy said in a slightly perplexed tone. 'I assume you didn't bring breakfast, though?' She waved a couple of paper bags at Rhona. 'Plus you haven't put the coffee on,' she added accusingly.

When Rhona didn't react to either humour or irritation, she asked outright. 'It's McNab, isn't it? What did he or didn't he do that lost you sleep? Last I got from him was a "sorry" at about half past midnight.'

'He visited me late last night,' Rhona said. 'Told me the whole story about this Holly girl . . . woman.'

'And that is?' Chrissy demanded.

'I wasn't sure how to take it. He's been weird since Ellie.'

'Let's face it, McNab's a law unto himself,' Chrissy said crossly as she set up the coffee machine. 'Nothing's changed on that front.' She threw Rhona a look. 'And you know that even better than I do. Tell me the full story while we eat.'

It didn't take long and, with each word she uttered, Rhona was reminded just how deep a hole McNab had dug for himself.

'He didn't assault this girl, whoever she is,' Chrissy said. 'You know that. And I know that,' she added firmly. 'She either took umbrage at the voicemail, or . . . he's being set up, probably as the fall guy for what's going on in the student strip.' Catching sight of Rhona's expression, she added, 'Don't look at me like that. I don't know anything about that except McNab is not a man to sexually assault anyone. Piss them off, maybe. He's done that often enough.' She paused. 'Assuming he tells the whole story to the boss this morning, it should get cleared up.'

Chrissy sounded as though she was persuading herself of that fact.

'Maybe I should call Janice?' Rhona said. 'Check if he did turn up?'

'Torture yourself if you must. Alternatively, we could look and see if there's anything back on the DNA samples from Achmelvich? Find out if it is our missing Callie?' Reading Rhona's expression, she gave in. 'Okay, you call Janice. I'll check if the results are through.'

Janice heard the door open and looked up in hope, but the welcome chorus wasn't for McNab. Where was the stupid bastard?

The last she'd heard of his whereabouts was a message from Rhona late last night saying he was with her. If he'd stayed there, Rhona would have had him up and in here well before this.

She checked her mobile for the umpteenth time, in the hope of a text at least, promising his imminent arrival. If he didn't show his face soon, it would be too late to speak to the boss before the interview scheduled with Derek Henderson.

If he wasn't here by interview time, would she have to reveal that, or do the interview alone?

She decided to make herself scarce in the interim. Hide out at the coffee machine, like McNab did, in case the boss appeared and asked questions she couldn't answer.

As she rose to leave, her mobile rang and, seeing Rhona's name on the screen, she quickly answered.

They both spoke at once. She to ask when Rhona had last seen McNab. Rhona to ask if he was with her.

'He left my place late last night,' Rhona told her. 'I tried to make him stay, but he was having none of it.'

'Well, he's not here now,' Janice told her. 'We have an

interview with Derek Henderson in ten minutes. If he's not here for that, I should speak to the boss.'

There was silence for a moment before Rhona said, 'Can you leave it a little longer? I think he may have gone round last night to see that guy Ollie in Tech, who forewarned him about the video. He seemed to be trying to put things right with everyone involved in this.'

Janice thought about that for a moment.

'Okay. If he's not here in time for the Henderson interview, I'll do it myself. But after that I have to go see the boss. And definitely before the strategy meeting.'

It was the best she could do, Janice decided as she rang off. McNab was her partner and she owed him that. Although at times he didn't act as though he needed or even wanted a partner.

She went by way of the coffee machine and, making a silent wish, bought two coffees. One of which was a two-shot espresso. All the way to the interview room she held out hope she might find McNab already there, but when the officer on duty outside opened the door for her, only Derek Henderson sat at the table.

And he definitely wasn't happy.

'You're late, officer . . . ?'

Janice sat down, placing the latte beside her and the espresso where McNab should have been.

'Detective Sergeant Clark,' she told him. 'My partner, Detective Sergeant McNab, has unfortunately been delayed.'

Henderson gave a little smile at that, and eased himself back in the seat.

Janice immediately had the impression he was glad it might be just the two of them and that Derek Henderson believed he had a way with the female of the species.

'I understand you want my statement on the incident at the croft campsite when my daughter, Lucy, disappeared?' he said pleasantly.

'I'd like to ask you a few questions about that, yes,' Janice agreed. 'Your wife and children came in yesterday to give their accounts.'

She watched as the truth of this dawned, wiping the semi-smile off his face, replacing it with anger.

'I was not informed that they were coming in,' he said in a stilted voice.

'The disappearance of Caillean Munro is being treated as an abduction, Mr Henderson. A serious crime which the children wished to speak to us about.'

'The children requested it or was it my wife?' he said icily.

'The children,' Janice confirmed. 'They also requested that Dr MacLeod be there.'

'The woman who dug up the body?' he said, sounding incredulous.

'The forensic scientist who exhumed the grave, yes. Lucy specifically asked for her. They had become friends as I understand it.'

He was staring at her, fury in his eyes. 'I did not agree to that. As her father, I should have been informed. I wish to make a formal complaint about this.'

Janice nodded. 'You're free to do that, of course. However, we did get permission from Mrs Henderson.'

The mention of his wife did nothing to lower his level of anger and his fists clenched. For a moment she thought he might hit her and questioned her stupidity at interviewing him alone.

'There is an officer just outside the door,' she said to defuse the situation. 'I could call him in?'

Henderson mustered himself. 'I'll answer your questions. Obviously, I want the missing girl found as soon as possible. Anything I can do to help, I will.'

'Good,' a male voice said as the door was flung open.

Janice's heart rose. 'My colleague Detective Sergeant McNab, who as I said was unavoidably delayed,' she said for McNab's benefit.

'Mr Henderson.' McNab gave him a nod of acknowledgement, then took his seat beside Janice and, picking up the coffee, drank it swiftly down. 'I apologize for my late appearance. I was with my superior, Detective Inspector Wilson, who is in charge of the case. He is very keen that we follow up on the information given to us by your children, Lucy and Orlando. We'd like to do that now.'

45

Day seven

On entry, McNab had immediately sensed the anger emanating from Henderson. He'd experienced such bottled-up anger himself many times, although rarely with a woman, but he suspected that wasn't the case with Henderson.

With his introduction and story about visiting the boss, he'd sensed Janice's relief. He'd also watched as Henderson's fury depleted. The clenched fists were released, the pulse which had been obvious in his neck had slowed. He had a hold of himself.

McNab looked to Janice, who gave him an almost imperceptible nod. Then he addressed Henderson.

'Your son, Orlando, told us he saw you enter Callie's van on the evening she disappeared.'

The look on Henderson's face moved from instant shock through calculation to certain denial.

'Orly couldn't have seen that, because it never happened,' he said, feigning bemusement.

'You did not enter Callie's van that night?' McNab said.

'I did not,' he replied, sounding more assured now. 'Or at any other time,' he added.

'So your DNA will not be found in there?' McNab said.

'I did not enter the girl's van,' he repeated.

He seemed pretty sure of himself, McNab thought, which suggested he was certain he'd left no trace behind.

'We will require a DNA swab and your fingerprints.'

'Of course, Sergeant. I'm happy to do that. As I was saying when you came in, I want to help in any way that I can.'

'So, Mr Henderson, have you any idea why your son would tell us he saw you enter the blue van if he hadn't?'

Eventually Henderson shook his head as though in complete bewilderment, then plumped for a sorrowful expression before saying, 'Francine mollycoddles Orly. He says and does things to get her attention.'

'How would that get her attention, exactly?'

Henderson folded his arms and gave a sigh of irritation.

'Francine and I are going through a rough patch. I lost my computer sales job a while back and things got difficult. I eventually got a new job . . .'

McNab interrupted him. 'Doing what exactly?'

'I work for a security firm now, CompuGuard. Anyway, I took my family on holiday to Arisaig to try and make it up to them. Although I think Orly's still angry with me.'

McNab didn't think the reason for Orly's disclosure was to get his mother's attention, and said so.

'You see, Orly didn't tell his mother that he saw you enter the blue van. He only told Dr MacLeod. In fact, when asked by Dr MacLeod why they hadn't told their mother this, he and Lucy said they didn't because it would make her cry.'

Henderson seemed briefly put out by this, then gave a dismissive shrug. 'I was seeing other women for a while. But not any more. The kids must have heard us arguing about it.'

Janice came in at this point. 'Your wife said you tried to

invite Callie to join you when she came back from her kayak trip. She said you'd been drinking and were quite insistent.'

He tutted his annoyance at this. 'My wife exaggerates. I was merely being neighbourly. The girl was on her own. It was a lovely evening and we were sitting outside. That's what happens at campsites. Folk are friendly.'

'But in Callie's case maybe not friendly enough?' McNab said.

'Just what are you insinuating?' Henderson said testily.

'That later that night you tried to get to know Caillean Munro a little better.'

'I've already told you, I did not visit her van. If Orly saw someone go in, it wasn't me.'

McNab signalled to Janice that she should move on to the next topic.

'Why did you walk to the burial site the morning Lucy disappeared?' she asked.

Henderson looked surprised by the question. 'Why does my walk along the beach matter?'

'Because Lucy followed you there.'

'What?' he said stupidly.

'Your daughter followed you there, shouted on you, but you seemed to be too interested in the deposition site and ignored her.'

'I went walking all the time when we were at the campsite. And fishing. And I never heard Lucy call after me. I had my earphones in listening to music a lot of the time.'

'You walked straight to the grave and stood there for a while, looking at it. Why did you do that, Mr Henderson?' Janice asked.

'The grass and wild flowers looked dead,' he said, as though the question had been nonsensical. 'I simply wondered why.'

It was a good answer. In fact, most of what he'd said had been credible.

Except the bit about entering Callie's van. McNab found himself believing the child on that and not the man.

The question was, could they prove it?

46

Day seven

Rhona looked round the meeting room, searching for McNab's auburn head among the gathered incident team, and eventually spotted it near the front, next to Janice.

So he had turned up, but had he talked to DI Wilson yet?

As she threaded her way through the crowd, Bill appeared to take centre stage. Behind him, the screen came alive and on it was the image of the three stick men she'd sent him earlier.

Bill had told her she would be on first, to bring them up to date with what she and Chrissy had discovered. If their findings were confirmed, then it would change the nature of the investigation.

Placed side by side, at first glance the stick men looked identical. Each fashioned from birch wood, with added alder twigs, all tied together with common garden twine. The gouged-out mouths gaping in what Rhona thought symbolized a silent scream.

Although they looked the same at this level of magnification, each had a different story to tell. A story only revealed in the forensic lab, through her and Chrissy's determined efforts.

Spotting her presence, Bill immediately called her forward.

'Dr MacLeod contacted me earlier with information that directly affects our investigation. I invited her here to explain how and why.'

Rhona stepped onto the low dais.

'Firstly, we have now identified the body on the beach as that of a young French woman called Eléa Martin from Nice, and not the missing Caillean Munro. We established this via the blood and articles of clothing found in her tent, and through the photograph taken at Gear Bikes where she hired her bike to cycle the NC500.

'Eléa, like Deirdre, was strangled. So the way they were killed was the same, although Eléa was then pushed off the cliff to the beach below and set up to appear as though she'd drowned. Both victims were, as you know, dressed in similar short wetsuits, and also looked very much alike.'

She continued. 'Now to the stick men you see behind me, which we believe form the signature of the killer.

'The first, to your left, is the stick man discovered hanging in Caillean Munro's campervan.

'Next to it is the one retrieved from the mouth of the first victim, Deirdre Reid, when we exhumed her body from the machair near Arisaig. By the state of the body's decomposition, and taking into account the nature and soil of the burial site, we believe she died approximately one month ago, although she was reported missing from Glasgow two months ago.

'The final image is of the stick man we found in the sand next to Eléa Martin at Achmelvich, north of Arisaig.

'Let's take a closer look at each one.'

Rhona magnified the first image, so that the rough bark and grooves in the wood became clearly visible together with the twine used in its construction.

'I can confirm that nothing of interest was found on this one, no DNA evidence of Callie, or whoever constructed it.'

She moved to the second image and magnified it, which brought a surprised murmur from her audience.

'Note the difference. On this one there are darker stained areas on both the bark and the twine. These, when examined, turned out to be a mixed profile of blood. One of which is Deirdre's. The second blood sample may have been deposited by someone snagging their finger when constructing the stick man, or perhaps bleeding from a dry skin hack or eczema. It is definitely not Deirdre's blood.'

Rhona paused there briefly as her audience absorbed and tried to comprehend what was being said.

She now switched the magnification to the third image, emphasizing that although it looked identical to the second, at closer quarters you could see that it was tied together somewhat differently.

'On this one, the dark patches of blood are also clearly visible and are a match for Eléa Martin, victim number two, adding weight to the idea that it may be part of the killer's signature to paint the stick man with the victim's blood. In this case there was no mixed profile. However, we did manage to retrieve skin flakes and blood from under Eléa's nails, which suggests she fought her assailant at some point.

'The most significant finding in all of this is that the DNA profile obtained from the secondary blood on the second stick man does not match that of the skin and blood we extracted from under Eléa Martin's nails.'

As the implication of this swept through the team, the babble grew. Bill let them voice their thoughts and emotions, before he quietened them, to clarify . . .

'This suggests we can no longer assume that we are chasing

a single perpetrator despite both the signature and modus operandi being the same. Since no details of these have been made public, then the likelihood of a copycat murderer seems unlikely. Which in turn suggests the abductions and killings could be the work of a group rather than an individual.

'A group who target young women of similar appearance who either live in the area of the student strip or, in the case of Eléa, are visitors to that area.'

When the surprised talking finally died down and the investigation team dispersed, Bill asked Rhona to come to his office. Waving her to a seat, he closed the door, then took his place across the desk from her in the well-worn leather chair she'd seen him use since they'd first met.

'So, there may be more than one killer?' he said.

'Forensically, it points that way. I felt we should be aware of the possibility. It doesn't mean for certain we don't have a copycat killing.'

Bill acknowledged that. 'Just because we haven't announced key details, doesn't mean they're not out there. Not every officer keeps his mouth shut, especially if the papers offer enough money. There are corrupt officers in every force.' He caught her eye and held it. 'And at the moment we, here in Glasgow, are under scrutiny. It took us too long to discover the truth about Deirdre Reid. Plus all the rumours and counter-rumours about goings-on at the student strip.'

Rhona wondered if this in essence was a conversation about McNab, but wasn't prepared to ask outright.

Bill sat back in the chair. She'd seen that look before. She mimicked it herself on occasion as though looking for divine inspiration, even when the answer could usually be found by looking through a microscope.

Eventually Bill broke the silence. 'I received a full disclosure from Detective Sergeant McNab last night regarding the CCTV footage taken at the Blue Arrow and subsequent voicemail sent to your mobile. And I have spoken to him in person this morning.'

Rhona's relief at this revelation was tempered only by her thoughts on what would come next.

'You can't think McNab would sexually assault a woman?' she heard herself say.

Bill's serious expression didn't change. 'In the light of the rumours focusing on the student strip, I have no choice but to launch an investigation. For that to happen, we must locate the young woman involved. At this moment, no accusation on her part has been made. As far as I am aware, she only sent McNab's voicemail to you. However, I suspect it may yet be circulated either online or sent to various newspapers.'

'Then she or someone with influence over her is pursuing a vendetta against McNab,' Rhona said sharply.

Bill didn't argue with her on that.

'Detective Sergeant McNab should not have been hanging about the clubbing scene in the hope, as he says, of uncovering more on Deirdre Reid's disappearance. Not without my permission,' Bill said. 'I believe he has you to thank for encouraging him to come clean?'

Rhona felt her anger swell at this. Why the hell give her the credit?

'Only because I was the first person to be told about the visits,' she said. 'DS Clark would have done the same if McNab had treated her like a partner. In fact, she tried after I received the voicemail.'

Bill nodded at this. 'I have already spoken to DS Clark about the situation.'

When silence fell between them, Rhona decided to ask the question she really needed the answer to.

'Is McNab to be suspended?'

Bill met her worried gaze.

'He is not, Dr MacLeod. There will be no formal action until the case has been fully investigated and all the facts have been considered. I'm only sharing details with you on a need-to-know basis.'

'And I can tell Chrissy about this?' Rhona said.

'If she hasn't heard it already.' Bill gave a wry smile. 'As we both know, Chrissy McInsh's ears have a long reach.' He paused briefly before adding, 'Let's hope the story goes no further than his immediate colleagues. If it does get out in a bigger way . . .'

He left the rest unsaid.

47

Loch Lomond

Day seven

The day was going well. As soon as the rain stopped, the kids had asked to go outside. Despite her concerns, Francine had put on a bright smile and agreed.

'Just stay where I can see you from the front window. And paddling only.'

'If the sun comes out, will you swim with us?' Lucy had asked, her blue eyes bright.

'Of course,' Francine had said, trying hard not to wish the sun would stay behind the clouds. Not a big water enthusiast herself, paddling was fine. Going any deeper was less alluring.

Despite not allowing swimming, Francine still insisted on water wings, for Lucy at least.

'Just until I join you,' she'd said to soften the blow.

Eventually she'd taken a sun chair down to the thin strip of sand and pebbles, together with a book. Although the sun still hid behind the clouds, it was pleasantly warm, and she was lulled into laying her head back and closing her eyes.

Listening to the laughter of the children and the chittering of birds in the nearby garden bushes, she realized this was the most serene she'd felt in a very long time.

When she opened her eyes a little later, she noted that the fisherman was back, sitting on his red boat, patiently waiting for a fish to take his bait. When he saw her sit up, the man gave her a friendly wave. She almost waved back, but at the last moment dropped her hand and took up her book again instead.

The last thing she wanted was to start up a conversation with locals or holidaymakers.

As she attempted to get back into her book, she suddenly realized that the children weren't there. How long had she dozed off for? Had they gone back inside?

She quickly rose, expecting them to emerge from behind the rocks along the shoreline, or the bushes that dotted the garden. When that didn't happen, she ran towards the house, calling their names, trying not to sound too frantic, knowing that for Orly, at least, that would cause real distress.

Eventually she heard Orly shout, 'In the kitchen, Mum.'

Her heart slowing, she called back, 'Is Lucy with you?'

There wasn't time for an answer before she was pushing open the kitchen door.

Orly's face appeared first, then a few seconds later she saw Lucy's blonde head.

'Why did you come inside without telling me?' She tried to sound unworried.

'You were sleeping, Mummy,' Lucy said, as though that was more than enough reason.

'I did fall asleep. Must be all this fresh air,' she said cheerfully. 'Are you hungry? I could put a pizza in the oven? It only takes minutes to heat up.'

When both heads nodded, she went to the fridge for the pizza.

As she did so, she had the distinct feeling she was being watched. The feeling was so strong, she felt the hairs on the back of her neck rise.

She moved swiftly towards the back door and turned the key. The door facing the road she had kept locked.

'What is it?' Orly, ever watchful, asked her.

She shook her head, trying to look unconcerned. 'Nothing, I thought I saw someone outside. Let's get this pizza going.' With trembling hands, she attacked the plastic covering with a knife, then slipped the pizza in the oven.

She stood for a moment, knife in hand, trying to sense if the watched feeling had dissipated, but still the hairs on the back of her neck were warning her . . . but of what?

Orly had risen and gone to the window. 'It's the fisherman,' he said. 'He keeps his boat along a bit from the garden. He's standing near the fence. D'you think he wants to speak to you?'

Francine shook her head. 'I don't think so.'

'But what if it's important?' he said.

Lucy looked up at this. 'If he leaves his boat there, he must know Auntie Marion,' she offered with childlike common sense.

Still Francine did not move. It was as though her feet had decided for her and stuck themselves firmly to the floor.

'He's coming over,' Orly said.

Almost immediately, the door was knocked firmly three times. Each time, her heart banged along with it.

'Mum?' Orly said, looking worried now.

She suddenly realized that they were fearful of their father and his many moods, but that didn't make them frightened of the entire world and the people in it.

She made herself smile reassuringly. 'I'd better see what our mysterious visitor wants, then.'

48

Glasgow

Day seven

McNab had shown the collage of photographs of the dark-haired Holly to the boss, together with the one where she looked like the Holly he'd met that fateful night in the rain.

He'd also pointed out the one taken in Nice N Sleazy, where the tall bloke had his arm about her shoulders.

'I thought I recognized him as a security guard I'd seen working there. When I checked in the club late last night they confirmed he'd worked for them in the past.'

'How far in the past?' DI Wilson had said.

'A couple of months ago. Around the time Deirdre Reid disappeared, sir.'

'Was this followed up at the time?'

'Jeff Broughton was questioned along with the dozen other security guards that work the clubs along the strip.'

DI Wilson had considered this for a moment. 'And you believe he's a possible link with this girl, Holly?'

'It looks like it from the photograph,' McNab had said.

McNab had been about to mention the shadowy figure behind Holly in the picture, but had decided not to. There was time enough for that when, or if, Ollie could furnish him with a better image. He knew who he thought it was, and was fully intent on finding out if he was right.

'You have twenty-four hours, Sergeant,' the boss had told him. 'If this thing escalates during that time, I will have no recourse other than to take you off duty.'

There was no answer to that, so McNab hadn't given one. As he'd left the boss's presence, he'd been only too relieved to get the time he'd been given, however short it might prove to be.

Now back out on the street after the Henderson interview, and a very long and uncomfortable chat with his partner, he felt much like he'd been to confession and told the truth for once.

Except he hadn't told *the whole truth, and nothing but the truth,* to either his partner or his boss.

He hadn't mentioned that the ghost guy in the photograph reminded him of someone he had tried to put away and failed. More than once. The most recent time being less than a week ago.

There's no way you could have identified what was little more than a spectre, he told himself. Even Ollie couldn't manage that.

As he drove to the address the bloke at Nice N Sleazy had given him for Jeff Broughton, he wondered if he was merely wishing it so, because managing to link his bête noire to Holly, and what she'd done, answered all his questions.

The Henderson interview still fresh in his mind, he moved his thoughts to the man's reaction to their questions.

The guy was a prick. That much was obvious. But was he more than that? The wife hadn't mentioned his affairs, although he'd casually revealed them as though they were on the same level as forgetting to stack the dishwasher or put the cat out.

McNab wondered briefly why such domestic pursuits should enter his head at all. Is that what he thought marriage consisted of?

He'd never really observed a good marriage, except perhaps the boss's to Margaret. He'd certainly seen what losing her to cancer had done to him. Any other relationships he'd observed in action, like Chrissy's, appeared fun and mostly short-lived, much like his own.

Except, he reminded himself, Janice and Paula seemed to get on well enough to get married.

He realized he'd kept the last relationship he had any real knowledge of until the end, because it both annoyed and perplexed him.

Rhona MacLeod and Sean Maguire. Still together. Sort of.

He forced his thoughts back to Derek Henderson. Something was definitely off there. Rhona had been convinced, as had Magnus, that the children had been telling the truth in the interview, although maybe not the whole story.

In the light of Henderson's statement, the children would have to be questioned again, as would Mrs Henderson. It was obvious there was stuff she wasn't yet ready to reveal. Although if she was sure she was safely away from her husband, she might then be willing to talk freely.

As for evidence that Henderson had been in the blue campervan, the man had seemed pretty certain they would find none. They now had his DNA and Janice had applied for a search warrant for the Henderson home and would remove his shoes for comparison with the footprint inside the van.

McNab could imagine Henderson coming on to the girl

that night, but what had happened after that? Did she head off in her kayak to avoid him, and something had happened to her? But how to explain the stick man hanging above the bed, plus the blood and vomit?

The revelation in the strategy meeting that there might be more than one perpetrator at work in all of this had changed his perception of the case. Male gangs preying on young women and girls for grooming purposes were by no means a new thing, but abducting and murdering them? Although more than one perpetrator might better explain the timeline and location of the three crimes.

And the whole thing surrounding the stick men and this film, which apparently only he hadn't seen.

Maybe Ollie was right and he should watch *The Blair Witch Project*?

Realizing he had reached his destination, McNab parked and took a look out to find a row of shopfronts, including a pharmacy, a bakery and a betting shop, with intermittent entry to the flats on the upper level. Climbing out of the car, the smell coming from the baker's reminded him that he hadn't eaten for some time.

Promising to remedy that after he checked on Broughton, he looked for number 10, which turned out to be above the bakery. The front door stood half open, with no entryphone system, which he realized might prove fortunate.

A tight set of stairs wound upwards. Even from here McNab could smell the warm pies he planned to savour after his visit.

Reaching the landing, he found two doors side by side, neither of which had names on them. He knocked both of them together, shouting, 'Open up, police,' loud enough for the folk below buying their pies to hear.

Seconds later, both doors were opened. One by a shell-shocked woman in her fifties, the other by a guy he immediately identified.

'Jeff Broughton, Detective Sergeant McNab, I'd like to come inside, if you don't mind. Don't want the neighbours to know all your business, do we?'

Broughton's face turned a dark shade of puce. 'What the fuck,' he muttered, but he did step aside to allow McNab entry. With an apologetic smile at the neighbour, McNab did so. Inside, he was assailed by even more delectable smells from downstairs and wondered how Broughton could avoid eating himself to death.

Broughton, having regained his composure, now assumed the stance of a security guard.

'How can I help you, Detective?' he offered.

'I'm looking for Holly Allan.'

Broughton attempted to cover his reaction to the name, which he obviously recognized, by looking bewildered and saying, 'Who?'

McNab produced his mobile and showed him the photo. 'This is you and Holly taken in Nice N Sleazy. You look pretty pally there, don't you think?'

'Lassies ask for selfies with security all the time.' He attempted a laugh. 'That doesn't mean I know her.'

McNab eyed him. 'The police are looking for her. Obstructing our enquiries . . .' He tailed off.

'What the fuck are you talking about?' Broughton's colour was on the rise again.

'Finding Holly.'

'I don't know where she is. And I don't work at Sleazy's any more.'

'So where do you work, then?' McNab said.

Broughton named a much more upmarket establishment in the Merchant City.

'Mmm.' McNab considered this. 'They definitely require police references. Not sure you'll be there long once I give them a visit.'

Broughton looked like he'd just been punched.

'You're sure now about Holly?' McNab tried again.

Broughton was replaying his options, trying to come to a decision. Eventually he did.

'Holly and I broke up when she started seeing Charlie Bonar.'

The name hit McNab like a fist in his face. 'Holly was seeing Charlie Bonar?'

Broughton's expression suggested he thought he'd maybe opened his mouth a bit too wide.

'When was she seeing Bonar?' McNab demanded.

'A couple of months back. That's all I know.' His voice had become more of a whine as the consequences of what he'd revealed hit home.

It was all McNab needed to know. 'Charlie Bonar,' he repeated, savouring the taste of that name on his tongue. Charlie had a way with the women. Only one of whom had had the courage to stand up in court and call him out for what he'd done to her. It hadn't made any difference because he'd walked away a free man anyway.

McNab recalled Bonar's smile as he'd heard the not proven verdict. But it seemed getting off with it hadn't been enough. Maybe he'd wanted more. Like revenge against the officer who'd put him in the dock in the first place.

'You have an address for Bonar?' he said.

Broughton, big man that he was, was visibly shrinking before McNab's eyes. 'No way, Detective. I haven't heard or seen him since I quit the Sleazy gig. And I don't want to.'

McNab decided to take pity on him. Broughton had left Nice N Sleazy well before the CCTV footage episode, so he couldn't have been part of the plan in which it appeared Holly had played the main role.

'Stay out of trouble, Broughton,' he offered as he made for the door.

'You have my word on that, Detective,' he said, his expression one of relief.

As the door closed behind him, McNab considered the possibility that Broughton could be straight on the blower to Bonar about his visit. If he did, his current job at the fancy club would definitely be on the line.

Sitting now in his vehicle with an extra-strong coffee and a Scotch pie, McNab considered what he'd just learnt.

He now knew why Holly had been so persuasive. With Bonar on your back, who wouldn't be? Although if Bonar had wanted him suspended, the CCTV footage wasn't enough. Not when he wasn't easily recognizable in it.

It seemed he'd played right into Bonar's hands when he'd left that begging voicemail for Holly. But had Holly actually told Bonar about it? Because if she had, surely the press would be all over it by now, playing it as part of the story of the police and the sexual assaults on the student strip?

Yet as far as he was aware it had gone no further than Rhona. Might Holly have sent it to Rhona to forewarn him?

He played with that idea.

He thought of Holly's paintings left in the empty flat and the note tucked under the pillow with the single word on it. *Sorry*.

He thought of what Bonar had done to the Russian girl.

What might he do to Holly if he discovered she'd crossed him in his desire for revenge?

Whether Holly had willingly set him up or not, she didn't deserve that.

McNab tossed the bag of bakery goodies onto the passenger seat and drank the remainder of his coffee.

'Charlie Bonar.' He licked the last taste of pie from his lips. 'I'm coming for you. And this time it's going to stick.'

How he would do that without harming Holly, he wasn't so sure.

49

Day seven

Rhona's unease, at both the strategy meeting and what had been spoken about afterwards with Bill, persisted all the way back to the lab.

Bill had allowed questions before he'd sent the team back to work, which she'd answered as truthfully as she could, all the time thinking that Magnus may well have had a different take on the evidence that appeared to suggest more than one perpetrator.

Even as she'd discussed the images of the three stick men and the forensic evidence they'd found on them, she'd questioned whether the killer or killers had in fact made the stick men themselves, or whether they'd simply purchased them from somewhere.

How many people had handled them before their victim's blood was applied?

The skin and blood found under Eléa's fingernails was by far the better evidence of her killer. In the first instance they could run that profile through both the Scottish and the UK databases and hope for a match.

Bill was pushing for fast-tracking, but that cost more, so would depend on the police budget. As she approached the university buildings, she decided she would give Magnus a call, run what they'd found past him. The stick man seemed key to all of this. Maybe also the key to the perpetrator or perpetrators.

Entering the lab, she spotted Chrissy through the glass and waved to her suited figure. She'd left her working on the wetsuit boots worn by Deirdre, the ribbed rubber soles of which had been caked with a mixture of soil and vegetation, which might give them a clue as to where she had been prior to her burial in the machair at Arisaig.

Spotting her arrival, Chrissy emerged and took off her mask.

'How'd it go?' she said, reading Rhona's expression.

'I think I caused a minor panic,' Rhona said. 'From one killer, they now fear they could have more.'

'It could explain the timeline and locations more easily,' Chrissy offered.

'McNab mentioned that in the meeting,' Rhona said.

'So he's still working?' Chrissy looked relieved.

'Bill says he received the video and voicemail in the early hours of the morning. They've talked and apparently McNab's been given twenty-four hours to try and locate Holly, provided it's kept under wraps. Only immediate colleagues to be made aware,' Rhona told her.

'Which must include me?' Chrissy said.

'Bill voiced the opinion that you probably already knew. His exact words were, "As we both know, Chrissy McInsh's ears have a long reach."'

'Cheek,' Chrissy said, although she looked pleased.

'So how did you get on with the wetsuit and boots?' Rhona asked.

'Most of what we recovered externally from the wetsuit

matches the sand and vegetation of the grave. The boots, however, were far more interesting.' Chrissy's eyes lit up. 'The soles are like car tyres. All those grooves. I was worried if she'd arrived by boat or kayak, any deposits might have been washed off. But no. The surface layer under the microscope looks like the beach sand at Arisaig. However, there's lots of interesting material underneath, suggesting she'd walked on different ground and vegetation. Dr Mackie will no doubt be able to point us in the direction of where it was picked up.'

Dr Jen Mackie was a colleague and an expert in soil forensics, and they'd worked together many times. Deirdre Reid had walked to her death in those boots. The material removed from them would hopefully help trace where she'd come from. And maybe where she was kept in the weeks before she was killed.

Chrissy continued. 'Also swabs were taken from Derek Henderson, although DS Clark said he maintained that he hadn't entered Callie's van, and showed no concern at giving a sample.'

Glancing at the wall clock, Rhona suggested Chrissy finish up for the day. 'I'm going to give Magnus a call,' she said. 'I'd like to hear his thoughts on what's just happened.'

Magnus answered on the third ring, sounding pleased to hear from her.

'Are you still at work?' she asked.

'Just arrived home. Why?'

'Has Bill been in touch yet?'

'No.' Magnus sounded intrigued.

'I wanted to speak to you about today's strategy meeting,' Rhona said.

'Okay. Do you want to come here? Or shall I come to you?'

Rhona considered this for a moment. 'I'll come to you,' she decided.

'Okay.' He sounded pleased. 'You know where I am.'

As she rang off, she found Chrissy checking her out. 'You're going to see the Prof,' she said, a twinkle in her eye.

'He's not all yours,' Rhona told her in return.

'What do you want to talk to him about?'

'Stick men and their significance in this case.'

'That sounds like a title for one of your forensic course talks,' Chrissy said.

'It no doubt will be in the future. As for now, it's not for the ears of the public.'

Magnus had chosen to live close to the river, so that he might stand on his veranda and view the constantly moving waters of the Clyde below, just as he looked out on Scapa Flow from his harbour home in Orkney.

They were seated in his main room, veranda doors open to the sounds of the river and city combined.

Magnus listened as Rhona repeated what she'd said at the strategy meeting, focusing on the forensic evidence retrieved from the stick men, omitting her own thoughts on the significance of this.

'I understand you've been working on a profile of the perpetrator?' she asked.

'I have.' He looked thoughtful. 'Although it may change after what you've just revealed.'

Rhona listened as he outlined his thinking.

'I must admit I've been puzzled by the timeline of the incidents together with the geography. Broadly speaking, our perceived perpetrator has focused on females who look alike, in age, height, build, hair colour, etc. All three either lived in the vicinity of what's called the student strip, or in the case of Eléa Martin, was a visitor there. Two have been found dead and one missing along the stretch of road known as the North Coast 500.

'The abduction either happened in Glasgow, as in Deirdre's case, or in Eléa and Callie's cases from campsites close to that route.

'The method of killing – strangling – was the same. In Deirdre's case she was kept alive for a month beforehand, and likely throttled on numerous occasions, which suggests the need for power and sexual gratification. Eléa was strangled the night she disappeared. Callie may well still be alive.

'Both murder victims had a Twana, a symbol of evil left with their body, which we believe symbolized something significant to the killer. In Callie's case one was left in her van.

'Now you say these stick men, although outwardly similar, were in fact not exactly the same. Each was bound slightly differently. Two had their victim's blood on them, but not in the case of the missing Callie. There was secondary blood on Deirdre's but no secondary blood on Eléa's. Is that correct?'

Rhona indicated that it was.

'Even before you explained about the scrapings from Eléa's fingernails, I suspected . . .' He halted there.

'You suspected the stick men might not be the work of one person?' Rhona said.

'Indeed. You can buy a variety of Twanas easily via the internet. Even if you buy a number of the same make, I imagine you could still pick up the DNA of those who have made or at the very least handled them, just as you can from a fencepost.' He smiled then, reminding her of something she had told him on a previous case.

He continued. 'It is possible that the crimes have been set up to look as though they have been carried out by a single perpetrator, although your recent forensic evidence, added to the timing and geography of the crimes, might point to a group activity rather than an individual. I suspect that was your interpretation?' He looked to Rhona for confirmation.

When she gave a nod, he carried on.

'If we're right and this is a group endeavour, they need not necessarily have ever met in person. All it requires is a shared hatred of women, or in particular those who look similar to the victims, and a meeting place online.'

'You're thinking of an incel-type group?' Rhona said.

Magnus nodded. 'Either way, they would have made a commitment and spurred each other on. They will be bound together by their decision. In that they would be one.'

They sat in silence, Rhona absorbing what had been said.

Eventually Magnus came back in. 'Remember, all this is conjecture. It's you, the scientist, who interprets the forensic evidence. What that tells you isn't the same as an unproven theory from a criminal psychologist like myself.' He gave her a wry smile. 'Detective Sergeant McNab, I think, would agree with me on that.'

It was clear from his expression that this contained an unspoken enquiry as to McNab's current position in the investigation.

Rhona told him. 'McNab has spoken to DI Wilson concerning the voicemail, and has leave to try and find the girl Holly.'

Magnus looked relieved about that.

'Can we discuss the Henderson family now?' Rhona said.

'I was hoping we would,' he told her.

'Derek Henderson's been in and given a statement and a

DNA sample,' Rhona told him. 'He maintains he never entered the blue van. That Orly made it up, to get his mother's attention.'

'Was he concerned about being swabbed?' Magnus asked.

'Apparently not.'

'Then he has either covered his tracks enough to feel confident, or it wasn't him that Orly saw,' Magnus said. 'I think we should have Mrs Henderson and the children in again. There's more going on there than either she or the children were willing to say.'

'This all began at that campsite,' Rhona said. 'If Lucy hadn't followed her father to the deposition site, Deirdre might never have been found.'

'Did Mr Henderson explain why the place interested him?'

'He said the machair had died and he wondered why,' Rhona said.

'It seems the man has an answer to everything.'

'Or we haven't asked him the right question yet.'

50

Loch Lomond

Day seven

Once she'd persuaded the children into bed, Francine had poured herself a glass of wine and gone out to sit in the garden. The sky showed no sign yet of darkening and the remaining light threw its long rays across the calm surface of the loch.

The earlier serenity that had been so swiftly removed by the arrival at the door of the unknown fisherman had returned when he'd shown her his ID and explained that he was a police officer who'd been given the job of keeping an eye on herself and the children.

'DI Wilson wanted you and the kids to feel safe,' he'd told her. 'So I'm your local fisherman for now.'

At that point she'd invited him inside, but he'd refused. 'I'm staying in the boathouse just along the shore. If you need me, just come along with the kids, or call this number.' He'd handed her his card.

'DI Wilson didn't mention this would happen,' she'd told him.

'I should have been more discreet with my fishing. Once

the kids spoke to me, I thought I'd better explain myself in case my presence frightened you.'

They'd said their goodbyes then, but not before he'd added, 'You can tell the children I'm a friend of Marion's if you don't want to alarm them with the police story.'

'I may just do that,' she'd said gratefully.

She'd re-entered the kitchen at that point to find the two children awaiting an explanation on the visitor.

'Our fisherman friend is a Mr Thompson,' she'd told them. 'He's a friend of Marion's. He's offered to give me some fresh fish, if he's lucky tomorrow.'

Orly made a face. 'You mean fish with eyes and bones? I wouldn't like that.'

Lucy had agreed with him. 'We'd rather have fish fingers.'

Francine had laughed at that. 'Well, you two can have fish fingers and I'll have the real fish.'

Now, watching the sun slowly sinking into the west, she thought she would look forward to another visit from PC Thompson, and was very glad that DI Wilson had arranged a bodyguard for her.

She would sleep a lot better tonight, knowing he wasn't far away.

51

Glasgow

Day seven

There was a light on in the front room which suggested that someone was at home, but who exactly? Bonar or some new tenant?

Sitting staring at the house, McNab recalled in detail the last time he'd been here. The Russian girl had managed to get out and flag down a taxi. The driver, seeing the state she was in, persuaded her to go to the police right away, and she'd done so.

After the duty doctor had checked her over, the police had photographed all her injuries: hair torn out by the roots, broken nose, the catalogue of bites and bruising. Then she'd given her statement.

When McNab and the duty officer had come here to arrest Bonar, he'd arrived at the door in his boxers, smelling of drink and shouting the odds at being woken up. He'd denied everything, of course. Said she'd come home drunk and bleeding after a girly fight with a mate.

The kitchen had told a different story, covered as it had been in her blood and clumps of hair.

The anger McNab had felt in that courtroom came flooding back. Bonar should have been put away for at least two years, but he hadn't been, and this is where it had led. Right back here.

Even as he contemplated this, he knew he shouldn't be here. He should have reported what he'd found out and left it to someone else to confront Bonar and check for Holly's presence.

But it was much too personal for that. With this final thought, he got out of the car.

The small front garden had been concreted over, an overflowing bin the only thing growing there. The curtains in the lighted room were tightly shut, and he could hear the TV on full blast, showing what sounded like an action movie, with revving engines and occasional blasts of gunfire.

Moving to the door, he tried the doorbell, wondering if whoever was inside was even likely to notice it.

At the second push of the button, he heard a raised voice order someone to answer the bloody door. At that point a curtain was flicked back. Anticipating such a move, McNab had already tucked himself out of sight.

He heard the door open and someone step out. 'No one here,' a male voice shouted.

'Fucking kids,' came a voice McNab immediately recognized as Bonar's. Then, just before the door was shut, he heard the voice he was hoping for . . .

Holly was in there.

Hearing the door close, his first instinct was to go bang on it and announce himself as the police, just as he'd done with Broughton. Although the outcome here was unlikely to be in his favour.

On the plus side, if they did choose to rough him up . . .

He wasn't here for a rammy, he reminded himself, but to rescue Holly.

But what if she didn't want to be rescued?

Even as he considered this, his mobile bleeped an incoming text. Staying in the shadows, he read the **Where the hell are you?** from Janice.

He'd promised to keep his partner up to date, but hadn't kept his word, worried she might talk him out of coming here.

Abandoning his post, he headed for the car to call her. She answered on the first ring.

'Thank God,' she said before he could speak. 'The shit's hit the fan. The video is out there and this time your face is clearly visible.'

'But how's that possible?' he said, stunned.

'Your friend Ollie says it's undoubtedly doctored. Deep fake, he says, but it's good, and it's bound to reach the media, alongside stories of alleged sexual assaults by police officers on the student strip. Where are you?'

'Following a lead on Holly's whereabouts.' He hesitated.

'And?' she demanded, sensing more.

'I may have found her.'

'Will she come in, d'you think?'

'I'm hoping so.'

'Let's pray she does, but don't get into more trouble trying to persuade her. The boss wants you in first thing. If you have Holly with you, even better.'

He headed back to the house and this time he beat on the door, and kept hammering until it was answered.

'What the fuck?' The guy who opened the door stared belligerently at him.

'Detective Sergeant McNab. I'm here to speak with Holly Allan.'

The man looked taken aback, then shook his head. 'There's no one of that name here, Detective.'

Ignoring his response, McNab pushed past him and shouted Holly's name. From somewhere nearby he heard Bonar shushing her.

'Holly Allan,' McNab called out. 'This is Detective Sergeant McNab. You are required to come to the station to give a statement regarding an incident at the Blue Arrow nightclub on Sauchiehall Street. If you don't come quietly, I will have no option but to arrest you.'

Following the sound of raised voices, McNab threw open the door and walked into the kitchen he remembered so well.

Bonar, standing just inside, regarded him in a surprised manner. 'DS McNab.' He gave a small laugh. 'Last I heard of you, you were in deep shit. Something about sexually assaulting young women?' He made a loud tutting noise.

McNab felt his fist clench with the desire to land one on Bonar's smug face, already anticipating the crunch as it met the cheekbone.

Don't go there, an inner voice warned, *because that's exactly what he wants.*

Holly was standing with her back against the sink. She looked terrified, but McNab couldn't read whether she was fearful of him or Bonar.

'Last time I was in here,' McNab said quietly, 'the place was covered in blood and clumps of a woman's hair torn out by the roots. That woman had twenty-six bites on her body and a broken nose.' He pointed to Bonar. 'He did that to her, and she wasn't the first. Nor will she be the last.' He tried to catch Holly's frightened eye. 'Whatever you've done, you're safer with me.'

He watched as she wrestled with her decision. She had betrayed him, he could see that in her eyes.

'I read your note,' he said. 'That's why I'm here.'

Bonar's face darkened as he grabbed Holly's wrist. 'What fucking note?' he spat at her.

In that moment, she appeared to make up her mind. 'I'll come with you,' she said, attempting to pull her wrist free of Bonar.

He fought this briefly, then suddenly let go, sending her flying across the room towards McNab.

Then the warning came. 'Be careful what you say, girl. Remember, we have ears on the inside.' Bonar smiled darkly at McNab. 'And some of them definitely don't like *you*, Detective Sergeant McNab.'

Blanking him, McNab took Holly by the arm and led her out of the kitchen, through the hall past the minder and out of the front door. Holly was visibly trembling as he helped her into the vehicle.

'Has he hurt you?' he asked as he joined her.

'He will,' she said, her voice shaking, 'now that I've come with you.'

'I won't let him.'

'You won't be a police officer much longer, after what he made me do to you,' she said, her face drained of colour. 'And what he said is true. He has police officers working with him on that.'

'Do you know who they are?' McNab asked.

She shook her head. 'I'm sorry, I did try to warn you.'

'I know.' He reached over and squeezed her hand.

As he drew away, he heard her begin to cry.

52

Day seven

Holly had gratefully accepted Rhona's offer of a glass of wine and some of the remaining pizza she'd ordered earlier. After which Tom had decided to curl up on her knee, which she obviously appreciated.

All things considered, she looked much improved from the frightened female Rhona had opened her door to an hour ago.

The call from McNab had come late, but she'd still been up and working. Her first thought when she'd seen his name on the screen was that it would be bad news, because it often was, especially when he got in touch so late.

'I offered to take her to my place, but I would have had to leave her on her own while I go to Ollie's,' McNab had told her. 'She didn't want that.'

It was at this point he'd explained about the doctoring of the CCTV clip and its posting online. 'Bonar says he has friends in the force who want me out. I suspect they're the ones behind the sexual assaults on the student strip.'

'Charlie Bonar? The man you gave evidence against recently in court?'

'That's the one,' McNab had confirmed.

Rhona had immediately told him to bring Holly here, and she would deliver her safely to the station in the morning.

And here she was.

Rhona hadn't questioned her at all, just offered food and drink and a loan of her cat. Although in truth it was Tom who had chosen to be Holly's comforter. The cat had a knack of reading sadness, worry and, in this case, fear in people.

There had been many times she herself had been a recipient of his tender care. Now the sound of his purring was the backdrop to the telling of Holly's story.

'You don't have to tell me, you know?' Rhona said, when she began.

'I'm going to have to say it all tomorrow,' Holly said. 'It might help if I try and explain myself now. Can you record me while I tell you? That way I can listen back and make sure I've covered everything.'

The story was a sad and distressing one. At first it seemed Bonar had been charming and affectionate towards her. When they'd met at Nice N Sleazy, she'd been broke and in serious debt. Her work wasn't selling so she'd taken a job at the club to help pay the rent. He'd been good to her, paid off her debts, and they'd begun a relationship.

'It was then he told me about a police officer who they suspected was sexually assaulting young women in the club. That they were trying to catch him, but because he was a cop, he was getting away with it. Charlie said the only way to stop him was to film him at it and he wanted me to help him do that.'

She stopped there for a moment, before making herself continue.

'I told him no at first. He wasn't pleased about that.' She

looked frightened by the memory. 'He threatened me about the debts he'd paid for me. So I did as he asked, making the excuse that maybe the guy I was to set up really was an abuser.'

She looked apologetically at Rhona.

'But when I met and got to know Michael, I didn't think he could be like that. I tried to back out, but Charlie got really angry so I did what he asked of me . . .'

When she fell silent, Rhona said, 'DI Wilson is McNab's boss. You can trust him to help you. Just tell him what you've told me and McNab will be okay.'

'But the stuff online?' she asked.

'The police already know it's a doctored video,' Rhona assured her.

She looked relieved at that. 'I want to put things right for Michael,' she said. 'But what about Charlie's friends in the police? What'll they do to me when they hear I've given evidence against him?'

Rhona found herself as concerned by that as Holly obviously was.

After Holly had been persuaded to go to bed in Sean's room, Rhona transferred the recording to her laptop and sent it on to Bill, thinking the sooner he heard it the better, including the warning of rogue officers.

After which she texted Sean to say she had a visitor staying over tonight and that she would catch up with him later tomorrow.

His reply was a simple Okay, with no questioning of who her visitor might be.

After the exchange, Rhona wondered if she'd made the right decision in turning Sean away tonight.

According to McNab, they had definitely not been followed

to her flat, so there was little likelihood of a nocturnal visit from Charlie Bonar.

And yet, Rhona thought, as she went through to her own room, she suspected she would have slept more easily if she'd known Sean would soon be alongside her.

53

Day eight

Once he'd seen Holly safely installed at Rhona's flat, he'd called Ollie, hoping the night owl was still up.

His call was swiftly answered. 'You've heard about the doctored footage?' Ollie said.

'I have,' McNab told him. 'And I'm on my way over.'

Ollie sounded pleased by that. 'There's other stuff you need to know before you face the music tomorrow.'

Well after midnight, he should have been tired, but wasn't, not with the amount of adrenaline coursing through his veins since his brush with Bonar. He thought back to his last time with Ollie and how he'd been fed pizza and strong coffee, and hoped there might be some sustenance available again.

As it was, he forgot all about his hunger and need for caffeine as soon as he sat down next to Ollie to view his array of screens and begin listening to his story.

His heart missed more than a few beats when Ollie played the recent footage on a big screen. In the original his face had been in shadow, as had Holly's. Not any more. Now there was no doubt as to who the supposed rapist was. It was also clear from Holly's expression that she wasn't in agreement with what was happening at all.

'Jesus,' McNab whispered, feeling nauseated. 'How the fuck did they do that?'

'Watch and I'll show you,' Ollie said.

The video was restarted and began to move slowly through the changes that had been made. First, the original shadowy image of them both. Then his face slowly began to form like some sort of reincarnation, shifting from nothing but shadow into the maniacal and determined face of a sexual predator enjoying his rape of a frightened woman.

The shock of what he had become on screen horrified McNab. It was like a re-enactment of *Jekyll and Hyde*.

'It's so fucking real,' he said. 'I'm a monster in that. And then that bloody voicemail asking her to—' He stopped there because it was unbearable to even think it, let alone say it out loud.

'It's undeniably fake. Good, though.' Ollie sounded impressed. 'Certainly done by someone with the skills and the appropriate software.'

Ollie glanced at McNab and, obviously seeing his wild expression, said, 'It's not the original and I can prove it. So no worries there. What about the girl, though? Will she say it is you and that's what actually happened?'

'Holly'll say what really went down. She's safe now and with Dr MacLeod, who'll take her into the station tomorrow to give a statement.'

'How did you find her?' Ollie said, obviously pleased by the news.

'Via a former bouncer at Nice N Sleazy. That photograph you showed me? That was Jeff Broughton with Holly . . . and the shadowy figure behind him I thought was someone I've tried to lock up a few times and failed, including recently.

His name is Charlie Bonar. He was the one behind setting me up, using Holly.'

'I thought you were likely the fall guy for whoever is behind the sexual assaults,' Ollie said.

'Bonar says he has friends in the force who want rid of me,' McNab told him. 'He threatened Holly to make her keep her mouth shut.'

'I have a couple of other things to show you. First of all, in our trawl of CCTV cameras along the student strip, I found something even more interesting than you and your girlfriend. Take a look at this.'

The screen to McNab's left came alive and on it was the usual grainy image which Ollie could interpret, much to McNab's continuing amazement.

'Where is that?' he said, squinting at what looked like a dark night with the added feature of rain pissing down.

'It's a black van by Nice N Sleazy. It's from way back. Recorded around the time Deirdre Reid went missing. Watch closely,' he ordered.

It was over in seconds. A female figure and a male, holding her up. They went behind the van and didn't reappear.

'Is that her? And who's the guy with her?' McNab said.

'Neither are distinguishable, even to me,' Ollie said. 'But considering where I found the clip I think it's likely to be Deirdre.'

'Where did you find it?'

'We've been trawling incel-type sites looking for anything anti-women that might be linked to the stick man motif. There are lots of sites talking about the *Blair Witch* franchise, but I eventually stumbled on a more interesting one where women – all women – are regarded as witches. And my, do the guys talking on there hate them.'

The screen was now framed by stick figures, similar to the ones found with the bodies. Within the frame was an array of comments that made McNab despair. The incitement to violence. Statements suggesting all women had rape fantasies. That they liked being choked. That without control they were a danger to men.

'Sick bastards,' McNab said.

'I suspect most of it's just talk, nasty though it is. Then deeper in I found this. One particular stick man being the entry point.'

The stick character he now clicked on became a door, leading into a narrow corridor and a dark, windowless room, where a blonde female figure, bound and gagged, was sitting against a wall.

The image was the quality of a 3D-computer game, and very close to looking real.

'That could be any of the stick man victims,' McNab said.

'I think it's meant to be,' Ollie said.

'Where did you find the van clip?'

'Posted here too, but choosing a different stick man as entry. So someone had access to the CCTV footage.'

'How many allow entry?' McNab demanded, knowing already what Ollie would say.

'Three so far,' Ollie confirmed. 'The room, the van and this one.' This time the image was of a beach with a rock face behind and the crumpled figure of a girl at its foot.

'There's no way anyone could know Eléa Martin was found exactly like that . . .' McNab tailed off, his brain going into overdrive.

'Unless you had access to police information regarding her discovery,' Ollie finished for him.

'You think there's an officer actually involved in the abduction of these women?'

'Maybe,' Ollie said. 'Or they're posting aspects of the case online in a forum they're a member of.'

McNab, noting Ollie's angry demeanour, wondered out loud how he survived, delving into such sick minds.

'Same as you do,' Ollie said, then nodded to the door that led into the bedroom. 'And Maria helps.'

'Maria's still with you?' McNab was pleased and a little jealous too.

'We rub along okay together.' Ollie sounded amazed that that was true. 'Although I'd never show her the stuff I have to do.'

They both lapsed into silence before McNab said, 'Is all this for the strategy meeting tomorrow?'

Ollie shook his head. 'Strictly between you, me and DI Wilson until further notice. Bonar says he has friends on the force. It certainly looks like it with regard to you being set up, but I haven't traced who's posting this shite on that forum. They may have no connection with Police Scotland.'

McNab rose, suddenly way beyond tired. 'I'd better go home and get some kip before the big day. Any chance you might identify a partial on the number plate of that black van?'

'That would be close to a miracle,' Ollie said. 'But miracles do happen.'

54

Achmelvich

Day eight

After the coastguard guys had arrived and told him he could leave, Trevor had come to the rocky outcrop above the cottage, where he had a clear view down to the cove and from there round the coast to the bay at Achmelvich.

He'd seen the helicopter land with the forensic woman, and had watched as she and the female police officer had arrived by car and made their way down to the beach to examine the body.

He hadn't been able to see exactly what they were doing, but he didn't really want to anyway. He wanted to forget the twisted, broken body, and the glassy-eyed stare that still haunted his dreams.

Driven to find out who she was, he'd eventually gone down to the cafe at the campsite thinking that Murdo or Esther would likely know if she'd been identified.

Finding out her name, Eléa Martin, and that she was French, somehow made things worse. Now she was real and not just a nightmarish memory that he wanted to dispel.

Esther had insisted on telling him everything they'd learnt

about her. How she had been over in Scotland on holiday. How she'd hired a bike in Glasgow to cycle the NC500, camping along the way.

'She thought she would be safe,' Esther had said, shaking her head.

At this point he'd broken his silence to say, 'It's not your fault it happened here.'

She'd nodded at that and given Meg a biscuit.

'I don't suppose you heard anything up near your place that night?' Esther had asked. 'Word is she fought her attacker before he threw her off the cliff. She must have screamed.' She'd looked at him then, as though willing him to add details to the developing story.

Trevor had shaken his head, struck dumb with fear. Although, ever since that conversation, he'd been asking himself if perhaps he had heard something, or Meg had.

He'd gone home by way of the cliff path that day, imagining the girl Eléa being forced to walk along there at knifepoint, because Esther had said that Murdo had found blood in the tent.

When he'd reached the point above where he'd found her, he'd leaned over so far, he might have fallen himself. There had been times in the past he might have chosen that route out of life. But not now, not with Meg dependent on him, and he on her.

He didn't think she had been taken along the cliff path. More likely she'd been brought in by sea. After all, she'd been wearing a wetsuit. He'd seen it through the netting. That was why he'd thought she'd drowned.

But she hadn't drowned, according to Esther. She'd been pushed off the cliff.

'Her killer wanted it to look as though she'd drowned,'

Esther had told him. 'The police think she was taken up there by car. They likely parked in that lay-by next to the old caravan you used to live in.'

At that point a sudden image had played out in his head. The girl managing to get away, running in the direction of the sea, only to find herself at the cliff edge.

If only she'd run down by way of his potato patch, she would have reached the beach and perhaps managed to swim away.

Esther had been studying him, willing him on to say he'd heard something. He'd shaken his head then, but was now beginning to question his memories of that fateful night. If he had heard her scream, what would he have done?

He hated that question because he suspected he would have ignored it.

The police had already been up the croft road, taking statements from folk staying in the Airbnbs, asking if they'd heard or seen anything that night. They'd spoken to him again too, but there was nothing more he could tell them.

Or was there?

He'd told the police that most of the holidaymakers were strangers, although one or two of the places had more regular visitors. Like the wooden hut tucked in the woods down by the wee fishing lochan.

He'd tried to rent the former shepherd's hut when he'd first come to Achmelvich, but had had no luck, so he'd stayed in the old caravan by the road until he'd got the cottage above the bay.

He was walking that way now. Meg liked to run in the nearby woods, and it made a change from the beach.

As he got closer he realized there was a van parked outside the hut with a blue double kayak on the roof. Somebody come to explore the coastline. He hoped they were aware it was a lot trickier here than further south near Arisaig.

As he watched from the edge of the wood, he saw a man emerge and take a look about.

Not keen to be spotted skulking nearby, he gave a low whistle to Meg and headed for home.

55

Loch Lomond

Day eight

She'd risen this morning knowing what she had to do about the T-shirt, especially after what the children had told her the previous evening.

It'd happened after her bodyguard had left and she'd fibbed to the children, telling them he was a fisherman and would bring her a share of his next catch.

How Orly had screwed up his face at that and said he preferred fish fingers. Lucy had agreed with him.

Francine wasn't a big fan of freshly caught fish herself, especially if it necessitated chopping off the head and gutting it, but she'd told them that Mr Thompson had promised to fillet the fish for her, ready for the frying pan.

At this point Orly and Lucy had exchanged glances, and she knew there was something they wanted to speak to her about. By the seriousness of their expressions, she'd realized that it was likely something to do with their father.

She'd listened in horror as Orly revealed that he'd seen his father go into Callie's blue van the night she'd disappeared.

'I saw Dad outside, walking about. Then he went over to Callie's van.' His voice had broken a little at that point.

Freaked, she'd not responded at first, her mind churning over what this might mean. Derek had certainly got into the habit of staying up late, drinking and growing more belligerent with every glass. He hadn't liked it when the girl, Callie, had turned down his invitation to sit with them.

Realizing the children were waiting for her to respond, she'd said, 'It would have been dark by then. How did you know it was your dad?'

'I just knew.' Orly looked worried that she didn't believe him.

Mustering herself, she'd asked if Orly had told Dr MacLeod this and he'd immediately nodded.

'And what did she say?' Francine had tried to keep her voice even, despite her thumping heart.

'She said she hoped we would be able to tell you about it ourselves.'

'So, now you have.' She'd tried to sound relieved and positive. 'The police will have spoken to Daddy and he'll have explained why he went in, if it was him,' she'd added.

'But they haven't found Callie yet. And there was blood.'

Orly's expression had made her reach out and hug him.

'Remember when you cut your finger with the bread knife and blood went everywhere? Callie probably did something like that, put a plaster on and went out for a night paddle.'

'But where did she go?' Lucy had said.

'I don't know,' she'd said honestly. 'But we have to hope she's all right, wherever she is.'

At that point the children had exchanged glances, and she'd realized there was more to come.

'What is it?' she'd urged, her anxiety beginning to mount again.

Lucy's response had made her stomach flip over. 'Daddy went to see the grave. I followed him.'

'But Daddy didn't know it was a grave,' she'd said then, her voice rising despite her efforts.

'There was a man there. Daddy was talking to him. That's why he didn't hear me calling.'

'Did you tell Dr MacLeod this?' she'd demanded.

'I told her I followed Daddy, but not about the man.'

'What did this man look like?'

'I don't know. He was too far away,' Lucy had said.

'Right,' she'd said, determined to bring this to an end. 'I'll be sure to let the police know about this man, although I'm certain he was just another camper like us,' she'd finished cheerily. 'Now, what about a board game? Marion said there are lots of them in the sideboard in the sitting room.'

Once she'd packed them off to bed, she'd sat down with a glass of wine and tried to work out what her response should be, and decided that she should write a note for DS Clark regarding what the children had told her. Plus send her the T-shirt with a note about finding it for Dr MacLeod.

She'd baulked at the thought of handling it again, remembering how keen Derek had been to locate it and how her suggestion that she bleach the fish blood stains out had pleased him so much.

But once she was rid of it, she would stop feeling so guilty.

The opportunity finally came late morning. The children were in the garden building a den with branches and a tarpaulin she'd found in the shed, when PC Thompson arrived at the door with his own parcel.

'Trout,' he'd told her with a smile. 'Filleted, of course.'

This time she invited him in and offered him a cup of tea.

He'd seemed reluctant to accept initially but finally agreed when she said she had something important to tell him.

She wasn't sure how much he knew about their background and why they were here, so she referred to them being on the campsite when the young kayaker Caillean Munro had disappeared.

At this point he gave a little nod as though he knew all about it, so she told him that she needed to send something important to DS Clark in Glasgow.

He'd assumed a serious expression at that and had suggested she bring it to the boathouse in half an hour. He would be changed and ready by then to make his report at the local station. They would deliver whatever it was to Glasgow for her.

With the T-shirt now safely wrapped up and addressed to DS Clark, with a note inside for Dr MacLeod, Francine allowed herself a sigh of relief.

She was doing the right thing. If Derek was innocent of harming Callie in any way, surely this would be the proof of that.

56

Glasgow

Day eight

She'd risen to find Holly already up and in the shower.

Rhona set to making the coffee, although with no fresh rolls or croissants, she had little in the way of food to offer. When Holly appeared, she suggested that she toast a couple of slices of the remaining loaf.

'Sorry. I usually have breakfast at the lab. Chrissy, my forensic assistant, brings filled rolls in for us.'

'Toast is fine,' Holly assured her.

Once showered herself, she returned to the kitchen to see Holly poring over her phone, the toast untouched on the plate beside her.

'Everything okay?' Rhona checked.

'Apart from messages from Charlie suggesting I come home now,' Holly told her. 'And we'll sort things out.' She looked despairingly at Rhona. 'He won't give up, you know. Men like Charlie never do.'

Rhona didn't try to dissuade her about that, because sadly she knew what Holly had said to be true. As did McNab, having tried his damnedest to put Bonar behind bars for his behaviour towards women, with no success up to now.

'You still okay to give your statement this morning?' she asked instead.

Holly nodded. 'I want to help Michael,' she said, reinforcing what she'd said last night.

'Well, if you're ready, I can drop you off at the station now.'

They drove in silence. Rhona could sense the fear emanating from Holly, but knew there was little she could do about it, except perhaps say that she had found herself in situations similar to this.

'What happened?' Holly said, her interest piqued.

'McNab saved me on more than one occasion. While putting himself in danger,' Rhona told her.

Holly looked round. 'He's like that, isn't he?' she said.

'Infuriatingly so,' Rhona said with a smile.

This small exchange appeared to bolster Holly, for afterwards the doubting expression was replaced by a determined look.

When they arrived at the police station, Rhona didn't leave until she saw Holly enter and approach the reception desk, hoping that whatever she said in her statement would save McNab's job and reputation.

After the overnight rain, Glasgow looked sparklingly fresh in the morning sunshine. Rhona contemplated returning the car to her parking spot at the flat, so that she might walk to the university through the park as usual, but noting the time, she decided to drive there instead. By now, Chrissy would have arrived with their breakfast and be keen for an update on anything she didn't already know about.

All of which Rhona found to be true with the addition of something more.

Chrissy, apparently unable to give voice to whatever news she had to impart, which was exceptional in itself, presented Rhona with the printed copy of an email she'd just received from Jen Mackie.

'Read it,' she managed, her eyes bright with excitement. 'Out loud,' she ordered.

Intrigued, Rhona did as asked.

'Subject to the material you sent me, and before my full report, I can confirm that the boots worn by Deirdre Reid contained biomarkers in their soles which did not come from the area where her body was discovered i.e. the machair near Arisaig.

'The same biomarkers were also identified from the samples taken from Eléa Martin's bare feet and boots, which suggests that Deirdre walked on the same ground as Eléa. Namely, the soil and vegetation to be found on the hill behind the bay where Eléa was discovered.'

'Does this mean that Deirdre was held somewhere near Achmelvich?'

Chrissy's question echoed Rhona's own unspoken one.

'But Eléa was killed shortly after she was abducted.' Chrissy was thinking out loud.

'Which means, unlike Deirdre, she wasn't kept prisoner,' Rhona said. 'Whoever took her killed her almost immediately – why, I wonder?'

'The police report says they believe she may have been driven up what they call the croft road, before being thrown over the cliff.'

'Maybe that wasn't the intention,' Rhona said. 'Maybe it was to hide her somewhere, but she managed to get away from them and tried to make her way down to the water.'

'But they caught up with her,' Chrissy added. 'Which changed the modus operandi.'

'I'll send this through to Bill, although the police up there reportedly checked out all the property in that area and found nothing untoward.'

'It'll all be Airbnb,' Chrissy said. 'Folk here today and gone tomorrow.'

'But rentals will be registered,' Rhona said.

'Only if they're officially rented out. There'll be second home owners too.'

It did feel like a breakthrough of sorts. If the killer or killers had a remote place on the west coast where they could hide their victims, then Callie might possibly still be alive somewhere.

Chrissy's hopeful expression suggested she might be nurturing a similar thought.

'I'll forward this to Bill,' Rhona said, sitting down at her desk. She wrote a covering email re. the strategy meeting later today and what might be discussed there, then sent it off.

As she did so, her mobile rang. Extracting it from her bag, Rhona saw McNab's name on the screen.

As she attempted a 'Good morning', he cut her off.

'Where is she?' he demanded. 'Where's Holly?'

Taken aback, Rhona explained that she'd delivered Holly to the station thirty minutes ago. 'I watched her walk in and up to the reception desk,' she said.

'You should have brought her in yourself,' he told her angrily.

'Why?' she said, puzzled. 'What's happened?'

'The guy on the desk said she left. Apparently, she changed her mind.'

'That can't be right,' Rhona said in surprise. 'She was adamant she wanted to give a statement.'

'Then she lied,' McNab said.

Rhona considered this. 'Or someone stopped her,' she told him. 'She was really worried about Bonar. He apparently sent messages overnight warning her that he had officers on the inside and that she wasn't to talk.'

'Well it worked.' McNab sounded exasperated.

'Wait,' said Rhona, suddenly remembering. 'Holly got me to record what she wanted to say in her statement last night,' she told him. 'I sent it on to Bill. My guess is she feared Bonar would try and stop her being interviewed, so that's why she recorded her statement in advance.'

McNab finally broke his stunned silence. 'And the boss definitely has this recording?'

'As do I,' Rhona assured him. 'Also, if she left the station it may have been because someone, Bonar's plant perhaps, approached her to get her to leave.'

'If you're right, someone may have spotted him,' McNab said, obviously buoyed up by this new development.

'Or *her*,' Rhona stressed. 'It could be a female officer. Remember, Bonar has a way with women.'

57

Day eight

So Holly hadn't let him down.

McNab allowed himself a few moments to savour that news, before he revisited his concerns as to what had frightened her enough to make her leave before giving her statement in person.

He'd already spoken, albeit briefly, to Sergeant Morris on duty at the front desk, so now headed back there.

'Any luck?' the officer said sympathetically on his return.

'Some,' McNab said. 'Did anyone speak to Miss Allan while she was in reception?'

'Apart from me, you mean?'

McNab tried to control his tongue at the silly question, and nodded instead.

'Not that I saw, Sarge.'

'Was she on her mobile?'

He shrugged. 'Who isn't nowadays? You only notice when they aren't.' He thought for a moment. 'She did ask where the Ladies were and I directed her there.'

'How long was she away for?' McNab asked.

The officer shook his head. 'Couldn't have been long.'

'Were there any female officers about when she was here?'

McNab was getting well pissed off by the painstaking expression Officer Morris adopted every time he asked him a question, but refrained with difficulty from saying so.

Eventually he got an answer.

'There was, in fact. Came in briefly, then exited again as though she'd forgotten something.'

'Name, rank?' McNab queried.

'No idea, Sarge. It was over in a second. I was on the phone at the time.' Now Officer Morris was the one sounding peeved.

As the phone rang on cue, McNab abandoned his interrogation and, taking advantage of the nearby coffee machine, purchased a double espresso for himself and a latte for Janice.

He found her keenly awaiting his return, but it wasn't because of the coffee.

'So?' she said, accepting it nonetheless.

'She stayed ten minutes, checked her phone and went to the Ladies. One female PO came in while Holly was there, then retreated, swiftly it seems,' McNab told her.

'Description?'

'Officer Morris couldn't say.'

'What about security cameras? Might they have picked up anything while Holly was in reception?'

McNab was running something through in his head and didn't answer.

'What are you thinking?' Janice demanded.

'If it was a female officer that put the frighteners on Holly, where would she do that?'

Janice's eyes lit up. 'If it were me, I'd choose the Ladies. No security cameras in there.'

'Exactly,' McNab said. 'But there is one in the corridor outside.'

Janice glanced at her watch. 'You're due in there now. Go, I'll check on the camera. And good luck.'

McNab rose, swallowing the final drops of his coffee, then braced himself and, with a nod to Janice, headed for the lion's den.

If he'd entered prior to his chat with Rhona, things would have been a great deal worse. He understood that. Nevertheless, he would be required to redeem himself in the eyes of someone he both respected and admired. Not an easy task, especially when he'd created the mess in the first place.

Had Holly not turned out to be the person she was, his career might well have come to an end at this moment. McNab reminded himself of that on entry.

The boss had earphones on and was listening intently to something. Eventually he took off the headset and focused his gaze on McNab.

'Miss Allan is here and ready to give her statement?'

'She was here, sir. She stayed at Dr MacLeod's place last night and Rhona, Dr MacLeod, brought her to the station this morning.'

'And?' DI Wilson's expression was becoming concerned.

'We believe it's likely that someone, an officer under the influence of Charlie Bonar, scared her off, sir.' He continued, keen to get his story out. 'Dr MacLeod thinks Holly expected that might happen and that's why she asked Rhona – Dr MacLeod – to record her statement last night, which was sent on to you, I believe, sir.'

DI Wilson considered this turn of events. 'You think she encountered this officer here in the station, this morning?'

'It's a possibility, sir. And, as Dr MacLeod rightly pointed out, it's just as likely to be a female officer as a male.'

'Before we discuss the reason for Miss Allan's sudden

change of mind, Detective Sergeant, I am given to understand that you tracked Holly Allan to the home of Charles Bonar, who you recently gave evidence against in court. Were you aware it was his place when you went there alone?'

McNab thought about prevaricating, then decided the question was being asked because the boss already knew the answer.

'I was aware of that, sir, but knowing what had gone down in that house previously, I was very concerned for Miss Allan's safety.'

DI Wilson assumed the ghost of a smile, or at least that's what McNab hoped it was.

'So, your bête noire took umbrage at your desire to have him put away and decided it should be the other way round.'

It wasn't a question but McNab decided to answer as though it was.

'I believe so, sir.'

'And your witness confirms this via her recorded statement, which I've just listened to. Of course, she could also be lying, Sergeant.' He paused there, while observing McNab closely. 'However, I believe she is telling the truth. I also do not consider you capable of what that doctored video suggested.'

The relief McNab felt at such a declaration cleansed his soul.

'So we proceed as planned. I am increasingly convinced we have one or more rogue officers involved in this, as Miss Allan implies. And perhaps also in the stick man case, which I believe you've been brought up to date with regarding the online developments?' When McNab nodded, he continued. 'DCI Sutherland has given orders that any further discussion should be on a need-to-know basis only. Understood, Detective Sergeant?'

'Understood, sir.'

'Therefore the strategy meeting this afternoon will be a closed-shop affair, for security purposes. We'll meet at two p.m. in the small conference room.' He paused for a moment. 'As for Miss Allan, I am concerned, as you must be, for her safety. However, I want you and DS Clark to concentrate on the stick man case. I will be the one to deal with Charles Bonar.'

McNab wanted to know exactly what his superior officer had in mind, but decided by the boss's expression it was wiser not to ask.

Janice barely waited until he'd sat down at his desk before she threw him a questioning look. McNab gave her an almost imperceptible nod, aware that her eyes weren't the only ones in the room that were fastened upon him.

Even now he was running the sequence of fellow officers through his head, wondering if any of them might be the plant in the room. Three women and twelve men, the same make-up as the jury that had let Bonar walk free.

How many did he really know? There were newbies in here he definitely didn't. Long-term players he'd worked with over years. How many of them disliked or even hated him?

Who knew?

He motioned to Janice and, getting up from his chair, indicated they were off out on a job.

Without asking where or what, she followed him. Neither spoke until they were outside and in their vehicle.

'So, what the hell happened in there?' Janice demanded.

McNab gave her a brief résumé of all he'd learnt. 'How

did you get on with the security camera outside the Ladies?' he asked.

'I had to lodge an official request to see this morning's recording. Not sure when that'll happen.' Janice looked suitably pissed off.

'We've been taken off anything to do with Holly and Bonar,' he told her. 'Stick man case only.'

'You did mention the female officer and the toilets?' Janice demanded.

'Of course. The boss is putting someone else on that,' McNab said, still trying to resign himself to what felt like abandoning Holly. 'Plus he's dealing with Bonar himself.'

'He'll bring him in?' Janice looked pleased about that.

'I suspect so. There's enough on that recording to make that possible. Although locating Holly and having her give a proper statement is still needed.'

Janice threw him a sympathetic look, before saying, 'I tried calling Francine Henderson earlier to arrange a time to speak to her and the children again. The number came up as not available.' Her look was one of concern. 'I was about to contact the nearest police station to ask that someone check in on them.'

In that moment McNab made up his mind and started up the car. 'We'll go see them ourselves. It's not far and we have time before the strategy meeting.'

'You want to go to Loch Lomond? I thought you hated the countryside?'

'I'll manage to thole it for a couple of hours,' McNab told her, while all the time thinking that looking for Holly was what he really wanted to do.

58

Achmelvich

Day eight

Even working on his potato patch didn't settle him, despite the pleasing sight of the burgeoning growth, promising a good crop.

Trevor began to wonder if living so close to the beach where he'd found the body, and within view of the clifftop where she'd lost her life, had tainted this place for him, perhaps forever.

Except she hadn't *lost* her life, he reminded himself. Eléa Martin had been murdered.

Not for the first time did he wish he hadn't walked on the beach that day. That he hadn't been the one to find her. Except . . . she might have lain there a long time and the police had said that discovering her so soon had made it easier for the forensic people to work out what had happened to her.

He began to consider if he should pay homage to the French girl. Perhaps build a cairn on the hilltop to her memory. He wondered if her family might visit this place to see where she'd died.

If they did, might it be better for them to find a mark of respect for Eléa here?

Or maybe it would be just for him to lay her ghost to rest.

According to Esther, the police believed Eléa's killer had also murdered the woman found buried in the machair near Arisaig and had likely abducted the young woman from a neighbouring campsite.

'They haven't found her yet,' she'd told him, shaking her head, 'probably because she's already dead and buried, along the NC500 somewhere. Let's face it, there's plenty of places there where no one will ever find her.'

By the time he reached the road, Meg had run ahead, thinking that they were making for the woods near the lochan.

The van with the kayak had disappeared from outside the shepherd's hut, so he decided it would be okay to follow the dog.

As he approached the little wooden structure, he wished, yet again, that he'd managed to rent the old hut, especially now, after what had happened. If he'd been living here, he reasoned, out of sight of the headland, he might have been able to put what had happened there to the back of his mind.

Meg, having run ahead, was now circling the cabin, as though following an enticing trail . . . Of what, he wondered?

Standing next to the open front porch, he decided to sit on the steps and take in the view while Meg followed her nose.

As he sat there, he made up his mind. He would gather stones from the foot of the cliff tomorrow and he would build a small cairn on the clifftop and put a plaque on it. On the plaque he would simply mark her name. Eléa.

Pleased with that thought, he rose to go and whistled for Meg, who presently appeared from round the side of the hut with something in her mouth.

'Drop that, Meg,' he ordered.

Even as he watched the object fall, he knew what it was and his heart lurched into his mouth.

He'd seen a stick doll like this in the sand close to Eléa's head on the beach. Back then, he hadn't examined it closely, but he remembered the gouged mouth and the body fashioned with twigs.

When he'd returned to the beach after Eléa had been taken away, everything on and around her body had also disappeared, including the net and buoys and the strange stick man. So the police must have thought it important.

Now here was another one, just like it, in a place not far from where Eléa had died.

He would, he realized, have to report this. Go to the police station and hand it in.

He glanced at the shepherd's hut, seeing it now as a bad place. Esther had said the first victim had been kept alive for a month before she was killed.

Did Eléa's killer have the same plan for her? And was it to incarcerate her here in the shepherd's hut by the lochan?

He stood for a moment, recalling the black van with the blue kayak recently parked outside, and a dreadful thought struck him.

There was still a girl missing. The one from the shore campsite at Arisaig. Might she be here?

He considered what to do next. He could perhaps force his way into the hut and the outbuildings. But that would be breaking the law, and he didn't want to do that.

As he stood thinking, the rain clouds that had been

threatening the western horizon arrived to pepper the surface of the loch.

Meg had already made her decision and was off, heading for home.

He decided to do the same. He would call the police station, identify himself as the man who'd discovered the French girl's body, and explain about the stick man he'd found at the shepherd's hut.

59

Loch Lomond

Day eight

They were winding their way up the side of the loch, with an occasional glimpse of water through the trees.

McNab had a vague memory of being taken to Balloch as a child by his mum. He hadn't liked being out of the city, although he remembered that she had.

It was weird, he thought, his dislike for the countryside, because as a boy he'd played in all the big parks that Glasgow was so famous for. But then, the image of the comforting city skyline had never been far away.

Unlike here.

'Are we nearly there?' he heard himself say.

Janice made a noise that sounded like exasperation. 'We are. Next entry on your right.'

It had taken longer to get here than he'd imagined, mainly because he'd got stuck behind a huge residential caravan being towed on a trailer to somewhere up the lochside.

McNab, irritated beyond belief, had been convinced that it was too big to be transported in such a manner, and was all for stopping the driver and challenging him on that.

Janice, ever the peacemaker, forbade him from doing such a thing.

Now turning into the track which supposedly led to wherever Francine and her children were staying, he was suddenly reminded of accompanying Rhona down a similar track, leading to her cottage overlooking the Sound of Sleat on Skye. Back then he'd been on his motorbike, with Rhona riding pillion.

When he'd seen how isolated her family cottage was, he'd been freaked. She, on the other hand, had extolled all its virtues, despite the nearest shop and, worst still, the pub being miles away.

Why anyone thought it better to live or even holiday in the wilderness was lost on him, and he said so.

'How is this safer? She'd have been better hidden in Glasgow,' he announced as he drew up outside a chalet-type building overlooking the loch.

'It belongs to a friend of Francine's,' Janice told him. 'Derek Henderson knows nothing about it.'

McNab grunted his continued disapproval as they got out of the vehicle. Janice was now checking her mobile.

'There's definitely a signal here,' she said.

'So how come you couldn't get her?' McNab said.

Janice didn't respond. Just headed down the short path to the front door. While she knocked, McNab took himself round the house to discover a wooden deck, a small beach and, of course, the grey-blue waters of the loch stretching out in front of him.

It looked as though the kids had been playing out here. There was evidence of a stone dam being built on the sand and, over towards the trees, a wigwam-shaped den made with fallen branches.

Seeing that, he briefly mused that for the kids maybe being here wasn't so bad after all.

At that moment the glass door to the deck was opened and Janice appeared, looking worried.

'They're not here, although Francine's car's round the side and the place wasn't locked up.'

'The kids have been playing by the loch,' he told her. 'Maybe they went for a walk. There's a path along the shoreline.'

Janice came out onto the deck and looked down at the dam on the beach, then where he'd pointed out the path.

'What's that further along through the trees?' she said.

'A boathouse maybe?' He peered down the path. 'And possibly a jetty. Maybe they're along there.'

Janice immediately set off in that direction, McNab following. The path wound through gorse bushes, eventually depositing them on a gravel beach next to a concrete jetty with a neat boathouse nearby.

McNab checked the double doors, but they were padlocked shut. Peering through the window, he saw that it was empty.

'There must be a way to drive in here, for when the boathouse is in use,' he said. 'I'll take a look round the back.'

The dirt entrance road was there all right and had obviously been used recently from the tracks cut into the surface, still wet after last night's rain.

Janice had followed him round.

'Looks like a vehicle and maybe a boat trailer have been here today,' he told her.

They walked back to the house in silence, although McNab could feel the wave of disquiet emanating from his partner, which he was now beginning to share.

If the family had gone for a walk so far from the house, why leave the door unlocked? McNab couldn't imagine Francine Henderson doing that. Not after everything that had happened to her family recently.

'Are there any neighbours in the other direction?' he said. 'With the tree cover, it's difficult to tell.'

'We didn't pass an entrance near to this one,' Janice told him. 'I was watching the road for the sign to this place.'

They were passing the children's den when McNab heard the crack of a twig nearby. Coming to a halt, he motioned to Janice to do the same, putting his finger to his lips, then pointing to the wigwam structure.

Someone was in that den, and most likely it would be the two children.

Janice obviously thought the same for she immediately called out their names and introduced herself.

'We met when you came to speak to Dr MacLeod. I chatted to your mum, Francine, while you were in with Rhona. Rhona said you were planning to swim together at Arisaig, but your dad wouldn't let you.'

The occupants of the den were heard to whisper to one another before the boy's head popped out.

'Hello, Orly,' Janice said. 'I'm Detective Sergeant Clark and this is my partner, Detective Sergeant McNab. We're here to see your mummy.'

While she'd been talking, Orly had emerged fully and stood up, his wee sister following him.

'Mummy went to see the fisherman, she told us to wait here,' Orly said.

'What fisherman?' Janice said gently.

'The one with the red boat.' He pointed along the shore-line. 'He keeps it at the jetty.'

'He isn't really a fisherman,' Lucy said in her usual forthright manner. 'He's a policeman sent here to protect us.'

'A policeman?' McNab looked to Janice, who shook her head, indicating she had no knowledge of this.

'Why do you say that?' Janice asked quietly.

'I heard him talking to Mummy at the door,' Lucy told her. 'He showed her his badge.'

'Shall we go into the kitchen and wait there for Mummy?' Janice suggested. 'And you can tell me all about this policeman.' She threw McNab a worried glance.

McNab listened to the expanded tale which now included a parcel Francine had apparently taken to the man at the boathouse, then, his concern continuing to mount by the minute, he went outside to call the station and check with the boss about this supposed policeman calling himself PC Thompson.

When he eventually got through, he explained about going to check on Mrs Henderson, since DS Clark hadn't been able to reach her by phone, to request she and the children come back in for a further interview.

'We found the kids here alone, sir, with a story about a PC Thompson, who was supposedly guarding them. They said their mum went to see him and hasn't come back.'

'No officer has been given that duty, Sergeant. How long has Mrs Henderson been gone?'

'A couple of hours, I think, sir. According to the girl, her mum had made up a parcel addressed to DS Clark. The man was going to take it to the nearest police station for delivery to us in Glasgow.'

McNab heard the boss mutter an expletive under his breath. For a man not known for cursing it was indicative of how serious this might be.

'You've checked the surrounding area?'

'The immediate area, yes. There's no sign of Mrs Henderson and her car's here. Her mobile also appears dead, sir.'

'I'll alert the nearest station at Helensburgh. When someone arrives from there, come back and bring the children with you. Their father will have to be contacted.'

'Derek Henderson still has questions to answer, sir.'

'Then we'll get him in here to answer them. Perhaps his wife's disappearance will encourage that.'

When McNab returned to the kitchen, the children were having juice and biscuits. There was also the smell of coffee on the go.

Janice poured him a mug and indicated that they should step outside.

'There was no one guarding them,' he told Janice, once out of earshot.

'Well it looks like there should have been,' she said angrily.

'How the fuck did they, whoever *they* are, know she and the kids were here?' McNab said.

'Because we have a rogue cop in our midst,' Janice said. 'Or more than one. That's pretty well confirmed.'

'The kid said her mother wanted to send you a parcel. Looks like whatever was in there was incriminating to someone.'

'Lucy said something else while you were out,' Janice told him. 'Something she hadn't told us up to now. She said her dad was talking to a man at the grave. That's why he didn't hear her. And she thought the man might be staying in an old caravan next to the campsite.'

60

Glasgow

Day eight

There were two soil maps on display on the big screen, side by side.

The first featured the landscape north of Arisaig. The second, the area around Achmelvich.

Rhona had no intention of doing Jen's job by describing in detail the individual soil types of each area where the two bodies were found. The team were only interested in why they were so important.

There were just ten officers in the committee room, including McNab, Janice, Bill Wilson and DCI Sutherland. Magnus had also been summoned. The rest, she assumed, had been selected by Bill.

Her job here today was to explain in simple terms to the smaller assembled group why she and Dr Mackie both believed that the two victims had trodden the same ground.

'Wheel tyres, as you all know, provide material indicating where that vehicle has been,' she began. 'In this case, the ribbed soles of the wetsuit boots worn by both victims have provided material which tells a similar story.'

She continued. 'Eléa, we believe, was abducted from her tent at Achmelvich. Probably taken by car up what is called the croft road. She may have escaped her abductor and run down through the vegetation, possibly trying to reach the sea. She was, we know, a strong swimmer and perhaps thought to escape that way. However, in the poor light she ended up on the clifftop, where she fought her attacker and was strangled then pushed to her death below.'

Rhona paused, conscious of all eyes, mainly male, upon her, reading the intensity of their expressions, sensing that many of them were currently visualizing exactly what she was describing. The female faces were different, as though reliving the trauma of the victim, or perhaps an uncomfortable memory of their own.

Every female knew or had heard of someone who'd been raped, or sexually assaulted, or simply coerced into doing something they didn't want to do, by someone stronger than themselves. For a brief moment, she herself was back running through that long black tunnel, her breath rasping through her throat, her heart pounding. Fear stabbing at her again.

Noting the concerned expressions at her silence, Rhona mustered herself before continuing. 'Deirdre Reid was incarcerated somewhere for up to a month before she was moved to an Arisaig beach, then strangled and buried. A detailed examination of her boots showed that she too had walked or been led over vegetation and soil similar to that found at Achmelvich.

'So, there is forensic soil evidence to suggest that Deirdre, having been abducted in Glasgow, with no sightings of her after that, may have been held for a time in the Achmelvich area.'

McNab spoke after her, bringing up a string of images supplied by Ollie. Beginning with one showing an enhanced CCTV clip of what looked like the apparent abduction of a blonde female on the student strip around the time of Deirdre Reid's disappearance.

That was difficult enough to view, but what followed was even worse, Rhona thought.

This was the incel website and its associated stick men figures, including the torrent of abuse unleashed against women, or witches, as they were referred to. Then worst of all. The fabricated image of one such figure of hate, a lone, bound and terrified female in a place of imprisonment, together with one of a similar female, lying broken on the sand below a towering cliff.

That final image, Rhona thought, demonstrated by its very existence that someone who was aware of the circumstances of Eléa's death was connected with the site and possibly too with the police force.

Magnus came in then, giving his thoughts on both the online material they'd just viewed and his belief that more than one perpetrator was involved in the crimes.

'I should stress that the killers may never have met in person, but nevertheless they share the same attitude to women, in particular to the women they choose as their victims. They follow the same modus operandi, as far as that is possible, and use the same signature, i.e. the stick man figure anointed after death with the victim's blood. I have come to believe that the wetsuit worn by each victim may also be a part of that signature, as is the repeated throttling, when that proves possible. Both throttling and rubber encasement of the victim being sexual.'

Bill spoke directly after that, revealing that he'd just

received a call from Lochinver police regarding the discovery of another stick man.

'It was found close to what's known as the shepherd's hut, not far from the east bay where Eléa Martin's body was discovered.' He paused as a ripple of voices reacted to this news.

'The finder was Trevor Wills, or at least his dog, Meg. He recognized the significance of the object because he had seen one like it in the sand next to Eléa Martin's body. Wills was the man who alerted the coastguard.'

Rhona watched as the implication of this swept through the assembled group.

'A team has been dispatched to Achmelvich to check out the hut. I have also decided to announce the importance of the stick man motif to the general public. We'll get a lot of crank calls no doubt, but if Trevor Wills hadn't linked his find to Eléa's death, he wouldn't have supplied us with this lead.'

Rhona was pleased to hear this. They were way past fears of copycat killings, and the release of such information to the general public would hopefully cause problems for the perpetrators.

McNab came in again at this point.

He made no mention of Holly or Charles Bonar, but spoke of the recent disappearance of Francine Henderson from her holiday cottage at Loch Lomondside. He spoke of a man who'd identified himself as a PC Thompson.

'This bogus officer apparently possessed identification which Mrs Henderson accepted as valid. We understand that she had taken him a parcel addressed to my partner, DS Clark. This parcel may have contained evidence relating to Callie Munro's disappearance.'

The increasing ripples of unease grew until DI Wilson came back in to silence them.

'The two children are with us and will be interviewed later this afternoon. We hope to know more about this man after we speak to them. Right, let's all get back to work.'

At this point Magnus caught Rhona's eye, indicating he'd like to speak to her. As he came over, Bill joined them.

'I take it you're both happy to stay around? The kids are in the family room, getting something to eat. We'll need you two after the social services have finished chatting to them.'

'Those poor kids,' Rhona said. 'Have you informed their father?'

'We're trying to reach him, but with no success so far. I have a feeling the missing piece of the puzzle regarding their father and Callie Munro may about to be put in place.'

'D'you want to head for the canteen and a decent coffee?' Rhona suggested when Bill had departed.

'Good idea,' Magnus said. 'You can fill me in on anything I didn't learn in the meeting.'

As they emerged from the conference room a few pairs of eyes registered that they'd been party to the closed-shop gathering.

'They'll all be suspicious of one another,' Rhona said in concern as they headed for the canteen.

'Psychologically demoralizing,' Magnus agreed, 'but I assume word is out already regarding McNab being set up by Bonar?'

'I would suspect so.'

'Then most officers will be with DI Wilson on this. No one wants a rogue policeman in their midst. Nor do they want to be accused of leaking information. So the less they know, the safer they feel.'

While Magnus elected to join the queue at the counter, Rhona found them an isolated table where they might talk freely. Checking her mobile, she found a missed call from an unknown number together with a voicemail message. She decided to listen to it.

Holly's voice was faint and a little breathless against the background rumble of traffic.

'I'm in London, staying with a friend. I'm happy to give a written statement to the Met police if it can be arranged. DI Wilson can reach me on this number. And thank you again for your help and advice.'

Rhona felt her heart lift, hoping this meant that Bonar couldn't get to Holly now.

'What is it?' Magnus said when he saw her smiling face.

Rhona told him.

'That is good news.'

He presented her with her coffee and an iced doughnut. 'A sugar rush is required after today's developments.'

Rhona agreed. 'So how do you want to proceed with the children?'

'I'm happy for you to chat to them. I'll watch from next door. Introducing me now may be counterproductive, initially at least.' Magnus thought for a moment. 'I suspected you weren't given the whole story the last time they were in, as we discussed. Since then, their mother has disappeared. They were, I believe, trying to protect her in what they said back then. Now the worst has happened. She's been taken from them. And by someone they thought was there to protect them.'

What had happened was terrible, especially when Magnus put it into words like that.

'Okay,' Rhona said. 'But I'm not a psychologist. I'm unsure of my ground here.'

'Do what you did before. That worked. Encourage them to tell you everything they remember about their stay at the cottage and about the fisherman. Then just listen. That's what psychologists do all the time,' Magnus told her.

Rhona didn't want to voice her fears as to what would be done with the children after they'd given their evidence. With their father not available, where would they go?

Perhaps sensing this, Magnus said, 'Social services will place them with short-term foster carers until they locate a willing relative or perhaps a family friend. This Marion who owns the Loch Lomond cottage would likely be a good place to start.'

In the short time she'd known the family, Rhona hadn't heard a mention of grandparents or any other family member. Derek Henderson, she thought, had appeared to be a man who liked to keep his wife and family on a tight leash. One that he held.

That had been painfully obvious at their one and only encounter in Arisaig.

61

Day eight

The van had stopped. The sudden screech to a halt had thrown her against the side, and her head had met the metal with a sharpness that had brought stars to her eyes.

She'd listened as her abductor had decoupled the red boat trailer. After which she heard him climb back in and they moved off again. This time without the rattle of the boat behind them.

How far had they come from the loch before he'd got rid of the trailer?

She realized she had no real idea. Closing her eyes, she tried to recall exactly what had happened before she'd passed out.

The smiling police officer who'd come to her front door to reassure her had suddenly metamorphosed into something else entirely on her delivery of the parcel to the boathouse.

He didn't even have to check what it contained, because she'd basically told him. She could still hear her voice as she said it.

'It's a T-shirt belonging to my husband with blood on it. He was wearing it at Arisaig when the girl Callie disappeared. I should have handed it in before, but . . .'

She'd tailed off then as she'd watched his face change.

They'd been standing next to the loaded trailer, coupled to his vehicle, and she'd been wondering why he should be towing the boat when he was only visiting the local police station to report in and deliver the parcel.

The blow, when it came, had knocked her out. She had come to here in the back of his van some time later.

What a fool she had been. She couldn't believe her own stupidity. One call. Just one call to DS Clark and she would have known he was an imposter.

Why had she not done that?

Too many years living with Derek had stripped her of the confidence that anything she did or even thought was sensible. She was regarded as a failure in thought and deed. A failure as a woman, a mother, a sexual partner . . .

And she had been.

The woman he'd apparently cherished when they'd first met had been placed in a glass case. And that glass case had continued to get smaller, until her limbs, her body, her brain had to be twisted and squashed to fit.

Anger rose up in her, filling her chest, attacking her limbs, so that she scrabbled and fought against her restraints until, eventually exhausted by the effort, she stopped and lay back gasping against the metal side of the van.

There was a smell in here. A smell she didn't want to identify. Sweat, urine, even blood maybe. Concentrating on it now, she felt her body begin to shake. Whatever had happened in here was about to happen to her.

And what about Orly and Lucy? All alone in that house. Why had she taken them there to that out-of-the-way place? She should have asked to stay with Marion.

DS Clark will try and check in with me. When she can't reach me, she'll go there. Please God, she'll go to the house.

She had to believe that to be true.

But what if Derek got there first and took the children? She would never see them again. He would make sure of that.

Her brain took off in a mad dance of what, why and how.

How had the man pretending to be a policeman known where she was?

Why was he looking for her in the first place? Had Derek put him up to it? She'd thought Derek didn't know about Marion's holiday cottage, but Derek made a point of knowing everything about her and the few friends she had. At least, the ones he allowed her to have.

She knew Derek would hate that she'd gone away. Disappeared. Would also be furious to discover she'd allowed the children to be interviewed by the police. Even madder when he was interviewed himself. That would be her fault. Always her fault.

And now the T-shirt with blood on it. Her letter to DS Clark. Her note for Dr MacLeod. Her abductor had seen them all and they'd changed him into a madman.

Why was that? How did Derek's behaviour at the campsite impact on this man?

The answer was there, of course. Had been from the moment he attacked her.

The man driving the van was somehow implicated in Callie's disappearance, and probably the other murders. Did that mean Derek was also involved?

What was it Orly and Lucy had tried so hard to tell her?

That Derek had gone into Callie's van. That Lucy had tried to follow her father to the gravesite. That he'd met and talked to a man there.

Who was that man?

Could it be the same man who'd pretended to be a policeman, who'd bound her and thrown her into this van?

But Derek wouldn't allow such a thing to happen. Would he?

She realized at that moment, if she proved to be a threat to Derek in any way, he would react very badly to that. She had been safe only for as long as she let him do what he liked, whenever he liked, with his life and with hers.

She thought about all those weekends away with the boys, supposedly fishing. Fishing for what? Young female campers like Callie?

The thought made her nauseated. She couldn't be sick. Not here.

With a will she didn't know she possessed, Francine forced herself to breathe more slowly.

Whatever she had to do to survive, she would do it. Not just for her, but for her children.

62

Glasgow

Day eight

Rhona stood for a moment outside the door of the family room, marshalling herself.

The last time she'd spoken with the children, their mother had been in the neighbouring room and their concern for her had been at the forefront of everything they'd said or didn't say.

They hadn't wanted to tell their mummy something that would make her cry. So they'd held it to themselves, so closely that for a while Lucy had lost either the will or the ability to speak.

'But Lucy chose to speak to you. She trusts you and so does her brother,' Magnus had reminded her when he'd left her at the door. 'Let them tell you everything they need to say.'

They were sitting together on the settee, Orly holding Lucy's hand. Both had been crying, the tears staining their cheeks.

The sight of them brought tears to her own eyes, plus the guilty feeling that if she and the rest of the team had been more aware of the danger to Francine and her children, this would never have happened. Having seen Bill's concern this morning, she knew he felt the same.

Rhona moved her own chair closer to the children and put her hands on theirs. She said nothing, just tried to show by her touch and her eyes how she felt.

Eventually Orly spoke. He told her that his dad had gone into Callie's van, then came out again and walked away in the direction of the old caravan, but he couldn't see him after that.

Lucy told her that her dad had met a man at the grave and spoken to him. After that he'd jumped the fence and come back through the field. She'd sat down, because she thought her daddy didn't want her following him. 'He was angry with me.'

'The fisherman at the loch . . .' Rhona began.

'He had a red boat. He waved at us and we waved back. He came to speak to Mummy. She went to the door. She said he'd offered us fish he'd caught.' Orly grimaced. 'I don't like real fish. Only fish fingers.'

Lucy nodded her agreement. 'I watched him from the window. He showed her his badge and told her he was PC Thompson and was there to protect us. Mummy believed him.'

'She didn't tell us that because she thought it would scare us,' Orly added. 'But we were pleased that you had sent us a policeman.'

Rhona's stomach flipped over at that. 'Can you describe the man?'

'He was like a soldier,' Lucy said.

'Why a soldier?' Rhona tried.

'He had big muscles in his arms,' Lucy told her.

They talked some more, about hiding in the wigwam when they heard McNab's car arrive. Then coming out when Janice had spoken to them.

'I thought Mummy was coming back,' Lucy said. 'She said she would.'

'I think she's trying,' Rhona found herself saying. 'And we're going to help her do that.'

'You promise?' Lucy said.

'I promise.'

When Magnus appeared at the door, Rhona introduced him. 'This is my friend Magnus.'

'Is he a policeman?' Lucy asked.

'No,' Magnus said. 'I just help the police sometimes.'

'Like Rhona?'

Magnus smiled. 'Yes, like Rhona. Can I ask you a question about the man who pretended to be a policeman?'

'Okay,' Orly said, after checking with Lucy.

'Could you help me make a picture of him on the computer?'

Orly's eyes lit up. 'Like a character in a computer game?'

'Yes.'

'You can choose his muscles,' Orly said to Lucy, who was looking equally keen.

'Okay, one more question before we do that,' Magnus said. 'Did you ever visit the boathouse?'

The two children observed one another before Orly replied. 'We did explore there, but we weren't supposed to leave the garden. Mummy told us not to.'

'That's okay. Did you see the man's car at the boathouse?'

'It was a van,' Lucy said, 'with a trailer.'

'Colour?' Magnus tried.

'Easy,' Lucy said. 'Black.'

'Number?'

Orly rattled off a plate number.

'It's a game with him,' Lucy said apologetically. 'It annoys Daddy, so he had to stop doing it.'

Magnus met Rhona's eye. 'Do you ever get it wrong, Orly?'

'Sometimes I mix up the letters,' he admitted.

'Okay, shall we have a go now at putting a face to the man who owns the van?'

'Yes,' the children chorused as Magnus produced his laptop. As they settled there, the faces eager to 'help' as they saw it, Rhona took her leave and went next door to where McNab and Janice had been watching.

'Traffic are already checking on versions of the number plate,' Janice said.

'How did he think to ask the boy that?' McNab said, obviously impressed.

'We spoke about Orly before I went in. Lucy, as you know, is the talker generally. Orly, Magnus sees as quite withdrawn, very serious, perhaps on the autistic spectrum. He'd already decided to get them to make up the face of the man, which would be more fun than trying to describe him. The possible van description, I believe, was a lucky shot in the dark, especially the number plate.' She paused. 'I have a feeling he'll show them images of vans to see if he can find a make and model too.'

She took out her mobile and, dialling her voicemail, handed it to McNab.

'Jesus, not again?' he said in horror.

'Take a listen,' she told him.

McNab accepted the mobile and walked out into the hall.

'What is it?' Janice said.

'A message from Holly. She's in London, staying with a friend. She wants to give her statement in person to the Met. She gave me her new number, although I suspect she really intended it for McNab.'

63

Achmelvich

Day eight

Trevor watched as the two police vehicles wound their way up the croft road. He was nervous and Meg, sensing this, pushed her nose into his palm to reassure him.

The police had asked to meet him at the old caravan and walk them to the place where he'd found the stick man. He still had it in his possession although he'd kept it outside the cottage in a plastic bag, not wishing to bring such a symbol of death into the house.

He'd imagined he could feel its power as he'd walked home to call the police on the landline, and was desperate to discard it from his pocket as soon as possible. By then he'd been so jumpy, he'd had difficulty speaking coherently to the person answering his call.

At first he'd babbled, so that they thought he was in shock and had been involved in an accident. The woman encouraged him in a calm voice and eventually he'd managed to tell her he was the man who'd found the French girl's body.

'Mr Wills,' she'd said then. 'What's happened?'

He'd explained about seeing the stick man in the sand beside the girl, and then finding one the same near the old shepherd's hut.

Not being from Achmelvich, she didn't know where he spoke of, but when he told her it wasn't far from the cliffs where the girl had died, she'd immediately passed the phone to a sergeant who told him he'd done the right thing in calling them and that they would be up with officers to search the area.

And here they were, coming up the hill.

'Right, Meg. Let's go meet them.'

There had been a heavy shower in the time since he'd come back to the cottage, but the rain clouds had now moved out to sea.

Underfoot the grass was wet and he could feel it brush his trousers, dampening them. It made him think again about that poor lassie running down the very hill he was climbing, desperate to escape her abductor.

The thought made him sick, because it was always followed by the image of her broken body on the beach.

He reached the road just as the first car pulled into the passing place. A burly police officer stepped out and came towards him, holding out his hand.

'Trevor Wills. Sergeant Marshall. Thanks for calling us. Do you have the stick man object you found?'

Trevor handed over the bag, glad to be rid of it.

After a brief look, the sergeant put it inside an evidence bag and stowed it in the vehicle.

'I assume you handled it?' he asked.

Trevor felt a shiver of fear. 'The dog brought it to me. I realized what it was and put it in my pocket.'

'No worries, Mr Wills. Forensics will be examining it, so

we'll need a DNA sample from you, so as to eliminate you from any findings.'

His answer didn't make Trevor feel any better. He was beginning to question why he'd called the police at all and Sergeant Marshall's scrutinizing look wasn't improving things.

'Right, can you lead us to the place your dog found it?'

He might be freaked by the proceedings, but it looked as though Meg was enjoying herself. She took off, instinct telling her they were heading back to the wee loch, the shepherd's hut and the surrounding woods, a favourite walk of hers, made even better by the four extra humans and a police dog.

Trevor, his stomach still turning somersaults, remained silent until he reached the steps leading to the porch, then said, 'I was sitting here looking at the loch when Meg appeared beside me with . . . the thing in her mouth. She'd been excited by a scent as we approached the hut. I thought she'd caught the smell of a vole. There's a hole in the bank there.'

Even as he spoke, Meg had made off again round the side of the hut, disappearing into a clump of gorse. After which, Sergeant Marshall nodded at the handler, who released the dog and followed it through the bushes.

'Are there any outhouses, sheds to this place?' the sergeant asked Trevor.

'One, I think, at the back, but the area's pretty overgrown and I normally don't go there.'

A shout and much barking suggested something might have been found. The sergeant ordered Trevor to stay where he was and set off through the bushes with the other two officers.

Trevor whistled on Meg, not wanting her to be near whatever it was they'd located. He was already painting a picture in his head of what any outhouse might contain.

Adding another image to his already horrific nightmares.

64

Glasgow

Day eight

McNab replayed Holly's voicemail three times.

He'd been nursing the terrible thought that she might be back in Bonar's hands or in the hands of the rogue cop or cops he was undoubtedly in league with.

Noting she'd included her new mobile number, he entered it in his own list.

There was so much he wanted to check with her, including asking whether anyone had approached her or behaved suspiciously while she'd been at the police station.

What she hadn't made clear in her message was exactly why she'd left when, according to Rhona, she'd been so determined to give her statement in person.

It was easy to be spooked on entry to a police station. Lots of folk felt it, even when they were innocent of any crime. That was why people often didn't report a crime, knowing they'd have to give a statement, explain themselves, and maybe even end up being required to give evidence in court.

He remembered the two young female jurors at Bonar's

trial. They'd wanted to be anywhere but in that court, and were never going to argue or even give voice to what they truly thought.

Holly may have been decided about coming in here, but the sight of uniforms everywhere, the bustle of the law at work, would, he thought, have been even more traumatic for her, because she'd been involved in framing a police officer.

His finger hovering over her number, he fought the desire to speak to her in person, to ask her the questions he needed an answer to.

Eventually good sense prevailed. He went back in and handed Rhona her mobile.

'Thanks, it's good to know she's okay.'

Rhona was waiting for him to say something else, which he wasn't planning on doing.

'Right,' he said, turning to Janice. 'Time to get back to work.'

As they headed off, Janice demanded to know if he'd taken Holly's new number down. 'Rhona said she intended it for you.'

'I can't call Holly. The case against me is still live. Bonar isn't in custody yet and no charges have been brought against him, or Holly for that matter,' he told her. 'You, on the other hand, could speak to Holly.'

Janice was eyeing him warily. 'What do you want me to say to her?'

'Not say. Ask. We need to know if she was approached while in here, and if so, what that officer looked like. Even if it seemed innocent, it probably wasn't. Also, Holly was with Bonar often at the club and at home. She saw and heard things, including who he was working with. One or more who may well be cops.'

They'd reached the coffee machine. McNab shut up and waited until its present customer had got his coffee and departed.

'Maybe the boss should bring Holly back here,' Janice said.

'If he does, they'll get to her,' McNab said. 'We know they have someone here on the inside. And now might be the time when we find out who that is.'

'How do you plan to do that?' Janice said, obviously sensing McNab was on a roll.

'You're going to have a talk with Holly. Find out who Bonar's mixed up with. One or more cops were at it in his favourite club, with me as the fall guy. Add in the fact that we have CCTV footage of Deirdre Reid being put in a black van nearby, and the next two victims were associated with the same area. My belief is that the French girl was selected in that club, like the others. Maybe they missed getting her that night, and had to follow her on her Scottish adventure. They didn't mind that since they'd already used the west coast to bury Deirdre. As for Callie, she liked those clubs too, and after heading north herself, ended up as luck or the devil would have it in the campsite near Deirdre's grave. Let's face it, the student strip was their happy hunting ground, full of those pesky witches that fuck men off by turning them down. You saw the footage from Ollie? Rhona's right. We're not dealing with a lone wolf here. It's a group endeavour. And the boss knows that.'

The idea had been fermenting for a while. Now that the boss had restricted access to the stick man case material, everyone was on edge. The public announcement regarding the signature of the killer had resulted in lots of contacts, which the boss had allotted to only a select few officers, including himself and Janice.

'Someone is going to be seriously pissed off about that, because they've lost access to vital information on what we know about the killer. So,' McNab said quietly, 'we pretend to have a lead on the rogue cop and see if we can flush him out. If it was me, I'd be shitting myself. Come to think of it, it was me, until quite recently,' he added with a grin, which he suspected looked maniacal.

It sounded neat and easy in his head, though it was anything but. Janice knew that, by the look she now bestowed on him.

'Let's head back into the lion's den.'

He'd been right about the atmosphere. On their entry, the room appeared unnaturally quiet. As they made for their desks, they noted that they and the rest of the chosen ones were now grouped together. Ostensibly because they were all working through the responses to the appeal on the stick man announcement.

McNab was pretty sure his fellow officers didn't see it that way, but decided he could live with that. After all, he'd been the one under suspicion himself not that long ago.

Any calls to the front desk were being immediately transferred through to the team, but emails with the stick man header proved to be the most popular method of communication.

Hours later, McNab was pretty sure his eyes were crossing, when one email eventually jumped out at him.

It was from a girl called Chelsea Grant, who'd been out of the country for the past three months and had only just learnt via the news announcement about what had happened to Deirdre. She'd known Deirdre through the film club, and had attended the special showing of *The Blair Witch Project* with her.

She wrote:

> These three blokes were giving out stick men, like the one in the police announcement, which we thought was weird but funny. They were targeting the females mostly. Either that or the men were rejecting them. Anyway, one of the guys really came on to Deirdre. She was okay about it at first, but it began to get creepy. We got away from him and after the film went into the bar for a drink. The place was really buzzing. The guy tried it on again, and when she told him to fuck off, he got really angry and said some pretty shitty things. Called her a fucking witch, like in the film.
>
> He wasn't shouting at her, more spitting it right in her face. Because I was standing next to her I heard and saw it all. Deirdre stood her ground, though. I remember thinking she was brave. Guys don't like being rejected or made fun of. Then his mates came over and dragged him away.

Signalling to Janice to come read his screen, McNab whooped, 'Bingo!' loud enough for the whole room to hear.

Minutes later they were in with the boss, where he was studying the email that had caused such excitement. They watched as he read it through once, twice, three times.

'It reads as genuine,' he confirmed. 'And matches what Deirdre's partner said about her visit to see *The Blair Witch Project*. No mobile number given though.

'It's best, I think, if DS Clark replies, making it obvious she's female. The word is out there that a police officer may be involved in the disappearances and that's why the perpetrator hasn't been apprehended.'

He continued. 'Urge Ms Grant to call you personally. Plus we get Tech to confirm the identity of the person with this email address.' He paused. 'It's a possible lead, if she can give us a description of the male who accosted Deirdre that night.'

'Maybe also issue a request to anyone who was in the bar and may have noticed the incident to come forward?' McNab suggested.

'We pursue this as far and as swiftly as possible, and on all fronts,' DI Wilson said. 'If we have a rogue cop involved, it may help us flush them out.'

Re-entering the room, McNab made a point of looking seriously pleased with himself. Janice took her seat and, with a nod and thumbs-up to those around her, proceeded to write her reply. Identifying herself, she urged the sender to call her as soon as possible.

65

Achmelvich

Day eight

Meg was back by his side, panting but apparently happy. The police dog had gone silent.

Trevor rose from his seat on the porch steps and ventured round the side of the cabin, keeping Meg to heel. The police had broken enough gorse branches to expose the door of a stone outhouse, probably an old byre.

Trevor suddenly remembered that he'd seen the small stone building on his first foray to the area in search of a new home, some years before. Back then the outhouse, with its red galvanized roof, had been easily accessible, and he'd imagined it as a good storeroom, or a place he might house a goat, back when he had the misguided notion that he might live off the land.

The door stood open, the padlock broken, but the officers were standing outside, deep in discussion.

He didn't think they'd found either a live person or a dead one, but they had found something that worried and upset them, that much was obvious.

Spotting his presence, the sergeant came over. 'Mr Wills, I'd prefer if you went back to the front of the cabin.'

'D'you think the girl missing from Arisaig might have been here?' Trevor said.

Sergeant Marshall was studying him intently. 'Why do you ask that?' he said.

'I think the French girl ran down from here trying to escape. That's why she was at the cliff. If her abductor tried to take her here, it was to keep her locked up like the first girl, Deirdre Reid.' He was aware he was babbling, but couldn't stop himself. It seemed so obvious to him now.

Before the sergeant could respond, he added, 'There was a van here earlier with a blue kayak on the roof. A man came out of the cabin and took a look around, as though checking if anyone was about. Me and Meg were trespassing, so I got out of sight.'

'Can you describe this van?' the sergeant immediately asked.

'A Ford Transit. Black.' That he was sure of.

'Any chance you took the registration number?' the sergeant said hopefully.

He only wished he had and said so. 'This is a wee place, Sergeant. Someone will have seen that van either arrive or leave, especially on the single-track road that leads into Achmelvich. The van was big enough to have trouble passing any oncoming vehicle on the rock-face section.'

He thought back to trying to pass the school bus, and how the driver often had to reverse down the hill for that to happen.

Then the question he had to know the answer to. 'Was she alive, d'you think, when he removed her?'

'It appears to be a crime scene, Mr Wills. That's all I'm permitted to say.'

He'd been thanked then and dismissed. Walking home,

the what-ifs began. All the things he might have done and hadn't. If only he'd checked round the back of the hut on his walks here, Meg might have indicated someone or something was inside.

If he'd taken note of the number plate . . . But why would he? He hadn't been suspicious at the time.

He tried to tell himself that she hadn't been dead when the guy in the black van had taken her away. Death hadn't been the smell from the open door of the outhouse, although he imagined he'd smelt other things.

Urine, faeces, but most of all, degradation and fear.

66

Day eight

He'd taken both her watch and her mobile phone, so she had no way of knowing how long they'd been travelling. How far had she come from the loch? Was her captor heading for Glasgow, or perhaps further to the north or west?

Every time she tried to identify the passing sounds, she was invariably drawn back to her fear for her children. Were they still alone at the cottage?

Surely when Sergeant Clark couldn't get through to her on her mobile, she would send a local officer to check she was okay? Or even come herself?

That thought had comforted her, until she realized that, discovering the children alone, the police would be obliged to take Orly and Lucy back to Glasgow with them.

To Derek, of course. He was their next of kin, and he wasn't under suspicion for anything. Especially since the T-shirt and her letters never got to Sergeant Clark or Dr MacLeod.

She castigated herself yet again for not handing in the T-shirt earlier. For not encouraging the children to tell her what was worrying them about their father.

The police were aware they hadn't been getting on as a couple, and that was why she was taking a break from her husband, but she hadn't told them that she thought him a danger to her and the kids.

So it would be natural for Derek to be given custody of them, at least while they searched for her.

That thought horrified her along with the idea that Derek might well have been instrumental in her kidnapping. His hatred towards her had been so obvious recently that she'd been stunned when he'd suggested they all go away on a holiday together.

Why, when he couldn't bear her company at home, had he decided on the spur of the moment to do that? And he'd been so persuasive. Telling her it would be good for them all. And then the location. His choice. Why had he taken them there?

Her mind immediately jumped to Lucy's story about why she'd been at the grave. She'd followed her father there, where he'd met a man.

Derek had no idea it was a grave, she'd told Lucy. And the man was just another camper like them.

'Daddy was angry that I followed him,' Lucy had said. 'That's why I sat down.'

Pieces of the jigsaw kept moving about the board she'd drawn in her head. Questions that couldn't be answered. Suspicions that couldn't be proved.

One thing was certain, though. She, like Callie, had been abducted. Why, she didn't know. Or by whom. Except, in her heart, she knew it had to be linked back to what had happened at the campsite.

At that moment the van slowed, then turned right, and she was thrown about as the wheels met an uneven surface.

They rattled on like this for a few more minutes, before the brakes were applied and the vehicle came to a halt.

Francine took a deep breath as the back door was eventually released and slowly swung open.

A man's figure stood with his back to her. For a terrible moment she thought, by the stance and dark hair, that it might be Derek, then he turned and she met the eyes of her fake policeman.

The kind, concerned look he'd worn when they'd first met face to face had gone, of course. Now his eyes shone with hate and a certain amount of pleasure at her obvious fear.

'Out,' he said. 'Now.'

He watched as she dragged herself forward. When she reached the open door, he caught her arm and wrenched her out. Her yelp as she hit the ground angered him still further.

He hated her, that much was obvious, but for what? That she didn't know.

Blinking in the daylight, she saw she was in a small courtyard, surrounded on three sides by a wall. She glanced upwards as, high above her, a plane passed over. Was it coming from an airport or heading towards one?

A shove from behind sent her staggering towards a half-open garage door. Propelled in by his next push, she stumbled and fell onto the stone floor, her knees crying out in pain.

Then the door was slammed shut and she lay face down, struggling for breath.

Where the hell was she now, and what did he plan to do to her?

It was then she sensed that she wasn't alone. There was someone else in there with her.

'Hello?' she cried out. 'Who are you? Who's in here?'

When the voice answered her, she recognized it right away.

Things had come full circle and she was back where it had all begun.

67

Glasgow

Day eight

Chelsea Grant had come into the station directly after she'd spoken to Janice on the phone, and was now sitting opposite them with a big mug of tea, looking calm and very determined.

According to Janice, her language during the phone call had been pretty forthright and colourful.

McNab was hoping it would prove to be the same here. One thing was certain, Chelsea Grant was made from the same mould as Chrissy McInsh. She might have been named after a district of London but she was Glasgow through and through.

'I was touring Europe the last three months,' she told him. 'Not easy now for musicians what with all the Brexit shite, but anyway. I sing and play saxophone in a jazz band. I've played the Blue Arrow on the strip a few times. It's a cool gig. I like it. I met Deirdre there. We got talking. Turns out she was a film buff, like me. We did a course in indie films. Some good. Some pure shite. *The Blair Witch Project* was on the list and there was a special showing. So we went along for a laugh.' She looked directly at McNab. 'D'you want me to go on, or answer questions?'

'Keep going,' Janice told her.

'Right. Well, as I said in my email, there were three guys hanging about the foyer, handing out these creepy stick dolls. Deirdre took one. Not me. Imagine taking that home with you. No thank you. My memories of the film were bad enough.' She pulled a face. 'Don't like woods at the best of times. After that movie, I'll stick with central Glasgow, parks *excluded*.'

At that moment McNab decided they were kindred spirits.

She waited. 'Are you going to ask me what these guys, especially the one that accosted Deirdre, looked like?'

'We were coming to that,' Janice said.

'Well we're at it now. And I can describe them, but in fact I can go one better. I have a photo and wee video clip of the creepy bastard. I took it when he was spitting pure shite in Deirdre's face.'

'You have an image of the male who verbally abused Deirdre Reid?' McNab asked.

'Sure do,' she said. 'I have the other two posers as well. I took it when they dragged the shitebag away. I wish, looking back, that I'd kneed at least one of them in the nuts, but it's too late now, isn't it?'

She pulled out her mobile and began to flick through screens of images, while all the time McNab's heart beat as though he'd just gulped down a large whisky.

'Here you go,' she said at last. 'Here's the shitebag.'

She handed the mobile to Janice, who, after a quick look, passed it to McNab.

He swallowed as the pulse in his neck took off to match his heart.

'You know him, don't you?' Chelsea said in an accusatory fashion. 'He's one of yours, isn't he? A fucking cop. I fucking knew it.'

'Why do you say that?' McNab said.

'Because he's one of the arseholes assaulting females along the strip. Before I left, I tried to complain about him to you lot. Lassies were talking about this guy feeling them up, sexually assaulting them. Then when they said they were going to report him, he flashes his badge and says, "Fuckin' try it and see what happens to you."'

'You gave a statement about this man to the police?' Janice asked.

'I tried. I called the station to report him. The officer on the desk promised me it would be dealt with. No one called back.'

'When was this?' McNab said, trying to control his anger.

'Before I went off on tour. Before Deirdre went missing.' She looked stricken. 'If you bastards had paid attention, she'd be alive today. And that French lassie too.'

'Will you make a statement giving details of this?' McNab said.

'Why do you think I'm here? I'm too late to save Deirdre, but there's still one girl missing who might well be alive.'

Every word she was saying was true. It was shameful that it had ever come to this.

McNab mustered himself. 'My partner here will stay with you while you give your statement. I promise you, it won't be ignored this time. I have to go and speak with my superior. Can you please send a copy of any relevant footage to the numbers DS Clark will give you?'

'Okay,' she said with a searching expression. 'Don't fob me off this time,' she warned.

McNab motioned Janice to the door and they stepped outside.

'You saw the bloke in the background?' he said quietly.

Janice nodded. 'I did. Is it really him? It's not that clear.'

'It would be to Ollie, though,' McNab said.

'Wouldn't it be better to speak to the boss first? This is way above our pay grade.'

McNab knew she was protecting him, from himself as much as anything, so he said, 'Okay, I'll speak to the boss first. Can you ask Chelsea what she knows, if anything, about Bonar and forward me the photos?'

The ping as the images arrived on his mobile hastened his steps. The atmosphere in the main room hadn't changed. 'Strained' would have been an understatement. McNab gave a nod to those still trawling through the responses to the stick man announcement and headed for the boss's office. He'd already knocked on the door before realizing that the boss had someone with him.

The murmuring continued, before eventually he was told to enter.

'DS McNab, Desk Sergeant Morris here was speaking to me about Ms Allan's visit to the station.'

McNab gritted his teeth to stop himself blurting out the wrong response to this.

'You can go, Sergeant Morris,' DI Wilson said.

McNab shut the door pointedly behind Morris and paused until he heard his footsteps move away. Then turned to find the boss waiting for an explanation for both his actions and his attitude.

McNab retrieved his mobile and brought up the image he most wanted the boss to see.

He watched as DI Wilson attempted to digest what he was looking at.

'The woman's Deirdre Reid. Who's the guy verbally abusing her?' he eventually asked.

'Check behind him, sir,' McNab urged.

A pregnant silence, followed by a voice of disbelief. 'Is that Sergeant Morris?'

'I'd say so, sir.'

'Okay, McNab. What the hell's going on here?'

McNab explained about the *Blair Witch* showing. 'Chelsea Grant, who's currently giving a statement to DS Clark, went there with Deirdre, who was hit on by one of the three guys giving out the stick men. Seems he wasn't willing to take no for an answer. According to Chelsea, Deirdre gave as good as she got, which didn't please him one little bit. His two mates eventually stepped in and pulled him off.'

'And you believe one of his pals was Sergeant Morris?'

'I believe Ollie will confirm that it's Sergeant Morris, who incidentally never reported what happened there that night, even after Deirdre Reid disappeared, then was found dead and buried two months later,' McNab said, anger deepening his voice.

DI Wilson's face was grey. 'You think he's the bent cop?'

'He was also on duty at reception when Holly changed her mind about giving her statement, sir.'

'And Deirdre Reid's abuser in the photograph? Any idea who he is?'

'Chelsea Grant thought he was a cop too. Says he's the one who's been assaulting women along the student strip and flashing a badge at them. If he's not a cop, then he's borrowing the badge. Maybe Sergeant Morris's badge.'

The enormity of what had just been revealed wasn't lost on the boss. That was clear from his furious expression.

'It's better if Sergeant Morris isn't made aware that we

suspect him. If this blows up now, there may be serious repercussions,' he said. 'You should also be aware that there have been developments in the search for Caillean Munro. Officers have found an outhouse close to Achmelvich where she may have been held until recently.'

McNab's heart lifted a little at that. 'You think there's a chance she's still alive?'

'It's a possibility, but it won't stay that way, if they think we're on to them.'

'What about the supposed police officer who took Francine Henderson?' McNab said. 'Might he be one of the three guys in Chelsea's photos?'

DI Wilson nodded. 'My thoughts exactly. Plus Francine Henderson could well be the next casualty if we're not careful about how we play this. Professor Pirie was attempting a photofit with her children. He needs to see these images. As do the children. Go, show them in person. I don't want them distributed any further than they have been already.'

68

Day eight

The family room was empty when McNab got there.

PC Wendy Cope, the family liaison officer, explained that since they could not locate their father, the children would be placed with a foster family overnight.

'And Professor Pirie?' he asked.

'I don't know where he went. Perhaps the Tech department? He mentioned something about the identikit picture the children had constructed for him,' she offered.

McNab thanked her and set off in that direction, hoping she was right.

The net was closing in, he told himself. The worry was it would move too quickly and they would lose some of their prey.

He couldn't believe that if Sergeant Morris was implicated in this, he was the only one. The likelihood was there were other officers involved. Maybe just turning a blind eye. Maybe complicit.

The boss, by restricting the number of officers with full knowledge of developments in the case, would have alerted anyone implicated that something was up. Already the traces were being wiped away.

Why had Sergeant Morris been in with the boss, if not to put himself on the right side of Holly's visit? Holly, of course, could have a different story. But something told him that it wasn't Morris who had frightened Holly away. That would have been too obvious.

The police service was no different from any other organization that held power. If you wanted to break the law, the best place to do that was from within. Recent events in the Met had shown that to be true.

On entry to what appeared to be a half-empty Tech suite, McNab suddenly realized how late it must be. Locating Ollie, thankfully still at work, he discovered the Prof alongside him.

Approaching, McNab noted that on one of the many screens Magnus and Ollie were viewing was what looked like the children's attempt at an identikit of PC Thompson, who did seem to have the build of a superhero.

'Can we tone down the arm muscles?' Magnus said as McNab joined them. 'I hope that's the only exaggeration, but Lucy was very keen to have them noted.'

'Recognize him as one of your own?' Ollie asked as McNab took a closer look.

He would have loved to say yes, but it was a definite no.

'Any luck with the number plate of the black van outside the club?' he tried.

'A partial maybe,' Ollie told him. 'You'll have heard about the black van spotted up near Achmelvich?'

'The boss told me they may have found where Callie's abductor was holding her. There's a forensic team on site,' McNab said. 'Once the material reaches the lab, we'll hopefully know if Callie was being held there.'

'There could be more than one black van involved,'

Magnus offered. 'They're common enough and popular with security companies.'

'What did you just say?' McNab demanded.

'Security companies use black vans,' Magnus said, puzzled.

McNab swore inwardly, aware just how significant that might be.

'What?' Magnus urged.

McNab eyed him. 'Francine Henderson said her husband had moved to work for a security firm. Made friends there who he went on fishing trips with,' he declared. 'And, as we all know, security firms are very keen to hire former cops.'

He turned to Ollie.

'The van at Achmelvich was a Ford Transit, according to the local who spotted it. What about the one in the CCTV footage?' he said.

'I'm better at faces than vans, but I believe so,' Ollie offered.

McNab, having gone down that avenue as far as possible, now produced his mobile with the images given him by Chelsea.

'These are the real thing.' He explained the context as Ollie downloaded them onto his system.

And then they were up on the big screen. It was mesmerizing. The static image of the altercation, alongside the snippet of video Chelsea had managed to record before Deirdre's abuser had been dragged away.

'The guy behind,' McNab said. 'I believe that's Desk Sergeant George Morris. I'd like you to check that image against his file to confirm.'

Ollie nodded. 'I'll do that, of course, but I already know it's him. I've seen him and chatted to him numerous times. That's Sergeant Morris all right, despite the quality of the image.'

'Might he just be intervening in this verbal assault as an onlooker?' Magnus suggested.

'If so, why not come forward and give a statement about it when Deirdre disappeared?' McNab said. 'He saw her picture often enough.'

'You're right,' Magnus nodded. 'That is deeply suspicious.'

Ollie set the short video clip on replay.

'Who the fuck is her attacker?' McNab said. 'Chelsea Grant, who filmed the altercation, thinks he's a police officer, because apparently he flashes a badge when women complain about his behaviour.' He explained about Chelsea's attempt to report him before Deirdre had disappeared.

'You think this might be the guy that you were set up to take the blame for?' Magnus asked.

'For the sexual assaults, probably yes, which means Bonar knows him,' McNab said.

The screen had changed and now had the official image of Sergeant Morris alongside the cropped one from the photo. It didn't take long for the comparison software to come to a decision.

'So what happens now?' Ollie said. 'Do we keep this under wraps?'

'We do,' McNab confirmed. 'We still have two missing women. Hopefully alive. We need to find them first.'

He looked to the screen displaying the identikit picture created by the two children.

'What say we show the children our group of three? See if they can recognize one of them as the would-be police officer who snatched their mother?'

When Magnus nodded his approval, McNab asked his next question.

'I take it you're still monitoring the incel site?'

'It's been down since earlier today.' Ollie looked worried. 'Around the time when the stick man announcement was made public.'

McNab swore under his breath. 'I suppose that was bound to happen. This film, *The Blair Witch Project*. How many folk are murdered in it?'

It was Magnus who responded. 'The Blair Witch of the title stalks and kills three young filmmakers, who ventured into the woods in search of her.'

A terrible thought was already playing out in his head. McNab decided to share it.

'Maybe they took the site down because they've already accomplished their goal. They've stalked and killed three women.'

Magnus contemplated this. 'That's possible, of course. But if the pattern was to replicate the movie, why snatch Francine Henderson? She's the odd one out in all of this. She doesn't fit the mould of the three chosen ones. She's an outlier. The only reason I can see for why she was taken is that she saw something, or knew something that endangers them. That's why she was being watched.'

'Her husband didn't know where she was, but we did,' McNab reminded them. 'Which is further proof they have an inside source.'

Magnus continued. 'The children said their mother was taking a parcel to the supposed policeman. It looks like the parcel was the trigger. What was in that parcel?'

'Did you ask the children that question?' McNab said.

'I did and they didn't know. Although Lucy did say her mother was writing letters to put in the parcel. One was for Dr MacLeod.'

'Whatever that parcel contained spooked the bastard enough to snatch her,' McNab said.

'Probably, yes, but remember he was already there watching her and the kids, so he suspected they knew something,' Magnus said. 'He started out by watching from the boat, then got closer. Eventually face to face. Why would he do that?'

'He was testing to see if they recognized him?' McNab said.

'Exactly,' Magnus said. 'I believe he thought there was a chance they'd seen him before and was checking that out . . .'

'So was it either here in the police station or on the campsite at Arisaig?' McNab finished for him.

'I can find out which officers were on duty the day the family came in,' Ollie offered. 'And match against anyone who took leave immediately after that?'

'I'd like to know the names of all officers who were on leave when the family went to Loch Lomond,' McNab said, 'and during the time the family were at Arisaig.'

69

Day eight

Rhona stepped out of her forensic suit and, tossing it in the bin, made for the shower.

The material recently delivered from Achmelvich had been itemized, logged and stored. According to the production officer, the SOCO team had basically stripped the scene in its entirety. The photos she'd seen of the before and after, and all moments in between, confirmed his words.

There had been plenty of human detritus, evidence that someone had been living, or more likely, incarcerated in that outhouse, including bodily fluids, waste and blood.

The thought that Callie and perhaps Deirdre may have been kept there in such conditions was too horrific to contemplate. Yet, Rhona reminded herself, there had been no body, which made her hold out a small hope that Callie might still be alive.

As for Eléa, she may also have been destined for that same outhouse when she'd been abducted from near the campsite at Achmelvich Bay. Sad to think that, if she hadn't managed to briefly escape her assailant and run towards the cliff, she might still be alive.

Stepping out of the shower, Rhona towelled herself dry.

Her intention was to head to the jazz club and hopefully meet with Sean, however briefly. Having finished so late, Chrissy had already gone home to see wee Michael before the toddler's bedtime.

The call from McNab arrived as she was heading down University Avenue towards Ashton Lane.

'Where are you?' McNab demanded.

'Almost at the jazz club,' Rhona told him, weaving her way through a throng of students intent on going in the opposite direction.

'Magnus and I are already here.'

'Are you and Magnus drinking buddies now?' she joked.

McNab made a sound she chose not to interpret, then said, 'I'll order your usual?'

'Do that,' Rhona said, already anticipating the taste of chilled white wine.

Before she joined them, she went through to the back office to see if Sean was about. His obvious delight when she walked in lifted her spirits.

'I was about to order pizza?' he said.

She returned his smile. 'Great, because I'm starving.'

'We can share it back here. Enjoy a little alone time?' he suggested.

'Give me half an hour to catch up with McNab and Magnus, and I'll be through,' she promised.

The two men, although seated together in a quiet corner, were not in conversation. Rhona wondered if she'd been invited to join them in order to be their intermediary. It wouldn't be the first time McNab had cast her in that role.

As she took her seat, she realized that she was wrong about that. McNab immediately looked to Magnus, who indicated that McNab should be the one to begin whatever it was they wanted to tell her.

Surprised at this turn of events, Rhona listened to McNab's story of an interview with a Ms Chelsea Grant, who'd apparently met Deirdre in the Blue Arrow, where she was playing, and had attended the *Blair Witch* showing with her.

'She was out of the country with her jazz band when Deirdre disappeared and only learnt about it via the stick man announcement,' he said.

McNab then told her about the fracas after the *Blair Witch* showing, caught on camera by Chelsea.

'Wow,' Rhona said at the end of his description. 'I like the sound of Ms Chelsea Grant. She sounds like Chrissy.'

'My thoughts exactly,' McNab said.

'So do I get to see this video?'

McNab produced his mobile and, bringing up the clip, handed it over.

During her time in the forensic tent with Deirdre, she'd imagined she'd got to know her, just a little. Where she had walked, what she had endured at the hands of her attacker. Now she could watch Deirdre come alive, see her determination, her anger, her fight against misogyny in its ugliest of forms.

The horrible part was the realization that it was likely Deirdre's decision to fight back that had led to her subsequent abduction and death.

The two men had remained silent as she'd played and replayed the short clip. Now McNab asked her if any of the three males in the scene seemed familiar to her.

She hadn't been focusing on the men, captivated as she had been by Deirdre. She now took a closer look at them. The one in the background whose features were a little fuzzy seemed vaguely familiar, but she couldn't be sure. The one verbally abusing Deirdre, his face twisted with hate, she didn't know. Then the one holding the radge one back . . .

'That one,' she said, pointing. 'I think I may have seen him somewhere before, although I'm not sure, to be honest.'

Her admission seemed to surprise them.

'Not the one in the background?' McNab checked.

Rhona took another look. 'I thought he looked vaguely familiar, but it's not a good image.'

'He's a cop, name of Sergeant George Morris, who works the desk in the station. He didn't report this incident when Deirdre Reid disappeared or even when you unearthed her body. Chelsea Grant says the main guy is the one sexually assaulting women along the student strip. She was convinced he was a cop, because he apparently flashes a badge if challenged and threatens the women involved.'

'So that's the one you were set up to take the fall for?' Rhona said.

She halted there as it suddenly struck her where she had seen the third man before.

'What?' McNab said, catching her expression.

'The one holding the radge guy back was in The Old Library in Arisaig. He was eating in the dining room when Chrissy, myself and DS MacDonald were there.'

Rhona recalled that he'd been sitting alone at a table set against the white-painted stone wall, next to the fireplace.

'He was staying there, you mean?' McNab asked.

'I don't know if that was the case. You don't have to be a resident to eat there. Lee's stationed at Mallaig. You need to speak to him and send him the image,' Rhona said. 'And Chrissy needs to see it too. She remembers everyone and everything. If it is that man, then he was in the vicinity of the campsite when we were exhuming the body.'

'I'll send you the image and video clip,' McNab said. 'You can check with Chrissy tomorrow.'

They parted company shortly after that, the men leaving individually, Rhona making for the office and, hopefully, food.

The pizza had already arrived. Rhona could smell the rich tomato and cheese aroma on approach.

Inside, Sean had cleared his desk, moved the laptop and set the large pizza box in the centre.

'I have a bottle of a very good red, but,' he said, noting her wine glass, 'I see you've chosen to bring your own.' He waved her to a seat. 'Help yourself.'

Rhona did as suggested and they munched in companionable silence, finishing one pizza before Sean revealed he had a second in reserve. 'Just in case.'

She managed two more slices of the pepperoni before she had to call it quits and move to the nearby couch with her wine. Sinking back against the cushions, she gave a satisfied sigh.

'I saw the announcement about the stick men on the news,' Sean said. 'Creepy stuff. I hope it produced results?'

'According to McNab, it did, one person in particular. Someone from a jazz band that plays the strip. She's been on tour in Europe the last three months. Only just found out about Deirdre's murder.'

'I don't suppose you can tell me her name?' Sean said.

Rhona shook her head. 'No doubt you'll work it out. Just don't repeat it to anyone,' she warned.

'Have I ever done that?' Sean looked mildly affronted.

'You're the soul of discretion,' she assured him, rising.

'Off back to work?'

When she confirmed that she was, he said, 'I could come by later? Make you breakfast in the morning?'

It was a pleasant thought. 'Do that,' she said, with a smile.

70

Day eight

On departing the jazz club, McNab contemplated heading for a curry at Ashoka.

He was definitely hungry and the aroma drifting out was like a beckoning finger, which, the nearer he got, the more difficult it became to resist.

He could have suggested that he and the Prof ate together. That thought had briefly crossed his mind, especially when it became obvious that Rhona was making for the back room and her Irishman.

But what would he and the Orkney bloke have to talk about? They'd about exhausted their discussion regarding the stick man case. They could, of course, reminisce about all those other times they'd worked together, when one or the other of them had screwed up.

McNab grimaced at such a thought.

Mind now made up, he entered the restaurant and allowed the warm smell of spices to envelop him. As the young waitress approached, he briefly considered ordering a carry-out, but the image of taking it home, only to eat it in an empty flat, didn't appeal, so he asked if she had a table for one.

'Of course,' she told him with a smile. 'Come upstairs, please.'

He couldn't decide as he followed her into the far reaches of the upper floor if she was intent on hiding him from the general public or allowing him the space to be alone.

Once she had him seated, with the large and varied menu to study, she immediately suggested a starter.

McNab found himself easily persuaded. After all, he could always take home what he didn't manage to eat here, and have Ashoka curry for breakfast too.

He was making his way through a large plate of vegetable pakora when his mobile, which he'd sat on the table, vibrated towards him.

The name on the screen was Holly.

The closer the mobile got, the more concerned he became about answering. On the boss's orders, he shouldn't be talking directly to Holly. That was Janice's job now.

But what if she and Holly had already spoken and this call was the product of that? Deciding that was reason enough to answer, he picked up.

'McNab here.'

The short silence that followed the utterance of his name seemed to last a lifetime.

Eventually, in a quiet voice, Holly said, 'Can you talk?'

'Am in Ashoka. So not really,' McNab said. 'But I can listen,' he added in what he hoped was an encouraging manner.

'Could we meet in person, then? I could come to you,' she said, sounding anxious.

McNab strove to understand what she might mean by that. 'But you're in London?' he said at last.

'I came back.'

McNab felt his heart beat harder. 'That isn't wise,' he told her. 'You should have stayed away from here.'

'I saw the stuff about the stick men on the news. Is Bonar mixed up in that?' she said.

'I suspect so,' McNab told her.

'Has he been arrested?'

'Not yet. That's why you should stay away.'

'But I'm already here.'

At that moment his main course arrived in a flurry of rice, curry and a large peshwari naan. As McNab thanked the waiter, he heard the click and buzz as Holly cut their connection.

Was she really back here in Glasgow? If so, where was she staying? With Bonar still out there, surely she wouldn't go back to her flat, even to see her paintings?

He immediately texted her. Grab an Uber. Come to Ashoka.

Convincing himself she would do as he said, McNab called the waiter over and asked him to bring another plate and also a dish of the vegan curry Holly had chosen on their visit here together.

He'd barely touched his food when she finally walked in. From his spot on the balcony, he saw her approach the desk and talk to the cashier, to eventually follow the waitress up the open staircase.

McNab rose to welcome her. 'I ordered your favourite from last time. It'll still be warm,' he said, trying to sound normal. 'What would you like to drink?'

'Water's fine, same as you,' she said, with the ghost of a smile.

Eating and drinking together again seemed to relax her, and eventually McNab felt able to ask how she'd been.

'Okay,' she told him. 'I'll probably move to London after

all this is over. There's more work for me down there,' she added.

He nodded, choosing not to say that she was better as far away as possible from Bonar, whether he ended up in prison or not.

'Where are you staying in Glasgow?' he said.

'Not at my flat. With a friend.' Reading his expression, she added, 'I told him I need to keep away from an abusive partner. Nothing about what I did . . . to you, or the police involvement.'

'May I know his name and address?' McNab said.

'I'll text you it. Plus I'll keep my head down. I have some paid work to finish which is good.'

'Janice, my partner,' he began, 'was going to be in touch with some questions. I thought it better she talk to you about Bonar and his associates, rather than me,' he explained.

When she acknowledged this, he added, 'Can I ask why you left the police station without giving your statement?'

'I lost my nerve,' she said. 'I was worried I would, which is why I recorded it earlier with Rhona.'

'No one persuaded you to leave?' he checked.

'The policeman on the desk asked who I had come to see. Then a female officer in the Ladies asked why I was there, in a friendly way. Why?'

'The desk sergeant. You'd never seen him before?'

She shook her head.

'And the female officer in the toilet, did you see her name badge?'

She considered this for a moment. 'You thought someone had tried to frighten me off?' she said.

'I wondered,' he admitted. 'After what Bonar said.'

'He has cop friends, or so he says. Not sure he has that

much influence on them. I suspect it's more likely the other way round.'

She had grown more confident and seemed ready to talk openly about things now.

McNab glanced round to find they were the only ones left at the far end of the balcony and decided to take a chance. 'Can I show you something?'

'Okay,' she said warily.

'I'll leave the sound down. The girl in the video clip is Deirdre Reid, the first girl to die. See if you recognize any of the men.'

He handed over the mobile. With a quick glance at him, she set it to play.

She did that three times, her face growing paler with each showing. Eventually she handed the mobile back.

'You believe that's why she was abducted and killed?' she said.

'We think so, yes. Did you recognize any of the men?'

She looked so frightened that McNab reached out and took her hand. 'It's okay. You're okay,' he told her.

She made an effort to muster herself, then said, 'The man at the back is the sergeant on the desk when I came into the station?'

When McNab nodded, she continued. 'The angry guy, that's the one I think you were set up to cover for. I never met him face to face, but I saw him at the club and at Bonar's place. I think he works for a security firm that Bonar has dealings with.'

'His name?' McNab tried.

She indicated that she didn't know. 'But I think the firm's called CompuGuard or something like that.'

'Do they use black Transit vans?'

'I wouldn't recognize the make, but they're black and are free of advertising. Maybe because they carry money sometimes?' she suggested.

There was a brief silence as she appeared to consider what she'd told him.

'The missing woman, Caillean Munro?' she asked.

'There's another one now,' McNab told her. 'A woman from the campsite where Callie was taken. We think she saw something. She has two young kids,' he added.

He watched as her face drained of all colour.

McNab sat back as the waitress arrived to clear their plates. When she left, he asked Holly if she was okay and if she wanted a coffee.

'A coffee would be good, but I need to go to the Ladies first.'

When she'd set off downstairs, McNab ordered two coffees and tried to decide what to do next. It was clear she'd been really shocked by the video with Deirdre. She would without a doubt know about the death of Eléa Martin. And now she knew about Francine going missing too.

He had really piled it on her, but he'd done it for a reason, he reminded himself. If Holly knew anything else, she would tell him now.

Ten minutes later, with no sign of her return, McNab grew concerned. It was then he noticed she'd taken her handbag with her.

Of course she had, he told himself. All women did that. But what about her jacket? It had gone too.

He headed downstairs and, standing outside the door of the Ladies, he tried shouting her name to no reply. Eventually a woman came out to tell him she'd been the only one in there.

'You're sure?' he said, pushing open the door so he might look inside.

'There's no one in there,' she repeated.

McNab headed for the desk and, describing Holly to the cashier, asked if he'd seen her leave.

'Five minutes ago. Someone was waiting for her outside.'

'Describe them,' McNab demanded, flashing his badge.

'Male, tall, dark hair, muscular. Wearing a T-shirt and jeans. She seemed pleased to see him.' The cashier threw McNab a sympathetic look. 'Looks like you just got stood up, pal.'

71

Day eight

It had taken a call to Ollie and a quick exchange of information to locate the place. While Ollie had done the tech work, he'd found a late-night cafe and topped up on enough caffeine to keep him going for a couple more hours.

Eventually Ollie had come back with the location of CompuGuard. Apparently it hadn't been easy. A security company with a lot of heavy security and no advertising.

'So only selected customers, then?' McNab had commented.

'I would say so,' Ollie told him. 'Explains the plain black vans.'

'And the radge guy?'

'Name's Keith Hamilton. Ex-army. As for the third man, I've been trawling his image in every database I can think of. I haven't found him yet. I have, though, matched the registration number the kid gave us to my partial from the night Deirdre was snatched.'

'The kid remembered right?' McNab had said, delighted.

'One switch of letter only. What are you planning?'

'Just a recce. Nothing more. I want to go back to the boss tomorrow with what I got from Holly.'

'You do know she may well have been lying and it's a trap?'

'I know,' McNab had admitted, the image of the muscled guy in the T-shirt and jeans still in his head. 'Any info on the new number Holly's using?'

'Am working on that and I'll get back to you,' Ollie told him.

Ollie's directions had taken him to the western outskirts of the city, not far from the airport. When he finally reached what he believed to be the CompuGuard security gates, the vehicle's arrival was drowned out by the sound of a plane overhead as it made a wide sweep before coming in to land.

Surrounded by a high wire fence, barbed on the top, in the semi-darkness he could make out a barn-size building probably holding the vans, the doors firmly shut. A single light shone in what might be a security office and a darker shape appeared to be a jumble of old stone outbuildings, probably from its previous existence as a farm.

The road he'd come in on had been tarred at one point in its life, but was now well-holed in places. With no signage indicating CompuGuard's existence, and nothing visible from the main road except what might be an abandoned set of buildings, they'd done a good job of discouraging visitors.

McNab sat there for a while, his mind ranging over what he might and might not do next.

Holly's shock at both the video and his revelation about Francine had, he thought, altered what she'd come there to tell him. Holly, he believed, was buried deep in this. How deep, he didn't know. He suspected that she was trying to play it both ways. Not get herself killed, and not allow anyone else to be killed either.

Much like himself.

The boss, he thought, would make his move shortly. Sergeant Morris would be first to go, but as soon as that happened, the shutters would come down, those involved would go to ground, maybe even AWOL. Most worrying of all, anyone who might give evidence against them would be removed, permanently. Callie and Francine being at the top of that list.

As he considered heading for home, Ollie called.

'What's up?' McNab said.

'I can tell you where the mobile Holly was using is currently located.'

'Where?' McNab demanded.

'Your place.'

'My place? You're sure?' he said, puzzled.

'She's either in there already, or hanging about outside waiting for you. It could be—' he began.

'A trap. I know,' McNab said. 'But there's only one way to find out.'

The road back seemed interminably long and filled with questions. None of which he could answer.

Two streets short of his block, he found a spot to park, then walked the rest, his senses on high alert. If she was there, she could already be inside, because he'd given her a key.

Maybe not such a wise move now, but . . .

There was no waiting car and no one hanging around at the front door. McNab rang his neighbour's buzzer and waited. Eventually she answered.

'DS McNab here. Any strange callers in the last hour or so, Mrs Campbell?'

The very respectable sixty-year-old lady who shared the landing with him was an avid reader of crime fiction. More than once she'd told him how much she liked having a detective living next door to her. It made her feel safe, or so she said.

'No, Mr McNab. All quiet in the close.'

'If you hear a disturbance in my flat in the next five minutes, will you call 999 for me?'

A pregnant silence followed. Then, 'For real?' she said.

'For real,' McNab assured her.

She didn't say 'How exciting', but McNab suspected she was thinking it.

The door released, McNab set off up the stairs. He gave Mrs Campbell's spyhole a thumbs-up as he inserted his key in the lock and entered as quietly as possible.

There was no sound except for his own muffled footsteps as he moved swiftly through the hall and into the main room. Flicking on the light switch revealed the same mess of takeaway cartons littering the coffee table that had been there for the past week, the kitchen area much the same.

Which only left the bedroom.

She was curled up on top of the bed in a foetal position. His first thought was that he couldn't hear her breathe in the silence. Neither did she move.

He switched on the ceiling light, almost blinding himself in the process, although it seemed to make no difference to Holly.

The words *she's dead* invaded his brain as he moved towards her, noting the terrible paleness of her skin.

As he felt for a pulse, her eyelids flickered open, albeit briefly, and he saw with horror the pinpoint size of her drug-filled pupils. What the hell had she taken and how much?

It was then he spotted the syringe, lying on the carpet next to the bed.

He'd seen her naked and there had definitely been no track marks on her arms or anywhere else. She'd admitted smoking dope and popping the occasional pill, but this was something else entirely.

The truth hit him then. Holly hadn't done this to herself.

He checked the pulse again, knowing it would barely be there. His brain careered between his two choices and which should come first.

Call 999 or use the naloxone to reverse the respiratory suppression caused by whatever she'd been given?

He heard the inevitable death rattle sound of the overdose as he scrabbled for the pouch they'd been issued with. Willing his trembling hand to do what was required, he freed the inhaler from its sachet and inserted it in her nostril with one hand while his other stabbed out 999.

When the call was answered, he spoke first.

'This is Police Officer DS Michael McNab. I have an overdose here and have used my standard issue of naloxone. I require an ambulance and police as quickly as possible to—'

He rattled off his address, then dropping the mobile, he took both of Holly's cold white hands in his own.

72

Day nine

Chrissy had recognized the guy in the video right away and had told Rhona that he'd been sitting at the small table against the wall to the left of the fireplace in The Old Library dining room.

'I can even tell you what he had to eat, because I'd fancied it myself,' Chrissy continued. 'It was venison with a sauce of rowan jelly and juniper.' She eyed Rhona at this point. 'I can tell you his pudding too, if you want?'

Despite the seriousness of the question and the answer, Rhona couldn't help but be amused.

'So the one holding radge guy back in the video was at The Old Library, sitting next to us. Maybe that was intentional?' Chrissy said thoughtfully. 'He maybe wanted to know about the excavation.'

'Who didn't?' Rhona said. 'Arisaig was alive with a desire to know what was going on. As for our meal with Lee, we didn't talk loud enough for him or anyone else to hear and we kept any discussion of what we were there to do until we were alone,' she reminded Chrissy.

'Lee will remember the guy too,' Chrissy said. 'Plus it's

likely his booking will be on the system. The staff might even have his name.'

'Which will probably be false,' Rhona added.

Chrissy shrugged. 'Maybe not. Why would he be worried about being a tourist who just happened to be at Arisaig when a mysterious body was found buried in the sand?'

'That's it,' Rhona said, a light dawning in the darkness.

When Chrissy looked baffled, Rhona tried to explain. 'Why was he in Arisaig? If we assume that he was part of the triumvirate and therefore complicit in Deirdre's abduction and murder, he would know where her body was buried. Did he come to revisit the scene for his own reasons, or did someone call to let him know the body had been found?'

'A rogue police officer, you mean?' Chrissy said. 'Or someone from Arisaig, or the campsite?'

Rhona ran through the sequence of events again. The call for her to come to Arisaig because a child had gone missing and a police dog had perhaps located a burial. How relieved she'd been to discover the child had been found safe and well.

Then her arrival at the campsite with Lee, only to discover that they also had a missing female, who, by the stick man in her campervan, may have been abducted. Possibly or probably by whoever killed and buried Deirdre.

'I think the third man's presence in Arisaig is connected to Callie's disappearance,' Chrissy said, mirroring Rhona's own thoughts.

'I agree and I don't think he was there by chance. Someone told him that the body had been found,' Rhona said.

'Are you thinking what I'm thinking?' Chrissy asked.

'If it involves the Henderson family, and Derek Henderson in particular, then yes,' Rhona said. 'According to Lucy, her father met a man near the grave. They talked to one another. Her father ignored her shouts and was angry with her. Then, when she went missing, he didn't mention any of that, but let the police and campers organize a search.'

'All of which is decidedly weird,' Chrissy agreed.

'They're bringing the kids back in today to look at the photo,' Rhona said. 'If Lucy and Orly identify one of the three men as their not-so-friendly fisherman, we can assume that's why Francine was snatched. They think she knows something. Or the parcel and note for me held incriminating evidence of some sort.'

'Maybe that something is about her husband,' Chrissy said. 'God, he hated it when you and Lucy got pally. And he was furious when Francine brought the children in for interview. That man has questions to answer.'

'Trouble is, he can no longer be found to answer them,' Rhona told her.

All in all, it felt like a breakthrough moment. The first thread that might possibly link the discovery of Deirdre's body to what had happened to Callie.

If one of the triumvirate had been there by chance and saw Callie, who fitted their chosen victim, might they make their move anyway?

'Lee should know all about it by now from McNab, and since your PC Murray was under his command, I've no doubt he'll be asked too.'

'I might call him anyway,' Chrissy said cheerily. 'We've been keeping in touch. I quite fancy a trip back to Arisaig that doesn't involve a body.'

As do I, Rhona thought, as they returned to their various jobs.

They had begun examining the Achmelvich evidence first

thing, Chrissy working on the recovery of trace and contact material from the clothing items, Rhona on the analysis of bodily fluids.

She would have preferred to have worked the locus herself, but since there had been no body to process, plus the volume of work outstanding on the previous two murders still to be dealt with, going north again hadn't been deemed a priority.

Had Callie's body been discovered, that would have changed things, of course. That didn't mean Callie was still alive, or Francine either, but the longer the absence of the next body went on, the more she'd decided to hope.

McNab called her mid-morning.

'What did Chrissy have to say?' he demanded.

'She recognized the third man from the video right away. She even remembered what he had to eat, for both courses.'

'That's my girl,' McNab said, impressed. 'She'll make a good witness. Your DS MacDonald confirms the sighting too. So the third man was definitely hanging about Arisaig when you were digging up the victim. The question is why. Did someone tip him off about what was happening? Or did he just fancy a visit to the scene of crime?'

Rhona told him their thoughts on Derek Henderson's part in all of this. And poor Callie's.

'Lucy saw her father talking to a man at the gravesite. Maybe he wasn't a stranger or a fellow camper,' she said.

'Are you suggesting Derek Henderson is part of this incel gang?'

'He fits the mode,' Rhona said. 'His wife and kids are afraid of him. He goes after Callie. She spurns him, like Deirdre did to the radge guy, so what does he do about that? Maybe points her out to his mate. Or perhaps they'd already seen Callie on the student strip and Henderson calls his friend to let him know she's there and all alone.'

Rhona could almost hear McNab's brain processing what she'd just said, before he came back in with, 'Holly's back in Glasgow. She called me and we met up. I showed her the video clip. She's seen the radge guy before too, with Bonar. She said he was the one I was set up to take the fall for. Plus she knew the company he works for, and guess what? Derek Henderson works for the same lot.'

'You've told DI Wilson all of this?' Rhona said.

'I will do, but I have somewhere to be first,' he told her.

'Where?' she demanded, her heart sinking.

There was a moment's silence on the other end of the line, then McNab cleared his throat.

'After I showed Holly the video, she said she was going to the Ladies. When she didn't appear back, the guy on the desk said she'd gone off with a tall, dark-haired, well-muscled bloke who was waiting outside.'

'The guy from The Old Library fits that description,' Rhona said worriedly. 'Plus it could also be the fake policeman the children described to Magnus. The one who took Francine?' She halted there, realizing the significance of all of this.

McNab came in again. 'They'd disappeared by the time I got down there, but Ollie tracked Holly's new mobile to my flat.'

'She was there?' Rhona said, surprised.

McNab's voice was dark and furious when he answered. 'Lying comatose on the bed. A syringe on the floor beside her. Either she tried to top herself or the bastards tried to kill her for talking to me.'

Before Rhona could ask the dreaded question, he added, 'I administered naloxone and called an ambulance.'

'She's alive?' Rhona said, willing that to be true.

'She was still out of it last night, so I'm headed there now to find out.'

73

Day nine

Francine lifted the girl's head onto her lap and, placing her fingers gently on the bruised and swollen neck, willed the pulse she found there to keep on beating.

In the poor light, the outline of the girl's face was barely visible, her blonde hair a matted and bloodied mass against her head.

Francine recalled Callie the first time she saw her. Arriving in her blue campervan, carefully parking it in the corner where she could look out on both bays and watch the sun setting in the west over Rum and Eigg.

She'd been so keen to be out on that blue lagoon in her kayak. Desperate, in fact.

Francine had envied her at that moment. For her youth and beauty. Her litheness and skill as she'd manoeuvred the kayak over the fence, then walked round by the gate to carry it into the waters of the bay.

The children had watched her in awe, and she'd spoken to them, promised to take them out in it the next day. Lucy could hardly contain her excitement and Orly . . . her pensive, worried boy had even shown his feelings by awarding her with a big smile.

Francine remembered thinking how wonderful it must be to take off alone in a campervan like that. Go kayaking whenever you wanted to. Be free and safe and happy in such a beautiful place.

Something she'd wanted for herself. Something Derek would never allow to happen.

And Derek had ended that for Callie too. Finally she could admit to herself that Derek was somehow implicated in all of this.

But how exactly?

Had Derek helped abduct Callie? Maybe with the man he'd met next to the grave of that other poor girl? Was it Callie's blood on his T-shirt?

She glanced down as the still figure shifted a little and the eyes flickered open to look up at her.

'Callie,' she said softly. 'It's me, Francine, Lucy and Orly's mum.'

Momentarily puzzled, the eyes seemed to clear a little as they focused on Francine's face, before fear swept through them and she tried desperately to free herself from the cradling arms.

Francine didn't try to prevent her.

She's afraid of you, she realized, *because of Derek.* The thought horrified her.

'I'm a prisoner too,' she said in between the muffled crying from the girl, now curled up alongside her. 'We can help each other get away from here.'

Callie fell still, as though processing Francine's words, before she drew herself up, trying to stifle the pain the movement caused.

In the poor light Francine could only imagine the extent of the girl's injuries to both body and soul.

'I'm sorry,' she said as the girl's eyes eventually met hers. 'I had no idea Derek had anything to do with your disappearance. It was the children, Orly in fact, who told the police that he'd seen his father go into your van.' She paused for a moment. 'Lucy desperately wanted you to be found alive after the body of another girl buried in the machair . . .' Francine tailed off at Callie's look of incomprehension.

'Who?' Callie said.

'Deirdre Reid, an art student, who disappeared from Glasgow two months ago,' Francine explained. 'They think she was kept alive somewhere for a month before she was killed and buried near our campsite.'

'So there *was* a girl in that place before me.' Callie looked stricken. 'I saw some of her things in the hut.'

'Can you tell me exactly what happened the night you were taken?' Francine said.

With a quick glance at Francine, she answered. 'I woke to find a masked man in the van. He had a knife. When I fought him, he cut me. Blood sprayed everywhere. I was sick,' she added with a grimace.

'Did Derek help this man?' Francine waited, dreading the answer.

'Your husband tried to come in earlier, but I sent him away. He wasn't happy about that.' She hesitated. 'I didn't hear him when I was blindfolded and taken across the fence to where the kayak was.'

Francine thought by Callie's expression that she might be trying to spare her feelings, so she told her what she already knew.

'I think Derek might have told your abductor that you were at the campsite. Lucy saw her father meet a man at what turned out to be Deirdre's grave.' She paused but only momentarily. 'Did Derek come to the place you were held?' Francine needed to know all of it, no matter how bad.

'It was dark and they always wore masks, but' – Callie hesitated – 'yes, I think he was one of the men that came.'

And there it was. The ugly truth.

Derek was an abuser of women, something she already knew, having been one of them. But was he also a killer?

Callie, perhaps reading her thoughts, came back in then. 'I left a partner like that. Escaped while he was in Hong Kong. That's why I was at the campsite. I thought I was safe there.'

Francine put her arms about the trembling girl. 'We're both still alive. I'm going to take a look round our prison. See if there's any way out of here.'

74

Day nine

The children were already in the family room. Glancing in through the glass panel, Rhona found her heart sinking. They looked so lost and alone. And completely powerless in the world they'd found themselves in.

She wondered if they thought their mother's disappearance might be their fault for speaking out against their father. Little wonder they had initially kept silent. With Lucy, even to the point of not talking at all. When they'd finally revealed the secrets they'd been keeping *so as not to make their mum cry,* look what had happened.

They must be wondering if what they were asked to do now might only make things worse for her.

As Rhona opened the door, both children looked up. This time, however, there were no smiles from Lucy, no excited calling out of her name. The adult world had let them down, and she was part of that world.

PC Hope came to greet her, together with a woman from social services. Rhona found herself huddled in this group away from the children, hearing of where they'd been placed last night and how the police were still unable to find their father.

She wanted to state that in no way should they be handed over to him, under any circumstances, but managed to keep her mouth shut on that subject, knowing that neither woman would be aware of Derek Henderson's possible role in all that had happened.

Magnus arrived minutes later and Rhona was pleased to see that he received a smile of welcome from Lucy, at least.

Reading the room, like the psychologist he was, Magnus suggested that he and Rhona be left alone with the children.

'If that's okay with you two?' He directed his question at Orly.

With a quick look to Lucy, using whatever unspoken language they had, Orly nodded their acceptance of this arrangement.

When both women left, the mood in the room improved immediately, demonstrated by Lucy asking if Magnus had found the man they'd drawn together the previous day.

Magnus explained that they might have found a photo of the man and did they want to see it?

It was obvious by the children's reaction to being given a task to do that this was far less threatening than being asked a series of questions.

Magnus set up his laptop as before and the children joined him at the table. Rhona approached but remained out of the inner circle, aware that whatever bond Magnus had established was important in what might happen next.

The image now showed the children's identikit picture to the left. On the right, a set of real photos appeared. Radge guy, Sergeant Morris and the third man, all the faces much clearer and more distinguishable than in the original still and video clip.

A pregnant silence fell as the two children studied the

photographs both individually then together in the silent way that they had.

Eventually Orly pointed to the third man. 'That's the man in the red boat. That's who Mum took the parcel to at the boathouse.'

The words 'and never came back' hung unspoken in the air between them, before Orly added, 'Will you find her?'

'Now that you've shown us who we're looking for, I believe we will,' Magnus told him.

A flicker of a smile crossed Orly's lips when this was said, and Lucy slipped her hand in his.

No doubt watching from the next room, and observing that a decision had been made, PC Hope arrived back.

'Juice and cake has been ordered and should be here very soon,' she told the children. 'You can go check out the computer games while you're waiting.'

They did as asked, rather than say their goodbyes, even to Magnus.

'Coffee?' he said as they exited. 'DI Wilson will have been watching and already know the outcome.'

They headed for the cafeteria and their usual table, Magnus opting once more to go buy the coffee. In truth, Rhona was glad to have a few moments to herself. It was probably unlikely that she would see either of the children again, at least not with reference to the ongoing case.

Her bond with Lucy in particular was obviously broken, so she could be of no further use in that way.

Should – *when* Francine was found and reunited with her children, then she might see them again. Somewhere, among all the horror, she'd imagined herself finally taking that swim with Lucy, which she'd promised back at the croft campsite.

'It went well,' Magnus said as he took a seat. 'So stop beating yourself up about Lucy.'

'You noticed?' Rhona said.

'You were in there from the beginning and Lucy trusted you then, and still does. Last time her mum was here with them, you were a little team together. You'd all been at the campsite when this began. They've lost their mother since then.'

Rhona acknowledged this with a nod.

'So we know who is at the heart of this,' Magnus said. 'Three men, who I believe formed a death bond of some sort. I suspect each of them was to kill a chosen female victim. Two young women are dead and the third one is still missing.'

'What about Derek Henderson?' Rhona said. 'What was his role?'

'With all such groups, there is the dark evil core, and the ones who play around the edges. Henderson's masculinity, as he saw it, was being questioned. He sought out others who felt the same. Every problem he faced was caused by women. They needed to be taught a lesson.'

He continued. 'I've never met the man, but I've viewed his interview with DS McNab and you've told me of your experience of him. My reading of what has happened is that Derek Henderson may have been responsible for bringing the third man to the campsite, leading to Callie's abduction.'

'But how does Francine's disappearance fit into all of this?' Rhona said.

'Derek Henderson, I suspect, is a coward at heart. Maybe her abduction was to threaten him into doing what they deemed necessary. Whatever that is.'

Rhona didn't like that thought. 'He will always save himself.'

Magnus nodded. 'I suspect so.'

'If they wanted to put pressure on him, would it not have been better to take one or both of the children?' Rhona voiced the horror she'd been hiding even from herself.

'Perhaps that was the plan and Francine persuaded the third man that it would be better to take her instead.'

Francine would do that, Rhona thought, even if it might mean her life being forfeited.

'There's perhaps another explanation,' she said. 'The third man was watching the family, but there was no sense of threat, as far as I can gather, until she wanted to post that parcel to DS Clark, with a note inside for me. I think that's what altered whatever plan was in motion.'

'So,' Magnus said, 'do we try and catch DI Wilson before we leave? He'll have the result of our meeting with the children by now, but he might like to hear our current thinking.'

As Rhona agreed, she suddenly remembered. 'McNab phoned me earlier.' She gave him a brief résumé of what she'd been told.

'He showed Holly the video?' Magnus said. 'After which she left and met someone outside who looked like the third man? Was it a set-up, do you think?'

'I suspect McNab thinks so. He was pretty angry about it,' Rhona said. 'Then Ollie traced Holly's mobile to McNab's place. He found her there, near to death. They'd pumped her full of drugs. If McNab hadn't had naloxone spray in the flat . . .' She halted there for a moment as Magnus absorbed this, before saying, 'When he left her at the hospital she was still in a bad way. He was heading back there earlier to see if she'd regained consciousness.'

'Let's hope she comes round soon. I suspect there's much

to tell when she does.' He rose. 'Shall we try to speak to DI Wilson now? I'm keen to know what's happening with Sergeant Morris.'

75

Day nine

Sergeant Morris was observing her with a kind, if slightly puzzled eye.

'Have you any idea what this is about, Detective Sergeant Clark?' he eventually ventured.

Janice knew exactly why Morris was sitting across the table from her in the interview room, and she suspected he did too. Yet he continued to address her in the manner he used on the front desk. Friendly and more than willing to help.

Getting him down here as quietly as possible hadn't been easy, but having McNab out of the office had helped. She felt a stab of anger on behalf of her partner and directed it at the man across from her.

How could both men be in the same job? *Semper vigilo* – always vigilant – the motto of Police Scotland. Not vigilant enough to suss out Sergeant Morris.

'If it's about Holly Allan,' he offered, 'I've already given my statement regarding her visit to the station.'

Morris looked round as another figure entered the room, then sat up straight when he realized who it was.

'Detective Inspector Wilson,' he acknowledged his superior

officer. 'I was just saying that I'd already spoken to you regarding Ms Allan's visit to the station.'

Without responding, DI Wilson took his seat alongside Janice and observed the man opposite. At first Morris appeared at ease, until the boss's direct stare began to chip away at the assumed facade.

Silence, Janice realized, could be as powerful as anger.

Morris couldn't demand or even request an explanation from his senior officer, but it was clear, as the pulse in his neck showed, that he desperately wanted to.

The stand-off ended when DI Wilson opened the file he'd brought in with him, laying out three photographs on the table. He pushed the first one towards Morris.

The sergeant didn't want to look at it but couldn't stop himself. After a moment he shook his head. 'What am I looking at, sir?' He adopted a puzzled tone.

'Deirdre Reid, being accosted by three men.' DI Wilson paused there to stare directly at Morris. 'One of which is you, Sergeant Morris.'

Morris, as though confused by the accusation, said, 'May I ask where this was taken, sir?'

Ignoring the question, DI Wilson fired up the nearby screen and on came the video captured by Deirdre's feisty film pal, Chelsea Grant. The short clip had been set on replay. Morris watched it only once, his expression moving from horrified surprise to defiance.

'Why, when Deirdre Reid went missing, did you not report this incident, Sergeant Morris?'

When no answer was forthcoming, DI Wilson pushed the second photograph forward.

'The interior of the location where Deirdre was incarcerated and sexually abused for up to a month prior to her murder and subsequent burial near Arisaig.'

This time Morris averted his gaze and stared, stony-faced, in front of him.

'Lots of forensic evidence found in there. And, of course, every contact leaves a trace . . . but you know that, Sergeant Morris, since you are an officer of the law and, of course, required to have your DNA on file as such.'

DI Wilson wasn't finished yet. He pushed the third photograph forward. This one had been captured by Rhona at the gravesite. The covering of soil removed, Deirdre Reid, unrecognizable from the first image, stared eyeless up at them, the stick man protruding from the remains of her mouth.

'Look at her, Sergeant,' DI Wilson ordered, when Morris continued to avert his gaze.

Morris did, and in that instant Janice saw him flinch.

The boss had remained calm throughout, his voice even, yet Janice could feel the waves of distaste and fury flow from him towards the man opposite.

The affable desk sergeant had gone. Morris marshalled himself and stared directly at DI Wilson.

'I did not kill Deirdre Reid, sir.'

DI Wilson sat back in his chair. 'Then tell me who did, Sergeant.'

76

Day nine

Callie was growing weaker by the minute. Francine realized that the effort to answer her questions, mainly centring on Derek's part in all of this, had taken its toll.

Feeling for her pulse, Francine could barely register it in her neck, or her limp wrist.

Callie needed water, that much was obvious from the parched lips, but there was none to give her.

If someone doesn't find us soon, it will all be over, for Callie at least, she mouthed silently.

Her exploration of their prison had yielded no hope of escape. She'd found the way she'd come in, and a locked door between this room and perhaps another outbuilding alongside. She'd listened at that door for a while, before anxiety had drawn her back to Callie.

Her belief that the girl was close to death was beginning to overwhelm her. And there was no way she would allow Callie to die alone.

Lying alongside her now, cradling the limp, far-too-cold body, she took the girl's hands in her own, willing her heat to flow into Callie.

She'd considered beating at the front entrance and calling

for help, but realized that her cries might bring her captor back and force him to make the decision on whether she lived or died.

Francine had no doubt that when he'd thrust her in here, he'd thought Callie was probably already dead.

'But he was wrong,' she whispered to the comatose girl. 'We're not dead yet,' she muttered defiantly, feeling the girl move against her as though seeking the comfort of her warmth and words.

Closing her eyes, Francine sought refuge in thoughts of her children. The police would have them by now, she told herself. They'll question them, hopefully with Dr MacLeod. Orly and Lucy trusted her. They would tell her what had happened at the cottage. About the fisherman and the boat-house. The kids knew she'd taken a parcel with her, but they hadn't known what was in it.

Francine cursed herself for the umpteenth time. Why had she not alerted the police to the T-shirt earlier? Then none of this would have happened.

It was at that moment she registered someone was in the adjoining building. Two voices, both male, were having an argument. And it might be about her and Callie.

Easing herself free, she tiptoed her way back to the intervening door and pressed her ear against it. What exactly they were arguing about she couldn't make out at first, but she recognized the voices. Both of them. The man who'd brought her here . . . and Derek.

The voices rose, one ordering, the other arguing against whatever he was being told to do.

She caught words that terrified her.

Fucking bitch. You fucking made this mess. Now fix it.

Derek's voice came back in, lower, pleading even. Whatever

he was being told to do, it sounded as if he didn't want to do it.

Then she heard the man say the kids' names. Orly and Lucy. Clear as day.

Why was he talking about Orly and Lucy?

All the times she had shrunk from Derek's fury about something she'd done or hadn't done, she had never been as terrified as she was now. They were intent on getting rid of everyone who might identify them, and the children were included in that.

But Derek would never harm his children. Regardless of what he'd done to her, he had never raised a hand to them.

But if her kidnapper wasn't caught, he might.

Her stomach rose into her mouth and she turned away to vomit its contents on the stone floor.

The sound of her retching must have been heard, because silence fell beyond the door. She heard footsteps approach. Then the lock was turned and the door eased open.

They were coming through. Panic at this drove her stumbling back to Callie. Sitting on guard in front of her still body, she waited, the crashing of her heart deafening her.

But no one came through that door. Instead, a fight seemed to have broken out and she suspected Derek was getting the worst of it.

If Derek was trying to save her, shouldn't she go and help him?

Even as she thought this she found herself rising to her feet again, staring into the gloom for anything she might use as a weapon.

Then silence fell, as sudden as death. But whose death?

She hated Derek for what he had become. What he had

done to Callie. What he had done to her and the kids. But if he was still alive . . .

She stumbled towards the open doorway, meeting the first spiral of smoke trailing its way in. Almost instantly she registered the crackle of flames as they took hold on whatever was in there, and she tasted the petrol in the air.

The smoke was billowing in now. The flames would soon follow. She should shut the door at least, to slow things down, and pray for the sound of a siren.

As she began to close the door again, she spotted the body just beyond the doorway. Even through the swirling smoke, she knew it was Derek, sprawled comatose on the stone floor.

She stood transfixed as the smoke billowed around him, reaching out to catch at her own throat. She had to check if he was alive, she told herself. But what if her captor was waiting for her to do just that?

There was a sudden roar and a burst of flame that lit up his face. A face she had once loved.

She threw herself forward to kneel alongside him. It was then she saw the syringe still embedded in his neck and the pool of blood seeping from below his head.

Had the syringe been meant for her? Was that what the fight had been about?

She checked for a pulse, already certain there would be none to find.

A fit of coughing told her she would have to get out of here, and fast. As she stood up, a thought came.

If Derek still had his mobile?

She began searching his pockets and eventually found it, but before she could check if it was functioning, another burst of flame drove her back to the intervening door. Pulling it shut behind her, she heard the sound of splintering glass as the windows of the neighbouring building exploded. The fire, breathing in the surge of oxygen, roared its approval.

Staggering back to Callie, she tried to bring the mobile to life, aware that if it was password or fingerprint protected, what little hope she had left was lost.

77

Day nine

McNab looked up as the nurse entered to check again on Holly.

'How's she doing?' he said, aware it must be the tenth time at least he'd asked that question.

She observed him with obvious sympathy. 'The doctor will be in shortly. He'll give you the full story. But I would say she's much improved. She was lucky you had naloxone to give her. You saved her life.'

He'd followed the ambulance here last night, after giving Mrs Campbell a quick visit to say a friend had fallen ill and not to worry.

She'd eyed him for a bit, before revealing she'd thought she'd heard folk on the landing earlier. A couple of male voices and maybe a female, but she'd been busy in the kitchen and hadn't checked the spyhole.

'I thought they'd gone up to the next landing, but maybe not.' She looked apologetically at him. 'Is your friend going to be all right?'

'I hope so,' McNab had told her.

It had been touch and go. He didn't need to be a detective to know that. He'd been around a few overdoses in his time on the beat, when naloxone hadn't been available to save them.

Pulling his chair a little closer, he noted that the fingerprint bruising on her throat had become more pronounced. As too had the accompanying bite marks, which had been swabbed and photographed on his direction.

He suspected he knew what the story would be when she was well enough to tell him. The hold Charlie Bonar had over Holly had brought her to this place. Bonar had a long memory and hatred for anyone he thought had denied him what he wanted.

In that, Holly and he were inextricably linked.

But she hadn't known Bonar's connection to the stick man murders. That had been obvious when he'd shown her the video clip. She'd gone so white that he'd assumed she'd made a hasty retreat to the Ladies because she was feeling sick.

What had happened then, he wondered? Had she called Bonar to report what they'd spoken about, or had she been the one to receive the summons?

As he gently lifted her hand to cradle in his, she stirred and opened her eyes. At first they appeared blind to where she was, then she slowly turned her head and saw him.

'Welcome back, Holly Allan,' he said with a smile. 'That was some trip you went on.'

She heard his words, but it was obvious they meant nothing at first, because she didn't remember.

'I found you at my flat,' he explained. 'You'd been given an overdose.'

She shook her head as if she had no idea what he was talking about. Then some memory took hold and she began to shake with fear.

'It's okay,' he said, holding her hand tightly. 'It's going to be okay.'

'It's not,' she said. 'They're going to kill those women.'

'You mean Callie and Francine?' McNab said. 'Who's going to kill them?'

'Her husband. They're making him do it, because he screwed up. Oh God, it's maybe too late.'

She shook her hand free of his and covered her face. The words came out in a rush. 'They told me I would be dead too, if I said anything.'

'And you came to see me anyway?' he said.

'They knew I would.' She glanced at her arm where the needle had bruised the skin. 'They wanted you to find me dead. That company I told you about. It's at an old farm out near—'

'The airport,' he finished for her. 'I know, you gave me the name of the company, remember?'

He gently released her hand from his and stepped into the corridor to call the boss.

'Holly came round,' he told him. 'She thinks they may have Francine and Callie at the CompuGuard compound. Ollie has directions. Can you send an officer to stand guard here? If Bonar finds out Holly survived . . .' He stopped there.

'DS Clark is on her way to you. She has an officer with her. I'll meet the two of you at the compound with armed back-up. Plus we've picked up Bonar, you'll be pleased to hear.'

'And Sergeant Morris?' McNab said.

'He's already in custody.'

'Then we have to move fast, sir.'

From the moment you decide you need to move fast,

everything shifts into slow motion, McNab thought. It was the same last night when he went for the naloxone. Every step he'd taken there and back had seemed to last forever. Even trying to wrench the inhaler from its packaging had turned him into an old man.

When he re-entered Holly's room, he found she'd drifted back into her drug-induced sleep, and he realized she'd only forced herself awake to speak to him, her brain fastened on the fear that the two women were shortly to die.

He couldn't leave her alone, he decided, even to go to the entrance to be picked up. He would have to wait until the replacement officer arrived to sit outside.

The nurse, seeing his agitation, offered to keep an eye on Holly until then, but McNab didn't want to take any chances. Instead, he paced the hallway, his mobile at the ready.

At last he spotted the jacketed officer just outside the ward door and went to greet him.

'DS Clark's waiting for you at the front door,' he was told.

McNab headed for the lift, which proved to be on the same go-slow as the world around him. Eventually exiting, the fresh air or perhaps the pelting rain seemed to speed time up a little as he jumped into the waiting car.

'Okay?' Janice said, pulling away even as he shut the car door.

'Are the other lot on the move?' he said.

'You know the time it takes to issue firearms.'

'Jesus, Mary and Joseph,' McNab pronounced.

'Let's hope they're with us soon,' Janice said. 'How's Holly?'

'She'll live if those bastards don't have a second try at her,' McNab voiced his fears.

Janice was driving well and the siren was already on, Glasgow punters drawing in to the side to let them past.

'Ten minutes to the airport. Four and a half miles,' Janice told him. 'You know the way after that?'

'I could take you there in the dark, in a snowstorm,' McNab told her.

'Maybe you should drive, then?' She pulled over and they switched seats.

The moments that took were regained as soon as McNab had his feet on the pedals.

As he exited the main road, he turned off the siren. 'We can't warn them we're coming,' he said. 'It's clear-up time down on the farm.'

They saw the smoke rising as McNab made a swift turn off the B road onto the holed track.

'They've fired the fucking place. Call 999 for an engine.'

As they bounced and rattled across the potholes, Janice made the call.

Smoke was drifting towards them through the intervening trees. That sense of time standing still was back with him. He'd driven this track in the dark and it had definitely not lasted this long.

As McNab put his foot down, the open security gates suddenly loomed out of the smoke. Ahead, the doors of the main structure were lying open too, suggesting whatever vans had been in there had since departed.

'Looks like they were warned we were coming,' McNab said as he drove straight through.

Smoke was billowing from two adjoined stone outbuildings, one of which had a double door. Jumping from the vehicle, McNab made for there first. On reaching the door, he thought he could hear coughing.

'Anyone in there?' he shouted, banging with his fist.

When a strangled voice managed, 'Yes, two of us,' he thought it might be Francine.

As he struggled to break the lock, the escaping smoke already catching at his throat, Janice appeared beside him with an enforcer. 'Use this.'

His eyes streaming, McNab manoeuvred himself into position and, with a count of three, let the enforcer do its job. The double door sprang apart, sending the chain and padlock flying.

The coughing, he guessed, was coming from the rear of the shed, the smoke pouring from an adjoining doorway.

'Francine,' he called, 'it's DS McNab. Where are you?'

As he peered into the smoke, Francine appeared like a wraith, coughing and spluttering. 'Callie's back here, but I don't think she's alive,' she managed.

McNab headed in the direction she'd pointed.

The body lay curled, just as Holly had. She was just as still, and despite the smoke, she wasn't coughing. As he drew her up and into his arms, he thought her dead.

His own lungs on fire, he forced his feet towards the open door and the two figures who stood outside.

It was perhaps the longest walk of his life. Longer than the one to fetch the naloxone for Holly. Even the billowing clouds of smoke became stretched in time. Every stumbling step he took, telling him that he carried a dead weight.

Reaching Janice and Francine, he laid Callie gently down and wrapped her in the foil survival blanket Janice handed him. As he did this, Francine sat down and took Callie's head in her lap.

'Has she been drugged?' he checked with Francine.

'Not since I've been with her. But—' She stopped as a burst of fire engulfed the part of the building they'd just escaped.

'What?' McNab demanded.

'Derek's in the other outbuilding where the fire began. I heard him and the man who took me arguing, I think the man wanted Derek to kill us. I went through and found Derek lying on the ground. I couldn't find a pulse. There was a syringe—' She stumbled to a halt.

McNab found himself heading back towards what was now an inferno. If he could pull Henderson out . . .

At that point he felt a hand grab his arm. 'You've no chance, Michael, and you know it,' Janice told him firmly.

The fire engine arrived at the same time as the back-up officers. Two ambulances minutes later. Perhaps the longest minutes of all.

McNab helped move Callie onto the stretcher. He realized, looking down at her, that this was the first time he'd seen this young woman's face in the flesh. She was, he saw, the embodiment of everything her abductors hated. One of the so-called witches they'd sought to torture and kill. Like Deirdre. Like Eléa.

Watching them transfer her into the first ambulance, he didn't dare ask if she was already dead. If he asked the question, he feared he might make it so.

Francine took his hand briefly before she went into the second ambulance to be checked over.

'Thank you,' she said. 'For everything.'

78

Day nine

When he asked for permission to follow Callie to the hospital, DI Wilson gave him the go-ahead. 'Take DS Clark with you. We'll finish up here and then take Francine back to her children,' he said.

McNab, now behind the wheel again, watched as the ambulance turned and, with its blue light flashing, made its way down the track to the sound of the siren.

Janice switched their lights and siren on to match. 'They wouldn't be doing that if Callie was already dead,' she assured him.

McNab chose to believe her, although the memory of the dead weight he'd carried from the burning building suggested otherwise.

They'd saved the two women for now, but if Callie was alive, she was still in danger. As was Francine. Both women were key witnesses to the men who'd made up the stick man gang. Callie, according to Francine, had been abused by all of them, including Derek Henderson.

She'd told him this as they'd awaited the arrival of the ambulance, and the distress it caused her was evident on her face.

Francine could identify her abductor, who she said had been the one to order her husband to kill her. By the description she'd given, together with the one supplied by her children, it confirmed him as the third man of the threesome who'd verbally abused Deirdre Reid that night at the film showing.

All of this he thought as they followed the ambulance the four miles back to the hospital, which felt more like forty.

On their final approach, Janice told McNab to get out and head into A&E while she parked the vehicle.

'Stay with Callie at all times,' she said. 'If word gets out that she's alive . . .'

McNab knew exactly what Janice meant. He suspected someone would have been put in place to watch the police arrival at the compound. Perhaps even one of their own officers currently attending the scene. They would know by now that she and Francine had got out of the burning building. He was more than convinced that what had gone down – the abduction, rape and murder of two young women – couldn't have happened without support from within the force itself. Sergeant Morris wasn't the only rogue cop in all of this.

Having caught up with the ambulance, McNab stood waiting while the two medics lifted Callie out and wheeled her inside.

'How is she?' he managed to ask.

'Alive, mate, but it's touch and go.'

McNab didn't register the crowd of humanity awaiting their turn to be treated in A&E, but followed the swiftly moving trolley, his badge in full view. All he could think of was, if Callie died, they might never find or catch all those who had hurt her. Might never have them pay for their crimes. Eventually Callie was wheeled into a cubicle in the assessment area and the curtain pulled shut.

McNab took the chair outside.

When Janice got here, he decided, he would head up to see Holly. Tell her what had gone down and thank her.

Janice made an appearance minutes later. 'How is she?'

'Touch and go,' McNab repeated the paramedic's assessment. 'If she isn't able to talk to us . . .' he added.

'We'll get them anyway,' Janice vowed. 'Go, check on Holly. Let the attending officer get some coffee.'

At the mention of coffee, McNab felt the caffeine pangs himself and went in search of the machine he'd passed in the casualty waiting area.

As he selected his double espresso, a man hanging about the entrance to the assessment area immediately headed for the male toilets. The sudden move, caused, McNab suspected, by his own arrival, set alarm bells ringing, because he'd seen such a reaction before, usually when someone had recognized him as a cop.

Abandoning his half-poured coffee, he swiftly followed the figure into the Gents.

There were a couple of men at the urinals, neither of whom were his guy. So he chose the cubicle next to the only occupied one and, easing the door shut, stood and listened.

He didn't recognize the voice, but he could make out a little of the conversation on the mobile call. As the man spoke, the swiftly moving figure heading for the Gents replayed in his head. Tall, dark-haired and muscled. Wearing a T-shirt and jeans. The third man.

The guy had been hanging about the entrance to the treatment area because he was very interested in who had just been taken inside. And that someone had been Callie.

Emerging from his cubicle, McNab realized he'd waited too long, his prey having already exited. Following, McNab caught a glimpse of him heading into the examination suite, after having flashed the famed badge at a nurse on entry.

McNab immediately sent a warning text to Janice, and followed his target into the emergency area.

If this guy, who he took to be the third man, was after Callie, that could only be to either establish she was dead or to make it so.

There was no sign of Janice outside cubicle six, which suggested that Callie, having been swiftly assessed, had been transferred elsewhere. But where?

With no sign of his suspect, McNab accosted a young female doctor and, presenting his ID, asked as to Caillean Munro's whereabouts.

'The young injured female that was brought in around twenty minutes ago?' she checked.

'Yes. There was a female officer with her,' he added.

She headed to the desk and began checking on the computer system. During which time, McNab's inner voice screamed at him to get moving if he didn't want to find Callie already dead.

'She was taken to Intensive Care five minutes ago. I believe your officer went there with her.'

But which officer? Janice or the fake one?

As he tried frantically to find a sign that pointed to Intensive Care, she appeared to take pity on him.

'Follow me,' she said briskly. 'I'll take you there.'

'The suspect in Callie's attempted murder is in the

building,' McNab told her as they walked quickly down a corridor towards a lift. 'I saw him in the reception area, and he's carrying fake police ID. He's tall, dark-haired and wearing a green T-shirt and jeans. You need to alert security and call 999.'

They'd reached the Intensive Care Unit. 'Do it now,' he ordered, before entering.

In here, the noise and bustle of the hospital faded to nothing. Approaching the desk, he explained who he was.

'But—' The woman looked perplexed. 'I believe there's an officer already with her.'

'Male or female?' he demanded.

She looked taken aback. 'I'm not sure.'

'Take me there now,' McNab ordered.

He wanted to sprint, but the ward sister, studiously aware of where she was, walked steadily and quietly. Everyone in here was seriously ill, some perhaps approaching their last moments.

McNab seriously didn't want Callie to be one of them.

When they reached the room, the nurse opened the door and whispered, 'Ah, I believe the doctor is in with her.'

Janice turned and, registering McNab's arrival, gave him a welcome nod and a reassuring smile. But Janice wasn't the one McNab was interested in.

His gut already screaming a warning, McNab threw himself at the tall, gowned figure bent over Callie and sent the syringe he held flying across the bed and onto the floor.

Janice, still not sure what was happening, went to pick it up as the two men tussled over Callie's body. Grabbing the mask, McNab tore it from the supposed doctor's face, and then Janice knew exactly who she was actually looking at.

She shouted to the nurse to press the emergency bell, then joined McNab in his attempt to wrestle the one they knew as the third man to the ground and handcuff him.

79

Day nine

'Go check on Holly,' Janice said, when Neil Innes had been led from the room by two officers. 'If she's awake you can tell her that Francine and Callie are both safe, thanks to her.'

McNab nodded. 'You're okay to stay here?'

'Of course. Go,' she ordered.

Exiting the Intensive Care Unit, McNab upped his pace. Holly, he knew, had a guard in place, plus there had been no release of information regarding what had happened to her. But that didn't mean word wasn't out there that she was alive and therefore a witness against the stick man trio and Bonar.

Bonar was already in custody and would be all about saving his own skin and that would most likely mean co-operation with the police. Bonar liked to bite and beat his women, but he wasn't a killer. And he would be very keen to make that plain.

His biggest concern, McNab registered as he navigated the Death Star, was that the ex-army radge guy, Keith Hamilton, was still unaccounted for. Innes had picked up Holly from Ashoka that night, but according to his vigilant neighbour there had been two male voices on the stairs. The second would be Hamilton's.

And Hamilton was a killer. Of that he was certain.

Holly had only surfaced long enough earlier to warn him about the danger to Francine and Callie. If she was awake now, she could tell him who'd tried to kill her.

The uniformed officer rose when he spotted McNab's approach.

'Everything okay, Constable?' McNab said.

'She's awake, sir. And sitting up,' he said with a smile.

'No visitors?'

'None.'

'Okay, Constable, you can take a fifteen-minute break.'

'Thank you, sir.'

McNab opened the door quietly, not wanting to startle her. After what Holly had been through, fear would be her constant companion for quite some time to come.

She *was* sitting up, he was pleased to see, even managed a flicker of a smile when she saw who it was.

McNab came to stand by the bed and took a good look at her. The auburn hair looked newly brushed, but the green eyes that had captivated him that first night were heavy – with what? The remains of the drugs meant to kill her or fear of what he had come to tell her?

He pulled the chair over and sat down, reaching out to take her hand.

'Francine and Callie are alive, thanks to you.'

She absorbed this in silence, then relief flooded her face and she squeezed his hand. 'I'm so glad,' she said. 'And Derek Henderson?'

'Dead. Likely from the overdose meant for them.'

She gave a little nod of acknowledgement. 'So he wouldn't do what was asked.' It didn't sound like a question.

'I suspect not,' McNab said. 'We've arrested Sergeant

Morris and Neil Innes. We believe Innes kidnapped Francine and was probably the one to inject Henderson.'

Another nod, as though she was putting together the pieces in her personal version of the jigsaw.

'Can you tell me who brought you back to my flat?' McNab said. 'My neighbour says she heard two male voices.'

'It was two of the men in the video you showed me of Deirdre.'

'Neil Innes and Keith Hamilton?' He paused as she flinched at the names. 'Innes came for you at Ashoka?' he asked quietly.

The little colour she had in her face appeared to drain away before she nodded.

'Was he the one to administer the drug?'

Her eyes were blank as though she was reliving those moments, before she eventually whispered, 'No, that was Hamilton.'

'Have you any idea where he might be?'

The question, which had to be asked, made it plain that the man who'd tried to kill her was still out there, despite all their efforts to find him.

'Is Charlie in custody?' she asked worriedly.

'He is. And as I said, we also have Sergeant Morris and Neil Innes,' he added, not mentioning Innes's presence in the hospital, which would have alarmed her even further.

'Then Hamilton's the only one left that I know about,' she said quietly. 'Does anyone know I'm alive?'

'No one knows what happened to you apart from my boss and a very small number of people.'

Relief flooded her face, albeit briefly. 'If he finds out I'm alive, he will come for me,' she said.

'That's why we won't let him find out,' McNab assured her.

'But if you don't catch him, I'll always be looking over my shoulder . . .' She stopped there, before adding, ' I don't want that,' in obvious horror at the thought.

An image of the video of Deirdre at the film showing being accosted by a rabid Hamilton came to mind. What Holly said was true. Hamilton might disappear for a while, but if or when he discovered she was alive, he would want to settle that score.

'Is there anything you remember which might point to where he could be?'

She laid her head back against the pillow and closed her eyes. For a moment McNab thought she was feeling ill again, before her eyes flicked open.

'He took my mobile that night he came to Ashoka. He might use it to try and find out what happened to me.' She looked at him. 'If he called any of the numbers . . . Bruce, the guy I was staying with, his number's on there. He'll be wondering what's happened to me.'

'Let's call him and see,' McNab said. He handed her his phone and watched as she punched in the number.

'Bruce, it's Holly. I'm using a friend's phone. I'm okay, thanks. Did anyone call you from my stolen mobile?'

A muffled voice seemed to answer in the affirmative.

'When exactly?' A pause. 'Today. Right. Thanks.' She told him she was fine and would be in touch later, before ringing off. 'Does that help?'

It might, McNab thought. Ollie had been monitoring Holly's mobile. Knowing Ollie, he wouldn't have stopped doing that.

'I need to go speak to our Tech department. See if they

can locate where your mobile was when it was used to make that call.'

McNab stepped out of the room to find the constable back in place, a coffee cup in hand.

'Don't leave her alone for any reason,' he ordered. 'I'll be back to check on her later.'

McNab headed for his vehicle to call Ollie.

80

Day nine

When Francine had described her journey from the boathouse to the CompuGuard compound, she'd said the only stop they'd made en route was to decouple the boat trailer. She'd estimated the time to get there from when they'd begun the journey to be around twenty minutes.

Wherever the boat had been left had to be linked to at least one of the gang, McNab reasoned. Another hideout perhaps, or simply where one of them actually lived.

The map Ollie had just sent placed the recent call from Holly's mobile six miles south of Balloch, which lay at the foot of Loch Lomond.

So Hamilton had been in that location and not long ago.

'What do you think?' McNab said to Janice.

'I think we head there now. I'll alert DI Wilson and ask for back-up while you drive. And put on the siren until we get close to the location.'

McNab's first instinct when he'd spoken to Ollie was to set off alone. For once common sense had urged him to include his partner. He was glad now he had.

They made the decision to head west this side of the river

and cross the Clyde via the Erskine bridge, in an attempt to avoid city traffic.

We were right, McNab thought, as they sped over the bridge, past the cars driven to the inside lane by the loud whine and flashing blue lights.

'We'll be in Bowling shortly. Turn off the siren and lights. Let's cruise into town as though we're not on the job,' Janice told him.

McNab did as requested.

'It's the ideal place to own a boat,' he said, glancing round. 'A harbour and plenty of shoreline. So how close are we to the location Ollie gave us?'

'Too close for a police car,' Janice said. 'I'll get out and take a look on foot.'

'It should be me doing that. Hamilton's not to be messed with and he's not a fan of females,' McNab reminded her. Which was an understatement to say the least.

'It's Bowling in the middle of the day, not Sauchiehall Street at night,' Janice said as she got out of the car. 'Park somewhere public. Outside a shop or cafe, as though we've stopped to pick up something to eat.'

McNab smiled despite himself. 'Okay, boss.'

He did as ordered then walked back to find Janice no longer in sight. 'Okay, partner,' he said glancing round, 'where exactly did you go?'

Moving more swiftly now, he walked further up the L-shaped cul-de-sac of bungalows she'd hopefully entered. At that moment his mobile vibrated in his pocket.

'Where are you?' he demanded.

'I found a red boat on a trailer at the end of the cul-de-sac. There's a black van too, number . . .' She quoted the registration plate.

'That's the one the wee boy remembered.'

'The van's in a garage,' she told him.

'You didn't enter the property?' McNab demanded.

'Call for back-up,' Janice told him. 'I'm going to knock on the door and see if anyone is at home.'

'No—' McNab mouthed as she rang off.

As far as he was aware, the other two stick men hadn't seen Janice in the flesh, but he had no doubt Sergeant Morris would have made a point of giving them the lowdown on his fellow officers.

His mobile buzzed again. This time it was the boss.

'Neil Innes's arrest has frightened the horses. Former Sergeant Morris is talking. He confirmed Hamilton's home address as Bowling. Local cops are on their way.'

'We're outside the house now, sir,' McNab said.

'Stay put, Sergeant, but don't approach. Hamilton is to be considered dangerous, especially to women.'

McNab assured him they wouldn't, aware that was already a lie, and rang off.

The high hedge that circled the garden was blocking a view of the house, which was probably the reason why Janice had entered the driveway. He could now see the red boat on its trailer parked alongside the garage in which sat the black van.

There was, however, no sign of Janice.

'What the fuck,' he muttered under his breath. 'She's supposed to be stopping *me* from going rogue.'

Caution told him to stay where he was and await back-up, just as the boss had ordered. But then again the boss had no idea that Janice might even now be in that house with Hamilton.

Skirting behind the trailer, he headed round the back.

The garden here was ringed by the same high hedge, the grass left uncut, and there was a mound of black rubbish bags piled round the kitchen door. There was also no one visible at the window.

Neither was there any sign of Janice, which could only mean she had gone inside.

Why would she do that?

He headed back the way he'd come, intent on knocking on that front door, regardless of the boss's order. As he passed the garage, his mobile vibrated in his pocket. Glancing at the screen, he saw Janice's message.

garage

Relief quashing his fear, he moved inside. She was behind the black van, close against the intervening door linking the garage with the house.

Seeing him, she placed a finger on her lips and pressed her ear to the door.

From where he was, McNab could make out only the rumbling of voices. One he thought female, the other male. He had the distinct feeling the male wasn't happy. The woman sounded frightened – and had McNab been the one right outside, he would have entered. By Janice's expression, she felt the same. When he nodded his agreement, she reached for the handle.

The door opened onto a hall, the increasing noise of the argument emerging from the furthest away room.

It was the scream followed by a crunching sound that launched them into action. Janice was first in, with McNab just behind.

Hamilton had the woman by the hair and was beating her head off a tabletop. Blood splattered the air as he swung her head up and then down again, pressing it hard against the surface. The white of a loosened tooth skirted across the table and landed on the floor.

Hamilton's face moved from fury to surprise when he finally registered his visitors.

'Let her go and stand back,' Janice ordered, her voice a steely calm.

'Or what, bitch?' Hamilton said in a mocking tone.

The PAVA spray aimed at Hamilton's face met its mark. He screamed and staggered back, his hands clawing at his agonized eyes.

As McNab handcuffed him, he heard the shriek of advancing sirens.

'Looks like the cavalry have arrived.'

Janice was checking out the woman, now slumped, crying, on a nearby chair. 'You recognize her?' she said quietly.

McNab shook his head, wondering how anyone could, among the mess of snot and blood.

'She's the staffer, Lindsay Gray, who the camera picked up entering the Ladies when Holly came into the station. My guess is Sergeant Morris called on her in case he needed help in getting rid of Holly.'

'So another one on the inside,' McNab said.

'Seems so, although I think she's grown to regret it,' Janice said as the woman was led out to a waiting ambulance.

'Well done, Detective Sergeant, although you had me worried for a while there,' McNab said as Hamilton was bundled into the waiting police car.

'So now you know what it feels like,' Janice told him firmly.

81

Day ten

'Now we have all three surviving perpetrators, plus Bonar, in custody,' Bill told Rhona, 'I think we can assume Francine and her children are safe.' He halted there for a moment. 'The question is, how much do we reveal of her husband's part in all of this? Especially since he can't be brought to trial.'

Rhona had been asking herself the same question.

'Callie did confirm that it was Neil Innes who attacked her in the caravan that night, not Derek,' she offered.

'But Tech say it was Henderson who'd alerted him by phone to Callie's presence on the site. Plus Henderson knew that Deirdre's grave was nearby.' He paused, a stricken look on his face. 'What kind of man takes his family on holiday to a campsite where he can view a murdered girl's grave?'

'An abusive one,' Rhona said.

Bill rose and went to stand by the window, as though to collect himself.

'Our first thought must be for the kids. And what story she can tell them,' he said. 'No child should be told their father was a monster. Even if he was.'

Rhona agreed wholeheartedly with that.

'I understand that Henderson died from an overdose?' Bill checked.

'The report came back this morning,' Rhona confirmed. 'The lab said the syringe held the same toxic mix that was used on Holly, and was probably destined for Callie and Francine. McNab thinks Henderson was given an ultimatum. If he wanted to live, he had to kill the women,' she said.

'Maybe he turned them down?' Bill said.

'Maybe he did,' Rhona confirmed.

Bill considered that for a moment. 'I think that's what you go with in your meeting with Francine. That's a story she can tell her children. Dad got in with a bad crowd, but he saved Callie's life and her own,' he finished. 'Right.' He checked his watch. 'Time to put all the pieces together.'

'Before we go in,' Rhona said, 'can you tell me what's happening with Bonar and McNab?'

'Bonar is very keen to tell us everything he knows. Including naming those officers involved in the sexual assaults. Also, Tech are doing a fine job in identifying contributors to that stick man site. Sadly, there are bad apples in the police service, just like everywhere else.'

'So McNab is clear of this?' Rhona checked.

'He is. Especially with what has happened since.'

The strategy room was full and buzzing when they entered. Rhona caught sight of McNab standing together with Janice. Spotting her, Janice raised a hand, indicating that they should meet for a drink later, and Rhona nodded and smiled her agreement.

Bill had no need to bring the meeting to order, because as soon as he'd reached the front, the crowd fell silent.

'I asked you all here so that you might hear the forensic

evidence that confirms what Callie Munro has said in her statement. Regardless of what the three accused profess happened, the science tells us otherwise. Dr MacLeod?'

Rhona gained the stage, and brought up the images she'd discussed the last time.

'As you know, Callie has identified the third man in the video as her attacker at the campsite, which has been confirmed forensically via deposits of blood, skin and fingerprints in the van, from when she tried to fight him off. He took her in her own kayak to a bay further east where his van was parked and from there to the cabin, known as the shepherd's hut, on the hill behind Achmelvich, where she was imprisoned, blindfolded and tied up.'

She paused briefly, checking to see if her audience was with her on this. When there were no questions, she continued.

'Callie remembers four distinct voices from her captivity and, as you are aware, after listening to recordings made of the suspects' voices, she has identified each of them accurately as Hamilton, Morris, Henderson and the man who we now know as the security guard for CompuGuard, Neil Innes.'

As she brought up an image of the hideous interior of the outhouse at the shepherd's hut, a rumble of anger went through the company.

'This is where she was held until she was transferred to the CompuGuard compound. As you can see, various items of clothing lie scattered about, including items worn by Deirdre when she disappeared from the student strip, as identified by her partner and friends.'

She continued. 'All such items, together with those worn by Callie when she was abducted, have been microscopically examined by my assistant Chrissy and myself, and a variety of forensic tests performed on them.

'I can report that semen from four different sources was retrieved and a number of human hairs. Each have found a match with one of the four accused. All four men have been present in this place at some time during Deirdre and Callie's incarceration. All four men are guilty of the sexual abuse or rape of both incarcerated women. Two of the men are guilty of murder.'

She waited until the babble of angry voices quietened before she spoke again.

'Let's take a closer look at the signature used by each killer, that is, the stick man left with their allotted victim. If you remember, in Deirdre's case there were two different deposits of blood. One came from the victim, the other unidentified and possibly not intended to be there. We thought the microscopic amounts probably came from a scratch caused when twisting the stick man into shape, via a cut, or from already broken skin, such as eczema. That blood has been identified as belonging to Keith Hamilton.'

Rhona let the chatter that followed this rise and fall again before she continued.

'Now to the second stick man located in the sand next to Eléa Martin's head, where she lay after being strangled then pushed from the cliff, not far from the shepherd's hut. On this stick man we found her blood only. However, we did retrieve skin flakes from under her fingernails, from when she tried to fight off her attacker, which were in fact a DNA match for Neil Innes.

'Derek Henderson's role in all of this is not clear, although we believe he did contact Neil Innes when he spotted Callie at the campsite. Chances were she'd already been identified as a possible victim, when she too visited the student strip. Discovering her alone at Arisaig, not far from the buried Deirdre, must have seemed too good an opportunity to miss.'

Her contribution over, Rhona made her way to the family room and the arranged meeting with Francine and the children.

When she reached the door, she stood outside for a moment, enjoying the sound of the children's laughter. Magnus was already there, she realized, on hearing the rumble of his deep Orcadian voice in response.

Magnus should be a father, she thought. *He would make a good one.*

When she finally brought herself to enter, the little gathering of a smiling Francine, Magnus, Orly and Lucy turned towards her.

Still unsure how to play this, Rhona hesitated in the doorway.

Until Lucy held up her hand in the sign they'd first shared in Arisaig, and she responded in kind.

When she and Magnus reached the jazz club, Sean was up on stage. As soon as Sean saw her he changed tunes, moving on to something he knew she liked as a welcome and saluting her with a raised saxophone.

Chrissy waved Rhona over. 'Well,' she said, looking her in the eye. 'How did it go with Francine and the kids?'

'Okay,' Rhona told her, glancing at Magnus, who nodded his agreement.

'Good,' Chrissy said.

'Janice says she'll be here shortly,' Rhona said as she accepted her drink.

'What about McNab?' Magnus asked. 'Is he coming?'

'You mean your drinking buddy?' Rhona laughed.

'What's this about drinking buddies?' Chrissy immediately demanded.

Janice arrived at that point and Chrissy's interest switched to the missing McNab.

'Where is he?' she demanded.

'I believe he's gone to check on Holly,' Janice said with a smile.

'Good,' Rhona said.

The High Court, Glasgow

Some months later

The jury, consisting of nine women and six men, filed back in.

McNab had observed them throughout the trial. The three younger women in the group were feisty, reminding him of Chrissy when she'd taken the stand to present the forensic evidence against Neil Innes, the third man who had remained unnamed for so long.

The forensic evidence was never in dispute. No male in the jury could argue that the throttling marks on Callie's neck had been inflicted via some sex game she'd asked for, or an imaginary fight with a girlfriend, as had happened in McNab's earlier thwarted attempt to have Bonar convicted of domestic abuse.

In this instance Innes had been charged with the abduction, rape and attempted murder of Caillean Munro.

It was the first of Innes's trials, of course, and would be followed by one for the abduction and murder of the French girl Eléa Martin, who had not survived to take the stand.

Not for the first time, McNab wished Eléa hadn't escaped

that day at Achmelvich only to run to her death on those cliffs. Then she, like Callie, might have survived her imprisonment and been able to take the stand and give evidence against her attacker.

Hamilton would be the next member of the stick man group to be tried and Callie's evidence of what had taken place in the shepherd's hut would put him away, together with that gathered by Rhona from Deirdre's body.

As for former Sergeant Morris . . . an internal investigation was ongoing with regard to his part in the stick man case. By the time he reached court, hopefully they would have rooted out those in the force who had aided and abetted him.

As it was, everyone was currently working in an atmosphere rife with suspicion and blame. Not helped by the tone and content of the press's reporting on the stick man case and its links to sexual assaults on the student strip.

They'd had some success in keeping Derek Henderson's part in all of this off the front page of the tabloids, mainly due to the boss's determined efforts to protect Francine Henderson and her children.

Francine's abduction by Innes, of course, was another crime, which Francine on reflection had decided she didn't want pursued in court, preferring to give the children her version of how their father had saved her and Callie from the bad man who'd kidnapped her at the boathouse.

The likelihood that the children might in the future discover the true nature of their father's involvement couldn't be foreseen of course. McNab was just grateful that at least at the moment they weren't being subjected to the media's version of events.

As the spokeswoman announced the guilty verdict for the

abduction, rape and attempted murder of Caillean Munro, McNab recalled a saying his religious mother was more than fond of using, especially when he, as a youth, had railed against the injustices of life.

The wheels of the Lord grind slowly, Michael, but they grind exceedingly fine.

Arisaig

One year later

She'd come further round the headland to the bay where Innes had left his black van in preparation for his kidnapping of Callie. There was no campsite here, only a few spaces along the single-track road where you could park for the night.

She'd hired the small camper, and was alone. She hadn't asked Sean to accompany her, because he would have accepted, despite the fact that he hated camping.

Besides, she had come here to reclaim this place in a way which was difficult to describe.

She supposed it was the equivalent of reclaiming the night in the city, which women did in defiance of male violence.

She'd promised herself a swim here when the investigation was over. She wanted to have a different memory of this place than what had been conjured up during that time.

Tomorrow, she would drive further north to Achmelvich and camp a night there too. Swim off the main beach. Perhaps even walk round to where Eléa had been found.

She was also considering a visit to Trevor Wills and his

dog, Meg, who had discovered Eléa's body and been instrumental in saving Callie from the same fate. She'd heard from Lee MacDonald that Trevor had built a cairn in memory of Eléa on the clifftop.

She would like to pay her respects there.

Her own ghosts laid to rest, on her way back to Glasgow she planned to meet someone at the Sands of Morar. Someone she'd once promised to swim with. A promise she could finally keep.

Francine, Lucy and Orly were holidaying there and they'd invited her to visit.

Something she had every intention of doing.

As the sun began its red descent, Rhona left the van to walk down to the white beach and enter the warm fringe of water that lay beyond.

Acknowledgements

With thanks to:

Dr Jennifer Miller who, being an expert in buried and hidden bodies, answered my questions on grave excavation in the machair of the west of Scotland.

Dr James H. K. Grieve, Emeritus Professor of Forensic Pathology at the University of Aberdeen, who is more than generous in answering my queries about modes of death.

Professor Lorna Dawson, of The James Hutton Institute, for her advice on the soils of North-West Scotland and for inspiring the creation of forensic soil scientist Dr Jen Mackie.

To Joe Allan, at Gear Bikes in Gibson Street, Glasgow, for his friendly advice on hiring bikes for the NC500 route.

A big thanks, too, to my wonderful editor Alex Saunders and the team at Pan Macmillan, who I believe now know Dr Rhona MacLeod and her team as well as I do.

Introducing Rhona MacLeod . . .

Lin Anderson's series of crime novels featuring forensic scientist Rhona MacLeod are set in and around Scotland. From the beautiful remoteness of the Orkney islands to the dark underbelly of urban Glasgow, the locations she chooses to write about play as much a role in her novels as the characters that she populates them with.

Go back to where it all began with the thrilling first novel in the Rhona MacLeod series. Read on for an extract now . . .

I

THE BOY DIDN'T expect to die.

When the guy put the tasselled cord round his neck, grinning at him, he thought it was just part of the usual game. The guy was excited, a dribble of saliva slithering down his chin and falling onto the boy's bare shoulder. He nodded his agreement. He was past feeling sick at their antics. He lay back down, turning his head sideways to the greyish pillow that smelt of other games, closed his eyes and shifted his thoughts to something else. There was a goal he liked to play out in his head.

On the right, the Frenchman, arrogant, the ball licking his feet, thrusting forward. The opposition starts to group and there's a scuffle. Bastards. But no worry 'cos the Frenchman's through and running, the ball anchored to him, like a child to its mother. The crowd breathes in. Time stretches like an elastic band. Then the ball's away, curving through the air.

Wham! It's in the net.

The boy can usually go home now. Not this time. This time, before the ball reaches the net, his head is pulled back, then up. The intense pressure bulges his eyes, bursting a myriad of tiny blood vessels to pattern the white. His body spasms as the cord bites deeper, slicing through skin, cutting the blood supply to his brain. At the moment of death his penis erupts, scattering silver strands of semen over the multicoloured cover.

2

SEAN WAS ALREADY asleep beside her. Rhona liked that about him. His baby sleep. His face lying smooth and untroubled against the pillow, his lips opened just enough to let the breath escape in soft noiseless puffs. No one, she thinks, should look that good after a bottle of red wine and three malt whiskies.

Rhona has given up watching Sean drink. It is too irritating, knowing the next morning he won't have a hangover. Instead he'll throw back the duvet (letting a draught enter the warm tent that had enclosed their bodies), slip out of bed and head for the kitchen. From the bed she will watch (a little guiltily), as he moves about; a glimpse of thigh, an arm reaching up, his penis swinging soft and vulnerable. He'll whistle while he makes the coffee and forever in her mind Rhona will match the bitter sweet smell of fresh coffee with the high clear notes of an Irish tune.

They have been together for seven months. The first night Rhona brought Sean home they never reached the bedroom. He held her against the front door, just looking at her. Then he began to unwrap her, piece by piece, peeling her like ripe fruit, his lips not meeting hers but close, so close that her mouth stretched up of its own accord, and her body with it. Then, with a flick of his tongue, he entered her life.

When the phone rang, Sean barely moved. Rhona knew once it rang four times the ansaphone would cut in. The caller would listen to Sean's amiable Irish voice and change their view of answering machines, thinking they might be human after all. Rhona lifted the receiver on the third ring. It would be an emergency or they wouldn't phone so late. When she suggested to the voice on the other end that she would need a taxi, the Sergeant told her that a police car was already on its way. Rhona grabbed last night's clothes from the end of the bed.

Constable William McGonigle had never been at a murder scene before. He had stretched the yellow tape across the tenement entrance like the Sergeant told him and chased away two drunks who thought that police activity constituted a better bit of entertainment than staggering home to hump the wife. Constable McGonigle didn't agree.

'Go home,' he told them. 'There's nothing to see here.'

He was peering up the stairwell, wondering how much longer he would have to stand there freezing his balls off when he heard the sound of high heels clipping the tarmac. A woman leaned over the tape and stared into the dimly lit stair.

'Sorry, Miss. You can't come in here.'

'Where's Detective Inspector Wilson?'

Constable McGonigle was surprised.

'Upstairs, Miss.'

'Good,' she said.

Her fair hair shone white in the darkness and Constable McGonigle could smell her perfume. She lifted a silken leg and straddled his yellow tape.

'I'd better go on up then,' she said.

The click of Rhona's heels echoed round the grimy stairwell, but if she was disturbing any of the residents, they didn't show it by opening their doors. No one here wanted to be seen. If there was a fire they might come out, she thought, in the unlikely event they weren't completely comatose.

A door on the second landing stood ajar. She could hear DI Wilson's voice inside. If Bill was here at least she wouldn't have to explain who she was. She could just get on with the job, go home and crawl back into bed.

The narrow hall was a fetid mix of damp and heat. The sound of her heels died in a dark mottled carpet, curled at the edge like some withered vegetable. She paused. Three doors, all half open. On her right a kitchen, on her left a bathroom. She caught a glimpse of a white suit and heard the whirr of a camera. The Scene of Crime Officers were already at work.

The end door opened fully and Detective Inspector Bill Wilson looked out.

'Bill.'

'Dr MacLeod.'

He nodded. 'It's in here.'

He allowed himself a tight smile. The two other men in the room turned and stared out at her. Dr MacLeod was not what either of them had expected.

Rhona looked down at her black dress and high-heeled sandals. 'I came out in a bit of a hurry.'

'McSween will get you some kit.'

Bill nodded to one of the men, who went out and came back minutes later with a plastic bag.

Rhona pulled out the scene suit and mask, put her coat into the bag and handed it to the officer. She took one shoe off at a time and, hitching up her skirt, slipped her feet into the suit. Only then did she step inside.

Rhona took in the small room at a glance. The hideous nicotine-stained curtains stretched tightly across the window. A wooden chair with a pair of jeans and a tee-shirt thrown over it. Two glasses on a formica table. A pair of trainers on the floor beside the bed. A divan, three-quarters width, no headboard but covered with heavy silken brocade in an expensive burst of swirling colours.

The boy's naked body lay face down across it, his head turned stiffly towards her, eyes bulging, tongue protruding slightly between blue lips. The dark silk cord knotted round the neck looked like a bow tie the wrong way round. The body showed signs of hypostasis, and the combination of dark purple patches and pale translucence reminded Rhona of marble. Below the hips blood soaked into the bedclothes.

'I turned the gas fire off when I arrived,' Bill said. 'The smell nearly finished off our young Constable, so I put him on duty outside for some fresh air.'

'Did anyone take the room temperature?'

'McSween has it.'

Rhona took a deep breath before she put on the mask. The smell of a crime scene was important. It might mean she would look for traces of a substance she would otherwise have missed. Here the nauseating odour of violent death mixed with stale sex and sweat masked something else, something fainter. She got it. An expensive men's cologne.

'McSween and Johnstone have covered the rest of the room. The photographer is working on the kitchen and bathroom.'

'What about a pathologist?'

'Dr Sissons came and certified death. Then suggested I get a decent forensic to take samples and bag the body because he needed to get back to his dinner party.'

'Important guests?'

'He did mention a "Sir" somewhere in the list.'

Rhona smiled. Dr Sissons preferred analysing death in the comfort of his mortuary. Taking samples of bodily fluids in the middle of the night he regarded as her territory.

'That's some bedcover!'

'We think it might be a curtain, but we'll get a better look once we take the body away.'

'Did the doctor turn him over?'

'Just enough to tell if he's been moved. He said the left side of the face, the upper chest and hips had been compressed since death occurred. He's lying where he was killed.'

Rhona opened her case and took out her gloves. She knelt down beside the bed.

'There's a lot of blood under the body.'

Bill nodded grimly. 'You'd better take a look underneath.'

Rhona lifted the right arm and rolled the body a little. The genitals had been gnawed, the penis severed by a jagged gash that ran from the left hand tip to halfway up the right side. One testicle was mashed and hanging by a thin strip of skin.

'This must have been done after he died or the blood would be all over the place.'

'That's what Sissons said.'

Rhona let the body roll back down. The boy's head nestled back into the dirty pillow.

'Any sign of a weapon?'

Bill shook his head. 'Maybe it wasn't a weapon.'

'A biter? Did Dr Sissons check for other bite marks?'

'He muttered something about bruising on the nipples and the shoulder.'

'I'll take some swabs.'

'How long do you think he's been dead?' Bill said.

Rhona pressed one of the deepening purple patches, and watched it slowly blanch under her finger. 'Maybe six, seven hours. Depends on the temperature of the room.'

Bill risked a satisfied smile.

'Matches the Doc.'

Rhona raised her eyebrows a little. She and Dr Sissons didn't usually agree. He had a habit of disagreeing with her on points like the exact time of death.

It was almost a matter of principle. Rhona had done three years' medicine before she switched to forensic science. She liked to practise now and again.

'How did you find him?'

'An anonymous phone call.'

'The murderer?'

'A young male voice. Very frightened. Maybe another rent boy came here to meet a client?'

'Alive, this one would have been pretty,' Rhona said.

Bill nodded. 'Not the usual type for this area,' he said. 'A bit more class, but rented all the same. I'll leave you to it? Just shout if you need anything.'

She was nearly an hour taking samples of everything that might prove useful later on. After she'd finished with the surrounds, she concentrated on the body, under the fingernails, the hair, the mouth. Dr Sissons would take the anal and penile swabs.

The skin felt cold through her gloves, but with the blond hair flopped over the empty eyes, he might have been any teenager fast asleep. Rhona lifted the hair and studied the face, trying to imagine what the boy would have looked like in life. There were none of the tell-tale signs of poor diet and drug abuse. This one had been healthy. So how did he end up here?

'Finished?' Bill's timing was immaculate. 'Mortuary boys are here.' He looked at her face. 'Go home and have a hot toddy,' he said.

A hot toddy was Bill's answer to almost any ailment.

Rhona got up from the bed and unwrapped her hands. 'Any idea who he is?' she said.

'Not yet. But I don't think he was Scottish.' He pointed to the hall. Behind the door hung a leather jacket and a football scarf. 'Manchester United,' he said in mock disgust.

'There are people up here who support Man U,' Rhona suggested cheekily, knowing Bill was a Celtic man.

'Yes, but they wouldn't flaunt it. Not in Glasgow anyway.'

Rhona laughed.

'All right then?'

'Yes.' She began to pack her samples in the case.

'The Sergeant will run you home.'

He walked with her to the front door.

'How's that Irishman of yours these days? Still playing at the club?'

'Yes, he is.'

'Must get down and hear him again soon. Good jazz player. You'll ring me as soon as you've got anything?'

'Of course.'

Sean was still asleep when Rhona got back. With the heavy curtains drawn the room was dark, although outside dawn was already touching the university rooftops. She had stopped at the lab on her way home and checked the swabs for saliva. It was there all right.

She left a note on the bench for Chrissy in case she got there first, giving her a brief history of the night's events, then she headed home for a few hours' sleep.

Rhona pulled her dress over her head, kicked off her shoes and slid under the duvet. She wrapped her chilled body round Sean's. He grunted and moved his arm over to take her hand.

'Okay?' he mumbled.

'Okay,' she said, but he was already back asleep.

Rhona closed her eyes and tried to relax into his warmth. She had been at many murder scenes, some more horrible than the one tonight. Death didn't scare her, not when it was reduced to tests and samples. But tonight was different. There was something about that particular boy. Something she hadn't been able to put her finger on. Not until the Sergeant had put it into words for her, coming back in the car.

The boy who had been abused and strangled in that hideous little room looked so like her, he could have been her brother.